PRAISE FOR BRADLEY K. MARTIN'S NUCLEAR BLUES

A daring story that is as unnerving as it is engrossing. Bradley K. Martin has the gift of making readers feel a place and fall in love with his characters. One of the best thrillers I have read with an international setting.

— ROMUALD DZEMO, READERS' FAVORITE

Bradley Martin wrote the book on North Korea — literally. His 2006 look at the inner workings of the Kim dynasty, all 912 pages of it, remains an unequaled primer on the most isolated regime. For his Kim family follow-up, Martin chose a thriller, titled *Nuclear Blues*. Turning to fiction has a perverse logic. Political scientists, after all, have failed to explain, predict or translate what's afoot in the Hermit Kingdom. The sprawling Central Intelligence Agency was just as shocked as investors in 2017 to find how much Kim's nuclear program leaped from theoretical to operational. There are no experts as the untested thirty-something Kim faces off with an unproven 71-year-old U.S. president. When basketballer Dennis Rodman knows more about Kim than Donald Trump's cabinet does, you might as well turn to a work of fiction. Martin's vivid read, centering on a journalist trying to get the real story in Pyongyang, has all the makings of a great Coen brothers film.

— WILLIAM PESEK, LIVEMINT

It's been said, perhaps apocryphally, that when Leo Tolstoy showed a friend the manuscript of his monumental 1,225-page masterpiece *War and Peace*, the friend read it and remarked that the book had everything but a horse race. Bradley K. Martin has stuffed an amazing series of coincidental and accidental relationships and bizarre events into his rambunctious, rollicking, dystopian novel *Nuclear Blues* — so many that he didn't need a horse race. This is a book that might cause Cubby Broccoli to abandon James Bond. It is a murderous, chaotic romp through a near-future North Korea by a Korean-American guitar picker, Bible thumper, bourbon drinker and burned out photojournalist from Mississippi now plying his musical trade in Japanese night clubs. Festus Park (Heck) Davis, born of a union between a South Korean woman and a Deep Southerner, is catapulted into an adventure that includes the obligatory pneumatic North Korean spy; a fundamentalist Christian university in North Korea operated by a dead ringer for Oral Roberts/Jimmy Swaggart/Billy James Hargis/Billy Graham/Pat Robertson; Iranian agents seeking a bomb; the noxious family of the Great Leader Kim Il-sung and his descendants; a behemoth investment bank that could be mistaken for Goldman Sachs. The book contains some of the clearest explanations of what credit default swaps are, and how they are used, outside of a financial textbook. It is an endlessly entertaining novel that also manages to impart, outside of the main narrative, a sense of what North Korea is about. It is not a pretty place. The book owes considerable to the reporting, research and news analysis that formed a major part of Martin's career as a Pyongyang-watcher. A Georgia boy himself, he has obviously heard enough gospel music and down-home preaching to add more veracity.

- JOHN BERTHELSEN, ASIA SENTINEL

Martin, who was chief North Korea watcher for Bloomberg News, clearly knows his subject, as was also evident in his nonfictional *Under the Loving Care of the Fatherly Leader: North Korea and the Kim Dynasty*.

- PUBLISHERS WEEKLY BOOKLIFE

The dark poetry of places, encounters, characters emerges slowly due to the fast tempo of the action prevailing over most everything else. I see a Roman Polanski film script. That's it.

- RUI PARADA, POET/TRANSLATOR

Most impressive is the way it builds from start to finish. The gentle beginning results in a last hundred pages that are gripping and surprising and original as hell. In all books of this nature, whether by John le Carré or Alan Furst or Philip Kerr or Bradley Martin, there is authority that pulls the reader in. *Nuclear Blues* is a book by a guy who knows what he's talking about. Bravo!

- PETER CARRY, FORMER EXECUTIVE EDITOR, SPORTS ILLUSTRATED AND DISCOVERY MAGAZINES

As one of Bradley Martin's characters asks his protagonist, "What's in your MIND?!" Whatever it is — and I think I recognize a lot of it from my own Southern upbringing — I loved co-inhabiting this author's world of intuition, imagination and wonderful writing. *Nuclear Blues* is one cool novel.

- ROBERT WADE, NOM DE PLUME

My first reaction was simply that this must be how things are in North Korea. The book is special and ambitious in portraying a place that many readers will find strange, shocking and perhaps hard to believe. People who stick with it will be richly rewarded. It's perhaps unusual that one of the main people in the story is dead before page ten. But I came to view this as part of a technique for building up character by setting, and gradually solving, puzzles. When Joe is shot we don't know why, but we begin to guess the reasons, and to understand the kind of person he was, when we hear from various sources about things he did and said during his trip. Protagonist Heck Davis struck me as a case of personal development, not de-mystification. I think the Heck character starts to mature abruptly when he finds he can kill a would-be assassin. He is cool and dynamic in the final drama, I would say very unlike himself at the start of the book. Kim Jong-un's appearance sets off a brilliant case of guessing who is who, especially as the historical person is frustratingly two dimensional. Here Kim has gained some depth, and even has some humor. The final scene in the cathedral is like the steepest plunge on a funicular railway. At first reading, the shock was a bit too much for me. But perhaps I should have realized from the narrow escapes in the early chapters that I would be facing some steep gradients.

- CHARLES SMITH, FORMER TOKYO BUREAU CHIEF, FINANCIAL TIMES

Tom Clancy meets Graham Greene.

- TODD CROWELL, NUMBER 1 SHIMBUN

NUCLEAR BLUES

BRADLEY K. MARTIN

GREAT
LEADER
BOOKS

Everybody wants to go to heaven, but no one wants to die to get there.

- B.B. KING

1 / PANMUNJOM, KOREAN DMZ

ON AN EARLY FALL day when Washington, Seoul, Tokyo and Beijing were in an uproar over the latest North Korean outrage, a U.S. Forces van propelled me and three other camera people past the scenic barbed wire and tank traps, fire bases and checkpoints of the Korean Demilitarized Zone. Once again I contemplated the zone's howling misnomer, but the thought no longer triggered a smile. That's how old the border story was. I couldn't complain. My band had no gigs scheduled for the next few days. All I was thinking was, I'd earn my shooting fee from *AsiaIntel* and get back to my music. I could use the money.

The South Korean sitting next to me finished some shots, closed his window and turned to me. "Chilly today." He and the others worked for the Seoul bureaus of international news agencies. Hearing from U.S. Forces Korea about my scheduled visit, with several spare van seats just waiting to be filled, they'd decided to tag along and get some stock images. Agencies liked to keep plenty of stock on hand so they'd be ready for spikes in client demand.

"Could use a little sun." The leaden sky blocked most of the light. Only later did it occur to me that it must have filtered out any vibes warning that things were about to turn truly awful.

GIs in Korea called the DMZ simply "the Z." A buffer strip two and a half miles wide with equal parts north and south of the Korean War ceasefire line, it snaked more than 150 miles across the waist of the Korean peninsula.

"Birds at three o'clock," the only woman in the van announced in Korean from the seat behind me. She swiveled to take the shot of Manchurian cranes flying low over a field. Rare wildlife flourished in the Z, thanks to the scarcity of humans. I joined the others in recording the image, not because it thrilled me but just in case Asia-Intel might have a use for it.

We passed through a checkpoint to enter Camp Bonifas, the razor-wire-fenced home of a few South Korean and American soldiers. I'd been there enough times to remember it was 440 yards south of the line. Our van rolled to a stop. A fine mist dampened my face as we stepped out to enter the single-story lecture hall for the usual briefing on history and stats.

"Heck Davis," I said, sticking my hand out to the crew-cut American public affairs officer who awaited us at the podium.

He lifted my mood by introducing himself as Major Player and then crinkling his eyes at my double take. "Frank Player is my name." Somewhere along the line, he'd acquired the good-humored wisdom to accept and even enjoy the certainty that this conversation would come up again and again.

I obliged him. "I bet you pray to your sweet Lord every night for a quick promotion to light colonel."

"Won't help much in view of my dad's sense of humor. The name on my birth certificate is Francis Scott Key Player." The major glanced down at his notes and cleared his throat — his signal to cut the chatter and take a seat so he could get on with the show.

A South Korean enlisted man projected a series of grainy photos and maps onto the screen. Player quickly got to the grisly highlight of his spiel. "Here's a photo of Northern soldiers using axes to hack Captain Arthur Bonifas and First Lieutenant Mark Barrett to death in 1976. American and ROK soldiers had gone out to trim a poplar tree because its branches blocked their view. The Northerners didn't want it trimmed."

ROK — he pronounced it rock — stood for Republic of Korea. That was the South's official English name. The North went by Democratic People's Republic of Korea, or DPRK. You had to spell out those initials. Nobody pronounced it dip-rock or de-prick, although the country's inhabitants were often called Norks.

The major recounted another fatal dust-up: the defection in 1984 of Vasily Yakovlevich Matuzok, a twenty-two-year-old Soviet citizen working as a diplomatic trainee at the Soviet Embassy in Pyongyang. Matuzok was a member of a tour group at Panmunjom. He handed his camera to another tourist, asking to have his photo taken. Then he sprinted across the line, zigzagging to keep from being shot by North Korean guards. Northerners in hot pursuit penetrated about a hundred and fifty yards into Southern territory. "One ROK soldier and three North Koreans were killed in a twenty-four-minute firefight."

It was a relief to get out of the lecture hall. Player led us into the Joint Security Area. The JSA occupied part of what once had been a farming community called Panmunjom — Plank Bridge Village. Negotiators meeting there had agreed on the 1953 armistice. The JSA's heart was a row of single-story, bright blue buildings that looked like temporary classrooms at an overflowing suburban school. The two sides' military representatives continued to meet there when they wanted to exchange insults and blow smoke in each other's faces. Every now and then they managed to iron out some problem, but in more than six decades they'd never gotten around to officially ending the war.

Each of the one-room buildings had two entrances, one in each side's territory. The border that had emerged from the contending armies' advances and retreats between 1950 and 1953 went down the middle of the conference tables. Negotiators could sit in their own territory and still face their adversaries.

If you thought of Panmunjom as a theme park, the theme was

intimidation. Each side had erected sky-high flagpoles, giant flags and grandiose building façades.

As we walked on the tarmac bordering the truce huts' southern ends, an opening between two of them gave me an opportunity to look across the line. It appeared that my reporter buddy Joe Hammond hadn't arrived yet. Joe was on the fourth day of a visit to North Korea. Because of Pyongyang's strong allergy to foreign news media, he'd gone in as a member of a group of ordinary sightseeing tourists. I'd timed my presence to coincide with his tour group's scheduled arrival at the northern side.

I envied Joe. I'd been in the North only once, to cover the New York Philharmonic concert in 2008. That visit had been even shorter than Joe's package tour. And instead of focusing mainly on the country and its people, my job had been to stick close to the American musicians. Still, even a brief taste had been enough to whet my interest in what was happening north of Panmunjom.

My current assignment to gather footage from the southern side of the Cold War border relic made plenty of sense from the editors' standpoint. It was one of those times when outsiders seriously wondered whether young ruler Kim Jong-un had gone full-scale, start-a-war bonkers — even as they worried that his Washington, D.C., counterpart was about to launch a preventive first strike.

The third-generation dictator disliked adult supervision and any hint of competition for power. He'd been on a roll since his headline-hogging liquidation of a mentor uncle in late 2013. His homicidal purges had peaked in early 2017 when hirelings smeared VX nerve agent on his older half-brother's face in a Malaysian airport terminal.

He had paused his barrage of external provocations the next year to promote a peace offensive that his enemies — at first cautiously welcoming it — had eventually denounced as "fake," another cynical Pyongyang trick. With the collapse of that latest "denuclearization and peace process," Kim had resumed lashing out at his enemies.

Once again, leaders of countries concerned were hyperventilating in helpless frustration. They needed to do *something*, but their advisors were unable to think of much of anything that wouldn't make matters worse. A preventive strike, against Kim personally or his nuclear program or both, quite likely would prompt a retaliatory Northern artillery attack wiping out the Southern capital, Seoul — restarting the Korean War.

So should politicians and diplomats call for yet another round of diplomatic talks? What would be the point? The North had made clearer than ever that it wasn't about to give up its nuclear weapons. Instead, the country was warning — and showing — that it was a force to be dealt with. There had been three major challenges within the previous two months alone.

Seventeen South Korean human-rights activists, preparing to launch balloons bearing leaflets and miniature radio receivers into Northern territory, had died when their fishing vessel exploded and sank. Even while denying that the cause was a Northern torpedo, Pyongyang's spokespersons had gloated that the puppet traitors deserved their fate.

A drone spewing out deadly sarin gas had penetrated an air-conditioning vent on the roof of the headquarters of a hawkish Tokyo newspaper known for demanding that Japan develop its own nuclear weapons arsenal as a deterrent. The attack clearly had been intended to terrorize any Japanese old enough to remember the Aum Shinrikyo cult's gassing of Tokyo subway passengers in 1995. (Coincidentally the number killed had been precisely the same, a dozen.)

Another obvious goal had been to remind the world that North Korea's weapons of mass destruction were not confined to nukes. Pyongyang had denied launching the drone. At the same time its propaganda outlets had advised the newspaper's personnel to get their affairs in order because their days were numbered.

And then — no doubt calculating that the just-launched U.S. invasion of Honduras would keep the American president's hands full for long enough that Pyongyang could get away with it — Kim had hatched an even more stunningly provocative stunt. He'd lobbed an unarmed intercontinental ballistic missile smack into the U.S.

missile testing range at Kwajalein Atoll, known as "the world's largest catcher's mitt," in the Republic of the Marshall Islands.

The only casualties had been a pair of young, tanned American contractor personnel shown struggling in photos that flashed around the world. The man and woman, Speedo- and bikini-clad respectively, had miscalculated and drowned in an attempt to body surf on the turbulence as the missile sank into the Kwajalein lagoon.

Inside-the-Beltway pundits had commenced wringing their hands over that demonstration of the enemy's aim. Pyongyang's spokespersons, meanwhile, hadn't bothered to suppress smirks while claiming for the record that North Korea, innocently, had been practicing for a satellite launch. It was purely "accidental" that the "rocket" had come down at a U.S. Army base and not at some other spot in the vast Pacific Ocean.

While the other camera people fanned out, I stationed myself near the entrance to an alley that ran between the two central Joint Security Area huts. The mist-dumping cloud had moved but the sky was still gray. Through the alley I saw, about twenty yards away, the Panmungak, a wide but shallow observation building atop which the North some years before had built an extra story as an additional symbol of national might.

Although my camera was set up to switch back and forth with the flick of a dial, my main assignment was to shoot video, not the stills that I'd taken for most of my news career and still preferred. Few people remember video as well as stills. Think Eddie Adams's South Vietnamese colonel executing Viet Cong suspect, or Malcolm Browne's burning monk. Black and white stills, especially, because you see them in the abstract, are the pictures that sear themselves into your brain. AsiaIntel, though, was an Internet-based news organization. Like many others using the same medium, the editors liked to post full-color moving pictures. I could handle that. I'd learned to make videos to promote my Tokyo band.

Preparing to drop my gear, I glanced at the forward guards. Maybe three yards in front of me, two ROK soldiers stood just inside the alley. They faced the North Korean side. Opposite them a Northern pair, instead of looking toward the South Koreans, faced each other. All the guards on both sides wore holstered pistols — Joint Security Area rules permitted only handguns. All the men were large and noticeably fit. All glowered. They'd been handpicked, I knew, for their menacing looks.

"Are they out on our account?" I asked the major, who stood a few feet away.

"I'm guessing there's a tour group visiting their side. The Northern guards always come out for the tourists who ride down from Pyongyang. Of course the ROK guards follow suit."

I set up my tripod.

"Ever since the Matuzok defection," Player added, "it's been the Norks' drill for the two guards in front to stare toward each other like that."

"I remembered that part. Peripheral vision. They can watch for any weirdness that might come down, either side of the line."

"Right."

As I fixed the camera to the tripod, a dozen or so non-Asians on the northern side entered my line of sight. Seeing Joe among them, I grinned at him. The Grand Korean People's Touring Company had brought him to the border right on schedule. If I followed my impulse to wave, his hosts might press him to explain why a tourist was acquainted with a news cameraman. Anyhow, the major had given us the usual warning not to gesture — it would be "provocative."

I started the camera rolling and focused on him. Joe didn't grin back but peered intently in my direction from the broad steps coming down to ground level from the Panmungak.

Spotting some Asians in civvies, I took them to be the North Korean tour group leaders. Three men ranging from youngish to middle-aged wore dark suits, white shirts and tightly knotted neckties.

The woman with them was so interesting looking that I zoomed in for a closer look. I judged she was in her thirties. She wore a conservative black dress — and a gold watch and necklace set with stones that glinted sufficiently even on that gloomy day to suggest they might be diamonds. But it wasn't just her getup and the fact she was pretty that made her so striking. The regal way she held herself bespoke a confidence I didn't detect in her colleagues. In her body language she was more like the big-hatted People's Army officer escorting the group, who gestured with command presence as he made his points.

Despite the chill in the air Joe wore no jacket, as usual. The bodybuilder's physique he liked to show off left no space for wrinkles to form in his green and white striped, short-sleeved shirt. Still, a closer look at him snapped me out of my boredom and put me on alert. There was something wild in his eyes, something coiled and edgy about his posture as he walked down the building's steps toward the principal conference hut, the one to my left. He kept darting nervous glances from side to side, instead of predictably gazing ahead to take in the unfamiliar view of the border looking north to south.

I kept my camera pointed at him. Our AsiaIntel editors liked footage that showed reporters expending shoe leather for on-the-scene reporting, as he was doing. As I looked through the viewfinder from my vantage point about ten yards from him, I felt something was dead wrong with the picture. I couldn't detect even the slightest hint of the sardonic smart-ass I'd been horsing around with since our days as middle school kids in Mississippi.

Moving right up to the main conference hut, crouching as if to look into a window, Joe gritted his teeth; he seemed to focus intently on something. Only later did I guess that what he'd been watching was the east-facing North Korean guard's reflection in the window glass.

That guard turned to check on him. Joe turned at the same time. Still crouching, he bent forward and, legs churning now, rammed his head into the guard's belly, knocking the wind out of him. Without breaking stride he scooped up the North Korean — who was taller than Joe but not as broad — and used him as a battering ram to knock over the west-facing guard, who had started to reach for his pistol.

"What the fuck!" I kept my camera pointed at Joe and rolling, not about to miss a frame of the action.

Dropping the first guard atop the second one on the sand, Joe dashed toward me. With his right hand he yanked his passport from his shirt pocket and waved the document, shouting, "U.S. citizen! U.S. citizen!"

The two North Korean forward guards scrambled to their knees, drew their pistols and fired in Joe's direction. Their backup had joined the fray.

Joe had surprised them all sufficiently that he made it around the South Korean end of the hut and angled right. I swiveled to keep him in the picture. Glancing at me, he flashed his trademark wry grin. Heading toward the rear area I'd just left, passing between me and the hut, he shouted, "Sixty-seven twenty!"

At that point he should have been out of the Northern guards' sight, the hut sheltering him from their fire. It was against JSA rules for them to cross the demarcation line in pursuit. Rules be damned, some were already over the line. Joe spotted them, zagged again and put on an extra burst of speed. The two South Korean forward guards, along with a backup patrolling behind them, pulled their own pistols and fired at the Northern guards. One Northerner went down. Another rounded the corner of the hut.

Joe crumpled and fell in front of me. Blood poured out of his back and a separate stream formed a pool under his chest. The bullet looked to have gone clean through his heart. I vocalized, loudly, my grief and outrage. "*Gaeseki ya!*" Sons of bitches! But my newsman's instinct kept me standing there, my camera following the continuing firefight. There wasn't a thing in the world I could do for my friend.

His left arm was splayed out so that the palm faced me. On it I saw three scrawled letters of the alphabet — looked like "CDs" was what he'd written.

Joe's "Keys to Success as a Foreign Correspondent," which he'd enjoyed enumerating to young wannabes, had numbered only two: "Always carry a pen, and never pass up an opportunity to take a leak." He was forever jotting notes, in his self-devised shorthand based on all-capital block letters, whether or not paper was handy.

I kept the camera rolling as reinforcements from both sides arrived on the scene. Two North Korean guards were down. A ROK loudspeaker spewed out an announcement in Korean, laced with so much static I could barely make out the message to Northerners: The border-crosser was dead. They should end the confrontation now and avoid further casualties.

Major Player rounded up us news people and hustled us to the rear. In moments we could no longer see the demarcation line. The shooting had stopped; now there was only shouting. I guessed some macho types on the other side were spoiling to continue the fight. In any case, the shouting ceased as well. Cooler heads had prevailed.

Ashen faced, Major Player tried to usher us into the van. "We'll get you folks back to Seoul."

I was still in shock, but not to the extent I'd stand for that. I tried to keep my voice steady. "No way are we going anywhere without filing first, Major. This is big news — 'American killed running across Korean DMZ' — and we're the ones to break it." The wire people nodded and grunted agreement.

Player considered. "OK, come to my office." While using his Internet connection to transmit what we'd shot, we phoned our editors.

I spoke softly when talking about the victim by name, so the others wouldn't hear that exclusive information. Lang Meyer typed a news flash as he questioned me. As he finished uploading it, he said he was dialing Joe's parents on another phone. He asked me to call the widow. He didn't want them to get the news first from the images that were about to appear on television sets everywhere. Before he ended our call I heard him speaking in a choked voice. "Colonel Hammond, this is Langan Meyer, editor of AsiaIntel, calling from Hong Kong. I'm afraid I have bad . . ."

I dialed Evelyn's number in Tokyo. I was close to losing it as I gave her the news.

Her end of the conversation was mostly sobs with only the occasional coherent phrase. "I had a bad feeling when he said he was going to that awful country and now . . ."

Bits of "Duncan and Brady," one of Joe's favorite songs, ran through my head: "Brady fell down on the barroom floor . . . Women all cryin'. . ."

When Evelyn caught her breath, I rang off with a promise to talk again later. The major had been on the phone, too. He stood up and announced that the dead man's passport identified him as an American citizen. The other three cameramen shot video of that announcement. Noticing that I hadn't done that, they eyed me with interest and asked Player for the name.

"Sorry but we have to withhold the name until next of kin have been informed."

One of the wire people, the woman, turned to me. "He yelled something to you. Did you know him?"

We four were competitors but I was also part of the story. Since I'd filed already and scored a scoop by being first to report Joe's identity, I couldn't begrudge the other three an impromptu press conference. I nodded. The Koreans pointed their cameras at me. Major Player grabbed a pencil and pad.

"He was Joseph Hammond, a staff reporter and editor for Asia-Intel specializing in financial stories. Next of kin have just now been notified."

"Seen that byline," said one of the Korean men. "Makes no sense — financial reporter runs across. Why not just wait, go home after four-five days' sightseeing?"

Noticing the photographer's round, black-rimmed Harry Potter eyeglasses, I couldn't help thinking of the incongruity: We were talking not about a magical fantasy, set at Hogwarts, but about a real person who had died. I put that out of my mind and gave him a straight answer. "Beats me all to hell."

He tapped his temple with an index finger. "Any problem in the head? Suicide on his mind?"

"I knew him well and there was no sign whatsoever of anything like that."

"What'd he yell at you?"

" 'Sixty-seven twenty.' "

"Means what?"

"Maybe something from scripture. He knew a lot of verses."

I visualized wire agency editors poring over desk Bibles to make sense of the doomed man's final utterance.

They asked me for Joe's hometown and current base. The answers — Gulf Springs, Mississippi, and Tokyo, Japan — would have been the same if I'd been the one killed.

"Did he have a family?"

"A wife, no kids" — yet. Evelyn was five months pregnant. Joe wouldn't be around to watch his child grow up. "I've got no idea how this came to happen — and I'm sure you'd get the same answer if you asked his parents and wife, so I hope you won't intrude on their private grief. But I can tell you he was one of the great reporters." I managed to keep my voice from breaking as I spoke but couldn't hide the tears.

The other newsies went to file updates. The major picked up the handset of an ancient Bakelite phone that had no dialing mechanism and relayed to someone on the other end of the line an account of what he'd heard from me.

When Player got off the phone I asked, "Can we talk with the post commander?"

"Commander's too busy. You can pose any questions for him to your escort, Mr. Cha, on the drive back to Seoul. We'll get back to you with the answers." He paused as a sympathetic expression replaced his officious one. "I'm sorry about your friend."

"I appreciate that."

The unavailability of the commander was OK with me. My task just now was to reclaim my van seat, pull out my laptop and write the obituary. Naturally I mentioned Joe's most notable series and the acclaimed book he'd based on it, *Burma Shave*, in which he'd laid out the details of vast, systematic corruption on the part of the Myanmar junta.

I told about a childhood spent on a series of Air Force bases, the last of which had been Mississippi's Keesler. I made note, since it was relevant to what he'd just done to the North Korean guards, that he'd won the state 150-pound high school wrestling championship. The final paragraph said an evening of remembrance would be scheduled at the Foreign Correspondents' Club of Japan.

2 / SEOUL

IN MY ROOM I emailed the draft obit to Lang Meyer. I had the TV on and was reliving the morning. I watched footage of Joe going down — including my close-up footage, which AsiaIntel had shared — and of the wire guys interviewing me. I heard talking heads and anchors offer their pretty much useless guidance. I took a bite out of a room-service sandwich, tasting only the bitterness of the knowledge that my friend was gone.

Lang phoned. "Thanks for the obit. It made me think about how close you two were. But there's a problem. Reporters all over the world are calling up demanding more information. 'Why'd he do it?' 'Did he go crazy?' 'Was it some bizarre way of committing suicide?' There's nothing to tell them except, 'We think he was perfectly sane.'" With his distinct North of England accent, Lang pronounced the first syllable of "perfectly" a little bit like the way the French say *un peu*.

"Yep. A wild man to the end but as sane as anybody I know."

"I saw you answering the competition's questions on TV. You looked admirably blank about the scriptural reference. You didn't fool me for a second since I remember that boffo routine you two had where you'd stand at attention, snap your heels and demonstrate the

Bible quoting competition you'd been into back in your Mississippi days."

"Sword Drill."

"Right. So you've had no trouble figuring out where 'Sixty seven twenty' came from."

"'Six thousand seven hundred and twenty asses.' Seventh chapter of Nehemiah, sixty-ninth verse."

"I wonder why those would be his last words."

"He meant, 'Don't let the bastards get you down.' "

"Some of the reporters who've phoned here wanted to know if he was some kind of religious fanatic, like that Kenneth Bae who got himself imprisoned in North Korea — you remember, the Korean-American missionary who'd been taped promoting a Joshua-at-Jericho scheme to pray down the walls of the regime. At least one paper, Murdoch's *New York Post*, has ignored my denial. They cast Joe as another Bae."

"Even the one's a bummer. I shouldn't have been so enigmatic."

"How long before your band's next gig?"

"Just over a week. Dry season."

"Any journalist visas in your passport?"

"Nope. Renewed last year, well after I'd gone full time with the music."

"How about the current trip to Seoul, for us?"

"Tourist stamp at the airport's good enough for the South Koreans if you're not staying long. Why?"

"You might be able to fool the North Koreans. I hope you'll accept an extension of your assignment."

"What you got in mind?"

"We need to track down what Joe was on to up there, and especially what sent him over the line. I'm thinking you might be able to get into Pyongyang with the same tour outfit that took Joe in. Retrace his steps, use any spare time to follow up whatever clues you find."

"Why not send one of your staff people?"

"They'd all have trouble getting in. We had to get Joe a clean passport, with no journalist visas, so the North Koreans would accept him for the trip. That took a while, and I want to move faster on this. One reason: Washington already had been moving toward reinstating its on-and-off ban on U.S. passport holders going to North Korea as tourists. What happened to Joe is bound to inspire a raft of political tweets and editorials saying lifting the ban was a mistake that urgently needs fixing — and not only the yanks but everyone else, too, should stay away. There could be a snowball effect on other countries' policies."

"I was always a camera guy, not a reporter."

"You have a reporter's instincts and your copy comes in clean. Anyhow, I've noticed that as a songwriter you do both music and lyrics. The news business in the Internet era is getting away from the old words-versus-pictures division of labor. If selfies by Joe at the DMZ had seemed sufficient, even the current North Korea story would have been strictly a one-journalist show. We would't have sent in a star shooter from Tokyo."

"It's tempting. I'd love to be the one to get the story — for Joe. But talk about suicidal behavior. The North Koreans have seen and heard me on TV."

"Disguise yourself. That's something you're good at, as I've noticed whenever I've seen you on stage. How many hats do you own, anyhow? With your grasp of the language and culture, maybe you could fly under the radar up there. Some of your family escaped from the North, as I recall."

"Place called Kaesong."

"You're fluent in Korean. That's the most important thing."

"My grandmother made sure of that. But I'm no expert, Lang. I've only been up north once — a quick in and out to photograph American fiddlers and percussionists in Pyongyang."

"I'm surprised."

"I looked for ways to get in for a serious visit. Almost copped a two-week journalist visa once. But when I went to their consulate in Beijing to pick it up, the authorities had changed their minds. They turned me back. After they started encouraging tourists, I thought of playing sightseer. But I didn't want the same old same old that other hacks were bringing back."

"Rare glimpses of the hidden reality of the Hermit Kingdom," Lang intoned in a spot-on parody of a pompous newscaster's mellifluous delivery.

"Exactly. I didn't want to spend my own money to produce some predictable piece of crap. I'd have gone in on a commercial tour if a news organization wanted to give me an assignment. But then I left the news business. First priority had to go to my performing career. That last part hasn't changed. As much as I want to see justice done for Joe, I wonder if doubling back is a good idea."

"I can understand that. And there's personal risk. They pulled an eighty-five-year-old American veteran off a tour and arrested him for his 'hostile actions' during the Korean War six decades before. And don't forget that fraternity boy, Warmbier, who thought it would be cool to steal a propaganda sign but got sentenced to fifteen years."

"I was just thinking of Warmbier. His coming home in a coma and dying was the immediate reason the State Department slapped on that tourism ban in the first place."

"Right. Give it some thought and let me know in a day or so. Evelyn is on her way to Seoul. Can you stick around long enough to help make arrangements for retrieving Joe's body."

"Will do. Was Joe working on a story on music discs?"

"Huh?"

"I've read that private traders in North Korean street markets deal in South Korean and Western CDs, along with video discs. Bothers the hell out of the authorities because they want to keep out subversive foreign culture."

"Old story. Discs wouldn't have been central to what Joe was planning.

"Maybe it was the kind of CDs banks sell."

"Is there something you haven't told me?"

"One of those palm-of-the-hand notations Joe would make when there weren't even any drink coasters for him to scribble on. I noticed it — just the three letters — when he fell. You may have to squint to see it in my footage."

"That's a serious clue." I heard excitement in Lang's voice. "The dude turned up something about certificates of deposit, something he thought might help track the Kim money. It was a long-term project of his."

We were saying goodbye when Lang added "We're going to miss Joe."

I wanted a drink but had one more duty. Why not combine the two? I put down a couple shots of duty-free bourbon, poured again and picked up the phone to call Mississippi.

It was past midnight in Gulf Springs but I knew the habits of Col. Pete Hammond, retired from the Air Force and currently selling real estate part time. He was still awake. He told me his wife Ruth had taken a sedative and gone to bed.

I went over again what he'd already heard from the government and seen on TV. Commiserating with him, I had to admit I couldn't think of answers to most of his questions, which were variations on: "Why'd he do it?" I didn't mention that Lang had asked me to look into that big question. I did ask him to explain to the rest of the family that there would've been nothing to gain by leaving my camera and rushing over to Joe after it happened.

"Don't worry about that, Heck. I heard from the Pentagon. Death was instantaneous. Ruth and I watched the footage you shot. There was nothing anyone could've done. Remember when you two were Boy Scouts practicing first aid? Joe came home repeating that old military crack that had made it into Scout lore: 'Shot through the heart? Just wrap a tourniquet around his neck.'"

The colonel's voice caught when he said that, but he resumed talking. He told me they really appreciated my parents' visit earlier in the evening, and the spicy Korean rice, meat and vegetable dish Mama had brought. "That *bibimbap* was still hot from the oven, in stone bowls — just the comfort food to get our bodies and minds through the evening. We almost felt we were there, with you, beside him."

That remark got to me, but following the grieving father's example I steeled myself. Then I called my parents, who had emailed to say they'd wait up for me to phone when I could. We went through much the same conversation. "It's almost like losing one of our own," Pop said.

Again I avoided mentioning Lang's request that I go north. Even so, the mere fact I was on the Korean peninsula was enough to worry Mama. "Festus, be careful!" She was one of the few people who refused to call me Heck, the nickname Joe had given me when we were in our early teens. "Those awful communists got your grandfather and uncle, and now they've killed Joe."

She had a point about danger. I'd been lucky, pretty much unscathed ever since I'd turbocharged my early career by covering the 1994 Rwandan genocide. Joe's luck, after much less exposure to the bang-bang, had run out.

The last call was to Fatback Hawkins, an old Mississippi bluesman pal. I'd meant to phone and check up on him anyhow. He'd been fighting lung cancer and I never knew whether a conversation would prove to be the last. He'd always been a night owl, and sure enough he answered on the first ring. From his slow, relaxed voice I could tell he'd likewise been at the bourbon.

Fatback had known Joe, encouraged his trumpet playing and even arranged some joint performing gigs for the three of us. He had a TV in his sickroom and he'd seen the news. "Heck, you spend your whole life living and learning and then you die and forget it all. Ain't that a shame?"

The last time I'd seen Fatback he'd been propped up in his bed, popping chemotherapy medications and washing them down with bourbon. "How's that wonder drug treatin' you? What they call it, again? Ni-something?"

"Nivolumab. Thought it helped for a while, Heck, but I feel like I ain't gonna make it."

I told him I might be headed to North Korea.

"You take care y'self, Heck. Anybody bother you, get 'em in the grits if you got to."

I took a cab to an Italian place in Itaewon and ordered pasta. Probably it would have been tasty enough, but when the waiter brought it I was preoccupied with remembering my old friends, one gone and one not much longer for this world.

By the time I snapped out of my funk and picked up the fork the food was cold. Leaving the restaurant, I dropped by a jazz joint down the street and took in the first set. The trumpeter's playing reminded me of Joe's. How we'd loved to fling trash talk at each other as we jammed at his home or mine. More than once I'd gotten his goat by teasing that he was actually playing not a heroic trumpet but a flugel-horn, a lowly sidekick of an instrument.

Fortunately the place was dimly lit. No one could see the moisture that collected around my eyes. I could have used the company of a fellow mourner to get me through the evening, but Evelyn wasn't due to land until a quarter to nine. By the time she reached the hotel after the long ride from Incheon Airport, she'd be exhausted. Back in the room I tried unsuccessfully to distract myself with television. Finally I gave up and decided to call it a day, see if I could get some sleep.

The phone rang at seven the next morning. It was Evelyn. "Meet me for breakfast?"

In the coffee shop I tried to keep the conversation focused on the boring but lulling details of *arrangements* until the plates were cleared away and she was on her third cup of coffee. Then I asked the big question: Could she manage with the child?

A decade younger than Joe and me, Evelyn was working in personnel for an American bank. I didn't know how well or poorly she was fixed. She was an attractive lady, a smart, funny strawberry blonde. I figured she'd find another partner eventually, but hoped she wouldn't feel financial pressure to make a premature commitment. I had no idea, because Joe hadn't made a habit of discussing family money matters even with me.

"Depends. The plan until yesterday was to quit my job and be a stay-at-home mom. It's not my style to hire a nanny and go right back to working full time. But you know Tokyo life. Joe and I like" — she caught herself — "we *liked* to travel and go out a lot. There's not much money saved up; no home equity, since the apartment is rented."

"You said it depends. On what?"

"As you know, Joe was investigating shady transactions and scary people in some not-so-stable countries. A few months ago the company gave him a nice life insurance policy. Joe never mentioned it, but Lang told me on the phone yesterday. The policy even covers getting killed reporting in a war zone. The payout would be enough for me to buy a little place somewhere, maybe near my parents or Joe's, stay home until it's time for him to start school — I checked; it's a boy — and then maybe start back to work part time or full time."

"Good."

"But there's a catch." She reached into her handbag for a tissue. "The policy has a suicide clause. If they decide Joe meant to get himself killed, the way those creeps on TV keep suggesting, we can end up getting nothing."

"Do you think that's what he did?"

"Absolutely not. He wasn't the type. You knew him as well as I did."

"That's what I think, too. He sure looked weird at the moment just before he made his run for it, but I figure that must have been because he saw himself as being in danger."

"What danger?"

"Lang wants me to head up to North Korea and try to find out. I've decided to go."

Now I'd said it. Evelyn's reaction was complicated. She seemed closer to tears. "I'm going to worry about you. Considering what happened to Joe, you'll be taking a big risk. I feel responsible because you'll be doing it for us — for Joe, for me, for our son." She patted her tummy. "I appreciate your friendship and your bravery, but isn't there some other way to figure out what was in Joe's mind?"

I looked her in the eyes. Didn't want her consumed with worry, so I had to make this speech a good one. "Sure, concern for my buddy, his widow and his child seem like good reasons to go and snoop around. But you shouldn't feel responsible, Evelyn. There are other factors that don't involve you at all. Start with my own family's abiding grief and bitterness since my grandfather and uncle disappeared in that same territory."

Right away I could see that focusing on me was distracting her from her own grief, so I plunged ahead. "And there's another factor. I didn't get into photography because I liked pretty pictures. What I liked was news stories — told with pictures or words or both. I used to be just as much of a news fiend as Joe. Until close to the end, I was relying on plain old denial to keep me from facing the fact that the supply of serious, untold stories I could tell well with photos had dropped drastically."

"I do know what you mean. Joe used to complain, too: 'Japan's going through a news drought.' "

"Ecclesiastes said it all: 'The thing that hath been, it is that which shall be; and that which is done is that which shall be done . . .' "

"And there's nothing new under the sun! Joe liked to quote that same verse."

"Eventually it got to the point where my typical assignment was showing up at an investment bank or hedge fund office and taking 'environmental' shots — nearly always in color — of some suit surrounded by the luxurious trappings of his position. My job was to capture his athletic figure, his determined visage and his perfect tailoring for the pages of a slick financial magazine that paid its way by peddling platinum watches and Lamborghinis to him and his fellow masters of the universe. It was male fashion photography for a mostly male readership."

My rant got a half-laugh out of Evelyn.

⸻

Evelyn left for her room while I signed the breakfast check. I reflected on my situation. Yielding now, temporarily, to the old pull of real news, I couldn't think of anybody better to work for than Langan Meyer.

Too many hotshot editors were in the habit of deciding ahead of time what the story would say. Only then would they assign people to assemble the evidence needed to back up their editorial presumptions. From talking with Joe I knew Lang was an old school, straight-down-the-middle editor. His approach was to start off by sending a journalist out with an open mind to learn on the ground what the story was, changing hypotheses as needed. Luckily the AsiaIntel owners — rich investors cheerfully covering substantial losses while trying to get the start-up on its feet — could afford the travel bills.

Bang-bang stories once had been my bread and butter. So any danger involved in Lang's assignment wasn't a serious deterrent; I was ready to go get the story — and hope that story would keep the insurance company from invoking the suicide clause.

I went to my room, called Lang and told him to count me in. He gave me a Beijing phone number for the tour booker, a South Korean woman who went by the name Barbara Lee. I phoned her and introduced myself as an American musician who had some free time.

"I had a cancellation on the tour leaving day after tomorrow. Can you get here in time?" After the previous day's news I was willing to bet she'd had more than one cancellation.

Letting her chatter on in her serviceable but heavily accented English, I quickly typed her as a power matron. "I lived in Los Angeles for fifteen years. You've come to the right place. I have high-level contacts in the DPRK."

She mentioned Joe. "That man was such a troublemaker. I wish I never heard of him."

She told me to fax her my details and documentation right away so she could get Pyongyang's approval. I needed to reach Beijing by the following mid-afternoon to present my passport at the North Korean consulate there, meet the group and, after we received our visas the next morning, fly to Pyongyang for our four-night tour.

China permitted U.S. citizens to transit with no visa, but I needed to get some dollar and euro cash and run a couple other errands. After I returned to the hotel, Evelyn and I went to keep our appointment in the U.S. Embassy consular section, whose duties included repatriating the remains of dead American civilians. The consular officer told her she could have the body shipped to Mississippi the following day. "We'll give you a notebook that was found in one of your husband's pockets."

Being Joe, I figured, he must have filled up several notebooks by the time he was shot. What had happened to the others?

We went to the mortuary to confirm his identity. Still visible on his left palm was the inked inscription I'd seen, a C, a slightly smaller D and an even smaller S.

━━━

I figured I needed to avoid calling my prospective hosts' attention to my part-Korean ancestry. Lang's assumption about my blending in was off the mark. Arrests of people such as evangelist Kenneth Bae illustrated that the North Koreans paid careful attention to ethnic Koreans and were especially inclined to accuse us of spying. I double-checked my passport. The only hint was my middle name, Park, my mother's maiden name. The North Korean spelling would have been Pak, but romanized in South Korean fashion it could just as well be an English name.

Six-foot-two and of medium build, I'd inherited a set of features thanks to which I didn't stand out from members of the dominant race on either side of the Pacific. (Put aside the fact I felt sufficient difference to give me an outsider's perspective toward both of them.) My nose was medium-sized, eyebrows dark and heavy, eyes double lidded. The high cheekbones and black hair could've come from a Cherokee ancestor on my father's side.

The braided ponytail I was about to have sliced off in the hotel barbershop was hidden behind my neck in my passport photo. I hated to part with the braid; it worked with my stage get-up. But it had to go, along with my mustache. Not only the wire service people who'd been with me at the Z but also, I assumed, North Koreans stationed in twin two hundred-foot watchtowers had captured the hirsute Heck with their cameras.

That passport photo dated back to a time when I'd been trying out a new look at the behest of a girlfriend. It showed me clean-shaven. The passport bore not a single stamp to identify me as a journalist. My credit line in the news business had always been Heck Davis, and that's the name I'd been identified with on TV the previous day. The passport name Festus Park Davis wouldn't give me away as being Heck.

Evelyn looked at me intently when I met her after my trip to the barbershop. Not only did she prefer the old me; now she was even more worried. "Don't get killed." It came out in a whisper.

"The North Koreans probably won't know who I am. Much less will they want to hurt me."

So far, so good — but in Beijing, Barbara Lee would turn out to be the tour-booking agent from hell.

3 / JOURNEY TO PYONGYANG

AT INCHEON INTERNATIONAL AIRPORT before checking in the next morning I found a facility where I could store my camera gear, laptop and phone for the duration of my trip so they wouldn't give me away as a journalist.

In Beijing I went straight to the North Korean consulate, arriving just before the deadline for handing in my passport. From the consulate, my taxi got me through rush-hour traffic to the hotel with ten minutes remaining before the itinerary called for the group to leave for supper. Time enough to take my luggage up and wash my face, that's what I thought. But a group of foreigners had already boarded a tour bus, whose motor was running. I suspected those were my tour companions.

Sure enough, a middle-aged Asian woman with a formidable prow of a bosom and a grimace on her round face was standing on the pavement by the bus's open door. Having seen my faxed passport photo, Barbara Lee spotted me as I alighted from the cab. She placed her hands on her ample hips. "I can see you're a trouble-maker," she complained, loudly enough for everybody on the bus to hear. "Probably another one of those journalists pretending to be a tourist like that one the other day. I bet you brought a fancy camera and a digital recorder, all that journalist equipment, didn't you?"

I couldn't get into a pissing match — too much was at stake. I needed to go to North Korea and she might be in a position to stop me.

"No, ma'am," I replied with as much false humility as I could muster. Koreans, especially older ones, tend toward a hierarchical cast of mind. I figured addressing Barbara Lee as ma'am might give her face and soothe her. "Here's my camera." I produced from my bag a fifteen-dollar, bottom-of-the-line, disposable model I'd bought in Seoul to complete my disguise. "I don't have any other equipment, except these." I reached in my jacket pockets and pulled out my traveling selection of Marine Band harmonicas in various keys, a double handful of them. "Like I said on the phone, I'm a musician."

"You claim to be a musician and what you play are those ridiculous toys?"

"I also play guitar, but my National Reso-Phonic is heavy. I left that behind since I came for sightseeing, not performing. These little harps here, well, I brought them along just to pass the time in case we get in a traffic jam."

I didn't quite shuffle as I was saying all that but, with downcast eyes, I assumed as respectful and subordinate a stance as I could manage. My parents had named me after the biblical governor of Judea. However, when I was growing up everybody was watching *Gunsmoke* on TV and associated the name Festus with Marshal Matt Dillon's slow-talking, illiterate deputy. It was Joe's nicknaming me Heck that saved me from always having to live down that image.

Barbara Lee showed no sign of being persuaded. "Troublemakers come up with such pitiful stories. That Joseph Hammond applied saying he was on the faculty of the University of Hard Knocks. After he got shot, the TV news called him a journalist. I did an Internet search. There is no University of Hard Knocks!" She huffed some more before telling me to get on the bus. I felt the eyes of my fellow tourists as we drove off through a cloud of air pollution so dark I could barely make out the newly constructed skyscrapers we were passing.

At the introductory banquet in a vast restaurant decorated with red paper lanterns and specializing in Peking duck, I made sure to sit as far away from Barbara Lee as I could get. Some fellow "tourists" seated on either side of me quickly let me know that the tour booker might just as well have singled them out for suspicious outbursts. Both were journalists, one from Germany and the other from Australia — and they had spent enough time with the rest of the bunch before my arrival to determine that in fact the majority of our group were journalists thinly disguised as consultants, professors, managers, clerks, whatever.

It was clear the pair assumed I was, indeed, one of them; but if I wanted to keep pretending otherwise, even with them, they were OK with that.

"I wouldn't have taken the risk of fudging my credentials if I hadn't heard it was expected," the Australian woman told me.

"Expected?"

"What I heard was that the North Koreans were seriously short of foreign currency, and a large percentage of the foreigners who were willing to pay their exorbitant rates for tours were journalists. Apparently a few years ago someone made the decision to allow people like us to visit, under conditions that let the minders keep control.

"Like what?"

"They don't want to organize real press tours more often than they have to — because then they would have to answer tough questions, respond to complaints about the itinerary, perhaps even tell us the truth on occasion. They just want to herd a docile crowd around to the usual sights. So they've hit on a 'Don't ask, don't tell' policy."

"How does it work?"

"We pretend to be ordinary tourists. If one of us starts making difficult demands, they can say, 'Look, you're here as a tourist. You told us you were a professor, not a journalist. Don't rock the boat. If you want to take a press tour later and set up special interviews, you can apply to such and such agency. Perhaps you will be accepted. On this tour, you're to go where we take you.' "

"That's it? Nobody gets expelled?"

"Normally, no. They don't want to drive away lucrative business. This way the North Koreans get their hard currency. We get to see at least the surface of a country that not many other people visit. Everyone is happy."

The German added: "I heard those rules of the game from an academic who recruits Western tour participants on commission. He sent me the brochure for this trip knowing what I do for a living, and he coached me on how to apply so that the North Koreans would have deniability — they can blame me in case I complain too loudly about how little we get to see."

"See no evil . . ."

"Yes. He told me Barbara Lee knew the rules as well as he did. We're not trying terribly hard to pretend not to be journalists, and she's seen enough of us today to have figured out pretty much who is and who isn't. Maybe she had caught some grief from the North Korean authorities for accepting Hammond on her tour. Even so, I don't know why she would pick you to dump on, instead of any of the rest of us."

I thanked my table mates for the explanation and let the matter lie. I really was what I'd said I was, I told myself. I'd left journalism. Taking this assignment was just one brief step backward. I would stick to my story and hope to be believed.

Fortunately, the hyper-suspicious Barbara Lee wasn't going to Pyongyang with us. Local guides from the tour agency she represented would take over there. Since I had no idea what to expect from them, though, simply knowing she'd be absent didn't chase away an unaccustomed case of pre-assignment jitters. After all, Joe had died on one of their tours.

━━━

I'd heard all the jokes about the rattletrap vintage planes of the North Korean state airline, but the Air Koryo jetliner we boarded at Beijing Airport the next day was a brand new Antonov. I vaguely wondered where the country — supposedly chafing under strict international economic sanctions to punish it for its bad behavior — had found the money to trade up. Selling overpriced tours to disguised journalists couldn't be bringing in anywhere near enough.

New as it was, the aircraft didn't exactly provide a high-end travel experience. Many North Korean passengers sat atop mounds of Chinese goods they were importing. The fact that they couldn't possibly fasten their seat belts didn't get them kicked off the flight. Even those of us who used our seats only for sitting weren't in the lap of luxury. All they brought us to snack on during the two-hour flight was hard candy. As if to compensate, the uniformed hostesses handed out piles of reading material. The newspapers and glossy magazines and pamphlets were all full of pictures of young ruler Kim Jong-un. Articles effusively praised him, his father and his grandparents.

The regime had built a gleaming new Pyongyang airport terminal building since my previous visit. Its similarity to modern airports else-where eliminated much of the feeling of otherness that a visitor in the past would have felt when disembarking at the old, tiny, bare-bones terminal. Still, despite my colleagues' assurances the night before, I worried as I stood in line at immigration. Would they find my name on a watch list and send me packing — or, worse, arrest me for trying to enter on false pretenses?

My turn at the window came. The immigration agent barely glanced at my documents before waving me through to customs. There, officials confiscated phones, which almost all the group's other members had brought along. Those went into a bag for return to their owners at the conclusion of our visit. My new journalist friends were upset, having understood that rules against bringing phones in had been relaxed. Apparently the regime had reversed itself again.

More than half of the group members had brought laptops. They had to line up and wait to have those checked by a pair of specialists.

I'd left mine behind on the theory that ordinary tourists wouldn't typically take such machines along for short tours in a country where the Internet made the authorities nervous. It turned out, though, that the North Korean computer inspectors weren't looking for journalists, especially, but for global positioning systems. I watched my traveling companions sympathetically as the officials confiscated, for the duration of the tour, every computer with built-in GPS — apparently for the protection of any sensitive areas we might pass.

They also took a Leica with every imaginable lens from a Brit shooter. The rest of the journalists had been careful to bring nothing better than high-end non-professional video or still cameras, all of which made the cut. I felt for the Leica guy and briefly thought of offering him my disposable. That would've been of almost zero use to a pro, though. Anyhow, I figured he would manage to borrow something better from somebody else in the group or find what he needed in a Pyongyang store carrying imports.

I scooped my harmonicas from my pockets and put them on the table. A uniformed contraband sleuth examined them at some length. I had to suppress a snort of laughter. Not wanting his inspection to reach the point of pulling them apart in search of nonexistent electronic components, I picked up one of the harps and blew a few bars of "Oh Susanna" — a tune way too chirpy to pose a cultural challenge. That drew smiles from a couple of North Koreans in dark civilian clothes, part of a group of four who evidently were waiting for us to complete the formalities. Recognizing the guides who'd led Joe's fatal tour, I felt a chill.

4 / PAY HIGH TRIBUTE

I TOOK a seat in the back of our tour bus and we set out. First stop in Pyongyang en route to our hotel was a pair of enormous bronze statues depicting Kim Il-sung, the president — he had kept the title despite his death in 1994 — and his son, Kim Jong-il, who'd ruled from then until his own death in 2011.

The chief guide, a spindly fellow whose name was Won, came back to me wearing a serious expression and carrying a basket, approximately a bushel in capacity, that contained an elaborate arrangement of fresh flowers. A great honor was in store for me, he told me. I would be the tour group's representative in presenting this basket to the Great Leader and the Dear Leader, as Kim the First and Kim the Second were known, respectively. I should watch through the window while the representative of the group just ahead of us made his presentation. That way I would learn the procedure. After he had spoken, Won looked at me anxiously. I guess he worried that I'd refuse.

"To what do I owe this unexpected request?" I asked, doing my best to hide the horror that almost any American would feel — magnified by my family's quite serious grudge against the regime.

"Booking agent Lee told us that although you are an American and thus our enemy you are a 'gentleman with good manners' who will know how to show proper respect," Won said, in correct but heavily accented English.

I pondered his reply for a second or two. Had I really fooled that piece of work, Barbara Lee? Or was this her cunning plan to punish me further for whatever pissed her off about me? In either case, refusing could attract unwanted attention and make it harder to carry out my mission. I was trapped.

"All right," I said, clenching my teeth but taking care to reveal no obvious sign of displeasure. We all alighted from the bus. With the other tour members assembled behind me, I marched up to the platform where the statues stood and bowed as my predecessor had done. I placed the flower basket against the platform, amid too many identical baskets to count. The flowers, and the bronze of the seventy-some-foot statues, made a brilliant contrast with the drab, lowering sky.

When I returned to my seat on the bus the female guide, Shin Mi-song, was in the next seat. She thanked me. "We sometimes have a problem finding someone willing to do that, and occasionally the person we ask even creates a scene. It happened just the other day. One of your fellow Americans poked fun at our Great Leader Kim Il-sung: 'He does have a Great Belly.' That hurt our feelings."

"Not the fellow who got shot running across the border?" I had no trouble imagining Joe speaking the words she'd quoted.

Several of the reporters sitting in that section of the bus had cocked their ears. They started taking notes as she replied.

"Yes. He was on our tour. I am sorry to have to report that he started off on the wrong foot here by offending our Highest Dignity."

Close up, she was not just pretty but drop-dead gorgeous — perfect, as far as I could tell, like a supermodel or one of those beauty contestants the Venezuelans groom from before puberty to become Miss Universe. I preferred women flawed at least sufficiently to show they were real — although I could imagine altering my standards if those moist, red lips of hers should ever pucker for me.

Her black dress was identical to the one she'd worn at the DMZ. Close up, the diamonds and gold of her necklace and watch looked real enough to my untutored eye but could have been good fakes. On her left breast she wore an enameled, gold-bordered pin bearing a portrait of Kim Il-sung. She spoke Oxbridge English as flawless as her looks. I wondered where she could have learned it. Maybe she was a diplomat's daughter?

I wanted to ask her about Joe, but I thought I'd better get the lay of the land before taking a chance on how far I could go with my questioning. I merely asked, "You say it hurts your feelings when foreigners make fun of President Kim?"

"We all love him as our parent. He led the victorious fight against the Japanese colonialists. He founded the DPRK. And he always showed such concern for the people. He used to crisscross the country on inspection tours to make sure the officials were doing their jobs and find out if the people were happy. While he was alive, a great many of our countrymen had the privilege of being in his presence."

"What about you? Did you have a chance to meet him?"

"I was an orphan. The Great Leader came to my village and asked how many of us had lost our parents. He gathered us and told us we could go to orphans' school, or not — it would be our decision. I was happy to go. At New Year's he visited us and said, 'You have no parents, so please think of me as your father.' And that is the way I have always thought of him. He said he would make sure we were treated as his own children." Her eyes glistened as she pointed. "We are passing the school now."

Turning to look out the bus window, I saw a gated compound. I could read the Korean inscription on the gate: Mangyongdae Revolutionary School. I considered what Ms. Shin had just said. Stilted as her wording had been, I thought I detected sincere affection and respect in her references to the founding leader.

The bus came to a stop in another parking lot and we stepped off to view the Kim ancestral home, a theme-park reconstruction of a mud-walled farmhouse with a thatched roof. Hundreds of North Koreans were lined up to walk past for viewing. Our guides insisted we break in at the head of the line.

"That American the other day also had some choice comments about this place," said Ms. Shin, who was walking with the German and Australian reporters and me. "It reminded him of a cross between the manger in Bethlehem and Abe Lincoln's log cabin."

Resisting the urge to smile, I wondered whether she wasn't taking a risk by talking so frankly to us. A tour guide couldn't rank very high in the Pyongyang pecking order. Wasn't she likely to get in trouble with the authorities for repeating remarks disrespectful of the regime?

The country's hall-of-mirrors atmosphere was getting to me already, and my imagination immediately leapt to a different interpretation: I wondered whether the authorities had assigned her to quote Joe to the journalists in our tour group, as part of an effort to spin the events of his visit. More ominously, was she trying to provoke us to spout disrespectful remarks of our own so we could be arrested and punished with prison terms or worse? Was chief guide Won in on it, too, his request that I present the flowers calculated to shock me into saying something they could punish me for? After all, with Washington reportedly moving closer to a decision on a preventive strike, the North Koreans might see some advantage in taking new American hostages.

Sooner or later my fellow journalists were sure to steer the topic back to Joe. I determined that I would keep my own mouth shut but listen carefully to whatever else Shin Mi-song or any of the other guides might say about him — anything that might help me get to the bottom of whatever had sent him across the border to his death. Had my friend, never a guy to hold his tongue, finally made one too many choice comments?

Further surprises awaited at the Koryo Hotel in downtown Pyongyang, where our group was billeted. The driveway and the sides of the street were lined with expensive, chauffeur-driven European sedans — Mercedes Benzes, BMWs, Jaguars, even a Maybach and a couple of Rolls Royces — all black, all apparently brand new, their motors idling as if the country had never heard of an energy shortage.

The hotel lobby swarmed with prosperous-looking Asians whose lapel pins, picturing members of the ruling dynasty, tagged them as North Koreans. Carrying shopping bags, they competed for the clerks' attention at stalls selling brand-name European luxury goods: cognac and other high-end booze, watches, jewelry, handbags, neckties and scarves. The prices were denominated in euros.

I found myself thinking back on our Mississippi church's youth pastor, who'd been fond of reciting Matthew 19:24. That's the verse that says it's easier for a camel to go through the eye of a needle than for a rich man to enter into the kingdom of God.

Of course I'd eventually realized that it wasn't the wealth itself that was to be seen as objectionable. Back when I'd met him, Reverend Bob, like every other young preacher, had been learning how to engineer wealth transfers from the corporeal kingdom to the spiritual. The biblical injunction to tithe was a major theme in our church.

Still, no doubt Reverend Bob's eye-of-the needle teachings had stayed with me, and played a part in my lack of enthusiasm for photographing self-regarding CEOs. But there was no way I could have stayed in Asia for so many years without seeing my bias worn down. The new rich and middle classes kept finding more and more resources they could use to ape their potentates in epic conspicuous consumption.

There were worse sins, I'd often reminded myself. Still, from what I had read, this was not supposed to be happening in Pyongyang. After the collapse of the denuclearization process, Washington had worked to round up international support for restoring the policy of "maximum pressure" — largely through sanctions — that the U.S. president had credited with bringing Kim to the negotiating table earlier. One of the main United Nations sanctions was a ban on exporting to North Korea the luxury goods the Kims loved so much that they had let people go hungry while the rulers and their henchmen bought more and more trinkets and baubles. Now there's a sin, I thought.

In an antiseptic-looking white-painted hall full of round dining tables we helped ourselves to a buffet offering a hybrid Western-Korean menu, including blandly seasoned mystery meat patties and a radish-and-water *kimchi*. Showing consideration for visitors unfamiliar with the pungent pickled vegetable dish, the chef had gone easy on the garlic and chili.

Presiding over the room were large portraits of the three generations of fleshy rulers, the current one portrayed as looking pretty much interchangeable with his grandpa. After eating, I strolled down the hall and looked through the hotel bookshop. Any wall space not covered with brightly colored propaganda posters was lined with shelves offering a selection of books and pamphlets. Most of those, like the stories in the newspapers and magazines on the plane, glorified members of the ruling family — particularly Kim Il-sung and Kim Jong-il but with a scattering also of recently published works about the current DPRK Supreme Leader, Workers' Party Chairman and Respected Marshal Kim Jong-un.

Back in the lobby I took a good look around and noticed, off to the side, something I had missed seeing earlier: a blue cloth banner hanging over a couple of desks. The banner's message was spelled out only in English, in gold letters. The larger letters above read: "Welcome Johnny Posey Evangelistic Mission Board." The smaller letters beneath those read: " 'Behold, he cometh with clouds; and every eye shall see him and they also which pierced him.' - Revelation 1:7."

The mission board for decades had handled arrangements for the most famous contemporary evangelist to preach to multitudes all over the world. A centenarian now, Johnny Posey lived in retirement awaiting his entrance into Heaven while his son Robert used the organization to handle not only preaching but also good works. It distributed food and medical aid to poor countries, on such a vast scale that the mission board operated its own fleet of cargo ships. Hardly a month went by without my encountering Robert Posey's name in the news.

I looked around hopefully for Robert Posey, the same preacher I'd just been thinking of, the one Joe and I had called Reverend Bob during the time early in his career that he'd spent as youth pastor of Calvary Baptist Church in Gulf Springs. Sure enough, I saw beneath the banner the familiar face and figure of our old Sword Drill coach, standing at least a head taller than the other necktie-wearing men who surrounded him. He had aged a lot. He was considerably thinner and looked haggard. His eyes were sunken.

Initially I was surprised that Posey organization members had come to town. But then I remembered they'd worked with both the eldest Kim and the middle Kim, on some highly publicized visits to North Korea by Johnny Posey and also on aid shipments. Still, I sensed a jarring contrast between the sober and earnest atmosphere in the corner they occupied and the shopping-mall feel elsewhere in the lobby.

Until that point I hadn't stopped for long enough to digest what I'd been going through, hadn't realized the extent to which I'd been on edge. That may help to explain why I felt considerable relief when I encountered Reverend Bob. It settled my nerves to see on his face that familiar expression combining kindliness and self-assurance.

As heir to the Johnny Posey empire, he'd certainly risen in the world — I'd read that he pulled down more than a million dollars in annual compensation for running the mission board. He had much more on his plate than guiding a few dozen teenagers into pious adulthood, and I'd long since moved away from the fundamentalist doctrines he'd taught me. Still, when I looked at him I saw the same man I'd turned to for wisdom in my youth.

I wondered what had brought him to North Korea this time. My understanding was that no real churches were permitted in the country — just a handful of congregations faked up by the regime to show off to any visiting foreigners who might ask on Sundays to go to services. There was no limit on North Koreans' worship as long as it was the Kims they worshipped. The authorities had permitted Johnny Posey to preach to a stadium full of locals some years before. No doubt that had been a carefully screened congregation of party members unlikely to be swept away by the Holy Spirit.

Six foot six and athletic enough to have been a standout in local church league basketball, Reverend Bob was a macho man who'd never considered a whole-leaf tobacco smoking habit a serious sin. At church youth camp he would come around at night to enforce curfew. We could smell him before we heard him. When I spotted him that evening in the Koryo Hotel lobby he was puffing on a baby-shit-green cigar. Cuba was one of the few countries that still claimed fraternal partnership with North Korea in what was left of the international communist community. Havanas were among the luxury items for sale in the hotel lobby stalls.

I caught his eye. Recognizing me, he flashed that sincere and incandescent grin of welcome that had encouraged many as they walked down the aisle to confess their sins and accept salvation. Breaking off a conversation, he strode over and hugged me. "You stayin' outta trouble, Heck?"

The four-inch height difference was enough that I found my nose pressed against his smoke-permeated suit lapel. I'd always liked the smell and its associations with comfort and help. "Reverend Bob, you've lost weight but you sure haven't gotten any shorter," I said as I hugged him back. I pointed to the banner and added, "You didn't include the end of the verse: 'and all kindreds of the earth shall wail because of him. Even so, Amen.'"

His grin grew even wider. "You got that right," he said, coughing and covering his mouth with a handkerchief he'd whipped from a trousers pocket. Then he looked at me appraisingly and said, "I guess you're with a tour."

"Yep. Just got in today."

He hugged me again, dragging me over to the clump of worthies and introducing me all around. He started with the Reverend John Hyon, a Korean-American cleric with a gentle, sweet expression, his hair starting to gray at the temples. If he'd replaced his suit jacket with a cardigan, Hyon could have starred in a children's TV show as an Asian-American Mister Rogers.

I recognized Hyon's name. He had a moderately high news media profile for lobbying in favor of U.S. diplomatic talks with Pyongyang, opposing Washington's prevailing hard line. He took a few moments to chat about how the two of of us separately had come to know Reverend Bob. Then he excused himself to resume a conversation with a North Korean.

Next up was United States Senator Fred Macon, a star of the tea party movement and its ideological offspring. The senator, a friendly African-American with a chocolate complexion, round, bespectacled face and unpretentious regular-guy manner, wore a suit that looked like he'd slept in it all the way from Dulles Airport. In person he didn't come across as being as extreme in his views as his television persona suggested. "What are your impressions of North Korea so far?" he asked me.

"Too soon to say."

He nodded approvingly — apparently he liked my unwillingness to jump to conclusions. In return, I liked his curiosity; unlike many politicians, he hadn't decided he knew it all already. I thought I detected in Macon a basic honesty.

And then there was Zack Nodding, Asia regional boss of Goldberg Stanton, the investment mega-bank. All he said was, "Hello," but he managed to make that sound unpleasant. Compensating for his tinny voice, he asserted his masculinity by giving me a bone-crunching handshake — he didn't change his neutral expression one iota when I grimaced. He handed me his business card, which identified him as Zacchaeus J. Nodding. I wondered if that J stood for Jerk.

Short and muscular like Joe, his face and hands deeply tanned,

Nodding was all sharp edges from the nose and jaw right down through the hand-tailored, precisely pressed pinstriped suit, blue-and-white striped shirt with starched white collar and Armani necktie — identical to a tie I'd seen at a lobby sales booth. He smelled of aftershave, the aroma so faint and unobjectionable that it had to be expensive. His banker wingtips were as highly polished as the fancy cars outside.

"Heck here, along with Joe Hammond, was one of my early souls, like you," Reverend Bob told Nodding while pulling from a jacket pocket a heavily worn volume bound in soft, dark brown leather.

"Yeah, you've told me." Nodding didn't smile.

Robert Posey's Souls Ledger, read the embossed silver gothic lettering on the book's cover. Extracting reading glasses from another pocket, Reverend Bob leafed through the gilt-edged onionskin pages at the beginning of the ledger until he found a one-line entry in his compact and tidy, copperplate-derived handwriting. He showed the entry to me with a triumphant grin and then read it aloud: "Festus Park Davis, July 18, 1988, Calvary Church Summer Youth Retreat: rededication to Christ."

Man, he was pulling up stuff from half a world away and decades before. I'd long since decided as a matter of principle to be up front about my problems with the theology I'd been brought up to believe in. This time, though, in the presence of Reverend Bob, I just grinned. Seeing that he took such pride in our once-upon-a-time spiritual connection, I didn't want to disappoint him or make him lose face among his colleagues. Besides, on this trip I was resolved not to rock any boats. I was here for information.

I didn't have to suffer the spotlight for long. Some North Koreans came up, smelling of the garlic they'd just consumed with supper, and changed the subject, consulting with Reverend Bob and Zack and John about their appointments for the following day.

The group began to disperse and Reverend Bob turned back to me. "Come up to my room, Heck," he said. "You and I got a lotta catchin' up to do."

As we rode an escalator up to the elevator bank on the mezzanine, he coughed and then said, almost whispering, "I saw you on CNN when Joe was killed — so tragic — but we'd better not get into that subject tonight. Rooms here are bugged, probably other parts of the hotel as well."

That required me to contemplate the bad ways in which my "tour" might end if I didn't watch myself. I felt my heart rate increase.

Fishing his room key out of a pocket as we stepped off the escalator, he resumed speaking in a normal voice. "Last time I was in Gulf Springs your folks told me you were leading a blues band in Tokyo. I guess things were pointing in that direction back toward the end of your high school senior year when you bought the motorcycle, camera and tape recorder and started spending weekends and vacation time following that black musician around the Delta — what was his name?"

"Fatback Hawkins." I affected blandness as I spoke the name of the legendary bluesman, who had worked with Muddy Waters. I remembered Reverend Bob registering mild but definite disapproval of the friendship that had developed after Fatback's return from Chicago to his Mississippi crossroads home. The reverend had feared that spending time in low dives listening to suggestive blues lyrics would endanger my immortal soul.

I'd listened politely to that advice and gone on doing what I wanted to do. Fatback had taught me a great deal — not all of it, of course, the sort of knowledge I'd want to boast of to a man of the cloth who, likewise, had taught me a lot. After all, it had taken not only musical talent but also street smarts for Fatback to survive decades of playing all night in Mississippi juke joints and Chicago clubs.

"My Tokyo band started off with mostly blues, but we've gradually branched out. Now I use the term 'American roots music.' " I reached into a pocket and handed him an unmarked, paper-jacketed disc. "Here's a CD we cut last month. I managed to get through airport customs without giving it up. You might want to play it some time, get an idea of what we're up to. We do rock, country, soul, spirituals, gospel, the occasional Dixieland. You'll recognize one song I adapted from that old-timey *Broadman Hymnal* we used to pull out of storage at Calvary for revivals and youth retreats."

He smiled. "Thank you. I'll listen to it, for sure." Ushering me into his room he said, "Let's kneel now." Down on the floor we both went and Reverend Bob held both my hands. He closed his eyes and, after one muffled cough, prayed aloud, "Lord, we rejoice in renewed fellowship and ask your blessings on Heck, who gladdens souls by praising your everlasting glorious name with the hymns of old. Grant him the faith to accept totally and act upon single-mindedly your eternal word as unerringly recorded in the scriptures. In the holy name of your only begotten son Jesus Christ we pray. Amen."

He was the one who changed the subject, as we stood up. "I imagine you're wondering what I'm doing in North Korea," he said.

"I sure am, although I do recall there's been some family involvement over here."

"Yes, Daddy's visits started in the nineteen nineties. Over the years since, we've quietly built on the contacts we made then with the first and second generation leaders. Two of the fellows you just met, John Hyon and Zack Nodding, have been the point men for us, keeping up relations with key DPRK officials. Several years ago Kim Jong-un agreed we could start a university in the northwestern part of the country. We did a lot of planning and preparation, built a rudimentary campus without any fanfare and populated it with a wonderful bunch of students."

"How about your teachers?"

"Around that point we encountered a serious problem. The State Department ruled against letting U.S. citizens use their passports to travel to North Korea. We wanted American professors who could teach in English."

"How'd you handle that?"

"We put the admitted students to work prettifying the grounds and waited for Washington to change course so we could bring in our teachers. Once State's ruling was withdrawn, we assembled the faculty and started teaching. Our board flew in last week to compare notes with the North Korean authorities as we prepare for the first full-length academic year. University is a fancy name for what we have at this point — it's a very small college, really — but it's developing nicely."

"I missed hearing about all that, somehow."

"There hasn't been much news coverage about it so far. The North Koreans haven't wanted us to make a big deal out of it in the media. I try to honor their request, make it a point not to speak on the record about it."

I reached down and rubbed my right knee, which throbbed a bit from the unaccustomed spell of prayerful kneeling. "Now that you mention it, I did read something about a Christian-sponsored university here, but I thought it was in the capital."

"Pyongyang University of Science and Technology. That's a different story, the high-profile one. Over there, they aren't allowed to teach or preach the Gospel."

"And you're allowed to do that at your university? Amazing. I thought the regime was dead set against Christianity."

"Maybe the Lord has touched someone's heart." He grinned conspiratorially, coughed and then continued talking. "More practically, there's a solid tradeoff for them. Whenever the regime decides to publicize what they're letting us do, it can help deal with human rights criticisms — the religious freedom issue. A lot of the students they're letting us take in are from families suspected of being secret Christians."

He pointed at the ceiling to remind me of the bugging as an explanation for the vagueness of what he was about to add. "I'm not in a position to say whether some of them had been punished for their supposed beliefs before this change of policy — or would be undergoing punishment now, if not for the new policy."

"So they're turning the religious dissidents over to you? Aren't they afraid you'll train evangelists who'll head out to preach and convert a third of the population?"

"They don't seem to have insurmountable worries on that account. North Koreans need special permission from the authorities to move around from place to place. For the time being, those assigned to our university can't move out of the local community. As for the non-Christian North Korean officials living there, policemen and so on, they're considered solidly loyal to the regime. The authorities in Pyongyang don't seem to worry they'd switch sides. But at least our students can practice their beliefs openly while they're on campus. For us, I can tell you, it's a joy to be in a position to nourish the hungry minds and souls in our flock."

"I bet it is. I've occasionally thought I'd like to try my hand at teaching."

"You'd be a fine teacher, Heck. I remember how well you did as youth minister of music during Youth Week." He stopped to cough twice. "I also remember when you used to sing and play your guitar at retreats. Although at other times you showed what I'd call a mild case of introversion, music dealt with that in a marvelous way. You didn't have to ask more than once for everybody to sing along. Performing, and caring enough about it to make sure you get through to your audience — that's a lot of what teaching, like preaching, is all about."

"Reverend Bob, why does your praise always make me want to say, 'Aw, shucks'? Anyhow, I especially appreciate it, coming as it does from one of the world's top practitioners of getting the word out."

He grinned.

"Here's another question for you. How are you paying for your university?"

"We trusted from the beginning that the Lord would provide. And because the Lord helps those who help themselves, we campaign for contributions. We get support from churches. Quite a few of them, especially in the U.S. and South Korea, have been taking up a special annual offering ever since we started the planning process. Calvary's one of those."

"Your voice is sounding a bit ragged," I said. "Hope your health is OK."

"Just a touch of bronchitis, occupational hazard for a preacher trying to reach out to every last soul while there's still time. Based on all the signs, it's becoming clearer day by day that the process leading up to Christ's return is under way. Each of us needs to prepare." He settled a gaze on me, but he didn't press me on what I thought about his argument. "There's also jet lag. I wear quite a few hats, have to fly back and forth a lot. But thanks for asking."

He looked at his watch and coughed. "I have another visitor coming in just a few minutes and need to get some things ready, so I'm afraid we'll have to continue this talk another time. Thanks so much for coming by, Heck. Give my love to your folks when you speak to them, and don't hesitate to holler if there's anything at all I can do for you."

As I let myself out I was thinking that the reverend was still quite a guy.

Looking down the hall, I saw the vague form of a man in a suit standing in a doorway, facing my way. In the semi-darkness of the corridor the glow of an exit sign reflected on his gold-bordered portrait pin, lighting up the man's face enough for me to see the East Asian features. Moving past him with caution I wondered what he was doing there. Surveillance? Or waiting to meet Reverend Bob?

———

I went to the hotel's front door with the idea I might slip out for a stroll in the downtown area. The youngest of our guides, who'd been lurking nearby, intercepted me and told me that wasn't in the cards. I'd known we'd be on short leashes. Still, by the time I got to my room the reaction to being back in the strange country, added to the tension resulting from my particular situation, had me fit to be tied.

Pouring a stiff bourbon from the duty-free bottle I'd bought at the airport in Beijing, I downed it. As I poured another, I turned on the television — Chinese made, I could see by the trademark — to catch the North Korean evening news. It was a good thing I'd fortified myself.

A middle-aged female anchor with a stagey, sing-song voice announced in a tone of operatically awestruck reverence that the huge Pyongyang statues of the first two Kim rulers — the statues we'd visited that afternoon — were receiving foreign admirers in record numbers. I cringed. It got worse. A camera zoomed in on a shot of the statues to show none other than yours truly, bowing after placing the floral tribute. "This visiting American pictured today," the anchor intoned, "is just one of the multitudes traveling from benighted countries around the world, humbly seeking enlightenment, hardly able to wait for their turns to pay high tribute to the peerlessly great men."

"Shit!" I gave the TV power button a vicious kick. I undressed, turned off the light and tried to sleep — but now I'd added another worry to my inventory. Had invisible monitors watched or listened as I'd lost my cool, and would they make me pay for it?

5 / PROFOUND VISION OF A
GREAT MAN

BY THE TIME we boarded the bus the following day I'd calmed down
— sufficiently, I hoped, to have a shot at succeeding in what I'd come
for. I knew we weren't going to get quality time with North Koreans
other than our traveling tour guides and the individual site guides.
What I needed to do was grasp whatever hints any of those might
offer regarding Joe's fate, and then probe for more.

Our hosts at each site obliged, to some extent, by getting in digs at
Joe and his behavior during his visit. My fellow journalists asked
follow-up questions, so I didn't need to show myself as the solitary
tour-group member obsessed with what had happened to Joe.

But I resumed stewing as I looked at the ridiculous sights we were
being shown. The Arch of Triumph, for example, a slightly larger
near-replica of the Paris original, commemorated Kim Il-sung's 1945
return to Korea after he'd purportedly routed the Japanese colonialists. Mama had made sure I'd never forget it was in fact the Americans and their allies, not Kim, who ended the decades of Japanese
rule over the Korean peninsula.

The real tourists snapping away for their Facebook and Insta-
gram postings were OK with the monuments. The journalists were
already grumbling, much as Joe would've done. They wanted to see

how the economy was faring, look for signs of policy changes. "Can't we visit one of the markets where private merchants peddle their wares?" "How about a stop at your computer center?" "Can we meet a high-ranking economic official?"

Hearing such questions, sometimes the other guides looked at Shin Mi-song — who'd replaced the previous day's black dress with a gray one. I was getting the impression they deferred to her, although Won was officially the lead guide and she looked younger than two of the three male guides. If she was the de facto boss of the group, maybe she was the one who had arranged my humiliation the previous day.

She presented a problem: From what I'd heard so far, she seemed to have more information about Joe than the others. But if she was in a position of authority she might well be the last to help me get to the bottom of his case and, if I pushed her for answers, the first to sniff me out and report me.

When Shin failed to respond to his questioning look, the chief guide spoke. "We must stick to the itinerary." The only exception was not a real exception. We stopped at an old, multi-story department store that happened to be on our route. It was almost devoid of customers. I had read that such establishments were mainly for show. Supposedly Pyongyang now had a newer store that had impressed some recent visitors as being more like the real thing. Still, most of the country's actual commerce in consumer goods was said to take place privately in the *jangmadang* — the markets that we weren't seeing.

There was little to tempt us in the drab old store. Much of one floor offered displays of cheap plastic household goods such as buckets and basins. Even avid shoppers in our group found nothing to interest them in the jewelry, footwear and ready-to-wear clothing departments, much less the electrical goods department. In a top-floor tailor shop, though, several of us — journalists all — did get measured for Mao suits, which North Koreans referred to as "people's clothing." The style had received a fashion boost from the third-generation leader, who, copying his late grandfather, wore such an outfit for many public appearances. I chose a dark blue fabric, figuring I could always use another stage costume.

We returned to ready-to-wear for just long enough to buy matching Lenin caps so we could truly unite in emulating the working masses. We'd drop by in our bus, en route to the airport on our last day, to pick up the finished garments.

That afternoon we headed north on a deserted highway past tree-less mountains. I asked Won where the trees had gone. The question seemed to fluster him. He replied only that we happened to have entered a national forest following a timber harvest. Before I could follow up, one of the tourists asked about itinerary details. That tree-less panorama continued to fill the bus windows for a couple of hours, the bleak landscape enlivened only by the occasional farming village. Finally we reached a forested area surrounding the resort hotel where we'd spend the night before seeing another monument to the leaders.

The journalists had all brought duty-free alcohol, figuring that among other uses it would be handy for smoothing relations with the North Koreans. Before supper, at lobby tables adjoining the bar in the resort hotel, we tried softening up the guides with our booze.

Shin Mi-song declined a drink. Saying she had some business to take care of, she left us. I worried that there might not be many more opportunities before our departure to pump her for information about Joe.

At least we made some progress with the men. Won told us he and the other guides were Pyongyang natives, and the three men were tall for North Koreans. Both factors were clues that they had enjoyed better-than-average nutrition. Those of us who had read about the North Korean class system could start with an assumption that the guides were members of the "loyal" class. Otherwise they wouldn't be permitted to live in the capital, whose citizens got prefer-ence in supplies of food and other goods — and they certainly wouldn't be trusted to guide Westerners.

Despite that relatively privileged background, I'd noticed —

starting with a handshake the first day — that Won was as frail and weak as an arthritic old man. After several glasses of Scotch, he spoke with apparent frankness about the famine of the nineteen nineties. According to outside estimates, hundreds of thousands of people had died.

"What was your family's experience during the hard times?" the German reporter asked him.

Won, like his colleagues, had a cigarette burning. He blew smoke from his nostrils before answering. "During the Arduous March — the March of Tribulation — we didn't have enough to eat," he said. "The factories weren't operating, so we couldn't get new clothing when our old clothes wore out."

"Why weren't the factories running?"

"Everything went wrong at the same time. There was no fuel, no power, no water."

Speaking of those hard times made his features sag — and what he said touched me. I'd never had any use for the regime, having read enough to know that its misrule was the basic cause of the country's troubles. But Won's words reminded me that those North Koreans outside the inner circle, the ones who had done the actual suffering, deserved sympathy.

"Things have improved," he said. "I have enough food to eat now. We have water for several hours a day and there's enough electricity. In my apartment I have a television and a refrigerator and a computer and a tape recorder." I hoped there was some truth to his dutiful spin.

One of the journalists asked Won to tell us his opinion of the work of the late Dear Leader and, now, the Respected Marshal in running the state and its economy. "What do you think of those leaders' visions for the country? How do you evaluate their competence in pursuing their visions?"

We all knew that the double-barreled question put him on the spot. The predictable response would have been to revert to the sort of lines we'd been hearing at every monumental stop along our way, about the greatness of the leaders and the perfection of the system they had built. I, for one, was not prepared for his actual non-answer — or for the evident agitation that propelled it.

He gasped audibly. "How can you ask me such a question? How could I, an ordinary person, comprehend the deep and profound vision of a great man? How can you ask me that?" He seemed almost to be hyperventilating.

I couldn't decide whether he sincerely bought into the notion that those two were great men, who dealt with matters of high state-craft far beyond his ken. Or, rather, had the question upset him by briefly tempting him to answer truthfully — and at his great peril — that the leaders had made a complete mess of his country?

He calmed down eventually and the group worked on the other two, trying with no success to draw out even a few basic facts such as when, why and how the situation had improved. I mostly stayed silent but spoke up at one point to say that the luxury goods stalls and expensive new European automobiles at the hotel had surprised me in view of the sanctions that had been imposed on the country.

The youngest guide, a square-jawed fellow who wore his thick black hair slicked back, gave the propaganda answer: "We are in the era of Respected Marshal Kim Jong-un, and the world will recognize the DPRK as a powerful and prosperous country."

"But how are you building up the economic resources that are needed for that to happen? Where is the money coming from?"

"Our enemies would love to know the answer to that question."

I wasn't sure what his smile signified. Did he know the answer himself — or did he simply not want to admit that he had no idea whatsoever?

━━━

The next day, still in the mountain resort area, they took us to a marble museum of seven hundred and fifty thousand square feet divided into two hundred rooms. We entered through four-ton bronze doors opening onto a red carpet. The museum staff provided us immaculate white cloth booties to wear over our shoes so we wouldn't track a speck of dust into the precincts. Once properly shod we were permitted to admire a chalk-white statue of Kim Il-sung, two stories high.

The museum housed gifts to the founder of the dynasty from well wishers representing a hundred and eighty countries. That fit with the propaganda line I'd been picking up on: Glorify the great man by portraying him as a leading world figure on whom the masses and prominent individuals from the four corners of the earth lavish admiration and reverence. Laughable as that might seem to us foreigners, it could play domestically to people deprived of contrary information.

A traditionally garbed young woman was hosting our group. "There are more than two hundred twenty thousand gifts in this building, far too many to be displayed at once. If you spend ninety seconds gazing at each gift, you will have to stay for a year and a half in the museum to see them all." We would see only highlights, including rooms devoted to gifts from countries represented in our tour group. This led to some amusing moments, as when the museum guide and Won explained to the Australian journalist what a boomerang is. Basically, though, I worried that I was wasting a big chunk of the limited time I had to find out what had happened to Joe.

Some foreign leaders seemed to have competed head to head in their giving. From Josef Stalin, who had installed Kim Il-sung in power, there was a bulletproof train carriage decorated like a Russian tearoom and with sit-down toilet. Mao Zedong later had given Kim a more proletarian bulletproof train carriage with characterless blond-wood Western furniture and Asian-style squat toilet.

My favorite gift was the stuffed head of a bear sent by Nicolae Ceaucescu. The Romanian communist leader had modeled his own dictatorship — including an extravagant cult of personality — on Kim's. Neither the Romanians nor the North Koreans had predicted at the time of the presentation that, in the same way Ceaucescu had gunned down the bear, his elite paratroopers on Christmas Day 1989 would shoot him and his wife and partner in tyranny, Elena. I was willing to bet that the young marshal, if he should ever realize the stuffed head was there, would see it as a bad omen and have it destroyed.

The quantity of the museum's ivory pieces suggested that vast herds of elephants had given their lives for Kim. A couple of those pieces and a few other items we saw showed exquisite craftsmanship or artistic sensibility. Most of what they showed us, though, was kitsch. The overall effect was like shopping in an enormous store that specializes in reselling unwanted wedding presents.

Finally we went to the holy of holies, an extremely lifelike Chinese-made wax statue of a smiling Kim Il-sung. Won told us that the custom for honoring the dead was to bow three times. Since Kim under the current constitution remained president for eternity, the guides bowed only once — as, following instructions, I had done at the big statues in Pyongyang.

After we'd finished the tour of Kim Il-sung's gift hall, they took us next door to a newer hall, a third the size. It housed a smaller collection of gifts — around eighty thousand of them — that had been presented to the middle member of the dynasty, Dear Leader Kim Jong-il. The booties routine was the same; the entryway statue, equally dazzling in its whiteness.

Impatient as I was to get information about Joe, I took note that one of Kim Jong-il's displayed gifts was from Reverend Bob. A realistic oil painting of a modern Middle Eastern pastoral scene pictured a barn where a cow had given birth to a remarkably unblemished calf of reddish brown color. It was apparent to me that the donor had seen his gift as a depiction of a sign that the Temple in Jerusalem was to be rebuilt. Reverend Bob in his Calvary Baptist Church days had cited Numbers 19:1-10 as telling us that in that case a red heifer, a rarity, would be needed. The creature must be sacrificed to provide blood for cleansing in order for the rebuilt temple to function according to Old Testament law. Then the structure, he'd told us, citing Matthew 24:15, could play its role in fulfilling End Times prophecy that foresaw the Temple's desecration by the Antichrist.

I thought it had been pretty ballsy of him to take the chance someone would let on to officials that his gift was one that the anti-religious regime could hardly accept — much less display. But I wasn't surprised to see evidence of that quality. Reverend Bob had always been an "I did it my way" kind of guy. He'd left Calvary Church over disagreements with the priggish and assertive chairman of the Board of Deacons. Barney Pietsch disapproved of cigar smoking and just about everything else, and he had his own ideas of how the church's youth ministry should be carried out. Pietsch, who had grown rich as a real estate investor, also had a limited tolerance for hearing his own children quote the needle's eye verse that the youth pastor liked to recite. "I'm outta here," Reverend Bob had told Joe and me, raising his arms like a boxer at the conclusion of a victorious bout.

My discovery about Reverend Bob's gift to Kim Jong-il entertained me, but I had other things on my mind. I'd figured out right away that the tasteless excess on display in the museums would have driven Joe up the wall. I'd been waiting patiently to see what the guides would tell us about my friend's visit there. So far, they'd failed to oblige. My patience was draining away.

The regime in 1996 had completed the Dear Leader's gift-hall annex, which had been built with the same expensive materials as his father's. As we trod a marble-floored hallway between exhibition rooms, I saw chilling confirmation that the famine and subsequent food shortages around that time had taken a heavy toll. We passed a platoon of uniformed soldiers, apparently sent from their base for sightseeing. Nearly all were conspicuously short. Several were under five feet tall.

I felt that I couldn't in good conscience swallow my feelings any longer — mission or no mission. I'd been speaking only English, hiding my Korean language ability. Shin Mi-song was doing most of the interpreting for us and she was standing nearby. Even a Tiffany's window dresser couldn't have arranged her black dress — the same one she'd worn two days before — more skillfully to produce a lush backdrop for her gold watch and necklace. With her jewelry, Ms. Shin herself could symbolize what I was finding obscene about the country – but I didn't want to get personal. Instead I had her ask the museum guide, "Why did you spend a fortune building this museum, using so many scarce resources, when people were starving?"

The museum guide's mouth flew open. Her eyes widened. But soon she came up with a breathless, high-pitched reply. "Precious new gifts were coming in and we could not exhibit them in a poor palace, so we built this palace with our best. It was the greatest desire of all the people. Why are you asking such a question? You must be a capitalist to care so much for money."

At that moment, as if imitating my mood, the room went completely dark. We tourists spoke quietly among ourselves. "No surprise here — forces of darkness and all that," the Australian correspondent muttered. The guides waited silently, any reactions invisible to us.

Even when the blackout ended a couple of minutes later, the museum guide didn't say a word about it. I was ready to resume my attack by pointing to the electrical shortage as further evidence that the rulers' spending priorities were skewed — but she had already started moving the crowd along to the last room in the annex, where we would be permitted to gaze upon the Chinese wax statue of Kim Jong-il.

Just as well, I reflected. She hadn't made the policies. If, thanks to eloquence or luck, I should manage to elicit a sign of agreement from her, she'd probably get in trouble. I didn't want to be responsible for that.

From the exit, where we took our booties off, she led us via an external stairway to an upper-floor roofed terrace where Won called for one volunteer from each of the nationalities represented on the tour to write down impressions in the guest book. I was determined not to be their dupe this time. Fortunately they didn't ask me. Instead they roped in a sixtyish American widow, a real tourist.

Shin Mi-song was standing beside me, along with a couple of reporters. I was acutely aware that spouting off was not what I had come to do, and I'd hoped my temper was cooling. But, no, here it came surging back. I made no effort to hide the bitter reproach that must have been evident in my eyes and voice as I remarked, "Joseph Hammond must have had a really choice comment about this place."

Shin glanced at me, poker faced, and then pointed toward the table that held the folio-sized guest book and a pen. "Here on the terrace he was asked to leave an inscription in the book. At first he refused, saying that if we required him to write down his views we would only be displeased with the results. But finally he gave in and wrote something, which I then translated for the museum guide. It was to this effect: 'I cannot tell the DPRK how to spend its money. But I would not wish my own government to spend this way.'"

"I bet that went over well."

"The museum guide — not this woman but another one who was showing us around — ripped the page out of the book and yelled at him that no other visitor had ever written any such insulting thing until that day. All the other visitors' comments had been very positive."

"From what you've told me about this Hammond character, I'm guessing he got in the last word."

"Yes. He told her, 'Other visitors go home and report to their countrymen pretty much as I have written but in blunter terms. Of course while they are here they try to be polite. I will be polite: You have a pretty dress and a nice face. The grounds are lovely.'"

I mentally applauded Joe, as a couple of the reporters jotted down the quote. But had he ultimately been busted for that sort of comment? I decided to try to get Shin off to the side so I could take a chance and try to talk with her frankly. Just then, though, our male minders rounded us up to board the bus.

━━━

I took an aisle seat in a back corner of the bus, hoping that Shin would join me in the window seat. As she boarded behind me, though, another member of the group sitting farther toward the front waylaid her with some questions about the remaining itinerary. Shin sat down there. The German reporter took the seat beside me.

Trying to look on the bright side, I thought about how glad I was to be out of the gaudy museums. On the landscaped museum grounds, leaves were just starting to turn red and yellow, pink and gold. But the welcome preview of autumn color soon gave way to the treeless countryside we'd passed through on the way up. It was a cloudy, dull day.

The German started talking to me about a theory he was developing: Joe, with critical remarks such as the ones that Shin and various site guides had quoted to us, had crossed some invisible red line. Then — whether merely registering his hosts' strong disapproval or actually receiving a reprimand from them — he had grown paranoid. By the time of his arrival at the DMZ, he'd imagined that his life was in danger and that he had no option but to run for it.

Not wanting to let on that I'd known Joe — or to reveal the clue I'd seen on his palm that suggested other possible reasons for his behavior — I grunted and nodded and shrugged. Eventually the German exhausted the topic. The tedium of the drive fed our need for sleep after several days of early rising. First he, and then I, nodded off. I awoke as we drove into Pyongyang.

That was our night to go to the capital's May Day Stadium. North Korea had made it almost an annual routine to invite visitors to a festival featuring tens of thousands of dancers, gymnasts, acrobats and musicians, along with card-flippers who created vast pictorial mosaics covering an entire side of the one hundred fifty thousand-seat stadium while the others performed on the field. The show was supposed to be taking a year off, but the authorities had decided to offer reruns during the height of the tourist season.

The nightly show combined the regime's version of history — including bloody scenes of fighting against first the Japanese and then the Americans — with a celebration of the paradise supposedly being built. The card-flippers formed pictures of a tractor factory and a hydroelectric plant. The leaders' idea of the economy seemed still stuck in the socialist past before the state-run enterprises had failed and the economy collapsed. There were no scenes of private traders buying and selling in the markets — the big factor that foreign experts had described as all that stood between the population and another huge disaster.

I managed to sit next to Shin in the stadium — but so did the Australian correspondent. And other journalists were sitting within earshot. Shin stayed busy answering questions about the display.

It was not even nine o'clock when we left the stadium. Most members of the group wanted to go out on the town, so we invited our minders to join us for some nightlife at any venue they might suggest — our treat. I figured this could be my opportunity to ask about Joe. The music might provide cover for private conversation.

The three male guides looked at Shin Mi-song when we first made the proposal. They looked at her again when I mentioned we'd prefer live music.

"Our nightspots have more karaoke than live music," she said, "but I do know one place where we may be able to go." It took her a few minutes on her mobile phone to organize the outing. After riding in our bus on what seemed a meandering, roundabout route, we arrived at a building that I suspected was actually within a pistol shot of the hotel.

Our group quickly found itself ensconced in the building's basement listening to a competent Chinese jazz ensemble. Some of my colleagues were puzzled: What about all the stories we'd read saying that jazz was banned in North Korea, on account of its anti-socialist decadence? I figured times changed — and, anyhow, rules were made to be broken by those of high enough status.

We were the only Westerners in what appeared to be an exclusive club, furnished with sofas and upholstered chairs. Among the Asians present, only about half were North Koreans as evidenced by their Kim portrait pins. Several groups consisting of both pinned and non-pinned were speaking among themselves in Chinese; one group spoke Japanese. Shin Mi-song sat down next to me. My opportunity finally having come, I leaned over and spoke into her ear: "Tell me more about Joe Hammond, please, Ms. Shin."

Her eyes registered that she'd heard me — but just then the band took a break. One of the other guides turned to Shin and, in Korean, urged her to play the piano. I've got to hear this, I thought.

She strolled forward with her perfect runway-model walk, and then seemed to prepare herself rather primly before arranging her perfect ass on the stool — sidesaddle. That was the clue, but I missed it. And then, without having given any other advance hint of what was coming, she started shaking the shapely right leg that was facing the audience, swaying and bobbing her head as she pounded out a number that I instantly recognized as "Great Balls of Fire."

She hit the notes right, both the boogie-woogie bass and the treble runs, and when she got to the middle she even kicked over the piano stool. Apparently totally uninhibited, she played standing up. She must have watched the old Jerry Lee Lewis film clips on YouTube to get that part right.

In no way did she resemble the brainwashed, lockstep, robotic North Korean of the media stereotype. I wondered, as I watched and listened, how that side of her fit in with the evidently sincere affection for the late Kim Il-sung she'd expressed in our conversation on the first day of the tour.

She wasn't singing, and it appeared she didn't plan to. Redneck twang must not have been part of the curriculum at the schools where they'd taught her the BBC English she spoke. But "Great

Balls" without the words is lamentably incomplete, so what was a musically inclined fellow supposed to do?

Figuring it was a way to ingratiate myself with her, I stood and sang as I repositioned myself next to the piano. The tourists and reporters were the first to start dancing, then some of the Chinese. Finally, half the people in the room including two of our male guides were up rocking and rolling.

When we finished that number she suggested we follow with "That's All Right Mama." I reached in my pocket and found the appropriate harp. When we'd finished that one, she suggested I pick our third and last number. Sonny Boy Williamson's "Help Me" offered great harmonica solo slots plus lyrics that, as Fatback Hawkins had pointed out to me, can be twisted tighter than two-dollar bed sheets around a fat hooker in a cheap hotel room.

The house band returned as we completed our mini-set. The crowd was going so wild by then, I judged Ms. Shin could've gotten away with setting the piano on fire — as, legend had it, Jerry Lee Lewis once had done to keep the great Chuck Berry from following his act.

With me, she could have gotten away with just about anything, I was thinking, my pants bulging, as we returned to our seats. *Concentrate on the mission, dude, not the woman.* As the house band began its set I was preparing to either hear her response to what I'd asked her or repeat the question.

A man appeared behind us, leaned over and said in Korean that the two of us were invited to the Number One Room. Ms. Shin translated for me, but called it the "VIP Room." We followed the man toward a door, flanked by a large mirror, on one side of the club's main room. Someone unlocked the heavy steel door. As we passed through, I could see that the mirror was a one-way viewing window through which those seated in the burgundy and gold brocade-wall-papered inner space could watch both the performers and the club's non-VIP patrons.

The group inside consisted mostly of young people, the women apparently still in their teens and every one of them as gorgeous as Shin. Three or four men wearing earphones and standing around the edges of the room clearly were armed, their suits not of sufficient quality to disguise the underarm bulges.

The VIP himself was a portly man seated at the center of the group and otherwise identifiable thanks to adoring expressions and body language displayed by those gathered around him. I figured him to be in his early thirties. Unlike his bodyguards, he wore no lapel pin. Like them, he was packing. His pinstriped charcoal-gray business suit was the second obscenely expensive bespoke model I'd noticed in Pyongyang. The tailoring was fine enough to disguise a shoulder holster — but he had pulled back his lapels and let his belly hang out, the better to attack his drink. I could see the butt of his pistol poking out.

With his girth and the roundness of his face the man bore some resemblance to the Kims whose portraits hung on walls, especially the oldest and the youngest. But this one wore a diamond stud in his left earlobe. The hairstyle was different, too — he wore his spiked — and to my eye he didn't look exactly like the pictures of any of them. I figured he might be secondary royalty — a brother, or maybe a cousin.

Seated next to him was the only old person in the group, a bald, lantern-jawed, khaki-uniformed officer with big, prominent teeth who looked to be in his sixties or seventies. Judging by all the ribbons and gold braid and medallions he wore, his rank had to be among the highest.

The VIP, obviously for my benefit, spoke to Shin in English — limited English, nowhere near her standard: "Every time, comrade, you surprise us. Last week, techno. American guy with you borrowed a trumpet and played. That was OK but then he went to Panmunjom, made a mess. This guy going to cause problems, too?"

He looked at me. Shin Mi-song looked at me. Was she taking heat on account of Joe's — and, now, my — behavior? I figured I was on my own. I thought I'd better start out playing the fool, the guise in which I'd apparently disarmed the loathsome Barbara Lee.

"I'm not a fellow who goes around looking for trouble," I lied in slow Mississippi English, a shit-eating grin on my face. "But I do know a recording company that would love to sign up Ms. Shin here if you wouldn't mind too much having her smuggled to Nashville, in my suitcase, so she can get started on winning her Grammy."

"Hah! We have export ban on Comrade Mi-song. But take a drink — consolation prize." One of his minions poured Johnnie Walker Blue Label. Asian high rollers preferred Blue. We still hadn't been invited to sit down. But I was so relieved that neither Ms. Shin nor I had been hauled off to face a firing squad, I didn't mind standing.

Before we'd had time to get down more than a swallow or two the VIP, who hadn't introduced himself, stood to signal that our time was up. "Come back, visit my country again." We started out the way we had come in. As we walked through the doorway and turned, I looked around. One of the bodyguards had opened a separate door in the back of the room. As our host and his retinue exited I caught a brief glimpse of an arched, brick-walled underground passageway in which stood a vehicle that reminded me of an amusement park railroad's open passenger car.

Soon it was time for our group to leave, since we'd have an early start the next day. Ms. Shin sat apart from me on the bus back to the hotel, but when we got off I went up to her and whispered, "Is he one of the Kim family?"

"Yes," she said, curtly enough to warn me not to pursue the matter. I headed up to my room after what I considered a mostly fruitless day. I'd confirmed only that Shin was personally known to someone in the ruling family. At least I was probably right to focus on getting her to talk, I told myself. But then a small voice grew louder, warning me that the way the evening had progressed wasn't an accident. Shin was no ordinary tour guide. I needed to avoid getting caught in a setup.

6 / IN YOUR FACE

THE NEXT MORNING we set out for Panmunjom. I was watching and listening intently for any clues to why and how this penultimate-day phase of the tour had cost Joe his life. We drove for an hour and were pulling into a midway rest stop when Won, as if reading from a script, made a chilling announcement through his microphone: "You are not permitted to stray from the road, due to the presence nearby of military installations. If you go where you are not supposed to go, it is permitted to shoot you."

My heart jumped up and made a lump in my throat as I thought of Joe. Shin Mi-song was sitting nearby, although not next to me, and she was looking straight into my eyes. It wouldn't have surprised me if my self-indulgent angry outburst at the gifts museum had led her to suspect that Joe and I were connected. I'd need to watch my step.

We stopped at the North's DMZ briefing hall. Inside, with Shin interpreting, an army captain — the same one I had seen with Joe and company in the Joint Security Area on the fateful day — filled us in on the layout and history, pointing to a tabletop scale model of the sector. His history was the officially faked-up North Korean version, in which the South had started the Korean War by attacking the North.

The captain then accompanied us on the short bus ride to the JSA. There we looked around while he fielded more questions. To avoid calling further attention to myself, I waited to see whether any of the other journalists would ask about the Joe Hammond incident. The German did, as we were standing on a balcony of the Panmungak observation building facing the conference huts.

"Two of my comrades died because of that crazy American," the captain spat out. "I have no idea what got into him. Even in our briefing room before we came to the Joint Security Area he said crazy things. He said my account of the start of the war was false. He lied that there is proof in the Soviet archives that Kim Il-sung went to Stalin three times and finally got permission to invade the south. I suggested to him that he and I restart the war right away, just the two of us. I also warned him that I could not guarantee his safety in our country if he insisted on saying such insulting things."

The captain's face grew red as he recalled the moment.

"That sounds like a threat," said the Australian journalist. "Do you think he ran across the line because you had made him afraid of staying in the North?"

"It was not a threat — just the normal reaction of any patriot who hears such slander. But who knows what he was thinking?"

"Did you have a further confrontation with him?"

"No. Although he was extremely provocative, I managed to pull myself together. In training they emphasize that we will receive the occasional difficult tourist. My way of keeping from overreacting is to do breathing exercises. I had calmed down by the time we came here to the Joint Security Area, but perhaps he had not done any deep breathing himself."

"So what did you see here that day?"

"I only noticed that he looked very strange, even before he acted. All of a sudden he attacked two of our men and started running. Our guards, quite understandably, pursued him. Two lost their lives. They were good soldiers and I miss them. One of them, a sergeant, left a wife and two children. I can never forgive that American bastard for what he did."

Shin Mi-song in her translation left out the word bastard. I looked over toward the spot where Joe had died, and my stomach churned. When I turned back, I saw that Shin, her face impassive as usual, was looking at me again.

En route back to Pyongyang the bus stopped in Kaesong at a traditional inn. The sprawling old single-story, tile-roofed masonry structure overlooked a canal. That stop might have been lost on me, so intently was I trying to sort through the accumulated evidence about Joe. But the aromas brought me out of my concentration, reminding me of home on nights when Mama and *Halmeoni* — my grandmother — cooked Korean.

Waiters ushered us into a dining room where we sat cross-legged on a heated floor that was covered with lacquered paper. The American widow, who had undergone hip replacement surgery not long before, wasn't up to floor-sitting and left for a chair in the lobby.

The staff rewarded those of us who stayed behind, serving us spicy roasted beef, rice, soup and a huge assortment of vegetable side dishes. I have to confess that I'd almost finished stuffing myself before I remembered the undersized soldiers at the gifts museum and reflected that there were a lot of hungry people in North Korea.

It made sense that the aromas and flavors seemed so familiar. After all, Kaesong was Halmeoni's and Mama's hometown. The 1945 post-World War II division of the peninsula along the thirty-eighth parallel had placed the ancient former capital city in South Korea. Then in 1950, in an early Korean War battle, enemy troops had captured the city. My grandfather and uncle had disappeared while the family was trying to evacuate southward. I wished I could ask somebody the location of the family home. Knowing I couldn't, I refocused my thoughts on the reason I had come.

The next morning we'd be flying back to China. The other journalists would file reports on what they'd learned about Joe's contentious encounters, adding to any already published accounts by other reporters who'd been on the earlier tour with him. I was inclined to hold off, because I had nothing better than some interesting anecdotes. I felt I hadn't drilled even close to the bottom of his story.

Had Joe died because of his proclivity for popping off with smart-ass remarks? I didn't imagine North Korean policymakers would want to take the risk of killing a U.S. civilian merely on that account. Had the army captain at the DMZ frightened him into bolting? To a stranger that might seem a plausible explanation, but I'd known Joe. He would never duck a fight. If he'd felt the captain's offer was a serious challenge he'd have been ready to go *mano a mano*.

Puzzled, fast running out of time, I needed to talk to somebody. As in my high school years, Robert Posey had made it clear he was available whenever such a need might come up. Hanging around the hotel lobby after supper, I saw him arrive accompanied by his board members. When I was able to break in for a moment, I asked if there was any place where he and I could talk without being overheard. He suggested a stroll among the lobby stalls, as if for shopping. We would in fact be doing just that, because he needed to buy more cigars. As we started off, I told him I'd been trying to work out what had happened to Joe.

"I figured as much, since you two were always so close. What have you found out about his stay here?"

"As always, he gave new meaning to the term, 'In your face.' "

"That's Joe, all right, literally. Remember when I sat with you and his parents at some of his wrestling matches, to offer support? Whenever he took down another wrestler he'd be poised there with his nose no more than an inch from the other guy's. It was all he could do to restrain himself from screaming 'Gotcha!' and then running a victory lap around the mat." Reverend Bob pumped his fist by way of illustration.

"Yep. Here in North Korea, he offered 'choice comments' at every stop. At the Z, I imagine they'd shoot him again, for emphasis and to make sure he's dead, if they had the chance."

"Why do you think he made a run for it?"

"I don't know, but he looked terrified before he started running. Something had spooked him. I guess he felt he was in some sort of danger."

"He could have felt that way without actually being in danger. I ran into him in the lobby here the night I arrived and again the next morning, just before he left for Panmunjom. Although he was glad to see me, I could tell he was agitated. This place has a way of driving visitors temporarily insane — all the unending propaganda: the Kim worship, the tall tales that are officially passed off as truth. That, plus being confined by your minders, watched and listened in on all the time — Americans aren't used to it."

A sheepish grin came to Reverend Bob's face as he recalled something. "I went temporarily nuts toward the end of my first visit here. When they were driving us down to look at the DMZ, the thought entered my head of making a run across the border to the Free World. But when I got to Panmunjom and saw those mean-looking guards on both sides I came to my senses."

The startling image made me smile, too, but I quickly turned serious. "The crazy man theory may be the one that a lot of people draw out of Joe's behavior while he was here but it doesn't jibe with the Joe that his wife Evelyn and I knew. Thinking of making a run is one thing. Doing it is another, as you know from your own experience. I can't see him going through with it out of that sort of momentary craziness — especially knowing his new life insurance policy had a suicide clause."

"Have you come up with a better explanation?"

"Joe wanted to know where the Kim wealth comes from and

where they're putting it. I was hoping I'd find some clues to what he'd dug up about that, but I've come up pretty much empty-handed. I can't give up yet, because I just have this feeling the money was involved somehow in what happened to him. For Joe, whatever story he was working on was always the big thing."

"I can see why you feel you need to go after that possibility. Tell you the truth, Heck, I don't know a whole lot about money. Zack Nodding and others on the board handle all that sort of thing and give me a salary."

"I understand that, Reverend Bob. It's just good to have you as a sounding board again."

"If you do learn something of a financial nature and you need help figuring it out, you can't go wrong consulting Zack. He was in my church in North Carolina after I left Gulf Springs, a crackerjack Sword Driller like you and Joe. Smart as a whip. Daddy was starting up the original Posey University in Virginia and wanted a standout freshman class to inaugurate it with a bang. Zack got nearly perfect SAT scores and could've gone anywhere. Daddy offered him a full scholarship."

"He took it?"

"He did, and he went on to graduate first in his class. By the way, you also met John Hyon. He ranked close second in that same class. We're training the best and the brightest of young Christians to become America's leaders. We'd noticed that the Mormons had started to account for a large percentage of career U.S. diplomats. That was thanks to their custom of sending youngsters abroad as lay missionaries. A kid was thrown into interacting with the local people and had to learn the language. We started our own program like that, and Zack and John were pioneers. The two of them went to South Korea for two years, preaching on street corners, wherever anybody would listen to them. John had grown up in Korea so he didn't have to study the language and was able to help Zack learn it. He sort of served as coordinator of our initial mission."

"So they were preparing to be diplomats?"

"Not John. We already knew he was cut out for the ministry. In Zack's case we prayed over it, and the decision was that he'd go on to the Wharton School for a master's in finance before getting a job on Wall Street. Now, nobody knows money better than he does. He went back to Hong Kong a couple days ago. Give him a shout or go see him in case you run up against something big and complicated with dollar signs all over it."

"Thanks. Maybe I'll do that."

"In the meantime, I suggest you think again about the temporary insanity possibility. Some of the tour guides are ringers, sent by the police or other spy agencies including State Security — that's the secret police outfit that corresponds to the old Soviet KGB. They watch not only the tourists but also the other tour guides. I'm not at liberty to tell you where I learned this, but I've been told there was somebody from one of the security agencies among Joe's guides. Maybe the spy scared Joe, accidentally or on purpose."

"We have the same group of guides."

"You may want to try to scope out who that person is — not that there's a whole lot you could do about it." Reverend Bob's face clouded. "Heck, it's a great sadness to me that Joe didn't come back to Christ before he lost his life. You remember when he wrote that letter?"

I nodded. Joe's letter of resignation had scandalized the Calvary Church membership and the story had spread to other Southern Baptist congregations in the generally conservative town. He'd written it after taking a New Testament course his first semester in college and concluding — as he had long suspected — that the Bible was very much the work of men.

"By then, I'd been called to the church in North Carolina," Reverend Bob said, "but Joe kept me in the loop — wrote a longer letter to me. People still sent handwritten letters then. In that personal letter he outlined all his arguments against our beliefs."

"He did tell me he'd written to you. I don't recall ever hearing you'd replied. I was afraid you'd felt offended."

Reverend Bob coughed again. "You were always the tactful one. I put that down to your upbringing as a Southerner."

He had a point. I'd always been somewhat less inclined than Joe to rock the boat. Even though Mama wasn't a native speaker of English, much less Mississippi English, she'd discovered a talent for picking up local dialects along with local customs. As a scholarship student at the state women's college, she'd become known for her Southern drawl and ladylike demeanor. She preferred I call her Mama, not *Eomma*, except when we were talking with Halmeoni, whose English was only rudimentary. Blending in with the local culture was important to Mama. Put all that together with her love of the Golden Rule, then factor in Korea's overlay of Confucian tradition, and you can see why she was always on Pop's wavelength when it came to raising mannerly youngsters.

I was by no means a youngster any more but I was still so well mannered I simply listened politely as Reverend Bob returned us to yesteryear.

"As for Joe," Reverend Bob continued, "like you, he called his elders sir and ma'am, but that's only because he was an Air Force brat — his term — who'd been raised on bases around the world before Colonel Hammond drew Keesler as his final career posting. Brash could've been Joe's middle name."

I laughed. "Nobody ever mistook Joe for a diplomat, that's for sure."

"But regarding that personal letter," Reverend Bob said, "I did start to draft a reply — never got it into shape to send to Joe before a big issue came up in my new church and distracted me. What my reply would've said is that I was touched that Joe had enough regard for me, as a friend and mentor, to try to save me from spending a lifetime preaching what he considered misguided doctrine. Besides, I could sympathize. I don't think I ever told this to either of you, but when I went off to college I had my own spell of doubting. Even Johnny Posey's son wondered if everything in the Bible was really the word of God."

Surprised, I replied lamely. "I guess it's what college students do." What I was thinking, knowing Reverend Bob, was that if he'd had doubts he wouldn't have taken them lightly. He'd always liked to do things in a big way.

"I read some things about evolution," he elaborated. "Had to sneak the materials into my dorm at the Bible college where I was enrolled, because they didn't approve. I started to doubt the biblical account of creation, including Adam and Eve's original sin. If evolution was right and our first ancestors were little specks of primitive life forms, no way were they intelligent enough to understand the concept of sin."

"Bet that upset your dad."

"You better believe it. Some Protestant evangelicals were getting interested in demonic possession and exorcism around that time. One of 'em was close to the college dean. The dean talked up that theory in regard to my lapse in faith. Daddy later turned sour on that sort of thing, but at that time the dean and his friend were able to persuade him to let the college tentatively schedule an exorcism for me — in case a month of prayer and intensive Bible study couldn't drive out the demon first. Daddy rearranged his workload so he could be with me for the month."

Reverend Bob coughed hard before continuing. "In between recitation of Bible verses I was on my knees for most of each day, my eyes closed tight in prayer — hearing stern reminders from Daddy of the fundamentals of what we believed. A week before the appointed day for my exorcism, thank the Lord, I concluded Genesis must have it right. The logic was irrefutable."

"How did you figure that?"

"After all, everything else we Christians believe springs from the truth of man's original sin. If that part weren't true, none of it could be true. So the account of Adam and Eve must be true. When I yielded, the Holy Spirit entered me, granting me joy and certainty. Ever since, I've known without a shadow of a doubt that God's word is true."

It hadn't taken me long to realize that what he was saying, rather than a simple reminiscence about Joe, was a sermonette tailored as a warning to me. Subtle as he tried to be, I could understand that he felt a sense of permanent responsibility for each of the individual souls he'd registered in his ledger, even though there must be many thousands of us by now. In our two meetings since we'd run into each other the other night, there'd been enough eloquent silences for him to suspect — if he didn't already know — that I, like Joe, was a backslider.

"I knew you weren't a Darwinist," I said.

"All that stuff about evolution, embryology, Big Bang theory is nothing but lies, straight from the pit of hell — lies to try to keep all the folks who are taught to believe such things from understanding that they need a savior. There's a lot of scientific data showing that this is really a young Earth, between six thousand and thirteen thousand years old. I believe it was created in six days. That's what the Bible says. And what I eventually learned is that the Bible is the manufacturer's handbook, that's what I call it. It teaches us how to run our lives individually, how to run our families, how to run our churches, how to run our country."

He paused to cough again. "That's a long way of saying that, having struggled with my own doubts, I certainly understood what Joe was going through."

"So you didn't take offense that time at the lake retreat, the summer after our high school graduation, when we swam to the raft and Joe hollered at you to walk out and join us?"

He laughed. "That's just the way Joe was — like you said, in your face. I had him figured out long before that and never took his comments personally. Even when he sent those letters to the church and me, I prayed he would see the light as I had done, rediscover God's purpose and be reborn in Jesus." He had lost his smile. "I'm afraid he never did and now it's too late."

Leaving Reverend Bob in the lobby, I thought over what he'd said about the tour guides. If there was one spook among them, my vote went to Shin Mi-song. Glancing over at the lobby beer hall I saw several of my tour mates and two of the male guides quaffing the local microbrew. I joined them for a farewell mug, hoping Shin would show up and join us. She didn't, so I went upstairs.

My room was at the end of a dogleg hallway. Approaching, I heard a door closing. As I rounded the hall corner, the North Korean man I'd seen lurking near Reverend Bob's room the first night walked by in the opposite direction. I unlocked my door and went in. On the bedside table was a Beijing Airport duty-free bag. Inside the bag were three spiral notebooks, the reporter's kind that flip open vertically. Opening one, I saw that it was filled with Joe's handwriting. I wanted to let out a happy whoop.

As I examined each of the notebooks, I sniffed to see if it gave off the telltale cigar odor. None of them did, but I figured nevertheless that my Santa must be a certain cleric, his heart as big as his frame. Joe — maybe nervous about something he'd jotted down, retaining his own fond recollections of Reverend Bob — must have handed the notes over for safekeeping that last morning when they'd met for the second time in the lobby.

Being a journalist, of course I had to ask myself why Reverend Bob hadn't mentioned the notebooks or passed them to me directly. Maybe for the sake of protecting his own enterprise he needed to keep as much distance as possible from Joe's case.

I faced an early wakeup the next morning so I left it at that, stuffing the notebooks into my bag and going to bed thinking grateful thoughts.

◻

On the bus to the airport, as Barbara Lee had instructed us was the custom, some of us presented our guides and driver duty-free loot we'd brought along, as farewell gifts. To the men went cigarettes —

Mevius, as Japan Tobacco had incomprehensibly renamed its Mild Seven brand, or Marlboro — along with any booze remaining in our bottles. To Shin Mi-song went chocolate in various forms.

As we said our farewells, it occurred to me to worry that an exit search would turn up the notebooks. Although I could make a strong guess, I couldn't be completely sure who'd given them to me and why. Just conceivably it was a setup. Langan Meyer had sent me to do a job, though. Other than those notebooks, there was nothing to show for my efforts. I had no choice but to tough it out.

In the end, no one opened my bag. Still, I didn't dare pull out the notebooks and look at them until after we had alighted from the plane at Beijing and completed our final meeting with Barbara Lee — who cocked her head flirtatiously and told me, "I hear you behaved yourself, mostly." Her erratic behavior annoyed and mystified me. Only with an effort could I hold my tongue.

Finally I boarded my flight to Incheon, where I would pick up my stored equipment and connect to a Tokyo flight. I had a window seat, next to a snoring man who'd covered his head with a Chinese newspaper to block the light. I opened my bag and got to work reading the notebooks. The first two proved disappointing, merely confirming what I'd heard about Joe's encounters in Pyongyang. Ditto for the third — until I reached the last entry: "N: NEVER HAPPEN. IRS, SEC, WRLD FIN SYST DWN TON/BRICKS. REP RISK 2HUGE!!!!"

Joe had scrawled those final notes in larger letters than he'd used earlier. That suggested that decoding the passage would be a good use of my time. I mouthed the word "Yes!"

For context I returned to the entry just before that one, "REVB FOUNDED COLLEGE!!??" Filling in the blanks I guessed that, having seen Reverend Bob in the lobby, he'd also met and put a question to financial specialist "N," the very same specialist Reverend Bob more recently had urged me to consult.

It was a clue. Still, knowing I was about to see Evelyn, I sorely wished I'd managed to come up with more.

⊏⊐

Joe's parents had arrived in Tokyo and were staying with Evelyn, awaiting the Foreign Correspondents' Club memorial gathering. There was only a day to go before the big evening but everything was under control.

Evelyn had contacted my agent and made sure I was free to play at the memorial. My only commercial gig for the week was scheduled for the night of my return. For that I didn't need to perform until nine, so there was time for an early supper with the family plus Lang Meyer. The next day the editor would interview candidates to fill the bureau's sudden opening. Then, in the evening, he'd show the Asia-Intel flag at the memorial.

They filled me in. The uncharacteristically helpful North Koreans, across a table at Panmunjom, had handed over to an American official Joe's luggage along with his phone, his laptop and his nonprofessional camera. As in the case of my tour group, the authorities had confiscated all phones and GPS-equipped laptops that members of Joe's group carried and kept them for the rest of the visit. Joe had left his camera on the bus while visiting the Panmunjom Joint Security Area.

"Maybe he figured he wouldn't need his own since you'd be there shooting with yours," Colonel Hammond said.

My hunch was different. "He could've decided already to make the run, and felt a need to travel light."

The consulate in Seoul had released Joe's gear to Evelyn, along with the notebook found in his pocket. "I've gone through the camera card and the notebook," Lang said, "but found no clues other than some notes on his argument with the army captain. Joe's account of that was pretty much the same as the one some reporters on your tour reported today based on the captain's version. Do you suppose that was what made him run?"

"It wouldn't have been like him to get scared off that easily."

Colonel Hammond agreed. "Joe could take care of himself in a fight."

Joe's parents had scheduled a funeral at Calvary Church to follow their return from Tokyo, with burial in a local family plot they'd bought. I could sense that Evelyn was OK with that, although she didn't say so. Joe had told the two of us one evening that he wanted to be cremated, with "no preacher permitted within a mile of the oven." But she didn't have to spell it out for me that she'd figured there could be no harm in letting the Hammonds do it their way. After all, Joe hadn't expected to be sentient as they disposed of his mortal remains. The family's arrangements, on top of what we were planning at the club, would make them feel better.

The Hammonds badly needed some sort of morale booster. News dispatches that day had reported details of Joe's reign of verbal terror in North Korea, adding fuel to the earlier speculation that he'd had a breakdown. Meanwhile I was there to tell the family I didn't buy that — but I'd failed to bring back the grail of contrary facts that they all wanted so badly.

I described my fortuitous receipt of Joe's first three notebooks. But as I told them, "The only clues to the meaning of the 'CDs' notation on his palm seem to be the last two entries." I read those to them.

"Who's N?" Colonel Hammond asked.

"My vote goes to Zack Nodding, the Goldberg Stanton Asia boss. He was in Pyongyang because he's also the financial honcho of the Poseys' mission board. We know from Joe's notes and from Reverend Bob himself that Joe had just spoken to the reverend in the hotel lobby. Joe then probably turned to Nodding to ask about a hypothetical financial scenario. The answer Joe got was that whatever scheme he imagined would be impossible. Government regulators would never allow it, and 'rep risk' — I don't know what sort of risk that is — was too great."

Whenever something pleased Lang, his ears shot up toward his buzz-cut hair and his green eyes twinkled. He raised his glass in a salute. "You're getting somewhere, Heck. Stay on it, first by flying down to Hong Kong to talk to Nodding."

━━━

We sent Joe out in style at the Correspondents' Club the next night. The club president got much of the serious part out of the way, talking about what a fine journalist Joe had been and how the Board of Directors and the Freedom of the Press Committee wanted answers about the mystery of his death.

A traditional club memorial was more roast than funeral — something on the order of an Irish wake, with the booze but without the body. Joe's friends knew that he, of all people, would have wanted things that way. In fact he had written it into his will, which he'd composed a year or two earlier while sitting in the club bar, making sure to finish before his second martini so the witnesses could certify he was of sound mind. He'd requested "a foot-tapping, dirty-dancing, good-humored, irreverent hoe-down in the club, with eats and drinks on the house all around, to be charged to my estate in case the board is too cheap to spring for them."

Mourners including me found it hard, at first, to put aside the still raw horror attending his death in order to move into the fun of celebrating his life. But after the first couple of speakers got things rolling, one after another of Joe's old friends and colleagues went to the microphone to tell tales about the Joe we were remembering. Most of those tales were funny, and each contained at least a little truth.

The Hammonds managed some smiles and even laughed several times. So did Evelyn. By the time she bravely if tearfully delivered an oral tribute to Joe, a couple of the guys from my band had joined me, gratis. We soon had the crowd whooping and hollering.

Our set featured Woody Guthrie's "Hard Travelin'," one of Joe's favorites. I couldn't help reflecting on all the hard traveling of the previous week, wondering if it was going to get harder.

FLYING to Hong Kong the next morning, I took along the newspapers that had piled up in my absence. The technologies of tablet devices and e-readers were impressive, but I still liked reading printed newspapers and magazines. A lot had happened around the world.

> Jerusalem — Senior rabbis today presided at a groundbreaking ceremony for the replacement of Judaism's main temple, on land that archeologists earlier had demonstrated was the site of the first two ancient Jewish temples.
>
> The archeologists had determined that the temple — last destroyed in 70 AD — was never on the Dome of the Rock as previously has been supposed. The evidence they had unearthed showed that the temple actually stood a short distance south of the Dome.
>
> The Dome of the Rock since 691 AD has been the site of Islam's third holiest shrine. Because there is no competing Islamic structure standing on the recently identified piece of land, rebuilding the temple is set to proceed with far less controversy than would be the case if it were attempted at the Dome.

The announcement by the archeologists and the ensuing preparations for rebuilding the temple have electrified evangelical Christian Zionists in the United States, who believe the temple must be rebuilt and its animal sacrifices resumed to fulfill Bible prophecies and pave the way for Jesus to return to earth.

Reverend Bob must feel vindicated, I thought, he and his red heifers.

There was news from Korea, too. A few days before, North Korean and South Korean officials had met to at least talk about coordinating plans in case of a widely predicted eruption of Mount Paektu on the China-North Korean border. The South's interest arose from its proximity to the volcano and fears that a major eruption could damage the Southern economy.

At more than 8,000 feet the highest mountain on the Korean peninsula, Paektu is sacred in national mythology. In North Korean propaganda, founding ruler Kim Il-sung is mythologized as having fought to victory over the Japanese on the slopes of the mountain.

The Northern regime claimed falsely, as part of its efforts to build a cult of personality, that the late second-generation leader Kim Jong-il had been born in a secret guerrilla camp on the mountain. Current ruler Kim Jong-un is officially described as the logical successor because he represents "the Paektu Line."

A serving cart bumped my left leg, which I had deployed into the plane's aisle to keep it from going numb while squeezed into the allotted economy-class legroom.

"Would you care for a beverage, sir?"

"Tomato juice, please."

The volcano's historic eruptions have kept to a cycle of roughly one per century, the last occurring in 1903. Earthquakes in the area have become more frequent and serious, and the mountain is growing measurably higher as its magma pool expands.

North Korea set off demolition explosions at its old testing site in May of 2018, announcing that it would cease testing. After the peace and denuclearization process failed, however, it resumed testing using secretly prepared facilities.

After each of the last several nuclear tests, a Russian satellite detected higher than normal temperatures atop Mount Paektu. Some scientists worry that the tests trigger changes in the volcano's core.

The North-South volcano coordination meeting had ended in an eruption of acrimony, the newspaper story said. The North side's delegates had walked out when a Southern delegate dared to bring up the possible connection to nuclear testing.

One of Reverend Bob's board members was mentioned in a short article about a "study session" in which activists from the American religious right discussed the Korean peninsula. Most speakers focused on the human rights situation in the North and favored harsher sanctions. Preacher and lobbyist John Jae-ho Hyon offered a contrarian view: "Negotiating a peace treaty with the DPRK is in the best interests of the United States — and as a welcome bonus it will help open the North to the word of Jesus." The accompanying photo captured Hyon's gentle visage.

That brought me to the end of my stash of print news. I checked the breaking news on my laptop screen and found that the top story was a doozey. A North Korean mouthpiece website, based in China, had threatened to attack the United States by using a nuclear explosion to trigger an electromagnetic pulse that would emit gamma rays to fry the imperialists' electric power grid from sea to shining sea.

Backing up that threat, foreign monitors had detected a brand new, unannounced North Korean nuclear test, carried out underground that very morning. Prior to launching its peace offensive the regime had announced creation of a hydrogen — thermonuclear — bomb, compact enough to use as the warhead of a missile. Some skeptics had questioned that claim, but foreign analysts unanimously judged that this new one was unquestionably a hydrogen bomb whose total energy released was vastly greater than the yield of bombs the North Koreans had tested before.

The regime said additional testing had been needed because of plots to invade North Korea from U.S. bases on the soil of neighboring countries. Its statement singled out Japan.

"If the Japanese think Hiroshima, Nagasaki and the 2011 earthquake, tsunami and nuclear meltdown were devastating, they have not seen anything yet," said North Korea's official Korean Central News Agency. "We warned earlier that we would sink all the islands of Japan. This is the weapon we will use to turn the entire archipelago from Hokkaido to Okinawa into a sea of fire."

U.S. financial markets had closed for the day, but Japanese markets were taking a major hit. I read enough to understand that the test and North Korea's commentary on it had united friend and foe alike in renewed outrage. As usual, it seemed no one could come up with an effective response that wouldn't risk a hugely destructive war — but that was not stopping the American president from using his Twitter account to warn that a preventive attack on North Korea was "on the table."

I still had time before our landing to do an Internet search on the man I was about to interview, Zack Nodding. He had enjoyed a whirlwind career with Goldberg Stanton in New York, Europe and Asia and was tipped to advance in due course from Asia CEO to the bank's top global job. Meanwhile, he served not only as vice chairman of the Posey organization but also as a member or officer of several Korea-interest groups in the United States. He'd been president, for example, of the Committee for Engagement with North Korea, and remained on its board. One article included a photo of Zack at a formal dinner hosted in New York by CENK, as the group called itself for short. He was presiding at the head table, seated between John Hyon and the ambassador who headed North Korea's United Nations mission.

My appointment with Nodding was for eleven thirty and I got to the Goldberg Stanton offices in a waterfront skyscraper by eleven ten. His secretary ushered me into the vast and opulently appointed room where we were to talk. She left me with nothing to do but gaze out the window at the drop-dead harbor view and roam around appraising the museum-quality Chinese antiques.

Eleven thirty came and went but Nodding didn't show up. Around 11:50 I finally started to suspect that intimidation was his game. I was used to it. He was by no means the first suit who'd played with me that way. At least Nodding, unlike a certain world-renowned Japanese management consultant I'd been sent to photograph, hadn't made me wait in front of a wall of books he'd authored so that I could look them over for forty minutes in stunned appreciation of his brilliance. Still, I was irritated. Normally I'd have let it go, simply filing a mental note to myself about this character, but maybe I was starting to channel Joe's in-your-face ways.

Nodding deigned to enter the room at three minutes past noon, offering no excuse for his tardiness as he gave me that bone-crunching handshake of his.

"Nice room, Zack," I said. "With the water view and the antiques and all, it reminds me of my getaway in Japan."

His face reddened. I'd ruined his power-strutting moment. I could almost hear the synapses popping in his brain.

"What brings you here?" he asked, jaw clenched.

"I've been retracing Joe Hammond's steps to find out what got him killed. In one of his notebooks he indicated you two spoke in the Koryo Hotel lobby — he tried out his hypothesis about the source of the Kims' money. He quoted you as pouring cold water on the theory, in view of regulatory problems and other risks. I was hoping you could reconstruct that conversation and tell me more about why you were skeptical."

"How detailed were his notes?" With his high-pitched voice, he brayed like a jackass.

"Not very — just a few key words. That's why I hope you can remember what you two said."

He looked at me intently. Finally he said, "I had never met Joe Hammond before that trip. I didn't get a good impression of him. He seemed to be reaching for a big story that was nothing more than a figment of his imagination. I wondered if, instead of a story, he was looking for a get-rich scheme to use for his own benefit." Zack stopped talking.

I kept looking at him. Joe had told me about that trick of the interviewer's trade. Silence makes interviewees uncomfortable, and eventually they speak.

Nodding finally did. "We only talked for a moment. I had to rush off. I don't remember much about his theory."

"Did he talk to you about certificates of deposit?"

Nodding raised his eyebrows. Again he took his time organizing his thoughts before replying, "I don't recall, but the news media keep reporting that the Kims have set up hidden accounts here and there at dodgy banks around the world. Those might be invested partly in CDs, but what would that tell us?" This guy was not being overly generous in dispensing information.

"So when he quoted you as saying the scheme he was thinking of was impossible because of regulatory reasons and risk, what did you mean?"

Nodding appeared deep in thought. "I'm having trouble dredging up anything specific, but I think his overall premise was that foreign financial institutions must be helping the North Koreans make money despite the international sanctions. I told him he was asking the wrong person." Zack stopped talking again, and looked at his watch.

I didn't take the hint but stood there until he picked up the thread again.

"My bank has a huge compliance department that works all day making sure we don't run afoul of regulators, especially U.S. regulators. That's true of all the other major banks, American or otherwise. I told that Hammond fellow as much. But my impression was that my answers didn't point to anything big enough for him — no Pulitzer Prize or instant riches, whatever it was he was looking for."

That irritated me. "Joe Hammond wouldn't have been after a Pulitzer. For one thing, AsiaIntel isn't an American organization and therefore isn't eligible. Anyway, he wasn't a prize-hound. Knowing he'd done his job well was the main reward he looked for. Certainly I never knew him to spend much thought on how he could make piles of money."

A phone beside Nodding's chair rang. He picked it up, listened a moment and hung up. "That was my secretary reminding me I have another appointment. I'm sorry I can't be of more help."

"If you think of something else, please let me know."

As I waited for an elevator, I realized that beyond confirming that Nodding was the person who'd spoken to Joe, I'd learned only one thing — but it could be important. Joe's premise, as Nodding characterized it, had been that "foreign financial institutions must be helping the North Koreans make money despite the international sanctions." But how would that relate to Nodding's suspicion that Joe had been looking for a get-rich scheme for his own benefit? I wished he'd given me more time for follow-up questions. Figured maybe he would have, if I hadn't started off with that smart-ass comment about his reception room.

An elevator door slid open and I got on. A TV monitor showed a financial network anchor interviewing someone. Glancing at the interviewee I recognized the tinted aviator glasses and thin-lipped smile of Helmut Fassler, the German head of the Hong Kong office of a London-based financial research company that prided itself on being independent, not part of any bank or brokerage company. I normally wouldn't pay much attention to the financial news, but Helmut was somebody I knew. He had been Joe's friend and regular news source. I had lifted a glass with the two of them in the club in Tokyo on more than one occasion.

Before the elevator door opened onto the lobby, I caught a snippet of what Helmut said: "In response to the accounting scandal, all the major red chip oil companies' CDS spreads have widened this morning."

Within an hour I was sitting in Helmut's Victoria Peak apartment. "I watched you on TV at the DMZ when Joe died," he said. "I'd been hoping to talk to you about that, but detected on the phone that whatever brought you here is more urgent. I have a lunch appointment, but I've postponed it."

"Much appreciated, Helmut. I'm trying to figure out why Joe imagined foreign investors would be interested in North Korea. How could anybody make money out of a country that sees farmers' markets as the sinister leading edge of capitalism?"

"You have a point. North Korea has no stock exchange, no bond market. Did Joe leave any clues to what he might have been after?"

"Not many. He did write on his hand, in ink, the letters C, D and S. I got all excited imagining that somebody had flogged thousands of my band's compact discs to the wholesalers who supply North Korean street markets."

"Yeah, yeah." Helmut gave me his tolerant grin. "Would you like a cup of tea?"

"No thanks. Financial illiterate that I am, I did know about certificates of deposit. I worked on that angle and didn't get anywhere. Then when I was coming out of the Goldberg Stanton office I saw you for just a second or two on TV talking about something called CDS, all the letters pronounced separately. That could have been what Joe wrote on his palm. The S was smaller than the D, but the D was also smaller than the C, so it could have been sort of a wedge-shaped scrawl of an all-capital-letters term."

I wrote it on a page of my notebook and showed him. "Problem is, I have no idea what it might refer to. That's why I'm here."

Helmut flashed me one of those kindly, pitying smiles that he reserved for people who weren't as smart as he was, meaning just about everybody in the world. "I don't suppose you know the term credit default swap."

"Nope."

"Not many do. These things weren't invented until 1994, didn't catch on until around 2003 and are still the province of financial specialists."

His phone rang. He glanced at it and shut off the ring. "My lunch date grows impatient, as beautiful women are inclined to do. Let me give you a simple explanation. Let's say you own Ford Motor bonds — you're lending Ford money in exchange for its documented promise to pay back the principal on a given date, along with interest at the stated percentage."

"Right."

"You've been hearing bad things about Ford and worry that Ford will default on those bonds. You consider selling, but others have the same concern, so the bond's price has dropped."

"Yeah."

"But on the other hand, the value of your bonds could soar. Rumor has it that Ford is close to a breakthrough on the alternative fuel front and the company might prosper.

Helmut's household servant, a middle-aged Chinese man, entered the spacious room, whose panoramic wraparound vista looked as expensive as the view from Goldberg Stanton's office. "Your lunch appointment has been trying to reach you. She says meet her at

Ritz-Carlton Lounge & Bar instead of Amber in Mandarin Oriental. She likes Ritz-Carlton pinky drinks better."

Helmut nodded agreement and turned back to me. "Because Ford might pull through, you're inclined to hang onto your bonds and buy more at bargain basement prices. But in case Ford fails, you buy a credit default swap to protect the bonds. The issuer promises that if Ford defaults within five years you can surrender the bonds and be paid their face value."

"So a CDS is a way to hedge my bet, an insurance policy with a fancy name?"

"Something like that."

"And the cost?"

"You pay an initial price for the CDS and an annual fee based on a percentage of the bond's current market value."

"To a high roller, wouldn't insurance seem like a dowdy, middle-aged, conservative, not-likely-to-make-him-a-billionaire-in-a-hurry kind of thing?"

"No. There are important differences between a CDS and an insurance policy. For one thing, the CDS issuer usually isn't an insurance company; most are banks."

"OK."

"And the bigger difference is that you can buy a CDS on something you don't own. A CDS on a particular bond can be bought and sold over and over with none of the buyers and sellers ever owning the bond itself. The swaps outstanding may total many times more than would be necessary to insure bondholders against loss."

"I don't see how that make sense."

"It makes infinite sense in the world of high finance. Let's change the scenario. You don't own any Ford bonds. The market consensus is that the future of Ford looks rosy because everyone knows Ford is on the verge of a breakthrough on the alternative fuel front. But you hear a rumor that the company is in such deep financial trouble no new car model will overcome its problems and Ford will likely default on its bonds. For a certain price you buy a 'naked' CDS. The negative rumor gets around, and the CDS price goes up. You sell yours for a profit."

"Where I come from they'd call that flat-out speculation."

"They would be correct. Naked swaps leave more room for speculation than stocks, bonds or currencies. And speculation is mostly what it's all about. The CDS, like the futures contract, is a type of derivative. CDS traders can be compared to the guys who have never seen a live pig but specialize in sitting in front of computer terminals, buying and selling contracts for future delivery of pork bellies."

"Was it Warren Buffett who said derivatives are 'financial weapons of mass destruction'?"

"In 2003." Helmut sipped at his tea. "He also called them 'time bombs.' By 2008 the financial crisis had quite a few others agreeing with him."

"Oh, yeah. I saw *The Big Short*. Great movie. There were a lot of losers."

"Some big winners, too, like John Paulson, who foresaw that subprime mortgages would turn out to be toxic."

"It shouldn't take a psychic to predict selling a house to someone who can't afford it isn't going to work out."

"True enough, but Paulson also had the vision to persuade Wall Street to package those mortgages and sell the mortgage-backed securities to others. That way, the banks could write credit default swaps insuring against default. Then Paulson went on a CDS buying spree, betting that the people buying the mortgage debt were suckers."

"The bastard must've hit the jackpot when the crash came."

"He made billions."

"And others are still cashing in big time?"

"Credit default swaps have been going out of fashion, but the market is still enormous. The total amount of credit protection at risk in case of default is counted in fourteen figures. The amount invested in the swaps themselves — the 'premiums' — is smaller but still in the trillions of dollars."

I stopped myself from remarking that Leadbelly's Twenty-Five

Cent Dude would be way above his pay grade messing with that stuff.

Helmut glanced at his watch. "It's time for me to leave. Why don't you come along and have lunch with us?"

"All right, thanks."

As we were leaving, Helmut's house man returned. "Your lunch engagement has cancelled. She became tired of waiting."

"Sorry, Helmut."

"Don't worry about it. There's an amusing spot we can go to, just us guys."

We exited the taxi in Wanchai's red light district and headed down a stairway, which discreet lettering on an arched overhead sign identified as Soi Awol. At the basement level, a small sign on a metal door told us we had arrived at Boon Doc's 2050 Club. After Helmut held his microchip membership card up to the peephole for inspection, a hostess in a skin-tight dress showing deep cleavage unlocked the door and exulted, "Oh, Dr. Fassler, we so happy you come back." Wiggling her tits and ass to the point she seemed about to spill out of her dress, she ushered us to a table, cooing, "You handsome man, me so horny."

Sober as I was, I recognized right away that she was a manufactured creation. But the quality was impressive enough that I figured if I'd been guzzling booze for a while I might not have caught on so quickly.

Once she'd seated us in a vinyl booth, with a ceiling fan sending a breeze our way and additional babes headed toward us, Helmut gave me a fill on the setup. "No humans work here. The Japanese were desperate to keep their lead in both robotics and love dolls. A joint venture brought the leading massage-chair designers in, as well, and they all worked long and hard developing secret proprietary techniques for mounting a love-doll body on a robot chassis. I bought a substantial shares holding last month, as soon as I learned about the breakthrough, and I'm recommending that relatively adventurous types among my clients do the same."

"These look Thai, not Japanese."

"Special order. The proprietor of this place is a fan of the Canadian novelist Collin Piprell, who features a generated-reality Bangkok girlie bar called Boon Doc's in his futuristic masterpiece *MOM*. The future is now and I think Piprell is getting a licensing fee."

Wall decorations included a neon Singha beer sign. Helmut ordered a Singha for each of us, and a few lunch items starting with fried grasshoppers.

Brushing away the gorgeous but programmed ladies, who kept calling us "butterfly" and promising to "love you long time," I urged Helmut to return to our earlier topic: "You said there's no North Korean bond market."

"No. There are no true North Korean bonds. There are a few billion dollars in outstanding debt and accumulated unpaid interest left over from Western bank loans to North Korea in the 1970s. The Norks quickly defaulted and no one has been willing to lend to them since."

"So I'm wondering if maybe they've skipped ahead and there's now a North Korean CDS market that's attracting speculators."

The creature snuggling against my right side chose that moment to grab my crotch and chirp, "You, me, short-time, go upstairs."

I looked up and saw that a staircase from beside the bar led to a second-story balcony with doors and windows, which presumably led to rooms. Back-lit window shades were showing shadow plays consisting of sexual gymnastics. "No detail too small," I remarked to Helmut, bowing my head briefly in tribute to his genius in choosing this venue.

He nodded acknowledgement. "There aren't any North Korean credit default swaps. No one would issue such a thing, *because* the North Koreans have already defaulted."

"Pardon me if I'm not getting it, but why would Joe have thought about the CDS market in connection with North Korea?"

From a curtained door behind the bar four more bar girls headed for our booth, each of them exquisitely beautiful. At that awkward time of day between normal people's lunchtime and the cocktail hour, we were the only customers. All the attention was coming to us automatically, along with the food and drink. I might've gone for a human version of one luscious member of the entering quartet — a ringer for my Pyongyang tour guide Shin Mi-song except that this one had a darker complexion, wore oversized round eyeglasses and carried a book. But I'd had my fill of the place.

So had Helmut. "I'll show you when we get to my office."

As we exited to find a taxi, I wondered briefly what the mentors of my youth would have said about Boon Doc's women. Reverend Bob, I imagined, might have cautioned against the sin of casting one's seed into a machine — although I'd never heard him sing the Monty Python song, "Every Sperm is Sacred." As for Fatback, I could practically hear him opining that, "in a pinch, poontang's poontang."

Helmut's office was packed with technological miracles somewhat longer in the tooth than the ones we'd experienced in Boon Doc's. He wheeled his chair around to face the keyboard and four monitors of his Bloomberg data terminal, which took up the top of his rear desk. "Although no North Korean CDS market exists, Joe was likely working under the assumption that what happens in North Korea affects financial markets in other countries."

"Can you get down to cases?"

"North Korea did a nuclear test early today and threatened Japan with nuclear destruction. Let's look at the effect on Japan Airlines bonds."

In the upper left corner of one of the middle monitors he typed WCDS, the letters glowing orange. Seconds later a new screen came up. He tapped away some more. Finally, happy with the page that appeared, he turned and beckoned me to lean forward.

"OK, I called up the world CDS market by country, narrowed it down to Japan and then to this graph, which shows the price fluctuation of credit default swaps on JAL bonds."

He pointed to a spike at the right end of the graph. "Here's the result, which I talked about this morning at the beginning of my TV interview. I guess you tuned in too late to catch that. But look. The reported trading price of the CDS on JAL debt went up by almost fifty bips."

"What's a bip?"

"A basis point: one hundredth of one percentage point. Fifty basis points is one half of one percent — of the price of the bond, *not* the price of the CDS. That translates into a huge percentage increase in the price of the CDS."

"So let me see if I analyze this right. The market thought the risk of a nuclear war against Japan increased. Therefore the risk that the flagship airline would default on its bonds increased. And so the CDS price went up?"

"You get the picture. And if we switched from JAL to some other Japanese corporate bonds you'd see movements in the graphs similar to what we saw here. There were large movements for South Korea, as well, although not as large as those for Japan."

"So could somebody have made a pile?"

"Yep, if he guessed ahead of time that the test — and the threat — would happen right around now, so he could buy enough swaps to make a killing. If he guessed — or if he . . . " Helmut gave me his cynical, conspiratorial grin.

"You mean if he was in receipt of the inside skinny, from the guy who pushes the button, that the test was coming soon and that North Korea would issue those explicit threats — and if, knowing what that would do to the CDS markets, he went out and bought himself a trainload of swaps?"

"Exactly. The ultimate insider trading."

"Maybe Joe was really on to something and getting so close somebody was after him, so he had to make a run for it. That would be good news for Evelyn — speaking of insurance. But I wonder how I'm going to prove that much."

"We can talk about that, but right now I need to get back to work. Can we continue the conversation over drinks tonight?"

━━━

I went to the AsiaIntel office and briefed Langan Meyer. Lang agreed that this could be the angle Joe had gone after. He wanted to hear an expert think aloud about how we could nail down the story. When the cocktail hour approached we went together to meet Helmut.

Holding forth in his favorite bar in Kowloon, Helmut began by reminiscing about Joe. Lang brought up Sword Drill and Helmut was curious; somehow he'd missed being treated to a demonstration. I briefed him on how the competition worked, explaining that the name came from Ephesians 6:17: "And take the helmet of salvation, and the sword of the Spirit, which is the word of God." Some commentators interpreted that to mean that the Bible is the Christian's sword.

"The way we did it to begin with, you'd stand at attention holding a stiff-backed King James Bible in one hand down at your side." I stood to demonstrate with my notebook. "On the command 'Draw swords,' you'd bring the Bible up to your waistline, one hand on the front cover and one on the back."

"Which hand where?" asked Helmut, a southpaw.

"Either hand could be the top one, but you couldn't extend your thumbs over the edge of the cover to the pages. The leader would call out the address of the verse — for the young kids it was likely to be a well known verse that they wanted you to learn by heart, like John 3:16. Then came the command, 'Charge!' You'd find it as quickly as you could" — I leafed frantically through my notebook — "and then hold the Bible up in the air with a finger on the verse to signal you'd found it. The one who found it first got to read it aloud."

"So it helps to pretty much memorize the Bible, I guess," Helmut said.

"Right. Joe and I kicked butt in Sword Drill from the start because we learned songs that listed the books of the Bible, in order, so we didn't have to waste time trying to figure out whether Obadiah was closer to Exodus or Corinthians. The church youth minister, Robert Posey, coached us: 'Remember that Psalms is halfway through the Bible; Matthew, three quarters.' Knowing all that kept us from wasting time flipping through the pages."

"*The* Robert Posey?" Helmut asked.

"Yeah. Our church was an early stop in his career. We called him Reverend Bob. I ran into him in Pyongyang, of all places. He's the one who sent me to Zack Nodding, who's vice-chairman of the Posey organization."

Lang smiled as he remembered something. "Joe said you and he had been the top Sword Drillers in coastal Mississippi — then you beat him out for the district title and went on to win the state championship."

"At that stage we were on our way to knowing the Bible well, so we competed according to more complicated rules that applied to older kids who stuck with the program — the unfinished quotation drill, for example. Or the doctrinal drill. 'Find a verse proving all have sinned.' The winner who came up with an appropriate verse first would call out the scripture reference before and after he read it."

Helmut, who'd begun his working career as a German naval cadet, was fascinated. "So you and Joe were like theological cadets. Looks like journalism's gain was the evangelicals' loss of a pair of major league Bible thumpers."

"Reverend Bob did see us as leader types and strong prospects for the ministry. He usually let people come to their own decisions, but he worked on the two of us, together and separately. He sat us down during a youth retreat our junior year in high school and told us we should become missionaries. Otherwise, think of all the souls who wouldn't hear the word that they needed to accept Jesus as their savior so as to avoid eternal damnation."

"I visualize the two of you preaching in Timbuktu." Lang smiled.

"Being missionaries hadn't figured in our career planning. But Joe and I agreed that Reverend Bob's logic was absolutely correct — assuming it was really God who'd laid down those rules. That was when we started taking a more questioning attitude toward the scriptures and church doctrine."

A blond Russian hooker who was passing by the table spoke to Helmut. He stood and accompanied her to a corner to chat privately. After she walked on and he sat down I remarked, "You're obviously well known in this establishment."

"She's a regular here who bugs me for investment advice whenever she sees me. She follows up with her broker. She's been on a roll. That emerald ankle bracelet is new."

"Speaking of advice, can we resume the finance lesson?"

"Where were we?"

"You follow the CDS market, I gather," Lang said.

"I keep an eye on it, mainly for macro research purposes. Most of the swaps trades are still OTC — over-the-counter — bilateral transactions. For my clients, who are conservative institutional investors, I stick to recommending less exotic — and more closely regulated — stuff."

He turned to me. "We were talking earlier about how the insurance analogy is appealing but limited. There's no one saying how much of a reserve you have to hold against the CDS contracts you've written. In insurance, you very much have to do that."

There was something I wanted him to expand on: "Earlier today you seemed to be telling me it's easier to screw around with the CDS market than with other markets."

"It's far more conducive to insider trading than stocks, bonds or currencies. For one thing, it would be much harder to get caught — especially if you had enough lead time to put together your CDS positions carefully, over a period of days or weeks or even months, giving you more reason to hope no one would catch on to what was happening."

Helmut told us that a sophisticated scammer would be placing trades on swaps keyed to as wide a variety of bond-issuing entities as could be usefully fit into the overall scam. The scammer would not do the trading only in one place but would spread it out in London, New York, Singapore and Hong Kong. Given the fragmented nature of the CDS market, it would be very difficult to find a paper trail across multiple cities and counterparties.

"As if anyone were watching," Lang said, looking disgusted.

"You have a point," Helmut said to him. He turned back to me. "The markets in stocks, bonds and currencies are more or less tightly regulated in developed countries around the world. The prime regulatory agency, I'm sure you know, has been the U.S. Securities and Exchange Commission, which does statistical analysis to look for clues that somebody's cheating. There hasn't been that sort of serious regulation of the CDS market."

"So much for Buffett's warnings," I said.

"There was talk of banning naked swaps after the sub-prime mortgage crisis started in 2007, but Wall Street blocked that. The pro-banks juggernaut in Congress pushed the street's argument that the CDS market is an efficient way to get early warning of a crisis that's developing. For example, they pointed out that bond rating agencies including Moody's and Standard & Poor's had lagged far behind the CDS market in detecting that Greek government debt needed to be downgraded drastically. There was something to that argument. I recall checking one day and finding that the Greek sovereign CDS was priced at almost 23 percent of the bond price."

"Naked swaps are still OK, then?"

"The European Union since 2012 has forbidden naked swaps on the bonds issued by its member country governments. But corporate bonds aren't affected. And in the U.S. and the rest of the world you can still do naked swaps on either corporate or sovereign debt. A ban didn't make it into the major U.S. law signed in 2010, the Dodd-Frank Wall Street Reform and Consumer Protection Act."

Lang turned to me. "Dodd-Frank was supposed to clean up the financial system. No one seems to think the results so far are any better than mixed."

"That's a fair assessment," Helmut chimed in. He explained that some credit was due to U.S. regulators trying to use Dodd-Frank to clean up the markets. The Commodity Futures Trading Commission in Chicago had issued final rules that would apply to "a variety of CDS involving indexing of multiple borrowers' debt instruments."

He got me there. "Huh?"

"You don't need to know."

"Ouch."

Moving right along, Helmut told us that the SEC had been working on rules to require more reporting, more transparency, more use of clearing houses for the CDS category that Joe probably was primarily interested in: the "single name" swaps covering debt of individual countries and companies.

"But the current administration in Washington is full of Wall Street veterans," he said, "and Congress is awash with their sympathizers. Whether or not they gut Dodd-Frank, as threatened, it's highly unlikely they'll let tough new regulations go into effect. Even if they did, I doubt that we would see much resulting change. After all, the very nature of the CDS beast is insider trading."

"You mean the sort of case we hypothesize regarding North Korea is routine?" I asked.

"No, what I mean is simply that the lenders who issue and trade swaps know far more of the intimate details about the credit-worthiness of the debtors than any investor would likely know. Given the failure to ban naked swaps I'd have to predict that CDS trading will remain the Wild West of the financial markets."

"You talk about needing more reporting and transparency," I said.

"But your Bloomberg terminal already seems to have an idea what's going on."

"It knows only up to a point. The bankers who broker the trades haven't been required to report much of anything. I showed you a graph. The truth is, nobody takes those numbers without a grain of salt. Individual brokers give their numbers voluntarily when the Bloomberg or Thomson-Reuters data people call and ask for current trading prices."

With no mandatory clearing house exposure, Helmut explained, there was no guarantee that the brokers polled would give the right numbers. "They may see it as in their interest to try to fool the rest of the market."

"So you call up the graph but the numbers it's based on are likely to be fake," Lang said. "That I did not know."

"A speculator can get a general idea of market direction from the data on his Bloomberg or Reuters data terminal, but you wouldn't trade on the basis of the specific number the terminal lists for today. Any savvy market player would follow up by calling a broker and asking directly for a price. The misreporting of CDS prices is an open secret among insiders — but it would be hard for the regulators to change that situation."

"Sounds like, at the moment, there's nothing whatsoever to stop someone from doing a huge insider trade through one of those banks," I said.

"There are some constraints. Swaps are legally subject to insider trading prohibitions. But to bring a case, the authorities not only have to find out about the insider trading and narrow down who's involved; they also need to assemble evidence to back up the charge. There are bound to be serious problems adjudicating a case because, as I said, insider trading is the essence of what the CDS is about."

"As if they were trying to ban sinners from hell?"

"You've got it. But the second constraint is more important. Bankers have to think constantly about their reputational risk."

"Ah! Now I know what Joe meant by that reference in his notebook to 'REP RISK 2HUGE.' Zack Nodding was telling Joe the risk to their reputation would keep banks from getting involved."

Helmut nodded. "Fewer than twenty banks are serious players in the over-the-counter single-name CDS market and just a handful take care of the majority of the trading. I can't think of even one bank whose managers would feel relaxed about doing a gigantic and obviously fraudulent trade — a trade that surely would come back to haunt them once word got out. The non-U.S. banks have their home country regulators to worry about. And banks around the world are scared to death of attracting the attention of the long-armed U.S. authorities."

"Or as Joe quoted Nodding as saying, the IRS and the SEC would come down like a ton of bricks."

"Nodding's right about that. And if a customer hit the jackpot more than once, going really big on days when some North Korean weirdness occurred and making multiple fortunes, the banker-brokers representing that customer might figure it was no coincidence. If they knew what was good for them they'd raise a public stink right away and make sure all the blame fell on the customer."

"So if someone wanted to make a killing in the CDS market using insider knowledge from North Korea," Lang said, "the first step would be to find a compliant banker-broker willing to take the risk of handling the trades?"

"Exactly. Next to impossible to find one, I'd say, especially after the first time the customer hits it big and it becomes obvious he had to have insider information. Otherwise we'd be talking about the perfect crime."

"If what the North Koreans are up to isn't a perfect crime," Lang reminded Helmut, "there's a way to expose it. Can you help us figure out what that is?"

That proved easier said than done. We agreed that the details we needed to nail down might not be available outside North Korea. Next step was to figure out how to get me in again, not for a sight-seeing tour but in some capacity that would permit me to sniff around. Coming up with no magic bullet for that, we agreed to give it a rest and think further. I'd return to being a musician in Tokyo for the time being. Lang's staff would watch CDS market movements, with advice from Helmut.

Back in Tokyo it turned out somebody had other ideas.

I WALKED to the subway station closest to my apartment, heading for lunch with Evelyn. One of the oldest in the city, the station hadn't yet been remodeled to install a protective barrier between the tracks and the platform. Waiting for a train there never failed to make me nervous. The entrance I used took me to the part of the platform where the back of the train would end up. The long train would still be racing along at close to full speed when the lead car reached that point.

Whenever I had to stand close to the tracks I always recalled an evening in a shabby wooden roadhouse near Greenville, Mississippi, when Fatback Hawkins, then a new friend, had come over between sets to join me at my table. "You got no enemies here, Heck, so how 'bout you lettin' me have your chair."

Upon my compliance he'd dropped his bulk in the chair I'd vacated, jamming it up against the establishment's back wall.

"Let's say some fella hear about you harvestin' a piece from his old lady and he come after you. You gotta make sure he can't creep up behind you, s'prise you. If you settin', you want to set way in the back, like this." He'd added that when walking or standing in a crowded place, like Chicago, "You gotta keep lookin' around behind you."

I'd long since applied that Fatback rule to the Tokyo subways, always making sure to keep focused on the possibility that some drunken or impatient passenger would blindside me.

This time, when I turned to look behind me, I was almost too late.

A hunched-over man, his arms straight out in front of him, was barreling toward me. He was so close —a few inches away — that I could hear him grunting from his exertion. I stepped out of his way. With a piercing scream he tumbled down onto the tracks. A second later, wheels of the lead car sliced him in half at the waist.

I exited the platform before the train came to a halt, not stopping to see what might happen next but darting looks behind me to make sure no other would-be assassin was following me. Out on the street I hailed a taxi to the restaurant. In the cab I tried deep breathing, the North Korean DMZ captain's recommendation for dealing with stress. It worked reasonably well.

My attacker had hidden behind one of those surgical face masks that Japanese liked to wear when they'd caught colds, or when they wanted to avoid catching others' colds or to keep from breathing otherwise polluted air. I'd seen his hair and hands, though. His hairdo was a tightly curled "punch perm," a style not so often seen since the nineteen nineties. He was missing the last joint of his left pinky, which I guessed he'd chopped off as a ritual apology to his boss for some foulup. Although I didn't recognize this particular specimen, I couldn't have been in the nightspot entertainment field in Tokyo without exposure to the general type.

Why would an aging, unreconstructed yakuza try to kill me? Somebody somewhere had to have taken out a hit on me. I felt pretty sure that the somebody in question was whoever had targeted Joe earlier, a somebody now sensing danger in my efforts to complete Joe's work. In the previous few days I'd been in North and South Korea, mainland China, Hong Kong and Japan. Somewhere along the way, I must have tipped my hand to the wrong person.

Evelyn would be flying out that afternoon to Mississippi for the Calvary Church funeral. I didn't want to freak her out any further, so I mentioned only that my train had been delayed when someone jumped or fell on the tracks. That was a common Tokyo occurrence.

The unruffled exterior I managed to present didn't reflect my feelings. I had dodged bullets and otherwise risked my life for news photos plenty of times, had been in more than my share of shoving matches and outright fistfights. But this was the first time somebody had tried to kill me.

I couldn't focus on my own problems for long, though, because I had to turn my attention to Evelyn's. She'd had a visit from an insurance investigator, one Hashimoto.

"He's determined to prove it was suicide and he was probing for anything he could use for that. He kept asking me about Joe's and my sex life. Telling him I'm pregnant didn't stop that line of questioning. He said men facing new responsibilities such as fatherhood are known to kill themselves because of the pressure."

"And unscrupulous insurance adjusters are known to become malignantly obnoxious."

"I haven't told you the half of it. He bragged that he had a *lot* of experience dealing with new widows. He kept running his eyes over my body and smacking his lips as if he were savoring a particularly nice slice of sashimi. He was coming on to me, Heck! Without saying a word that I could report to the authorities or his boss, he was signaling that I could buy him off by sleeping with him. I'd rather be penniless and homeless, live under an overpass with my son."

Speaking of the pressures that come from new responsibilities . . .

All I could do was assure her that Lang and I were doing our best to find out what was behind Joe's run. I didn't have the heart to tell her we had come up with zero ideas on how to proceed.

———

Still feeling queasy after Evelyn left to catch her plane, I wondered how quickly whoever had sent the gangster to kill me would dispatch reinforcements to finish the job. The thought of going to the police occurred to me, of course, but I needed to think through my options. Instead of returning to my apartment, I went straight to Tokyo Station and headed for my mountain cabin.

I found a vacant pair of seats in an unreserved car of the bullet train where I could press my back to the window, bend one leg up onto the aisle seat and be in position to watch comings and goings up or down the aisle, in case anybody might be following me. Knowing that deep breathing would carry me only so far, I'd thought to buy from a platform kiosk a couple jars of saké and some salted nuts.

An hour into my journey, word of the attack made it to the electronic news display in the front of the car. A headline in Japanese kept scrolling into view: " . . . Korean resident killed in mysterious subway incident . . . " I resumed my focus on the aisle and sipped the saké.

Changing from the bullet train in the city closest to my cabin, I waited on a sparsely populated platform for a local commuter train. No dangerous-looking characters appeared. My fellow passengers were office workers, uniformed students and elderly shoppers heading back home near the end of the day. Once the train started the climb up the river valley, I relaxed enough to gaze at the countryside, marveling as always at the tiny and oddly shaped rice paddies tucked into the forest wherever there was water and fertile soil. The rice was ripening nicely as harvest time approached. The bucolic scenery normally would trigger a delicious relaxation, but that day was different.

A hissing sound at my rural station signaled that I could slide the door open and step out. I swept my eyes over the almost empty platform as I breathed in the chilly air.

A two-mile taxi ride took me to the hilltop where the dirt road ended and the stone stairway down toward the lake began. Passing the other summer cabins, most of which were boarded up until the following season, I reached my place before dark. I took the precaution of pulling from the ground and carrying inside the wooden stake marker that bore the house number and identified me by family name as the occupant. No use announcing myself to another gangster who might come looking for me in those woods.

Although my Korean chests and Chinese tables in truth didn't remotely approach a caliber that would excite Goldberg Stanton's office decorators, the lake view as always was spectacular. Gazing from the deck with drink in hand soothed me.

I went back inside, pulled a tray of lasagna from the freezer to nuke in the microwave and turned on the NHK radio evening news. The lead story was the one I needed to hear. The national broadcaster's announcer identified the man who'd been run over in the subway as an ethnic Korean who'd been a member of Kodo-kai — a financial mafia known as the underworld's bank. Kodo-kai was a branch of Yamaguchi Gumi, the largest and most vicious of gangland syndicates. Witnesses told police the gangster had appeared to fall while attempting to shove an unidentified man of uncertain ethnicity and undetermined nationality. The intended victim had left the scene immediately.

During and after supper I considered my situation but didn't come up with any easy answers. My pursuers weren't going to give up after the one failed attempt. What if they managed to scare me enough to make me contemplate abandoning my quest? I wouldn't know where to go to raise a white flag. I realized I should've had better sense than to try to hide out in the cabin. They might need a little time to reconnoiter after the day's failed effort, but then they'd find me fairly easily.

A moderately comforting factor was that Japan's restrictions on guns were extremely tight. Even gangsters generally had to make do with other weapons, such as knives. To kill me they'd probably need to get close. I sharpened my biggest kitchen knives, brought up some rusty golf clubs, a baseball bat and a heavy iron mallet from the basement storeroom and made sure all the windows and doors were latched.

Probably a waste of time since I'd be no match for a professional killer. I really needed some warning in case they should show up during the night. Looking around, I glimpsed a bell, similar to a cowbell, that sat on a kitchen shelf. Local authorities had alerted us to a sharp increase in bear sightings near the lake. They'd advised everyone to buy a bell and ring it when walking alone to notify any foraging bears that we weren't their normal prey. Carrying an electric lantern, I went outside and tied the bell to a still leafy tree branch, in need of trimming, that hung low over the entrance to my property. Anyone coming in would have to disturb the branch and ring the bell.

Thus alerted, I figured, I should have time to crawl into a storage space, above my bedroom closet, whose door the Japanese builder back in the 1920s had cleverly disguised as part of the wood-paneled wall. I placed the longest of my knives inside the *tendana*, in case my pursuers happened to know that design trick.

It was hard getting to sleep. For a long while all I could do was worry and listen for the bell. Assuming I lived till morning, I decided, I'd need to come up with a better hideout. The really discouraging thought was that yakuza had networks capable of finding me, sooner or later, anywhere in Japan. I had boxed myself in.

I finally managed to sleep but the price was a terrifying dream. I was sitting on a toilet. Everything was blood red: the room, the toilet, myself and all the things coming out of my body. In volcanic eruptions I was shitting blood, puking blood, pissing blood, ejaculating blood. Blood was spurting from my nose and ears and eyes and the pores in my skin. In another corner of the room I saw Joe lying face up on the floor. He, likewise, was all red. Tears of blood streamed down his cheeks. Out of his wound shot a stream of blood of such volume and velocity as might have issued from a fire hose. There came an immensely loud explosion. In a flushing whirlpool that resembled a tornado, Joe and I and the room went down the toilet.

Waking to find I was sick, I ran for the real toilet. My nausea didn't last much longer but the stomach cramps, headache and diarrhea continued for much of the night and the nightmare recurred whenever, in the short spaces between toilet runs, I nodded off.

At least the bell didn't ring. The symptoms abated enough by dawn for me to brew and drink a mug of tea. Then I phoned a neighbor. Whenever he had days off from teaching English to Japanese college freshmen, Larry came up from Nagoya to carry out his responsibilities as our international community's volunteer forestry chief. I asked him if there'd been a power failure lately.

"Weekend before last a whole lot of trees fell in a storm. I heard from the electric company crew they'd take days to get all the lines back up, so I filled my ice chests. You better trash anything perishable in your fridge. You can ride with me to the store if you want. I'm going anyway to get some milk and bread. Meet me at the top of the hill in half an hour. Bring the garbage. We can drop it in the store's bin."

As I approached the top of the hill I heard a chainsaw start up. A few steps farther and I could see Larry, waving his screaming saw to chase off a mother bear and her cub. The creatures quickly disappeared into the woods. Larry — himself a bear of a man in lumberjack garb — switched off the saw.

I took in the rest of the scene. Two vehicles were parked along the narrow roadway. One was Larry's ancient, lovingly restored Toyota pickup. The other, next to the garbage shed, was a black, left-hand-drive Buick with deeply tinted windows, bearing license plates issued by the local prefecture. The driver's door stood open. The shed, for summer use only, was padlocked to emphasize what the sign said in Japanese and English: "Take your garbage home off season!" Someone renting or borrowing a cabin, either an illiterate or a thoughtless slob, had left a pile of filled bags propped against the shed's door. The bears had torn them apart.

The scattered garbage was a mess — but by no means as awful a mess as the dead man who lay face down on the road. His right hand, still attached to the body, held a bloody knife – a throwing knife, by the looks of it, but he had bled on it without managing to throw it. His left arm, detached from his shoulder, lay nearby. I could see by counting missing finger joints that he had committed not just one, not just two, but three major screwups requiring him to make ritual atonement to his boss during what must have been a long criminal career.

Next to the arm lay the chewed carcass of a miniature poodle. Yakuza and their women liked such creatures, for some reason. To bring the little white dog along he would have had to consider this a fairly routine assignment with scant risk of distraction, I figured. Or maybe he was a henpecked gangster whose girlfriend's insistence that the pet needed an early morning outing had trumped workmanlike caution.

Kobayashi, a caretaker en route to start his day's work repairing someone's cabin, drove up. He phoned the authorities. Then as Larry and Kobayashi stood and talked, facing toward the body and away from the Buick, I removed from atop the console separating its front seats a sheet of notepaper. On it were written my name and address and directions to my place.

I folded and pocketed the paper, which had concealed the vehicle's front cup-holders. In one of them I noticed a metal object that looked like a baseball-sized golf ball turned into a samovar. Grenades smuggled from the Philippines, I now recalled having read, were the latest addition to the yakuza arsenal. Most of the imports were just stun grenades, more useful for terrorizing than for killing. In view of the previous day's events I figured the one in the Buick must be the real thing, a fragmentation grenade. In that case, none of my precautions would have saved me from being blown to bits if the gangster had made it down the hill to my cabin.

I considered taking the device home for self-defense but thought better of the idea. Leaving the grenade for the police to deal with, I joined the other two men.

"This hoodlum must have been headed somewhere else on the

main road and pulled off onto our side road so he and his dog could pee," Kobayashi was suggesting to Larry. "Maybe the bears were in the shadows when he drove up and he didn't see them at first."

"Yeah," said Larry. "Those yip-yip-yippy little dogs have a tendency to overreach. This one must've gone into attack mode against that bear cub. When the mother bear started to make breakfast of the poodle, the dog's master pulled his knife and attracted mama bear's attention — instead of getting the hell away, like a sensible person." He glanced down at the chainsaw he still held in his right hand. "But who am I to talk?"

The previous day I'd thought I might confide in Larry and ask if I could hide out in his cabin for a bit while I came up with something better. This bloody scene rendered that idea completely out of the question. Now that a local gang was on my trail, it would be worse than stupid to hang around waiting for the next move.

I dropped my bagged garbage onto Larry's truck bed, thanked him for taking care of it and walked back down to the cabin. My tentative plan was to hop a train for Niigata, a city on the Japan Sea coast where I had friends who'd no doubt take me in. I went on the Internet to message them but found I had an email from Reverend Bob:

Dear Heck,

We have a fresh opening on our faculty, and you're the person who comes to mind. I had a chance to listen to the CD you gave me. It's really good. I realized you would fit perfectly in a new role of teaching music performance to our students, with an emphasis on gospel, spirituals and Christian rock.

We can't pay large salaries, but we would give you room and board and a local spending allowance while depositing some dollars in your bank account abroad that you could use after your return.

I hope you can do this, Heck, even if you can't stay longer than a semester. During our conversations I sensed in you a need for change. I certainly don't want to put any pressure on you. But I've prayed over it and I am convinced the Lord wants you to come to Posey Korea University. What do you say? The new term starts next week, so the sooner you could get over here the better.

Reverend Bob had a history of stepping in, unasked, when he was most needed. Still, my eyes grew moist as I contemplated the way he had illuminated the way ahead this time by hitting his send button. I called for a taxi to meet me at the top of the hill in forty minutes. That would get me to the station in time for the next train down to the flatlands.

I phoned Lang at home — woke him up. "The bad news was the gangster attacks. The good news is this email. With all the shit that's been coming down, it seems like the answer to our prayers."

"I know you studied a lot of Bible, but do you actually think the Big Guy personally orders these earthly events?"

"No, but I wouldn't be surprised if Reverend Bob had enough empathy — whatever you want to call it — to feel my pain and offer a way out. He's a special fellow."

"Why not just talk to the police and ask them to find whoever sent the hit men?"

"Considered it" — I patted the pocket where I'd stowed the evidence — "but I have no confidence they'd be helpful. Japanese cops have a lousy record when it comes to the yakuza. Live and let live is a common arrangement. Some places, they're more partners than enemies. Besides, news could get out and keep us from nailing the exclusive story Joe was after."

"That's a valid point, but going back to North Korea is a really dangerous plan. I know I was urging you to go, but that was before this happened. There aren't many stories worth a journalist's life."

"I don't have much choice. I can't hide out in Japan permanently, and I don't want to disappear somewhere else like the jungles of New Guinea. Better to go on the offensive. Reverend Bob's provided the break we needed. The university's not in Pyongyang, but at least I'll be inside North Korea. I doubt yakuza are going to follow me over there."

An employment application form was attached to Reverend Bob's email. Reading it, I found that Posey Korea University was by no stretch of the imagination an equal opportunity employer. The fourth question, after name, date and place of birth, was, "On what date were you born again?"

Fortunately I didn't need to rack my brain figuring out how to answer that one honestly and still qualify for the job. Reverend Bob had already consulted his Souls Ledger, found the date July 18, 1988, and typed it into the form along with my name.

Back in Tokyo I didn't return home. I figured a lookout might be posted near my apartment building, watching the lobby door. While making my travel arrangements I crashed with Hiro, who played banjo and mandolin in my band. I made a list — almost forgot the "people's clothing" — and gave him my key for a one-bag, one-guitar packing run. He took the luggage straight to Tokyo Station by taxi and disappeared into an enormous crowd there before handing it off to me on the platform for the Narita Express airport train. I watched, but saw no sign of gangsters following him or me.

9 / CHINA BORDERLAND

I FLEW INTO SHENYANG, whose international airport was China's closest to the North Korean border. Still watching carefully, I saw nothing en route to suggest I was being followed.

Riding a taxi into the heart of the industrial city of nearly five million, I found that the pollution, at least that day, was almost as bad as what I remembered from Beijing. I recalled the clear mountain air I'd left behind in Japan. But my top priority for the time being was simply to keep breathing, whether well or not so well.

I followed Lang's suggestion and stopped at the U.S. consulate-general to advise on my North Korea teaching plans. I didn't hide the fact I'd been a journalist.

The vice-consul, a Foreign Service officer whose job included watching North Korea, pushed aside what he told me was a stack of United Nations and U.S. sanctions documents to make space on his desk for writing. When he'd finished noting down my passport information, he thanked me for coming. "I wish there were more like you in that Posey crew. The consul-general asked the university officials to give us a list of U.S. citizens they had hired, but they refused. We don't know the names of the Americans over at the Posey campus or even how many there are. You're the first who's checked in with us."

He frowned. "It's hard enough for us to help American citizens who have trouble over there when we know who they are. The United States has no diplomatic relations with North Korea. If there's any problem involving one of our citizens we have to ask the Swedish ambassador — who represents our interests in Pyongyang — to handle it. Imagine the hassle for the Swedes, and the grief for us, if there arose a situation involving dozens of nameless American university professors."

"Why didn't the consul-general insist?"

"Off the record, he did. The State Department told him to suck it up. The Poseys have powerful connections in Washington. Robert Posey prayed at the president's inauguration, you may recall. His organization lobbied, successfully, to reverse the North Korea travel ban."

"Why do you suppose they didn't want to give you the faculty list?"

"Their office in Washington told us they were deferring to their hosts. Pyongyang supposedly was afraid official dealings with the U.S. government would lead to leaks to the media and publicity about North Korea's change of policy."

"Why would that be a bad thing?"

"My impression is that cooperation with the Posey organization is so inconsistent with the country's ideology and previous policy, the top guys are afraid it would make them look weak to their enemies, external or internal. Yes, they had dealt with foreign Christian groups in the past — but never before to the extent of encouraging the Christians to practice and teach religion inside the country on an ongoing basis."

He shrugged and changed the subject. "The Chinese are proud of their new, fast train — up to 148 miles an hour. But the scenery goes by so fast you can hardly see it. My advice for your first trip to the border, if you haven't bought a ticket yet, is to hire a car and driver." He stood up and pointed out his office window. "They congregate down the street outside that restaurant."

As my driver picked his way through city traffic toward the outskirts of Shenyang, I wondered again just how Reverend Bob had managed to make the university happen. He'd suggested some practical reasons the North Koreans might have gone for the plan. Probably there'd be no point in asking him for an in-depth explanation, though. He'd downplay any worldly factors and, once again, cite the possibility that God had touched some hearts high in the Pyongyang apparatus.

Once we got out of the city I turned my attention to the landscape. My survival could depend on knowing the territory. The journey took us through a vast mountainous area, largely forested, with few signs of habitation. It presented quite a contrast to the crowds packed into much of China. The northeastern reach of the country had once been a separate territory called Manchuria, the reserved homeland of the horsemen who'd conquered China in 1644 to form its last imperial dynasty.

Tens of thousands of refugees from North Korea were said to live on the Chinese side of the border. Hunting them were both North Korean agents and Chinese cops whose job was to arrest them and send them back. The remoteness and forest cover would help conceal any escapees who made it into these mountains.

Yang, my driver, was an ethnic Korean whose family had lived in Dandong, the border city where we were headed, and held Chinese nationality for three generations. We chatted in Korean. He'd turned to driving for a living after the failure of a larger business — a bakery to make bread and cakes — that he'd started on the North Korean side of the border, in Sinuiju. Authorities there had failed to follow through with a promise to provide industrial-strength 380-volt power. That had left him holding the bag after he'd invested a couple hundred thousand Chinese yuan in plant and equipment.

Nevertheless, he said, "One day North Korea's going to be a good investment opportunity, with the new special economic zone they started building just across the border from Dandong. Construction's on hold for now but I'm lined up to go back in when the time comes."

Dandong, with a population half the size of Shenyang's, proved to be a bustling city with construction projects everywhere. On the waterfront main drag I checked into the Renmin International Hotel, where a university representative was to contact me. The curtains were open in my seventh-floor room and I took in the view of the Yalu, as the Chinese called the river. To the Koreans it was the Amnok. On the other side I could see Sinuiju, whose skyline consisted of dull and nondescript low-rise buildings. Off to my left was the combined highway-and-railway Friendship Bridge connecting Dandong and Sinuiju.

I showered quickly and went out to explore the city center — looking for a way to follow the money, as investigative reporters like Joe made it their business to do. The vice consul in Shenyang had reminded me that China remained North Korea's number one trade partner. He'd told me that most of that commerce — mainly private — shipped via Dandong.

The hotel desk clerk said the Chinese were putting the finishing touches on a new, wider bridge. Meanwhile, incoming and outgoing truck traffic alternated using the old bridge's single highway lane — mornings one way, afternoons the other. The new bridge site would be quite a hike, the clerk said, but I could easily take in the old one on a relaxed pre-supper stroll.

I passed the bridge and came to a dusty parking lot, where Chinese customs officials checked trucks coming from the North Korean side either empty or loaded. I knew little about the overall North Korean economy, even less about Chinese-North Korean trade. I needed to learn. Since money was at the root of the story I was after, I needed to be able to explain why the international sanctions weren't working as planned, and why the North Koreans had failed to build and maintain a thriving legitimate economy — failed so miserably that, at times, they'd resorted to international criminal activities such as counterfeiting and drug trafficking.

I passed a block of storefront offices whose windows bore painted multilingual signs proclaiming them to be trading and freight forwarding companies. A man sitting at a desk inside one of them didn't look busy, so I went in and started chatting with him. A Chinese named Cheng, he spoke Korean. He told me the loaded incoming trucks carried mainly raw materials including minerals, silkworm cocoons and unprocessed seafood. "Come around tomorrow morning and you'll see the outgoing, which is primarily manufactured goods," he said.

"When I was in Pyongyang the other day," I said, "I saw a lot of fancy European automobiles, Louis Vuitton handbags, Havana cigars, two-hundred-dollar bottles of Cognac. Is that the sort of manufactured goods you're sending across?"

Cheng grinned. "That is what the American vice-consul from Shenyang asked me when he came in the other day. You wouldn't be an undercover sanctions inspector, would you? I'm not saying those embargoed items don't go across, but my company doesn't handle them. We supply the North Koreans daily necessities, home electrical appliances and, in season, farming tools and chemical fertilizer."

Cheng told me it was his policy to require payment up front in Chinese yuan, U.S. dollars or euros, not DPRK won. Even the North Koreans didn't have much use for won, he said, especially after the so-called re-denomination of the currency in 2009 when the government confiscated most of the traders' savings.

Cheng said he accepted bank transfers only after establishing good relations. "Even then the North Koreans try to cheat us. They cheat a lot. Every trading company that does business with them has to be cautious."

He seemed happy to have somebody listening to his rant, so I pressed him for details. A typical scam, he said, was for the North Korean side to provide extra performance at first, to establish a good relationship — and then, when the other side relaxed its guard, to plead lack of cash and ask for shipment in advance of payment. A

Chinese trader who complied and then tried to get his money back would be told that the North Korean trading official he had dealt with was no longer employed and his former employers refused to be responsible.

I walked back through the truck inspection yard, confirming that much of the incoming consisted of piles of raw materials, covered or otherwise. The vice-consul had told me the Chinese had stopped buying coal and iron ore for the time being but could reverse the policy at any time. Thinking of that remark reminded me of something else he'd said: "Dandong is full of refugees, spies, missionaries, dealmakers, crooks and assassins." That last category bothered me.

The vice-consul hadn't mentioned sidewalk tradesmen, but I soon encountered one of those on the riverbank. The man rented telescopes to tourists so they could view the North Korean side of the river. I paid to take a look, and what I saw jibed with my earlier impression: Sinuiju looked dead, almost devoid of color except for propaganda signs and murals. Dusk had fallen and the streetlights and neon on the Chinese side were glowing — but the North Koreans weren't lighting up.

The vendor stocked items of memorabilia. Tourists could buy crisp new North Korean currency notes in various denominations, North Korean postage stamps and enameled pins — including Kim portrait pins. I had no way of telling whether they were Chinese knock-offs or the real thing. There were singles picturing Kim Il-sung or Kim Jong-il and doubles in which the two were pictured against a red flag.

"Is there a triple, with the new, younger ruler included?"

"Those are fairly new and rare; only top-level cadre wear them so far. I'm sorry I don't have any in stock."

I bought a Kim Il-sung single. It had been a long day and I wanted a drink. I wandered back past the hotel through the built-up downtown waterfront area until I found a large storefront restaurant. A neon sign in Korean proclaimed that I had reached Arirang. That name, I knew, came from a folk song that for modern Koreans symbolized the hope for reunification. The North Korean regime had appropriated the song's name for the annual mass games festival that I'd watched as a tourist in Pyongyang.

I spotted Yang, the driver, through the plate glass window. The wannabe entrepreneur saw me and gestured for me to join him at the bar. He was sitting with a bespectacled, mop-haired man. Figuring I had lucked into a popular watering hole, I went in and sat with them and ordered a beer. The other fellow, also ethnically Korean, worked as a reporter for a local newspaper.

Talking with them, I got the picture that the main pastime in Dandong was imagining all the riches that would unfold locally if North Korea seriously opened up to the outside and reformed its economy.

"The trade zone could be big," the reporter said, "but only if the North Koreans would do their part. Their pattern has been to ease up on the command economy — then suddenly reverse themselves. They need to have consistent policies. They must offer credible assurances that they won't swoop in again and confiscate the private sector's profits."

"They have your example. Why don't they emulate China?"

"We wonder about precisely that. We were hoping we could show the new young leader how to do it right — the way China did it. But then he had his uncle, Jang Song-taek, put to death. There are reports Jang got caught plotting a coup. Whether that's true or not, he was widely alleged to be dealing corruptly with Chinese companies. His death left a big vacuum. There was one other family member who knew China well, Kim Jong-nam, half-brother of the current leader Jong-un. Jong-un had Jong-nam assassinated, in Malaysia. We haven't heard of anyone still alive in the North Korean ruling family who understands what needs to be done as well as the two dead guys did. For a while during the peace offensive it did start to look as though Kim Jong-un himself might be coming around, but lately we've seen less evidence of that."

I finished readjusting my butt on the backless, uncomfortable bar stool and took a swig of my beer. "Even without copying you, the North Koreans seem to be pulling in some big money."

"We've heard that, but we don't know where it comes from." The reporter signaled for his bill. "Whatever it is, it can't be as sustainable as what they could achieve with consistent reform and opening."

"The new bridge should be at least some help."

The reporter looked at Yang and rolled his eyes. "Apparently you haven't heard. We finished building the bridge long ago. They were supposed to be building a road connecting to it on their side of the river. There's no road. It's a bridge to nowhere. Kim Jong-un has other spending priorities."

The men left to keep other appointments. I turned to a wall-mounted television screen, which was showing the official North Korean evening news. The woman reading the news looked familiar, and I quickly realized why. She was the same anchor who'd thrown me into a rage on my first evening in Pyongyang. The big news today was that Supreme Leader Kim Jong-un had visited an army base to give guidance. He wore a midnight blue Mao-style tunic and his haircut was a whitewall, shaved above the ears but long on top, the forelock flapping against his forehead. He looked like the late Great Leader Kim Il-sung, but he also resembled the VIP I'd met in Pyongyang with Shin Mi-song.

That thought reminded me that Ms. Shin, with her high-level contacts, might well be a spy and might know something she hadn't told me about the background of Joe's death. I couldn't eliminate her as a suspect in the plot against my own life. I just hoped her tour guide assignment — cover job or not — would keep her in the capital for the time being. Happily, I found it hard to imagine I'd need to worry about encountering her at the university.

I finished my beer, perused the lined-up bottles of Western and Asian booze and spotted an unopened fifth of Four Roses. It wasn't my favorite bourbon, but Fatback was partial to it. I ordered a double, on the rocks. When it arrived in the hands of the bar maid, graceful in her flowing traditional Korean costume of *chima-chogori*, I silently toasted Fatback and wondered what he'd do in my situation. I guessed he'd just pick up his guitar and start playing and singing and dancing. "When the blues get you down, get down with the blues," he'd say.

An East Asian man wearing a windbreaker over an open-necked sports shirt sat down on a nearby stool. Turning toward him I was astonished by his resemblance to both Kim Jong-un and Kim Il-sung. Not sure he wasn't Chinese, I took a chance and addressed him in Korean anyway. "Do you work as a double for North Korean leaders?"

"People have been asking me that ever since I started studying Korean in Seoul in the nineteen nineties." He asked the barmaid for a Scotch and she moved down the bar to pour it.

I introduced myself as an American soon-to-be music teacher at Posey Korea University and the man switched to English.

"Paul Crisostomo, from the Philippines. I teach English at a university here in Dandong." He lowered his voice. "Soon one of the waitresses will ask your nationality. It's part of their job. Tell them you're Canadian. You'll attract less suspicion that way. By the way, I'm a Roman Catholic priest. I normally don't call attention to that. The Chinese are at odds with the Vatican and would kick me out if they decided I was making serious trouble. I tell you only because your boss Robert Posey and I are in the same line of work, even if he doesn't recognize it."

"Doesn't recognize it?" I looked at him quizzically.

"Do you know how he started his career in the ministry?"

"After he got out of seminary and before he came to our church in Mississippi as youth pastor, he was a missionary — in your country, as a matter of fact."

"So you knew him back then. Maybe you heard him say he'd gone to the Philippines 'to convert the Catholics to Christianity.'"

"You're right that he has — or at least used to have — a pretty narrow definition." I smiled. "Although I consider myself a follower of Jesus, currently there's no way I'd meet Reverend Bob's criteria to be considered a Christian. But he seems to be looking the other way. Maybe he's going soft and ecumenical."

"He tried the ecumenical thing in my country, but by no means in any of the normal ways. He volunteered to have himself crucified on Good Friday as an act of devotion. They rejected him: 'Sorry, you're a foreigner and a Protestant.' I can't swear the next part happened exactly this way, but I hear he got a tetanus shot, sterilized some nails, hired a group of assistants, showed up in the middle of the night at an already vacated cross and had his crew nail him up. The story is that he stayed up there not just for a couple of hours but for fourteen or so before another group of men, sent by his father, pulled him down — and within a few days he had left the country. I haven't managed to confirm the details. It was hushed up at a high level."

I felt a chill, recalling a day at church youth camp when we were all at the lake for swimming. As I'd peered through my sunglasses at Carolyn Close, hoping like a lot of other guys that her loose wet swimsuit top would fall down, she'd pointed to marks on Reverend Bob's palms and asked if they were stigmata. He'd responded with a faint smile. "Think what you like." From that moment on, as far as we kids were concerned, he'd had an air of sacred mystery about him – not a bad tool for a youth pastor, working in a pious community, to carry in his kit.

"Wow." I was silent for a moment, unable to come up with a proper response. Then I steered our conversation back to Father Paul's uncanny resemblance to the first- and third-generation Kims. "At first, I guess, it was only Kim Il-sung they compared you to."

"Yes, Kim Jong-un was only a boy then and his existence was unknown to most Koreans and foreigners. Judging from pictures taken when he was at school in Switzerland, he didn't look particularly like the Great Leader. After his first adult public appearance and his promotion to four-star general in 2010, at the advanced age of twenty-seven, there were rumors they had done plastic surgery and put him on a reverse diet so he would gain weight and look just like his late grandfather. Makeup could also be involved."

"Why would they do that?"

"Political branding. Kim Il-sung is still revered as the regime's founding god-king."

Father Paul's remark about makeup brought back the memory of the only time I'd seen Reverend Bob's father in person. Johnny Posey had flown to Mississippi to launch a televised revival in the local stadium. Joe and I were among those waiting at the airport to meet him. The makeup assistant had been at work during the flight. The goo on the world-famous preacher's face appeared to be a quarter of an inch thick.

We were there because we'd been helping with the local advance work. "Boys," Reverend Bob had told us, a bit feverishly, "when Daddy gets here I want him to see that our preparations have been the best and most complete that any community anywhere has ever laid on for one of his crusades."

Johnny Posey had indeed been generous with his compliments, but had directed them to the chairman of the local committee rather than to the son who'd done most of the work. Now, sitting with Father Paul, I wondered if Reverend Bob had ever won the unqualified paternal approval he'd wanted so badly — and whether he went in for makeup, now that he was the active televangelist in the family.

Father Paul downed his Scotch and signaled for another. "The hair style is the easy part for Kim Jong-un. A 'Chinese waiter's haircut' is what somebody called it back in 1945 when Kim Il-sung returned from the Soviet Union and made his maiden political speech in Pyongyang."

"You have your hair cut the same way, so I guess you encourage people to notice the resemblance."

"It's good salesmanship. Even years after they've left their home country, the Koreans I work with still more or less worship Kim Il-sung."

"Why?"

"Partly decades of brainwashing by the regime. But there's an element of reality, too. Kim Jong-il, the second-generation leader, stuck with his father's policies long after they had passed the point of diminishing returns. Economic failure came on the Dear Leader's watch. He got the popular blame for ruining what his father had built. People look back on the period when the Great Leader ruled alone as a golden age when the state provided for the needs of the people."

I thought of the tears I'd seen in Shin Mi-song's eyes my first day on the package tour, as she'd described the original Kim.

"So looking like granddaddy Kim is useful for you?"

"When North Korean expatriates are told that there's an even higher power, they find that claim more believable if it's coming from someone who looks like the Beloved and Respected Great Leader."

"And over there" — I pointed in the direction of the river and the North Korean shore beyond — "the regime hopes the grandson can trade on physical resemblance to the grandfather to keep the dynasty in power?"

"That is the plan, apparently. But I'm skeptical. In my mission we feed those of our flock who cannot feed themselves. Young Kim talks about doing the same, but so far has not come up with a way to feed the non-elite. His advisors have done a first-class branding job on him, but branding can take a political leader only so far when the masses are hungry."

I told him about the soldiers I'd seen at the gift museum, who showed effects of childhood malnutrition. "But I didn't see any signs of current food shortages anywhere they took us — definitely nobody dying of starvation."

"You wouldn't see that at a tourist stop like Mount Myohyang, or anywhere in Pyongyang. Despite the fact the recent drought has worsened the food shortages, you're not likely to see it even where you're going. Such sights are not for foreigners. The regime will make sure you and the rest of the Posey community have enough to eat, for the time being. If they let you out to roam around in other nearby communities you may see starving people — but I'd be quite surprised if they let you out. I hear security over there is as tight as in a prison camp, no outsiders permitted in and no one from inside allowed to go out, except along a sanitized route where you won't see anything alarming."

"I might have known. Sounds like what my tour guides showed me — and didn't show me."

"Precisely."

"Another question. The Koreans you're working with are refugees?"

"The Chinese see no refugees — only illegal aliens. They want them out. So, for the record, I just happen to have some friends of Korean ethnicity who are 'residents' of China." He winked.

"So from those 'residents,' what more do you hear about Posey Korea University?"

"The university has ethnic Korean recruiters, who are citizens of China. For several years they've been scouring China's Korean border region, urging refugees who have become Christian or shown an interest in Christianity to return to North Korea and go to the Posey site."

I felt a presence behind me and turned. Shocked, I took a second look. It was Shin Mi-song. Like the waitresses, she wore a traditional Korean ensemble consisting of a short jacket over a long, wraparound skirt. But her outfit was white with a red sash, not the waitresses' red with white sash. As I reeled, in near panic, wondering what the hell she could be doing here — and how dangerous this renewed contact might prove — she pretended not to know me. She spoke to Father Paul: "How are your classes going, Professor Crisostomo?"

"Very well, thank you, Ms. Kim. I'd like to introduce you to a new customer, Professor Davis, who will be teaching music at Posey Korea University." He turned to me. "Ms. Kim is assistant manager here —

when she's not traveling, which is more often than you might imagine."

I had no difficulty believing that she traveled often. That would fit right into the profile, as would the name change. Kim is the real surname of more than a fifth of Koreans, making it the easiest choice if a fake name is needed.

"How nice to meet you, Professor Davis," she said. "My co-workers tell me you are from Canada. Lately, our restaurant seems to be attracting a great many Canadian customers." Decoded, those words meant: I *may* keep your little secret about your nationality if you will keep quiet about the fact I am two totally different people.

I felt exasperated at first; it hardly seemed a fair exchange. But then I reflected that all three of us had dual identities. "Glad to meet you, Ms. Kim."

"How was your trip to Pyongyang?" the priest asked.

"Busier than I had expected." She turned to me and said, "Since you are a music teacher, Professor Davis, you may enjoy our live entertainment, which starts in about forty-five minutes. Shall I find you and Professor Crisostomo a table where you can order supper in the meantime?"

She seated us at the largest table. Unfortunately, I noted, it was smack in the middle of the restaurant. No seats were even remotely suited for following the Fatback rule, in case she meant for me to die where I sat.

Under the circumstances, I didn't feel hungry. My stomach was jumping. Was she or wasn't she on the same team as the people who'd tried to kill me? If she was, I'd fallen into her trap. Would she poison my food? I put that fear aside when I saw Father Paul, with no apparent ill effects, eating heartily from our platter of braised crab claws and the accompanying communal serving bowls of Korean side dishes including three kinds of kimchi. Maybe she'll wait and kill me where there's no taster and no witness, I thought. I tucked into the spread, skipping only my individual bowl of rice.

Father Paul looked up and said, "Here's one of them now."

"One of what?"

"The Posey recruiters. This one covers the Dandong area, and doubles as university logistics man."

A slight, slender, hunched-over East Asian man came toward us, looking at me. He stopped at the table and said, in excellent English, "From the photo, I think you must be Professor Davis. The hotel people said you had gone for a walk. It's my assignment to take you to Posey Korea University tomorrow."

"How did you know where to find me?"

"Sooner or later, everyone comes to Arirang. Good evening, Father Paul. May I join you gentlemen?"

The man sat down. I asked him not to mention my real nationality in front of the waitresses, since I'd told them I was Canadian.

"Right," he said, "just as I don't call our friend here Father Paul in front of them. You may call me Byon, if you wish, bearing in mind that few of the people one meets in Arirang are precisely who they say they are." He didn't smile when he said it. He called a waitress over and ordered an orange soda. Father Paul invited him to dine with us on our enormous meal. He grabbed chopsticks and a spoon and dug right in.

The waitresses were lining up on the stage. Management had been picky in its hiring: Every one of the women was a serious looker. Some started playing Korean music on traditional instruments. Led by Shin Mi-song, others broke into a fluid Korean traditional dance, swirling as they snapped long pieces of brightly colored fabric as if cracking whips. I'd seen similar performances in Seoul.

Everything was professional even after the musicians changed instruments for a transition to Western pops. One tiny woman put away her *kayagum*, a traditional Korean zither, and switched to harp — not a harmonica but a real, golden harp bigger than she was, with long strings. They segued into Western classical, Shin soloing on piano with "Moonlight Sonata." Finally her crew transformed itself into a rock band. The dancers came out to the tables and dragged diners out of their chairs and onto the floor. I could see where this was leading.

The little harpist took me by the hand and pulled me up to the stage, where she handed me a guitar just as the assistant manager started belting out Adele's "Rolling in the Deep." The woman could sing, after all. That song wasn't in my repertoire, but I'd heard it enough times that I had no trouble providing driving chords to accompany her. They kept me up there for several numbers.

After we'd finished playing and singing — and talking; I'd done the "Mean Talking Blues" — the entertainers insisted I join them to take bows. At least we weren't bowing to graven images of the leaders, I thought — until I looked up and saw that we were. High on the opposite wall were lined up large portraits of all three dynastic Kims.

After our second bow, our beautiful bandleader walked backstage while the applause continued. I figured she'd return to the stage for an individual bow, the way conductors do in the West. Then, at long last, would come the moment when she'd take me aside and tell me who she really was. It wasn't that I needed more evidence she was a spy. But we did make nice music together, and I was having trouble figuring whether I should run for my life.

She didn't come back. We musicians bowed for the third and final time, without her. It wouldn't be prudent to burst through the doorway to find and confront her in the unfamiliar back-office area. I'd have to proceed on the working assumption that meeting her again would mean trouble.

━━

When I returned to my table another surprise awaited me. Behind a post was Senator Macon, seated next to an aide and chatting with Father Paul and Byon. The two Washingtonians had visited the Posey campus following their Pyongyang meetings and were on their way home. Byon had brought them down to Dandong. They were staying in the Renmin Hotel and would take the train to Shenyang and fly out the next day.

The senator seemed to have consulted the hotel's valet service. His suit looked pressed, and he wore it with a crisp, open-necked dress shirt. Macon's presence temporarily reassured me. Nobody with any sensitivity to the potential repercussions of international incidents was likely to murder me while a United States senator was watching. I could hang out for a while in this well lighted, public portion of the restaurant and get a fill from him on what to expect up at the university campus.

He greeted me as soon as I sat down. "Some of my fellow African Americans complain that not only do I belong to what they call white political groups — the GOP, the tea party movement — but I also talk like a white man," he said. "And here we find you — a mix of Korean and Caucasian, according to Bob Posey — and you sing black and, when it suits you, you talk black." He chuckled. "It takes all kinds."

I gave him the short answer: "I guess we search for authenticity where we hope to find it."

"I see you like a drink. So do I. Take my advice and schlep some of your favorite hooch up to the campus or you'll have nothing to do at night but attend the prayer meetings. Bob is no Johnny Posey, and I feel for him as I watch him trying to fill his old man's very large shoes. But I like his preaching all right. I'm sorry I can't say as much for his hospitality. Buy what you want on the China side. Byon here will help you get it through North Korean customs. Right, Byon?"

Byon pretended for a moment not to have heard, then looked up from his orange soda and nodded. He didn't look happy about it.

"Thanks, I'll do that," I said. The tea party wasn't my cup, but I liked the senator. He was bright, and as plainspoken as Joe. I asked him, "Other than a dry county — we still have quite a lot of those back in Mississippi — what else should I expect?"

"Bob is doing wonderful work up there. In the early twentieth century they called Pyongyang the Jerusalem of the East. American Protestant missionaries — Methodists and Presbyterians, mainly —

made huge inroads in Korea, especially the northern part. Kim Il-sung grew up in a Christian family, even played organ in church. Church was a big part of his training in how to make himself a god, which is pretty much what he did after he got control. And then he banned other religions including Christianity. Now Bob is bringing Christianity back. He tells us that the Korean Christians up there are full of joy to be able to practice their religion."

"I still don't see what's in it for the regime," I said. "Reverend Bob told me there's a human rights angle — hosting the university should help the North Koreans deal with critics who say there's no freedom of religion. But if that's the case, where are the foreign news stories?"

"I imagine the North Koreans are waiting to time any major publicity for when the news will do them the most good. We American politicians aren't the only ones with spin doctors on staff, you know." He glanced at his aide, a slender white guy, who responded by cocking his head to the left and offering a toothy, beauty-queen sort of smile.

━━━

There seemed no point in resuming my Pyongyang act and pretending, for the benefit of Ms. Shin, that I didn't speak the language. A spy would know — especially since I had ordered in Korean when I first arrived in the restaurant. Hell, she'd known I played guitar. The waitress came back and I asked her in Korean to replace my drink, which I'd emptied after deciding I was safe as long as Macon was around. There was still no sign of the multi-talented assistant manager.

A few minutes later, Macon and his aide stood to leave, saying they had to get an early start in the morning. I joined them for the walk back to the hotel, through a forest of neon. When I got to my room I didn't turn on the lights immediately but went to the window and looked across the river. Sinuiju was nearly dark, only a few dim lights flickering here and there. What a contrast with high-rise, happening Dandong.

I was about to walk over and flip the room switch but I changed my mind when I glanced down on the street and saw a man on the sidewalk looking straight toward my window. I closed the room curtains tightly, but still didn't get much sleep that night. I had no clear idea what the North Korean woman's reappearance in my life meant but I feared nothing good would come of it.

10 / IN THE BOONDOCKS

In the light of a sunny and crisp early autumn day, about to cross into North Korea, I felt slightly less apprehensive. Reverend Bob seemed to have the ear of the country's authorities. I would keep my eyes open but, with luck, maybe I wouldn't be in much danger on his cloistered campus.

In the hotel lobby Byon met me, bearing my visa — a separate document. As I knew from my previous trips, North Korea didn't stamp visas into the passports of imperialists. We packed my bag and my guitar into a chauffeured van. The driver already had loaded a shipment of Chinese-made guitars, a couple of banjos, a mandolin and a gross of harmonicas, all ordered for the students at my request, but there was still room for more cargo. Byon gave me a look of distaste, but he did have the driver stop so I could stock up on bourbon.

As the senator had assured me, the border formalities presented no problems. We drove across the Friendship Bridge and headed east-northeast, soon leaving the built-up parts of Sinuiju behind. I didn't say much, since the driver was North Korean and I figured there was a good chance he'd been assigned to spy on us. Thinking about that reminded me of Shin Mi-song, who was in my thoughts more than I liked.

The scenery was similar to what our tour group had encountered on our side trips outside Pyongyang: an odd patchwork pattern on the hills and mountains. The coloration of each geometric tract — they ranged from brown through yellow to deep green — apparently depended on what crop, or which weeds, had replaced the absent trees and when. These were nothing like the forested mountains I'd seen on the Chinese side of the border.

This mountainous terrain wasn't rice country. Many of the farmers had planted potatoes. Harvest time would come soon, but the scrawny plants didn't look promising. In each of the few settlements we passed, people sat, stood or moved in desultory fashion in the fields. Their work besides weeding seemed to consist of picking up stones and moving them to piles. There were few signs of mechanization — only the occasional truck or tractor. Some oxen but mostly people were doing the heavy work.

Although everyone looked poor, I didn't see anyone in a posture suggesting late-stage starvation. Maybe starving people were inside, dying. That would make sense, especially assuming we were following the "sanitized" route that Father Paul had told me about.

Enormous characters on the mountainsides, in the Korean *hangul* writing system, spelled out political slogans. One, far off and visible for only a moment as we rounded a bend, said, "Long Live the Youth Commander!" That must have been an earlier title for Kim Jong-un before his father's death. Maybe the area, due to its remoteness, was far down on the regime's priority list for updating the propaganda signs.

The evidence was piling up that I'd made a mistake. Personal danger aside, I could hardly expect to learn anything about a sophisticated financial scheme while isolated in a remote part of the country that was noticeably poor even by North Korea's abysmal standards.

We pressed on, moving higher into the mountains and seeing yet fewer signs of human habitation. I checked my watch when we saw one car go by. It was just under an hour before we encountered another. Then, as I wondered what we'd do in the event of a break-down, sirens sounded, our driver pulled over and a motorcade of large, black European sedans with tinted windows passed us at high speed. It looked like a gangsters' funeral procession.

We stopped for a fueling and lunch break. The gas station was a one-man operation: no billboards or logos, just a concrete block hut and a pump. I might have missed seeing it if we hadn't stopped there.

While the driver filled the tank, Byon and I chatted at a lone concrete picnic table. I asked why the North Korean mountains had been deforested. It had occurred to me that maybe timber sales could be a partial source of the money influx I'd seen evidenced in Pyongyang.

Byon disabused me of that notion. "Originally it was Kim Il-sung's policy. North Korea had plenty of ore and coal and other raw materials but it didn't have enough land fit for agriculture. The South was agriculturally rich, lacked mineral resources but decided to import them so it could build a manufacturing industry. Meanwhile Kim wanted the North to be self-sufficient all around; instead of importing food, he was always urging the people to expand farmland. They filled in swamps and tidal basins and started up the mountains, cutting the trees and burning them for fuel, planting crops to replace them. They were supposed to terrace as they went but most of the terraces were poorly built, too weak to last."

The driver had started walking in our direction. Byon opened the lunch bag from the Renmin Hotel and began distributing the contents.

"The economy collapsed after the Soviet Union and Eastern Europe abandoned communism and stopped sending aid in the early nineteen nineties. People were desperate. They climbed still higher into the mountains, cutting even scraggly, thin trees for fuel and culti-vating private plots on slopes as steep as sixty degrees. Rains came and washed the terraces and their contents down into the valleys, covering good farmland below with stones and clogging the rivers with silt, making the flooding far worse. It was a terrible mess and they still haven't finished cleaning it up in some places." Byon raised his arms in a gesture of dismay.

"Sounds like a self-inflicted wound." I took a bite of my sandwich, processed cheese on hard white bread.

"The regime blames nature for the flood damage. It also blames the United States — for choking off the country's economy so that people had to scrounge for food and fuel in the mountains. No one mentions the Great Leader's policy that started it all."

Is his policy still the regime's policy?

"Current policy is to replant the forests, but as you can see there's been almost no progress. Arbor Day, when everyone has to turn out to plant trees, used to be on April 6. For propaganda purposes, to make the date correspond to an event in the manufactured Kim family legend, they changed it starting in 1999 to March 2, when the ground in much of the country is still frozen. Of course many trees, planted with great ceremony on that day, die and have to be replanted. And even if the seedlings are put in later, at the right time, transplants don't grow for long before people cut them down, or at least tie their branches to the trunks so that the trees won't block the sun from shining on the subsistence crops they're planting."

The driver rejoined us and scarfed down his sandwich. We ate our hard East Asian pears in silence before resuming the journey. I reflected on what I'd just learned. Eliminating one alternate notion of how the country's leaders might be getting rich — exporting timber — brought me closer to understanding why they might resort to a nefarious financial scam. It could be pure desperation: They had to face the fact that their versions of conventional means of creating wealth weren't working.

Around mid-afternoon we pulled off the paved highway and drove for ten minutes or so over a rutted gravel road, following a rocky stream up into yet higher mountains. Finally we came to a stop at a steel gate, around 10 feet high, that was surmounted by a modest sign painted in red and gold. In English only, the sign proclaimed that this was Posey Korea University.

Even though Father Paul had alerted me that the place was under tight security, I was surprised to find the gate guarded by armed, uniformed men. Looking off to either side I saw a chain-link fence, also around 10 feet high if you included the barbed wire at the top. Based on what I had come to know about North Korea I supposed the fence and gate were there to keep non-university people out and to keep us in.

First to greet me was the dean of faculty, a slender, fortyish woman from Kentucky named Sable Pugmire who wore corduroy pants and a cable-knit sweater. We walked past the classroom buildings and the labs and gym. All were of unpainted wood construction, nothing over two stories. It looked like a quickly erected military camp. There were no ivy-covered masonry buildings, much less ivory towers.

Sable led me toward the administration building, no fancier than the others. "Assuming everything continues to work out, we can worry about raising money to put up more permanent buildings later," she said. The North Korean government had sent soldiers to build the structures —"although the Posey organization had to ship the lumber here from abroad."

"I did notice the tree shortage."

In her office, she filled me in on my teaching responsibilities. "All our classes should be conducted in English, but it's good that you have Korean language ability. You can lead singing in Korean and help the students when they don't understand something in English." She pointed down the corridor. "Dr. Posey is busy but he'll see you later in his office."

She gave me a campus walking tour. The classroom building was two stories high with various one-story extensions. Next was the single-story library. "We're so proud to have a full line of Christian books here along with a complete collection of the Western classics."

The library looked small to me but I gave her an encouraging nod.

She stopped to show me the dining hall, which backed up on a large vegetable garden. "Supper is at six. Please be on time. Dr. Posey is a stickler for saying grace with everyone present."

"He hasn't changed."

We peeked into the kitchen. The staff members were preparing supper. Two of the cooks, tears streaming down their faces, were chopping onions. My eyes fell on a worker pouring rice out of a big sack that hung from the ceiling by a hook. The action brought back a memory of Fatback. We'd finished off a bottle of whiskey in his Mississippi kitchen. I'd finally gotten around to telling him I had accepted a war photography assignment.

As I'd anticipated, Fatback had shown even more disapproval than Mama had. "I done put too much into teachin' you how to play guitar and harp for you to go gettin' killed and make me feel like I done spent all that time on you for nothin'. You a musician, not a fighter."

"I can take care of myself if I need to. Been doing it for years — ever since Reverend Bob taught me boxing."

"Never heard about that."

"That was before I knew you. I was a high school freshman. A big bully of an upperclassman named Arnold took a dislike to me and gave me a cherry belly out behind the stadium."

"You mean he held you down and beat the back of a toothbrush on your belly real fast, like he was a drummer, till that belly swoll up bright red?"

"Yeah, the sadist. Kept the toothbrush in his locker for just that purpose. Judging by the smell of his breath, he never used it on his teeth. Reverend Bob heard about it and just happened to have a couple pair of boxing gloves in his office. He took me out behind the church and taught me what I needed to know."

"I s'pose the reverend taught you no hittin' below the belt, gotta stick to them gentleman-like Marquess of Queensberry boxin' rules."

"He did, and it worked just fine. Back at school, the next time Arnold pulled out his toothbrush I gave him a bloody nose before some other upperclassmen pulled us apart. He didn't bother me any more. I've had more fistfights since then and won more than I lost."

"Listen, Heck. You run into trouble in the real world, I want you to forget all about what that preacher told you 'bout fightin' fair. Say a man come after you with a knife. You got to use anything handy."

Maybe I'd looked doubtful. Or maybe, regardless of my initial response, Fatback had wanted to show me, memorably, what his point was.

In one swift and fluid movement he'd grabbed our empty bottle by its neck, smashed the bottom on the stove and crouched, thrusting the jagged weapon out in front of him, moving way faster than prudent Mississippians normally permitted ourselves to do when the temperature in the shade was ninety-eight degrees Fahrenheit.

Demonstrating on what was left of a fifty-pound sack of grits that hung from a hook, he'd instructed me: "Duck when he first come at you. Move in low. Stick it in hard above his pecker, far as you can shove it, and pull up with both hands. Turn that edge so you gouge along one side of his rib cage. Turn it again when you get to the top. Then slice down the other side."

A stream of grits had flowed out through the foot-wide flap he'd made as I watched them pile high on the floor.

"Maybe you do time, Heck, but you still alive."

The yakuza hit men had cleared up any doubts I might have had about the value of Fatback's advice. I wondered if they were still watching my Tokyo and mountain places.

━━

Finally Sable and I reached a faculty apartment building, another unpainted wood-frame structure — this one with a roofed, open-air passageway along one side. There Sable assigned me my quarters: a sitting room, which would also serve as my office, and a bedroom with attached bath.

"How about Internet and telephone? I don't see any facilities here. Come to think of it, I didn't see any in your office, either."

"Those aren't available except to Dr. Posey. The North Koreans insisted on that. For what they call security reasons, the rest of us are limited to snail mail. DPRK postage stamps are available at the campus snack stand — and some of them are stunningly beautiful. Your family and friends and any stamp collectors among your acquaintances will be happy to receive them. If there's an emergency we can arrange for you to use the electronic communications facilities in Dr. Posey's office."

When Sable left, I opened a bottle of bourbon, poured three fingers and drank it neat, shaking my head and mentally pointing one of those fingers at myself. Getting the story or image wasn't the end of a news assignment. Whatever we got we had to file to our editors. Snail mail! That hadn't been the journalist's transmission choice since the nineteenth century advent of the electrical telegraph and transoceanic cables. I'd brought my laptop this time, figuring that a professor's having one shouldn't arouse suspicion. Failing to check ahead on the availability of transmission facilities was the sort of mistake I'd never have made, no matter how short the notice, if the hit men in the subway and at the lake hadn't rattled me.

It had come to seem wildly improbable that I'd get the story I needed while confined in the rural cocoon of Posey Korea University. Still, if only for my safety, I'd need to do some more deep breathing, calm down and stop making mistakes. Meanwhile, at least I'd have a chance to try something new — teaching. Maybe that would prove interesting enough to keep the overall experience from driving me batty. Maybe I'd make some new friends. Maybe I *would* get the story, somehow.

When I went into the dining hall, with its rustic tables and benches, its unfinished wooden floor, walls and ceiling, it felt as if I were back at a Calvary Church youth retreat held in some back-woods Mississippi camp — except for the food, which proved to be an appetizing blend of Korean and American cuisines. To go with our meatloaf and fried chicken we had a choice of five kinds of kimchi, collard greens cooked with pork, broccoli with cream sauce, string beans, navy beans and mashed potatoes.

It was six sharp and I was the last to arrive. As soon as I plopped down in the seat Sable had saved for me, we all bowed our heads and Reverend Bob, up on the stage, said grace. "Lord, with the signs multiplying that your only begotten son will soon return to rule the earth for a thousand years, we give thanks that you have permitted us to gather in Christian fellowship here in formerly godless North Korea." He stopped to cough. "We thank you for the food that we are about to eat and ask that you bless it to the nourishment of our earthly bodies." He coughed again. "In the name of Jesus Christ we pray. Amen."

Amens echoed around the room. As platters, bowls and utensils clattered, Sable introduced me to her husband, Ezra, and their three daughters. The oldest, Shirley, a brunette, looked about fourteen physically but seemed older because she had a permanently worried look on her scrubbed face and wore a long, shapeless granny dress over her sneakers. The other two, effervescent identical-twin blondes around eight years old, were named Goodness and Mercy.

"Ah," I said. "Twenty third Psalm, sixth verse."

Cocking their heads and pointing to each girl as her name was uttered, the twins delightedly spoke in unison: "Shirley, Goodness and Mercy shall follow me all the days of my life and I will dwell in the house of the Lord forever."

Sable and Ezra beamed. Shirley looked sullen, and I felt for her.

Sable taught biology and chemistry; Ezra, physics and math. Their teaching hours were staggered so they could take turns home-schooling their daughters. Back in Kentucky, they'd been involved with a museum, research institute and theme park devoted to promoting the accounts of creation set forth in the book of Genesis.

So excited that they both talked at once, they told me all about the organization's Australian founder. "Atheists, even the biggest names in secular science, are no match for Ken Ham," Sable boasted.

A pale, thirty-something Caucasian man sitting nearby rolled his eyes. We introduced ourselves; he was Bartow Toombs, an English teacher from Savannah.

The Pugmires were still talking to me, waxing rhapsodic about Posey Korea University and the miraculous change in North Korean policy that had permitted them to witness for Jesus inside the country. They kept that up until Shirley interrupted with a whiney complaint. "There's nothing to do here. Not even a store, much less a mall." I figured she'd gladly leave this remote locale to return to Kentucky and dwell in the house of the Pugmires, if not forever then at least through high school.

Feeling there weren't likely to be many promising topics for conversation between me and the Pugmire couple, I was relieved when Lindsey Harrold joined the conversation. A drawling, white-mustached Texan in his seventies or eighties who taught theology, Lindsey introduced himself by cracking a joke at Reverend Bob's expense. "Bob might have chosen some other context than the End Times for giving thanks at your first meal with us, considering you probably felt already that you'd come to the end of the earth."

I laughed, and Lindsey went on to assure me that things weren't too bad at the university. There were movie nights, the little library had a decent selection of books and the students were enthusiastic.

Bartow Toombs looked up from his kimchi. "You always think the glass is half full, Lindsey."

The meal ended. Reverend Bob came over to welcome me with a big grin and a hug. "You got here quick, Heck. That's great. I'm headed off first thing in the morning on a trip to the States, but come by my office around eight tonight and we can have a chat. Sable will get you squared away in the meantime."

Sable took me over to another table and introduced me to several students. Male and female students alike wore jeans. Sable told me in an aside that the Christian head of a South Korean department store chain had donated the clothing. The students looked like their counterparts anywhere else in northeastern Asia, except for their generally small stature and what I took to be stress lines around the eyes and mouths of many of them.

The student body president, who had topped his jeans with a white dress shirt, looked to be considerably older than a traditional college student — maybe thirty-five. He mentioned there was a long waiting list for my class.

Leaving her family to walk out with me, Sable told me the campus was a restricted area. We were not to venture off the main paths or into the mountains without security people escorting us. "This is for our own protection. The DPRK is not accustomed to religious people exercising their faith openly, and there are fears it could cause problems." She stopped at a security post near my building and introduced me to the unsmiling plainclothes cops who manned it.

By the time I got to Reverend Bob's office I'd decided to level with him. My youthful experiences had taught me that a frank chat with him could produce ideas that might not have occurred to me. Even if the problem I'd run into this time turned out to be too far from his own experience for him to think of anything helpful, it was worth a try. I had nothing to lose.

"You probably saved my life inviting me over here," I told him. "I respect you too much not to be honest about this. I have to confess: the prospect of teaching was not the only reason I came. A couple of really bad things happened. First, a man tried to push me in front of a train in the Tokyo subway the day before I got your email."

"Tried to kill you?! Why? Did they catch him?"

"He ended up being the one run over by the train. Turned out to be Korean-Japanese, a gangster. I left Tokyo for my safety, but another gangster came after me the next morning. He got sidetracked before he could find me, but he was close." I didn't want to mention the second yakuza's fatal fight with the mama bear — it was so preposterous I had trouble believing it myself.

"But why? What in the world could make you a target for Japanese gangsters?"

"I figured it was because I'd been sniffing around trying to scope out what happened to Joe. I told you in Pyongyang I suspected his death was related to some sort of complicated financial scheme run by persons unknown. I got a further clue suggesting that scenario from reading Joe's notebooks, which some kind soul provided me. Am I right that he gave them to you for safekeeping when he met you in the lobby his last morning in Pyongyang? And then you made sure I got them?"

Reverend Bob smiled and puffed on his after-dinner Havana. "God moves in a mysterious way his wonders to perform." He coughed, then added, "That's always been one of Daddy's favorite hymns."

"Don't get me wrong. I like the idea of teaching here, but I also thought if I came over to your campus I could pursue the story and maybe find out who wants to kill me. Now that I've arrived, I'm afraid that's impossible up here, so far from Pyongyang and any other settlement of more than a few hundred people. I hadn't realized just how remote your campus is. So I'm pretty much at a loss about what to do."

"You did the right thing to come. The authorities wouldn't want to let anything happen here that would discourage our project, and I'm sure they know letting someone attack an American teacher would do just that, in a big way. They keep extremely tight control, as I'm sure you realized during your time as a tourist. Besides being safe here, who knows? Maybe you'll get a sudden insight that leads you to a big story. You know, Zack Nodding thinks our friend Joe may have turned greedy."

I didn't say anything.

He took a puff on his Havana and coughed. "Zack mentioned a case to me that he thought might be similar to Joe's, even sent me copies of some old news stories to show you. Let's see where I put those." He rummaged in the top drawer of his desk until he found some printouts. "They're about a young reporter whose job in the nineteen eighties was writing the *Wall Street Journal*'s 'Heard on the Street' financial gossip column. When he got some information likely to 'move the market,' as they say in the financial world, he passed it along to broker friends who capitalized on it before the column got into print. Do you know the name R. Foster Winans?"

"Yeah. I heard about him more than once from none other than Joe, who used to work for the Journal and despised Winans, as does every other journalist who ever worked there."

"I just read these clippings quickly, but Zack wonders if Joe could have been at least thinking about doing something similar."

"I don't see any logic in that, and I can't picture Joe involved in an insider trading scheme even if he was desperate. He was an honest reporter." I couldn't fight the anger that was making my face flush. "I'm sure Zack knows finance and all that, but . . ." I stopped myself from saying more.

"I gather you two haven't exactly hit it off. You're different types. You're like John Hyon — a pleaser, generally easygoing, considerate and well liked. Zack, on the other hand, tends to rub people the wrong way. He doesn't always know how to act, although his heart's in the right place. Let me share with you some of the circumstances behind that and maybe you can find it in your own heart to think better of him."

I nodded.

He coughed before continuing. "We encourage homeschooling, but it has to be done right. Zack's mother homeschooled him all the way from kindergarten through high school. He was an only child. He was a baby when his father abandoned them. The boy would have benefited from more and earlier social interaction with other children. He's a bit intense, sometimes lacking in sweetness of spirit. But Zack loves the Lord — he's one of a remarkable few among the faithful who've never shown any signs of doubt. And he does know finance, inside and out. I depend on him as my right hand in practical matters."

I considered what he'd said. Maybe I'd been too hard on Zack. Maybe he'd had bad experiences with journalists and was ready to imagine the worst about Joe — although for the life of me I couldn't visualize how the scheme, as Zack imagined it, might work. Insider trading based on what information? Oh, well.

━━━

Back in my apartment, what really stuck with me from the conversation was Reverend Bob's description of me as a "pleaser." The word stung. It was an acceptable description of an entertainer, but not of a newsman. Even while floating in a sea of brotherly love at Posey Korea University, watched over by a guardian angel whose initials were RB, I needed to keep my body in shape, my instincts and technique sharp.

I pondered that as I fell asleep. The next morning I awoke early. In sweats and running shoes I went out to the security post. "It's my custom to run in the morning, for my health," I said in Korean. "You're welcome to come along."

One of the security guys took me up on it. About my age but a smoker and not terribly healthy looking, he wore a business suit and necktie and vinyl dress shoes. We ran along the campus trails back and forth, the agent huffing and puffing, until he got a blister and dropped off at his post saying I could continue alone.

I considered the effort a success: In case I should ever need it, I now had some latitude to roam around a bit without the cops bothering me.

When I entered the dining hall that morning Reverend Bob was there, but only for long enough to say grace. Carrying breakfast in a paper box, he made a hasty departure to begin his journey.

I was determined not to disappoint him. I'd throw myself into teaching. Remembering what the student body president had said about the waiting list, I told Sable I'd be happy to teach as many hours as it took to permit all comers to enroll.

"Thank you!" she said with a big smile. " 'The hand of the diligent will rule.' "

"Proverbs 12:24, English Standard Version. Well, there's also good advice for a newly minted professor in the second chapter of Titus: 'Show yourself in all respects to be a model of good works, and in your teaching show integrity, dignity and sound speech that cannot be condemned.' "

"You certainly know your Bible." Sable seemed to have developed new respect for me.

We agreed I'd teach instrumental music in small weekly sections so I could work closely with the students. I'd also bring them together in larger groups, for choral music. Early in each week I'd hold one session comprising all of the students to prepare choral and instrumental numbers for performance.

On the first day I walked into the campus's auditorium — the space also used for Sunday services. Rustic like all the other buildings but theater-like with its rows of chairs slanting up from the stage, it was packed with students. Evidently there was a lot of interest in music. We'd need to order more instruments once they got close to the point where they were ready to perform en masse.

At the lectern I proved to be just as much of a ham — OK, a pleaser — as I was on stage. I told them my story, mentioning that my own Korean mother and grandmother, like many of my listeners and their families, had been refugees. I described my upbringing in Mississippi, a place they'd never heard of, and how on Sundays I would spend up to seven hours at Calvary Church — I'd needed that much time to attend morning and evening Bible study sessions and worship services plus choir practice, youth council meeting and the teen social that capped off the day. I told them how each Saturday, at the local Korean church, morning language classes had given way to afternoon games and sports with the children of Korean couples who'd moved into the area.

Part of my role was to help the students learn English. Still, I didn't want to push them too far, too fast. I spoke alternately in

English and Korean, translating English terms into Korean for them. I found that I also had to translate modern South Korean terms I'd grown up using into more basic Korean to make myself understood. The Northern and Southern vocabularies had diverged considerably since the 1945 division of the country.

Much of the substance of what I had to say was new to the students. I told them that first day how I had developed the habit of attending African-American churches that honored the traditions of spirituals and gospel music. Some students had never met a black person and none had any idea what the term African-American meant. But when I explained the background of slavery, their eyes signaled recognition of the subject. North Korean propaganda had zeroed in on whatever was disgraceful in American history.

Explaining how the slaves had expressed their pain and longing in spirituals, I began singing slow and soft:

> *Nobody knows*
> *The trouble I've seen,*
> *Nobody knows*
> *My sorrow . . .*

I sped up the tempo and raised the volume

> *Sometimes I'm up.*
> *Sometimes I'm down.*
> *Oh, yes, Lord.*

. . . and then sang softly again:

Sometimes I'm almost
Down to the ground.
Oh, yes, Lord.

After that sank in, I foolishly tried to lighten up the session. "I don't know if you've heard of foot washing Baptists. I became a foot *stomping* Baptist." Only a couple of the students — who had been influenced by Pentecostal missionaries in China — knew about the ritual of foot washing. I let them explain. Then I demonstrated foot stomping while I played some appropriate music. Finally I told them that "foot stomping Baptist" was my joking play on "foot washing Baptist." None of them laughed.

I told them about bluesmen I had met and learned from. If the students had heard of the blues they might consider the genre strictly secular, I said — and I knew Posey Korea University was an explicitly Christian institution. But as Fatback Hawkins had told me, "You can't sing the blues unless you been to church."

The traditions were all tied up together, I told them. I launched into a rendition of Son House's "Preachin' Blues," a sinner's lament about how booze and women have kept him from realizing his ambition of becoming a preacher so he won't need to work for a living.

When most of their expressions showed they had not the foggiest notion of what on earth I was going on about, I decided to shift to more orthodox examples. First I sang the spiritual "Go Down, Moses." I pointed out that the biblical exodus and the freeing of African-American slaves offered parallels to the students' own travails as they wandered between two countries in search of a promised land that they might now think was Posey Korea University:

Go down, Moses,
Way, way down in Egypt's land.
Tell ol'
Pharaoh:
Let my people go.

They started to get it. Pretty soon they were clapping and swaying and tapping — or even stomping — their feet.

Then I gave them a gospel song from the first third of the twentieth century:

Jesus on the main line,
Tell him what you want.
Just call him up and tell him
What you want.

They liked the beat but didn't understand the lyrics. The reference, I told them, was to the then-newly invented telephone and the wiring that connected users to one another. Discussion revealed that a land-line phone never had been a fixture in the typical North Korean home. But nearly all the students who'd been in China had used mobile phones.

⸺

I asked for volunteers to tell their own stories. Although it had seemed the class was already starting to click as a group, only a couple of hands went up. When the student body president stood and in under a minute gave us the CliffsNotes version of his life, I sensed that more than shyness was involved in their reticence. I could see how he and probably most of the others had been conditioned to hold things in, for fear of arousing suspicion. They probably figured the class included at least one spy assigned to remember or even record any remarks that might be construed as anti-regime. Who was I to say that wasn't the case?

Anyhow, looking at my watch I saw that my time was about up. We'd made a decent start.

"You've heard today," I said, "how some great music came out of people's hard lives. In this class I want to hear you make stand-up music out of your memories of low-down times."

I convened the first of many guitar sections the following Monday. Only one of the three students showed signs of real talent, but I assured them they all could learn to play the instrument if they'd practice.

At the end of that class Pak, the student I'd spotted as a natural, stayed behind for a chat in the hallway where I was sending the other students off. "My father thinks we're related," Pak said in Korean. "His family was from Kaesong. I passed along what you told us about your missing grandfather and uncle who didn't make it to the South. He believes he's your first cousin."

"Wow! Wouldn't that be something? I was in Kaesong just the other day. Wondered if any of the family might still live there."

"My grandfather left there soon after the war. With Kaesong part of the North, communist officials didn't want people suspected of disloyalty living that close to the border. They kicked tens of thousands of people like my grandfather out of Kaesong and sent members of the 'loyal' class from other parts of the country to take their places as new residents." They banished my grandfather to a mine in the mountains of North Hamgyong province. That's where my father was born."

"Where is your family now?" I envisioned them still hiding in China, or imprisoned in a North Korean camp. If so, though, how would they stay in touch with young Pak?

"I'm not supposed to talk about it. Perhaps later I can. Please don't mention what I've said."

"All right. I do hope to meet him."

Maybe I was in the right place after all, even if I was no closer to unraveling the Joe mystery. Nobody had tried to kill me since I'd arrived. I was already developing real affection for my students, and deeper concern about the country they were introducing to me. And now came this news. I'd grown up knowing a lot of cousins on my father's side but I'd missed having any on my mother's side. If it turned out that Pak's father was really my cousin, that would go a long way toward justifying the bumps in my road to Posey Korea University. And as a bonus, that dining hall food was excellent. If I weren't running every morning I'd be putting on weight for sure.

11 / USE ANYTHING HANDY

BYON DROVE up from Dandong with a new student, a young woman named Yu. She joined a harmonica class section. I recognized her as the petite waitress-musician who'd performed on kayagum and harp the night I visited Arirang.

I didn't think it showed me up as wildly paranoid to suspect she was a spy sent by Shin Mi-song — either to finish, by herself, or to help someone else finish the job the yakuza had botched. I asked her to stay behind after class. "Welcome, Ms. Yu. It's an honor to have one of Arirang's fine musicians join us. What brings you to Posey University?"

Her smile was half the size of her face and genuine enough in appearance — but people could be trained to smile sincerely before pulling the trigger.

"I often waited on Mr. Byon. I told him my family had been Christians and I wanted to study here."

"How did your assistant manager, Ms. Kim, feel about losing one of her stars?"

"She has been away, traveling."

I couldn't read Ms. Yu with any certainty, but figured there was nothing to stop even a pint-sized cheerleader type from becoming an assassin given all the killing methods that had been devised.

"Well, no doubt you'll be a fine addition to the campus. Don't forget to practice *bending* the notes the way I showed you today, to get that good blues sound. You're making fine progress already. I have a feeling you're going to master the harmonica quickly and move on to add, say, the banjo."

Although Sable Pugmire was always pleasant, and had been even more so since my offer to handle a heavy teaching load, I hadn't gone out of my way to spend time with her. For one thing, I didn't want to get into a discussion of the propaganda leaflets promoting young-earth creationism that kept appearing in my mailbox. That day, after I returned from the classroom to my apartment-office, Sable paid me a visit. She told me I had a summons to take some students and perform for someone "very high up."

"We've only had the classes going for a couple of weeks."

"I know, but we have no choice. When I say very high up, I mean really, really high up."

"Like who? The county sheriff?" I remembered that cavalcade of black cars that had passed us on the road coming up. "The local mafia boss?"

"Even higher. For security reasons I'm not supposed to tell you now. It's set for Saturday evening. You'll be performing near the university."

It was going to be a severe test of my teaching ability to prepare a small ensemble, made up of students with musical training or experience plus Pak and a couple of other beginners who were naturally gifted. I wondered what else might await me. Was this a plot to get me out of the campus grounds and into a place where it would be convenient to kill me? Did that explain the timing of Yu's arrival? Should I fear the personage we would be performing for?

On the other hand, I reasoned, there might be something in this for me — and Joe, and Evelyn. If someone in this remote region possessed such stature or power that he or she must go unnamed for security reasons, by keeping my eyes and ears open maybe I could, after all, learn something that would help me get the story I was after.

―――

On Saturday evening the seven students and I packed ourselves into the university van. We rode out onto the highway and headed north briefly before the driver turned through a checkpoint onto an immaculate, smoothly paved road. In another minute we came to a high-walled compound guarded by a conspicuously large contingent of armed security men. Tall, wearing military uniforms, they stood stiff as wax figures. Inside the gate was a lush garden in which the abundant maples showed gloriously red and gold. We crossed a railroad spur and saw, to our right, what appeared to be a one-room passenger station. The garden opened up into a lawn, cropped close like a golf green, that surrounded a spread-out, three-story, white masonry mansion of basically utilitarian Western architecture. A chunky fringe of traditional Korean tiled roof surrounded a flat heliport where several camouflage-painted helicopters were parked. The whole effect was of graceless opulence backed by unlimited power and money. If the owner of this place meant me harm, I had a lot to worry about.

An attendant ushered us into a high-ceilinged anteroom decorated with a patterned beige Chinese carpet and a giant painting of Kim the First as a young warrior on horseback. On a table awaiting us were egg sandwiches, fruit — more of those hard pears, which were in season, but in this case of exceptionally good quality — and bottled water and soft drinks. A waiter in a white jacket poured me — and me alone — a stiff drink from a bottle of JW Blue.

Through the doors that led to the performance venue we could hear a band doing a decent imitation of South Korean K-pop. The finale after twenty minutes was "Gangnam Style," which I'd heard was banned in the North as decadent "puppet" music. Someone here was above the rules.

We entered the ballroom where we were to perform, an imposingly large, centrally heated space with crystal chandeliers dangling from a ceiling even higher than the one in the anteroom. There we saw the same chubby young fellow who had hosted Shin Mi-song and me in the Number One Room at that Pyongyang nightclub. I could hear the wide-eyed students closest to me sucking in their breath as they recognized him.

His costume validated our decision to wear casual clothes for the performance. Diamond stud in his earlobe, his hair spiked just as when I'd met him in Pyongyang, he was in jeans with no shirt but only a leather vest so as to show off elaborate yakuza-style tattoos — real or fake, I couldn't tell — that covered his left shoulder and arm.

He was seated in the centermost of a row of upholstered chairs featuring well provisioned built-in cup-holders and snack trays. Beside him sat a round-faced man in his sixties or seventies who was sporting a plaid flannel shirt. A bevy of gorgeous, mini-skirted young women flanked them to fill out the front row. The people behind them on non-upholstered chairs looked more businesslike, some in military uniforms, others in business suits, only one wearing people's garb. Regardless of costume, several were armed. The leather vest was too roomily cut for me to tell whether our host was carrying.

The VIP spoke to me in English. "I heard from Comrade Mi-song you returned to my country. Welcome back, Mr. Davis."

What followed were by no means my finest moments on stage. The youngsters and I performed with gusto, and I was surprised they'd done as well as they had, but there hadn't been time to prepare enough pieces. Too soon, we ran out of material. When we took our bows in hopes of leaving quickly, our host — mimicked by his minions — raised shouts of "Encore!"

Yu, a fast learner as I'd expected, had put in plenty of time practicing harmonica. During the encore, I found I could rely on her musically as she accompanied me on a few more numbers that otherwise would have been solos.

Not a show of shows, but our host seemed satisfied. My guess was that not too many foreign artists trekked up to his mountain villa for command performances. He had his entourage applaud long and hard. Then, standing, he thanked me and said he hoped we'd return and perform again. "I like oldies. Next time do some Doors and Jimi Hendrix, then send students home, stay here to party, enjoy karaoke and women."

———

On the ride back to campus I pondered an urgent issue. My VIP host — who I now realized was the Respected Marshal himself — seemed to welcome my presence in the country. Hell, if I understood him correctly he was suggesting I take over from retired basketball star Dennis Rodman as his American drinking buddy.

Add the fact that Ms. Shin was the one who'd given Kim the word that I'd returned, apparently in non-alarmist terms. Did they welcome me to North Korea because I'd be easier to kill there? Or was it someone else who'd wanted me dead? In either case, I was relieved to find myself still among the living when we reached the university gate.

They say nothing's darker than a North Korean night, and there was no light on the walkway in front of my apartment. The bulb had burned out, I figured. The apartment door was slightly ajar. Relieved at having made it this far into the night without meeting an assassin, I was ready — too ready — to assume that this could be simply a matter of a cleaning person having neglected to lock up. Propping my guitar against the outside wall, I pushed the door open, took one step in — and saw the thin stream of a penlight making a glow line in the corner of the sitting room. Someone seemed to be going through my desk.

Following my first — irrational — impulse, I flipped the switch for the overhead light. I should have turned and run instead. The light didn't come on. The intruder turned off the penlight and quickly, without a sound, moved between me and the doorway. By the dim light filtering through the walkway from a gibbous moon I could see the glint of a knife blade held by a short-haired intruder, not much smaller than myself. He was coming to kill me.

By feel I grabbed the bottle standing on a bookcase next to me, which I knew still held a couple inches of bourbon. Fragrant droplets splashed on my face when I smashed it against the doorjamb. I couldn't help thinking what a shame it was to waste good bourbon like that. I ducked low as he stabbed at me. His knife nicked my left ear. Then, starting with a two-handed upward thrust of the bottle, I gutted him.

It was over in no more than five seconds. As I listened to the dying screams and gasps of the man whose innards were spilling out, it hit me that I had killed a human being. I wanted to be sick.

The noise attracted the attention of everyone around, and the campus security detail soon arrived bearing large handguns and bright flashlights. The dead man on the floor turned out to be a North Korean named Min, a worker in the university dining hall. Min was a man we'd all known — or, rather, had thought we knew. He was the same worker I'd seen in the kitchen, on my first day, pouring rice out of a hanging sack.

Min had turned off the apartment's electricity. A diagram showing the main power switch's location was in his pocket. Nevertheless, looking at the expressions on the faces of Sable, Ezra and other neighbor-colleagues who got a whiff of the whiskey-soaked sitting-room floor, you'd have judged I was at fault.

Maybe the security men felt the same way. After bandaging my ear, they hauled me off to a small, bare room in their hut for interrogation, in Korean, that lasted the rest of the night. "Had you spoken personally with Min?" "How did you learn to kill a man with a bottle?" "Do you work for the American government?" Seated on a low stool under a large overhead light fixture, I stuck to my story: I couldn't imagine why anyone would want to break into my room, much less try to kill me.

———

Around daybreak the interrogators left me alone with tea and bread on a dining hall tray. Famished, I gulped it down and wished for more. A half hour or so later, the man in charge re-entered and said, "You may go now. Someone important is waiting for you."

I emerged from the detention cell and found Shin Mi-song, wearing her gray dress and a light coat that was open far enough for me to see that she'd switched to a different loyalty pin. Instead of the single portrait of Kim Il-sung she'd worn on duty both as a tour guide and as Arirang assistant manager, this was the new model, exclusively for higher-ups, that pictured all three Kim dynasty rulers.

"Let us go."

I couldn't read her face.

As we walked to a black Mercedes, she added, in a low, flat voice, "Do not speak until I dismiss the driver."

We rode out of the campus gate, the uniformed guards waving us through without formalities. Ten minutes later I found myself reentering the walled compound that had been the scene of the previous night's performance. The driver took us to a corner of the garden, not to the mansion. He parked, then walked into a two-story concrete structure that appeared to be an office building. I guessed it might be the headquarters of the villa's security operations.

Shin led the way as we walked to a glade. Looking around I saw that, in addition to maples, other mature trees, both hardwoods and evergreens, stood on the nicely landscaped property. Apparently deforestation stopped at the estate's walls. Birds of various species were singing their morning refrains. She motioned me to a concrete bench. "You must be tired after your all-nighter."

She was right. But sleep deprivation had intensified my feeling of helplessness. "Who are you, really?" I hoped my tone didn't reveal how irritated I was to be at her mercy.

"What if I asked you that question?"

"You must know the answer already. It's clear you're a high-level spy."

"That is only part of who I am. To make you understand the rest I shall have to tell you my story. First I must warn you that if you repeat this we are both toast, as your American phrase goes. Put another way, in the jargon of one of your professions, what I shall tell you is off the record."

So she did know I was a newsman. I nodded. "Understood. Could you start by telling me your real name?"

"I have used several fake names, but Kim Mi-song and Shin Mi-song are both real. You should call me Mi-song. I had an adoptive father named Shin. My real father was Kim Il-sung, the late president."

I guess my jaw dropped, which was not cool. "That orphan yarn you told me?"

"All of the Great Leader's unofficial children tell the same story. There are scores of us. I am the youngest."

Why was she telling me all this? Was she playing good cop to lull me into getting myself in worse trouble? Best to play along and see if the answers became apparent, I figured. "This is going to take some time for me to digest, and it raises a lot of other questions. Meanwhile, let's go back to the subject of spying. I know you run a gin joint and guide foreign tourists but I assume those are just incidental to your main occupation. What variety of spook are you and how did you get where you are?"

"Those of us who are backdoor royalty, if we exhibit talent along those lines, are encouraged to volunteer for a sort of bastards' honor guard. I have the talent. My career so far has been with a special, small intelligence organization set up by the party that focuses on rooting out any challenge to the leader's one-man rule. We are noted for our surveillance skills and technology."

"Are you the boss?"

"My official title is deputy director. The director is a general in his nineties who, as a teenager in the nineteen thirties, fought alongside my father against the Japanese colonialists. He is senile, a figurehead; that is the case with many other titular heads of organizations. Another deputy director is actually functioning and more senior than I; he currently runs the agency. The plan is to place me in charge eventually, but for now I carry out missions of my own devising — such as the restaurant, which I set up as a border listening post."

"Are you the real boss at Arirang even though your title is assistant manager?"

"In terms of ultimate authority, yes. The person with the title of manager runs the day-to-day aspects of the restaurant business. I focus on how to make it all work as a source of intelligence."

"Since you're a spy, tell me why that kitchen worker Min came after me last night."

"I do not know."

"This doesn't strike me as the sort of country where freelance criminals, without solid connections to the powers that be, would get very far."

"I have not had time to check on Min's connections. I traveled for much of the night to arrive ahead of anyone from another agency who might wish to take over your case from campus security. I avoid leaping to conclusions, preferring a methodical approach. But I imagine we are dealing here with the same people who tried to have you killed earlier, in Japan."

"You know about that."

"My agents were slow reporting to me on the two failed hits, but as soon as I heard about them I sent Ms. Yu to the campus to keep an eye on you."

"So who tried to kill me in Japan? And why do you care what happens to me?"

"Let us go back and continue my own story. The important benefit from my combination of job and bloodline has been that my half-brother Jong-il placed trust in me and so does my nephew Jong-un, Jong-il's third son and successor."

"Jong-un being that dude I met for the second time last night — not just any VIP but Number One, the current grand wizard and exalted cyclops."

She smiled. "You assume I would not know that those are titles in the Ku Klux Klan. But, yes, you met Kim Jong-un."

She paused and looked at me, maybe reconsidering my own trustworthiness. Then she continued. "What neither Jong-il nor Jong-un managed to discover is that the country is more important to me than the Kim family. Along with some other people, I am determined to overthrow the regime and end the people's misery."

Again I was speechless, but not for long. "What does this have to do with getting me out of detention. What's going on?"

"You are a journalist looking for a story and it is in my interest for you to get it. Kim Jong-un is gaming the international market in financial instruments called credit default swaps."

Pleased to hear my suspicions confirmed, I relaxed a little.

"Didn't know it went all the way to the top but we'd guessed about the CDS scam."

"Then you have some idea how enormous it can be. I want Jong-un to fail. I want you to expose him."

"If Kim's the one behind it, I definitely want to expose him. I'll be grateful for any help fleshing out what has to be a very complicated financial story."

She nodded but didn't speak, apparently sensing that I had more to say.

"But I'd be uncomfortable if you tried to enlist me directly in your plot, as much as I might privately sympathize with what you're trying to do. Aside from questions of journalistic ethics, there are practical limitations: I have zero experience or competence as a spy or saboteur. That sort of thing is not in any of my job descriptions."

"You are resourceful enough to deal with assassins." Her eyes shone. "But you need not worry. I expected that you would wish to keep a separation between journalism and revolution. Politics is my department. News is yours."

Somehow I didn't need more time to think her offer over. My response was immediate, instinctive. "It's a deal. Please don't exaggerate my ability to scope out the CDS scheme further. I'm going to need a *lot* of help. In fact I've already had help, from someone who understands finance, to learn what I know so far. Also, Joe left clues. He carried one when he died, and then I got another one when a friend gave me Joe's notebooks."

"I am that friend."

"You? I thought it was Reverend Bob — Dr. Posey, the head of the university. How did you end up with the notebooks?"

"At Panmunjom I warned your friend Joe that his life was in danger. After the guards killed him I went back to the bus to secure the notebooks from his bag."

"Thanks for rescuing them."

"You are welcome. Knowing that Joe Hammond was a respected investigative reporter who had exposed the secret finances of another pariah state, I had hoped to enlist his help. I had assigned myself as one of the guides for his tour. When reporting to the party on what I was about to do, I had not mentioned him individually. My explanation had been that I needed to assess the security situation regarding tours that tacitly accepted reporters."

Seeing her innocent expression, I could understand how she got away with such duplicity.

"As our tour bus arrived back at the hotel the evening before the group's visit to Panmunjom, I was unsure whether there would be another chance to talk with him privately during the remaining day and a half of his stay. When he stepped off the bus I whispered in his ear: 'Watch the CDS market.' Already he had placed his notebook in his bag. He scribbled a note on the palm of his hand. He wanted to ask me some questions. I felt I had placed both of us in more than enough risk. I rushed off."

"That scribbling on his palm was our first clue."

"I had meant for him to wait and put it all together after he returned home. But I should have known from his earlier behavior on the tour that your friend was neither slow nor patient. Apparently he worked out the basics of the scheme quickly and tried to learn more in his few remaining hours in the country. Somehow, by the time we were en route to Panmunjom the next morning, the wrong people had found out about his inquiries. He was marked for death."

"I'm wondering how he could have been in danger when he had you, a top-level spy, on his side."

"There are several intelligence agencies in this country and we all spy on one another. That is the way my father set it up. My brother and nephew continued the system, to give them the best possible chance of learning about even the tiniest germ of a plot against them. One agency put a hit on Joe Hammond. I have my own spies in that organization. I learned about it in a phone call I received during the group's rest stop halfway to Pyongyang. I feared that he had virtually no chance to leave the country alive, but he deserved at least to know the situation."

Her face conveyed something akin to grief as she recalled Joe's plight. A softhearted spy? I wondered if she was doing an actress number on me. But according to her account she had taken an enormous chance by leveling with Joe, and now she seemed to be risking even more by talking to me. I said nothing and let her continue.

"I was last to reboard the bus at the rest station, immediately after I had heard the news, and by then all the seats close to him were taken. My opportunity did not come until we exited the briefing hall at Panmunjom – after he argued with the army captain."

"That's when you warned him?"

"Yes, as we were about to board the bus for the short ride into the Joint Security Area. You saw what happened when we arrived at the JSA. He wasted no time before making his escape attempt."

"Or 'made a mess,' as Kim Jong-un put it when we were in the nightclub."

"Yes. After the killing, as a cover story to protect the sources who had sent word to me about his targeting, I reported to Jong-un that Joe seemed to have taken the argument too seriously — imagining that the captain actually would shoot him. Neither Jong-un nor others who heard that version doubted it. The notion that we can frighten an American literally to death fits well with our ideology. Propaganda is so much a part of daily life that even the man at the top starts to believe it. When some of the journalists taking the same tour went home and wrote articles speculating that this was what had happened, it quickly became the official explanation here. The case was closed."

"Looks like the killing didn't hurt the captain's career. He's still on the job."

"Things worked out well from the point of view of those who had put out the hit. Your friend's run provided an unexpected opportunity to eliminate him without serious diplomatic complications. It would have been awkward to explain the mysterious death of a healthy American."

"Well, that answers one of the big questions that brought me to your country in the first place. Joe didn't commit suicide. But I guess you're in no position to tell that to the life insurance company so his widow can collect on the policy."

"Larger matters are at stake for me and my country. I am sorry."

The way she said it made me feel she really was sorry.

"There's something else I wonder about. How did you find out I am, or was, a journalist?"

"The first clue was that you booked the tour immediately after Joe Hammond was killed, when others were terrified and canceling. Barbara Lee was all right with that when you called her, but she started to worry later when she heard from Pyongyang. The Hammond incident had given ammunition to elements in the regime that were calling for a crackdown on journalists disguised as tourists. The tour company conveyed that to Barbara Lee and told her she had better be careful about whom she included. She feared she would lose her business."

"Why didn't she call me back and tell me to forget it?"

"I told her not to worry. But she still felt pressure from elsewhere, and you made her nervous."

"If that's what you call nervous, I don't care to see seriously disturbed, not to mention vicious. I wanted to throttle Barbara Lee when your colleague Mr. Won said it was her recommendation that got me chosen to deliver the flowers at the statues."

"You are right. Barbara Lee is a total pain even on her good days. I have a confession to make, though, and you will not like this."

I looked at her quizzically. "Yeah?"

"It was my idea to ask you to present the flowers at the statues. I had a feeling that you would agree, to maintain your cover. I knew that the gesture would defuse some of the suspicion harbored by those who had wanted you barred from the tour. I am also the person who tipped off Central Television that an American would be doing the honors. I learned from one of my people that there was a noticeable uproar in your hotel room just at the moment when you would have seen yourself on the telly."

"Arrrrgggggghhhh!" I glared at her. "I damned well hope the results were up to your expectations."

"They were. Without your televised tribute at the statues, most probably a second spy — not from my agency — would have been assigned to join your tour as a 'guide.' We never would have received clearance to take you into that nightclub, where you were able to meet Kim Jong-un and use your charm and wit to assuage his suspicions. Later, you might have been denied re-entry to the country in your new guise as a music professor. Even if you had managed to be re-admitted, Kim Jong-un would not have known you and thus would not have been available to serve as a character reference when you killed Min. So . . . do you forgive me?"

"Well, OK." I felt sheepish. "Sounds reasonable."

"To answer your original question, I compared the photo you sent to Barbara Lee with the television footage of you at the DMZ." Mi-song pronounced it the British way, Dee Em Zed. "You called yourself Heck on the telly, and I did some research on just who Heck Davis was. Your earlier visa applications came up from our records. I learned you are of mixed ancestry and speak Korean. You were cuter with the braid and mustache."

The smile dazzled me, as intended. My thoughts alternated between impulses. Should I run like hell — or grab her in a tight embrace, to shield her not only from the foggy, foggy dew, as the song goes, but also from the unimaginably powerful enemies she had decided to make?

"Why didn't you tell me all this earlier — like when you saw me in Dandong, before I came up here?"

"Although I knew that you were focused on completing your friend's work, I failed to anticipate that you would manage to find your way back to this country so quickly. The report about the DPRK visa that Byon was arranging for you reached me on the very day you arrived at the border. I did not yet know about the assassination attempts in Japan. Besides, I felt unprepared to have this conversation with you. I had not determined precisely how to use the truth about the CDS scheme to bring Jong-un down. I still have not figured that out. But clearly, after what happened last night, there is no delaying matters further."

A chilly wind had come up. My irritation had long since subsided but still I was mystified. "As you can imagine, I have more questions."

She looked at her watch. "I must go into the villa now. Jong-un ought to have awakened. Before certain other people gain his ear I need to speak to him and give him a plausible explanation of why I drove up here and arranged for you to be released."

"What's your excuse?"

"I shall tell him that I had planned to come to this area on another matter. Since you had been his special guest at the villa, I knew he would want every courtesy provided. And, after all, you did surprise the burglar in your room; the killing was in self-defense."

"That's true. And we don't even know whether Min went there

specifically to kill me. Who knows what he was looking for with that penlight?"

"Both you and I have had a long night. I shall instruct my driver to return you to your campus. Clean up and have a nap while I do likewise. Later you will hear from me and we shall continue our conversation."

I'd already yawned several times.

She rose to go. "You should not mention to anyone on campus that we have talked."

I looked at my watch. "Pretty much everybody will be in church for much of the morning. When they get back they'll figure I was just released from detention."

She turned toward the villa, her jacket open. Focused as I thought I was on matters of life and death, I realized I was unable to avoid noticing how inviting her smiling lips were and how nicely she filled out that gray dress.

I PICKED up sandwiches from the Sunday brunch buffet in the dining hall and returned to my apartment to set about making the place habitable. Squatting on the wooden floor, I wielded a towel to wipe up bourbon and broken glass and dried blood. I heard footsteps and a shadow appeared on the wall. I grabbed the gore-caked remains of my weapon, turning and rising to a crouch so I could use it again on whoever had come for another crack at me.

"Easy, big guy." Bartow Toombs, the bookish English professor, backed up and pushed his open palms in front of him. "Just wanted to know if the campus renegade Baptist got out of stir. I knew church wasn't the place to look for you."

"Oh, hey, Bart. Sorry, I'm a little shaky still. Probably could use a drink to settle down. Can I get you one? There's plenty more where this bottle came from. Come on in. Just walk around this mess. Just don't ask me what's been going on around here. As I told the guards, it's a mystery to me."

"I could use a snort. I would've attended today's monthly communion service in exchange for a few drops of sacramental wine, but I knew those teetotalers would serve grape juice instead."

I chuckled as I poured for both of us. But there was no mistaking the troubled look on his face. Bad vibrations in the dining hall had made it clear that other faculty members were unhappy with Toombs, a worldly Episcopalian who made no effort to hide the fact he didn't buy into the campus's hyper-religiosity. With something of a start, I realized I might be cruising for similar problems. While I was too new to have earned a rap sheet as long as Bart's, he wouldn't be the only one who'd noticed my failure thus far to attend Sunday services. I replied: "Going through a rough patch?"

"For one thing, they want me out."

"Oh, for God's sake." This was worse than I'd imagined. I lifted my drink in a toast. "Here's to your finding a new gig, pronto." We clinked glasses. "Did they give you any reason?"

"Sable said they have a problem with my attitude. They're not renewing my contract next year. They've already got a replacement lined up, a woman from Bob Jones University."

"Bummer."

"I can't complain too much about getting canned. I don't fit in with most of the faculty. The problem is, I need to start hunting for a job and I'm blocked from doing that."

"You mean because of that emergencies-only rule for using Reverend Bob's Internet and phone connections?"

"That, yeah. But I had a workaround in mind. I was hoping to take the long weekend that's coming up and fly to a civilized country with unlimited communications where I could hole up in a hotel room, do an online search and send some applications out. Now my passport's missing. I can't leave North Korea until I get a new one, and that's going to be complicated."

"Because North Korea and the U.S. don't have diplomatic relations."

"That's it. Sable did arrange for me to use the phone to call the American interests section in the Swedish embassy in Pyongyang. They said they'll work on it, but it's going to take time. I'll go down and fill out the papers at the embassy during the long weekend, and then it'll be Christmas break before I can leave the country."

"Sometimes things turn up. Maybe you'll luck out and find your old passport."

Pointing to the ceiling, he gestured for me to go out on the walkway with him. "I think it was stolen," he said in a low voice. "And now, after your experience last night, I think Min must've been the one who stole it, for whatever reason."

I pricked up my ears. "Where were you keeping it."

"With my diary and other papers, in my desk."

"Diary?"

"I was thinking I should publish a memoir once I got back home. Not many English lit minors from the U.S. get to spend time in North Korea. It's not that I was having torrid affairs with campus beauties — or any other adventures that would justify the term, for that matter. But I'd been keeping a diary here in notebooks, writing down in longhand a record of everything that did happen, however mundane. Had almost three notebooks filled up. I didn't have much else to do with my spare time."

"Might as well — can't dance. That's what we used to say back in Mississippi when we were debating whether to go to youth fellowship after the Sunday evening church service."

"What I heard was, there's a reason you Baptists disapprove of sex."

"Yeah?"

"Yeah. Reason is, it could lead to dancing." He chortled and took a swig of his bourbon. "Anyhow, on Tuesday I wanted to write an entry about the outstanding quality of the kimchi they serve in the dining hall. When I opened the drawer, my passport and the diary notebooks were missing. I'm not the neatest person, so I couldn't rule out the possibility I'd just forgotten where I put them. I finally went ahead and made the call to the Swedish diplomats just in case the items didn't turn up. I still hoped I'd find them — but once I heard Min had been rummaging through your desk, I figured he must have stolen them."

"Too much of a coincidence."

"Yeah. I know they have a lot of spies in this country and I'm guessing he was one of them. Good thing I didn't interrupt him or I might be dead from that knife of his. I didn't have even a bourbon bottle to fight him with." He grinned ruefully. "I can't go to the authorities with my suspicion since I imagine the powers that be were behind it."

"Anything in your diary that might have set them off?"

"That's what I've been trying to figure out. I knew people don't get a whole lot of privacy in this country. Sable had put me on notice from day one that we're all under surveillance by the campus security men. Being forewarned, I was discreet. I tried to write just enough detail so I could remember the full stories later. I even avoided using insulting terms for faculty members I disagreed with — namely, just about everybody except you. I was putting down nothing but bare facts."

"D'you reckon you'd written about something you weren't supposed to know?"

"There's one thing I wrote about that I definitely hadn't been cleared to hear. One of my students, when she was talking to me privately about her course work, let drop that her parents and the parents of other students live close to the university, in a separate compound. The students visit them on certain designated weekends and during breaks. That's great, I told her — family togetherness and all that — but I wonder why they wouldn't have told the faculty about it. She didn't know the answer."

"Where exactly do they live?"

"She wouldn't tell me. She got flustered, asked me not to mention what she *had* told me. I wrote an account of that conversation just a day before my diary went missing."

I silently pondered what he'd said. It reminded me of my still unanswered question about where student Pak's father, who might be my first cousin, lived.

Bartow reached back through the doorway and set his empty glass on the bookshelf. "Well, I'm dying to hear your theory on what's behind the recent crime wave at Posey Korea University, but that can wait. I imagine you need some quiet time."

"I do, indeed. See you in church."

"You're joking, but I did go to the first service of the semester and I plan to attend some more. With my time here so short, I need to gather new material for my book."

"Don't be too hard on the faculty in your tell-all. There are decent folks here, trying to do their best for the kids. I was starting to relax among y'all until Min made me realize I'd better not get too comfortable."

"Doesn't their absolute certitude bother you? I mean, from Robert Posey right on down they are so sure they know precisely what God thinks about everything."

"Guess I got used to it growing up."

"Not I, my friend. I'm accustomed to priests who show more humility about the unknowable, acknowledge the difference between mythology and fact."

"Substituting Genesis for science, the way Sable and Ezra teach, does bother me," I admitted.

"That's a big part of my beef. Students will suffer from those big holes in their knowledge, once they graduate and go out in the world."

"Other than that, I'm not so sure much harm comes from a literalist approach to scripture. Take my field. Over the centuries, literal-minded believers have been responsible for some wondrous musical compositions and lyrics. J.S. Bach, for example, was a total religious fanatic."

"Closed mindsets are dangerous. After all, people don't live inside bubbles."

"Well, look at all the good the Posey organization does with its aid shipments. Of course I have my disagreements with Reverend Bob, but if evangelicals mind their own business — if they aren't active theocrats, working to change the laws so we all have to agree with them — it seems to me the positives often outweigh the negatives."

"In the States Robert Posey *is* an active theocrat. He told his followers how to vote, and after his side won he announced that the victory was God's doing. I'd be inclined to assume he's also a fraud, like most televangelists. And there are signs of mental instability."

"Oh, I'd almost forgotten. You were a psychologist before you switched to academia."

"Yep, for seven years. I think you were abroad most of that time so maybe you weren't paying so much attention. After everybody started to see him as the successor to his father, Robert Posey became a celebrity. The whole world is his pulpit. That's not enough, apparently. His feelings get hurt, publicly, because he still isn't taken seriously in some quarters. He had a lot of trouble dealing with that episode a while back when the news media treated him as a rube and an ignoramus, after he publicly called Islam a demonic religion. He just huffed and puffed: 'Demonic is exactly what it is.' "

"And obviously you don't like him one bit, which is your right. But I'm curious to hear your psychological evaluation."

"The short diagnosis is, he has a monumental daddy complex. He couldn't match his old man as a preacher — or, until 2016, as a presidential advisor — so he always looked for other ways to compete. That's my theory of why he got into international charities big time."

"What's the harm in trying to live up to a distinguished family name?"

"Nothing, up to a point, but . . ." Bartow paused. "Hey, you've known him all your life and I haven't, so you could be completely right about him and I could have him all wrong. Anyhow, I'll head along now."

Just as well. I'd started to grow irritated listening to his pop psychoanalysis — pun intended — of my old friend and benefactor. It wasn't as if I didn't have enough else to think about.

13 / FAR MORE THAN A SPY

I'D TAKEN A TWO-HOUR NAP, showered and dressed, and was about to pay a second visit to the brunch table, when there was a knock on the door. It was Ms. Yu. She spoke softly. "You should go to the far corner of the athletic field, behind the spectator seats."

I nodded and she disappeared. Her mention of athletics had reminded me of my scheme for keeping minders off my trail. I changed into sweats and loped off toward the bleachers, affecting a runner's expression of dutiful righteousness.

Seeing the ravishing spy in the distance caused me to pound the ground harder and faster. When I reached her I was grinning and panting at the same time.

"Crawl under quickly." Wire cutters in one hand, she used the other to hold up a section of chain-link fence. She saw me hesitate and added, "It will not electrocute you." Once I was under, she disguised the cut in the fence with a log.

We got into her Mercedes, the front seat this time. "I left my driver to enjoy his rest. It seemed a pleasant day for a picnic." We started up a rutted mountain road, not passing the campus gate — or, for that matter, any other sign of human activity. "This is an unfamiliar road and I must concentrate on navigating, so please wait before asking more questions."

I dutifully shut up. She was wearing black pants and a red and blue striped sweater. It was the first time I'd seen her in casual clothes. I was happy to keep my eyes on her, largely ignoring the typical cleared mountainsides with their crudely terraced, rocky plots.

Finally she pulled off of what passed for the main road onto what looked to be no more than an oxcart path. Driving for a minute or two more, she stopped the car. "No one will bother us here."

From the trunk she retrieved a blue blanket and a box of food she'd scored at Number One's villa. "It is Swiss Day there. Jong-un is nostalgic for his school years in Switzerland. The main course is geschetzeltes and rösti."

I spread out the blanket. She arranged the chopped veal in white wine and cream over the hash browns and served us.

No longer hot, it was at least warm, fragrant and plentiful. I dug in. "Did young Kim give you any trouble about turning me loose?"

"My explanation satisfied him. During weekends he does not keep affairs of state much on his mind."

"I'm still having trouble with his identity. The guy I met doesn't look all that much like Kim Jong-un's pictures."

"The pictures are taken when he makes public appearances. The two times you saw him, he was relaxing."

"I don't know how relaxed he was, but he certainly acted like a guy with a lot of power."

"He relishes that power. He is very much his father's son — aggressive, bossy and cruel. That is precisely why Jong-il chose him, over the two older sons."

"I guess a dictator needs to be a mean son of a bitch. But the fellow seems *really* young to be running a country."

She opened a bottle of domestic beer, brand name Haean, and poured some into plastic picnic cups. We touched cups and sipped. It proved to be quite a decent Czech-style pilsner.

"Jong-il specified in his will that more experienced hands would help out with the transition by providing counsel. But Jong-un soon began to dislike being beholden to the regents. He purged his mentors at a rapid clip."

"Nobody, anywhere in the world, who was paying attention failed to hear the news when he had that uncle put to death. One of the regents?"

"Jang Song-taek was his uncle by marriage, as the husband of my half-sister Kim Kyong-hui, Jong-il's only full sibling. And, yes, Jang was considered chief regent until his downfall."

"'Downfall' seems like an understatement. Who's left among the regents?"

"Choe Ryong-hae is the only mentor assigned to the task by Kim Jong-il who is still standing. I understand he was seated next to Jong-un at your performance last night."

"Civilian clothes? Round-faced older guy?"

"Yes. He was demoted a while ago, only to bounce back into Jong-un's favor. But I would say that it is only a matter of time before Jong-un pushes Choe out permanently."

"What sort of background made him mentor material?"

"He is the son of a close guerrilla comrade of Kim Il-sung's, and in his youth he was part of the group of princelings that hung around Kim Jong-il. Illustrating how much a part of the junior power structure he was, that gang gave Choe a rude nickname."

"I'm cleared for rude, even for filthy. What was Choe Ryong-hae's nickname as a youngster?"

"Ryong-du."

"Ryong-du. Head moving toward the sky? I don't get it as a nickname."

"It is a slang term for masturbation. In English you might call him Wanker Choe."

"Ha. I missed that when I was studying Korean. Certainly didn't hear it from either Halmeoni or Mama. Are you going to tell me why they called him that?"

"He was several years younger than Jong-il but lived in the same elite neighborhood in Pyongyang. One day Jong-il, who was then a college student, had a group of male and female friends visiting at the mansion. He expressed doubts about the manliness of Choe, who was shy and not yet dating. Jong-il ordered Choe to drop his pants, then pointed out his lack of an erection despite the presence of the girls. To make a long story short, some of the boys held Choe down while a girl was enlisted to massage him. He grew aroused. According to those who were there Jong-il said, "Oh, you are capable. I am satisfied.""

Mi-song recounted all that matter-of-factly, with no accompanying blushes.

"Wanker Choe! He seemed to be having a good time with the girls last night."

"Despite physical problems related to tobacco, alcohol and aging, he is quite the ladies' man. My nephew has arranged for him to receive twenty milligrams of Cialis per day."

"And what does Wanker do in return?"

"His specialty is domestic politics. He handled the transition when Jong-il took over and then again for Jong-un. He is skilled at political agitation and control — and branding. Among American political operatives you might compare Roger Stone, who served Republicans from Nixon to Trump. It was Choe who proposed changing Jong-un's appearance to achieve a closer resemblance to his grandfather."

"There was one more guy I noticed both places, in the nightclub VIP room and again last night at the villa: crew-cut, square-jawed, looked a little like John Travolta without the smile. Wore the same civilian clothes both times: blue shirt, striped necktie. Big bulge under the left lapel of his suit jacket. Seated behind the kid both times. Bodyguard?"

"*Chief personal* bodyguard — first to Jong-il and now to Jong-un, who refuses to go anywhere without him."

"I'm lucky to have you as my tutor regarding the ins and outs of the North Korean elite. Guess your family connection makes you quite the big shot."

"Not many know that I am Kim Il-sung's daughter. Those few who know dare not spread the information beyond the inner circle. The leader's sexual exploits are a totally taboo topic."

"You seem quite powerful."

"That is because of my position with the agency. Normally membership in the ruling family does not come with many practical perquisites unless one is among the official offspring.

"I don't get the impression you're poor."

"I am remunerated according to my rank, which is comparable to three-star general. The pay is nothing by your country's standards or by the standards of the North Koreans who work in foreign trade. My apartment in Pyongyang is modest — three rooms. When I work I wear, if not my Arirang uniform of *chima-chogori*, either my black dress or my gray dress. They are the only Western business outfits that I own."

"You'd be a knockout in a croker sack." As soon as I'd spoken I regretted it. Keep it in your pants, Heck. We're after information here. I was as relieved as I was disappointed when, after the briefest smile, she adopted the patient expression of someone who's waiting for the next question. So I asked it.

"Whose idea was the CDS scheme?"

"Mine, I am sorry to say."

I whistled. "That's some sophisticated swindle for a spy to have come up with."

"For my work I often read material from enemy countries. Around the time of Kim Jong-il's death I came upon a paper from the Samsung Economic Research Institute in Seoul. I remember the exact title: 'North Korea's Provocations and South Korea's Stock Market.'"

I took another bite of veal.

"The study examined ten of our previous provocations and explained why eight of them had moved the Seoul bourse's KOSPI index more than the other two. It occurred to me that for those with superior information there was money to be made by trading in sizable, high-volume markets around the world. While I was thinking about that, I read something from the United States about how the financial reform law had given a pass to naked CDS trading. I read enough to realize that the swaps market would be much easier to manipulate without detection than the stock market."

I put down my fork. "You must be a financial whiz to have figured that out."

"My adoptive father understood real-world economics better than most North Korean officials, and some of his concerns rubbed off on me. I took secondary school economics courses in Europe, and later majored in political economy at university in Pyongyang."

"Learn anything at the university?"

"I realized that my North Korean professors had little idea of how prosperity had come to the West and to South Korea. Their job was to give us a vision of an ideal top-down economy as it was supposed to have existed under my biological father in the 1960s. Faculty careers would have suffered if the professors had switched from outlining the evils of capitalism to enthusing about the advantages of reforming and opening up in the style of China or Vietnam."

"Was that training supposed to help you as a spy?"

"In theory, yes. Political economy is a prestigious major — it was the major of Kim Jong-il himself. My degree was a factor in my rise in the agency. It helped me again some years ago when an opportunity arose for a small group of exchange students to study economics and finance in New Zealand."

"You went for it?"

"I applied, and that was one occasion when my royal bloodline was beneficial. People like me have been overrepresented among the country's exchange students, no matter the destination, because of our presumed loyalty to the ruler in the face of overseas temptations to the contrary."

I chuckled. "Meaning, by extension, spies are also overrepresented among exchange students."

"Precisely. At least one student in our group needed to be an undercover minder, keeping tabs on the rest of the group. I was a natural to go in that role, and to learn about the capitalist imperialists so that we could use their methods against them. In the end, however, my Kiwi professors brought me to an understanding of why so many of our people are in dire straits."

"Dangerous knowledge once you came home, I imagine."

"Kim Jong-il was still alive then. I knew better than to try to push him to reform and open the economy. He would never do it. He feared that one result would be a middle class that would demand freedom and a share in power. As long as he lived, it simply could not happen."

"How about Jong-un? I read some articles, around the time he took over and again later when he launched his peace offensive, speculating that he wanted to fix the economy."

"Jong-un at the outset hinted of major changes to come. He raised hopes that something along the lines of China's opening and reform under Deng Xiaoping might occur here. Jong-un even gave a speech saying he would make sure the people would not need to 'tighten their belts' again."

I helped myself to a third plate of chopped veal. Mi-song had stopped eating long before.

"The possible implications were intriguing. If he had asked my opinion, I probably would have taken a chance and advised him to go for it. But very little of substance happened and soon I could see that he possessed neither the vision nor the fortitude that he would have needed to jettison the system his grandfather and father had built. He talked the talk, but I had to face facts: He was loath to do more than fiddle around the edges of the old system. Knowing that I could end up in big trouble if I pushed for reform when the supreme leader was not ready for it, I came up with Plan B."

"The CDS scam. And when Kim resumed making noises about

economic development in connection with the peace offensive, I guess you weren't buying."

She shook her head, frowning.

<hr />

After I'd savored the last bite of veal and potato, we bagged the trash and put it in the trunk of her car.

She glanced at her watch. "It is still early. We can continue our conversation here. I have not yet briefed you fully."

That was fine with me. I stretched out on the blanket, positioning myself so my eyes could take in every inch of her. "So how'd you sell Jong-un on your Plan B?"

"I told him that I had devised a way for him to feed the people, earn their love, ensure a smooth succession and, at the same time, play a nasty trick on the imperialists."

"Nice."

"What I proposed fit into his needs as he perceived them. To cement hardliners' support for his succession, he felt he must show his mettle — must demonstrate how tough he was by standing up to our enemies. That fits into the long-term strategy of wearing down the enemy, gradually making South Koreans and Americans believe we are so strong it would be futile to resist our demands further."

"So he would have stepped up the pace of military provocations in any case?"

"Yes, but he might have emphasized verbal threats to a greater extent than he has done. I advised him that the markets would adjust to mere mouthing off. Canny investors eventually would conclude he was bluffing, and would start buying on the dips. For him to make the big money, frightening words needed to be accompanied by concrete evidence that he had achieved the ability and had the will to do what he threatened to do. If you analyze the provocations you can pick out the ones that were most closely tailored to advancing the CDS scheme. Words in those cases were combined with demonstrations."

"Making money at the same time he impressed his generals must have appealed to Kim when you proposed the idea."

"He asked me for all the details. I told him how to calibrate a series of provocations and explained which swaps to buy in each case."

The woman had proved to be far more than a spy.

"It occurred to me that for a provocation to move a market drastically, we needed to get under the skin of some major figure — a president or prime minister, a television star, an often quoted billionaire. If we could provoke such an opinion leader into a major, intemperate outburst, that would spook investors."

"Haha. Let me guess: That tactic really came into its own with the 2016 American election."

She smiled and nodded. "I also suggested sabotaging Pyongyang-watchers abroad by manipulating the output of the Central News Agency, editing the lists of officials accompanying the leader on inspection tours. Foreign analysts would be fooled into thinking hard-liners were taking over, then soft-liners, then hard-liners. Muddying the waters that way would make foreign markets especially jittery about what our country might be up to. Jong-un thought that was a particularly delicious touch."

"Impressive! Well, the provocations came to a halt during Kim's peace offensive, but they resumed with a vengeance once things between your country and its old enemies went sour again. There's talk again in Washington about launching a preventive attack on your nuclear facilities or leadership or both. I suppose your CDS trades are going great guns in this toxic atmosphere. Are you going to tell me next that you planned the peace offensive — say, to cover your tracks before regulators or anybody else in the financial world might get suspicious and start checking into CDS market movements?"

"How did you know?" She smiled. "I did advise Jong-un that he should not keep up a breakneck pace indefinitely — not only because of the danger that the CDS scheme would be discovered, but also because enemy countries would not tolerate the escalation of our provocations forever. He would need to take a break at some point and let things calm down before resuming."

"I think Pyongyang has taken breaks like that several times over the decades."

"Yes. I did not need to remind Jong-un more than once that a peace offensive is the regime's tried and true tactic for resetting the clock when the pressure to denuclearize starts to become too great. And that reset is a bonus benefit. The tactic invariably has helped us gain on our enemies, moving us toward the strategic goal of weakening the U.S.-South Korean alliance to the point where our leader can rule over the entire peninsula."

"Kim Jong-un went through quite a dramatic image change for the peace offensive. For a while there, South Koreans and Americans were starting to think he was a really cool guy. If it had gone on much longer he could have become a rock star and gotten on the cover of *People* magazine."

"Choe Ryong-hae was primarily responsible for fine-tuning the image change, although I had suggested the general outlines of what was needed.

My admiration was growing. I wanted to pull her down on the blanket. Instead I said, "I don't get it. It's your wildly successful scheme, and you want it exposed?"

"It was not my scheme for long. Jong-un thanked me for the idea and told me not to mention it to anyone else. He said he did not wish for me to be distracted from my main job of spying to protect him and his regime. He assigned it instead to his uncle to carry out."

"Jang Song-taek?"

"Jang had a long history of being close to most of the organizations that dealt abroad using foreign currency. He had been looking for new ways to pull in foreign exchange in the face of the international sanctions. To that extent, he was an obvious choice for the added role."

"Yet it's clear something went wrong — or we wouldn't be here on this blanket together."

She got the hint but her reaction wasn't as I'd hoped. "We could probably use an after-lunch stroll."

I glanced around at the desolate countryside and up at the steel gray sky.

She sprang up and started climbing the hill.

I pushed myself off the blanket with reluctance and joined her. "Something about your expression suggests you didn't like the uncle."

"For one thing, he was a dirty old man. He started hitting on me when I was thirteen, home on school vacation. Until the day he died, I made sure never again to be in a room alone with him." She grimaced. "Looking on the bright side, keeping the creep's hands off me was good training for my spy career."

"You said, 'for one thing' . . . "

"A big problem with Jong-un's turning my scheme over to him was that Jang Song-taek was deeply corrupt. Throughout his career he had connived to cut himself in on a huge variety of deals. Behind his back, foreign businessmen called him 'North Korea's Mr. Ten Percent,' borrowing the nickname of the late Pakistani President Benazir Bhutto's greedy husband, Asif Ali Zardari."

We neared the peak. The mountains beyond stretched as far as we could see, even becoming pretty as their patchwork grids went out of focus. No settlements were visible. Against that background Misong, her hair blowing in the wind, looked even less like a top agent of one of the world's most repressive regimes. She looked like an angel.

"Did Uncle Jang skim the profits of the CDS scheme?"

"That was one of the secret charges against him when everything finally caught up with him and Jong-un had him put to death. Jang was also blamed secretly for taking cuts from another scheme that had shown promise before the country's enemies caught on to it — using our computer hackers to steal from overseas banks. But the biggest charge, one that was publicized, if vaguely, was that he had been plotting a coup against Jong-un."

"So after Jang's killing did you finally get to take over your brainchild and run it?"

"No. Jong-un assigned me to identify anyone who had fallen through the cracks in the original takedown of Jang's associates and dig up any overlooked dirt. Oversight of the CDS scheme went to a unit of the Workers' Party's Bureau 39, which is in charge of raising slush funds for Jong-un. That particular unit was relatively uninfected by Jang's influence."

"Do the Bureau 39 people handle the money directly?"

"No. To get around sanctions, apparently it goes through a front corporation registered in a Caribbean tax haven. I have not been able to identify the corporation."

I asked the big question: "Which banker-brokers are handling the trades?"

"I have not yet learned their identity. You must be thinking that I cannot be much of a spy if these matters have eluded me. Let me explain. The DPRK has a stovepipe organizational structure. Orders come from the top and information from each agency goes up the chimney directly to the ruler. There is very little communication across organizational lines. The people handling the CDS operation were ordered to keep it top secret."

"Makes sense."

"Let us wend our way back to the motorcar."

We walked down. To improve my view, I let her lead the way.

"Although I don't know the name or other details," she said, "I have heard that a high-level overseas operative working for General Ri Jang-byong acted as go-between with the bankers who ultimately agreed to handle brokerage. And I understand that the portion of Bureau 39 that deals with the CDS scheme has been placed under General Ri's de facto control."

"Who's General Ri?"

We had reached the clearing where we'd picnicked. She turned to me.

"He was in the VIP room the evening of our duet at the nightclub in Pyongyang."

"Oh, that skinny, uniformed guy weighed down with medals,

teeth like a horse's, who sat beside the grand youth kleagle?" I grinned, hoping to make her smile. I liked her smile a lot.

She didn't oblige. Instead, her expression turned somber. "The heavily decorated soldier was General Ri. He spent most of his career building the nuclear, chemical and biological weapons programs. He is now second in command of the People's Armed Forces, under Jong-un. Among the organizations that he oversees is the security agency that ordered Joe killed."

I gulped, stopped talking and squeezed my eyes shut, visualizing Joe running for his life from a pack led by the wolfish looking Ri.

"The same agency hired the gangsters who tried to kill you in Japan."

I sucked in my breath. "And the same spy outfit would be suspect number one in what happened last night?"

"I should not be surprised to learn that Ri's organization had given Min the assignment."

"If so, would Ri have been acting under Jong-un's orders?"

"When I spoke with Jong-un today he showed no sign of knowing that there had been a hit out on you. Certainly Ri would not report failures, for fear of appearing incompetent. Typically he would tell Jong-un nothing before accomplishing the mission. Then he would boast about having killed one of Jong-un's enemies."

"So getting back to the matter that interests us most, how do we find out which bankers are handling the CDS trades for Ri?"

"The identities of the go-between and those broker/bankers are extremely closely held. Of course I have my agents watching for any information they can glean, but most of my people are based inside the country. Since the brokers must be foreigners, working for a big bank abroad, I thought that an American journalist such as Joe — or, now, you — might be able to discover the answer."

"Fat chance, while I'm stuck here at Posey University. Anyhow, I think I need to know more about Kim Jong-un."

"Where would you like to start?"

The blanket was still on the ground and I wanted us to tumble onto it and start something right then and there. While I managed to force my words into debriefing mode, my underlying focus must have dictated the topic. "There were a lot of — I want to say girls, they were so young — women with him, both times I met him. Was one of them his wife?"

"No. When he first came to power he set out to make a show of being a devoted husband. But the temptation of having palace wenches available to him at any time quickly overcame any real resolve he might have felt. When he goes for after-hours entertainment, and for weekends in his villas in the provinces, he typically frolics with his Pleasure Corps."

"They follow him around?"

"Some especially favored women do. But each of his residences has a separate contingent, with full wardrobe. The local villa's crew are all wearing their Heidi dresses today, and when I was leaving he had put on his shepherd's outfit with embroidered jacket and flat-brimmed hat for this afternoon's let's-pretend."

"What's that all about?"

"The custom of 'country days' dates back to his father. Kim Jong-il feared that if he were known to travel anywhere by plane he would be shot down. That fear was based partly on what happened to Mao Zedong's rival Lin Biao in 1971. Jong-il tried to limit his publicized trips abroad to countries he could reach easily by armored train, usually China and Russia. In his palace and his villas he indulged in make-believe travel. Jong-un has continued the custom even though he has less of an air travel phobia."

"How do they find the women?"

"There is a bureaucracy that recruits the prettiest girls in their early teens from middle schools all over the country. They undergo rigorous training in how to please a ruler of large ego and strong libido."

"Are the Pleasure Corps women considered permanent members of the harem — treated as minor wives?"

"Not usually. Once the bloom is off, they typically retire in their early twenties. Kim Jong-il's custom was to arrange a retiree's marriage as if he were her doting uncle, whether or not he had impregnated her."

"Speaking of rulers and their women, may I ask who's your mother?"

"That is a story within the very framework that we have been discussing. Jong-il had to compete with his younger half-brother, Pyong-il, to become the eventual successor to my father. Pyong-il held one enormous advantage. His mother was the first lady, with the ear of the president. Jong-il's mother was long since dead. Jong-il set out to neutralize that factor by driving a wedge into my father's marriage. He did that by introducing my mother-to-be to my father. She was very beautiful, I am told. Kim Il-sung was old then, but not too old to fall for her."

"I seem to recall that Pyong-il has avoided forfeiting his life despite all the palace intrigue."

"He has been prudent enough to maintain a low profile in virtual exile — as an ambassador posted to a series of European countries, most of them in what used to be the Soviet bloc."

"Did your father take a hand in raising you?"

"Not directly. He had a great many women during his lifetime, but it was good politics for him to pretend to follow conventional morality. There was a need to keep tongues from wagging after he impregnated my mother. Jong-il, as I told you, had considerable experience dealing with such situations. He married her off to an army officer who had been stationed for ten years in remote mountains near the front, with no chance to meet a prospective bride.

"Nice surprise for the bridegroom."

"The drill was for the bride to pretend on her wedding night that she was a virgin and then tell the supposed father that the baby came prematurely. But I was a normally sized full-term baby. The officer who had married my mother was no fool. He badgered her until she broke down and told him the truth. He got drunk and complained to his friends that the Dear Leader had tricked him, with the complicity of the Great Leader. In a group of friends, usually there is at least one who is reporting to the authorities. Those comments quickly got back to Kim Jong-il, who by then was my father's right-hand man. Jong-il sent both my mother and her husband to a political prison camp."

"What I heard is that three generations of a political offender's family, including his children and his parents, would be sent away at once — but I'm guessing you didn't go with your mother, in view of who your biological papa was."

"No, Kim Jong-il had me adopted by Shin Dal-hyon, our relative by marriage and a prominent technocrat. I grew up partly in his house, partly at international schools in Switzerland where I studied using the name Shin."

"You said Kim the elder took an indirect hand in your raising."

"He received reports on my progress and met me once a year to give me a present — the last one was this necklace, which he gave me the year I entered secondary school. He died shortly after that. Shin Dal-hyon actually brought me up, along with his wife, and I feel he was more of a father to me than Kim Il-sung."

"Did you ever see your mother again?"

"I was an infant when they took her away. They never told me that she had gone to a camp. The story for my benefit was that she had died in an automobile accident. I learned only much later what really had happened. Both she and her husband died in the prison camp after enduring years of overwork, brutal treatment and malnutrition. Shin Dal-hyon's widow is all the family I have now."

"So Shin himself is no longer among the living."

"Correct. When he was named vice premier he devised grand plans to reform the economy. Foreign countries and international organizations were ready to help. His plans would have taken resources away from the military. Some generals went behind his back to complain that he was hurting our readiness for war. Jong-il listened to the generals and demoted him, assigning him to revive and manage a huge chemicals and synthetic fiber factory complex that had fallen into ruin during the Arduous March."

"The great famine of the nineties."

"It was far worse than that — a general and total breakdown of the economy. There was no machinery remaining at the factory complex, not even electrical wiring, not a scrap of wood or any other usable material. The plant had sat idle due to lack of fuel and raw materials. Desperate looters had removed and sold or consumed everything of value. There was no way that Shin Dal-hyon could succeed in reviving it with the modest resources at his command. He despaired and took his own life."

"I'm getting the picture that you didn't much like Kim Jong-il."

"Not only did he deprive me of my birth mother and my adoptive father. It is believed within the top elite that Kim Il-sung died of apoplexy because of the inconsiderate way Kim Jong-il treated him after he retired."

"And now Kim Jong-il's long since dead."

"I cannot relax, even when I view the preserved corpse. Kim Jong-il is like a poisonous snake that you run over with your motorcar. Get out to look and you may be bitten."

She checked the time. "We ought to go now."

Probably not only the tone of my voice but my face, as well, showed my feelings of disappointment bordering on panic. "But I don't know enough yet to do more than blunder around blindly in your country. Can't you spare a few more minutes to brief me? For starters, why are you plotting to overthrow your own family's regime? What your half brother did to your mother, and to both of your fathers, might explain part of your motivation. But since Kim Jong-il's death, Junior's been in charge. I'm guessing there's more to it."

"There is more. Showing you is the next item on our itinerary." We folded the blanket and put it back into the trunk.

WE DROVE DOWN THE MOUNTAIN, turning off onto a route that was new to me. A few people walked along the road, some carrying loads. They didn't turn to stare. That close to the ruler's villa, local people must have grown accustomed to seeing black Benzes whizzing past. With the dark tint on the windows, even heading directly into the afternoon sun we had no need of sunglasses. The people we passed couldn't have seen much of us if they'd tried.

On the edge of a village, Mi-song turned off the road and drove into a shed attached to a ramshackle freestanding wood and masonry house. "Let us speak Korean in here," she said. "I should like to avoid starting rumors that a foreigner is loose in the village." She knocked on the door of the house and, when it opened, motioned for me to join her inside. Once my vision adjusted to the gloom, I saw an emaciated girl lying on a pallet and staring straight up through one blank, glassy eye. The other eye was missing, replaced by a scabrous sore that leaked pus. She seemed incapable of movement. A kneeling middle-aged woman bent to try to raise her head and feed her some soup.

"My driver nearly ran over her early this morning when we were driving up," Mi-song whispered. "She is so thin, he almost did not see her. She was lying on the edge of the road a few kilometers from here. Rats or crows had eaten one eyeball. The hospitals available to ordinary people up here have no supplies, no food, no medicine. We stopped to check on her and brought her to this place, the nearest village. I asked around and found this woman, who had known the family well and agreed to look after her. How old would you estimate she is?"

"Maybe twelve?"

"Ask her. She seems to be conscious now."

I walked over and asked her.

"Twenty three," she croaked.

"What happened to you?"

She stared at me from the single eye and replied, "Big trouble."

To avoid tiring her, Mi-song suggested that I get the rest of the story from the *ajumma* attending her.

As the young woman closed her good eye and dropped off to sleep, the auntie told me that things had gone from awful to horrible for the patient's family when the regime imposed a currency re-denomination scheme, knocking two zeroes off the replacement currency — but only accepting for exchange a few hundred dollars' worth of the old currency per family. "The people, almost every family, lost their savings. Her family" — she gestured toward the young woman — "lost their house, trading it for food that did not last them long. The parents starved to death."

The daughter had subsisted for years on what she could earn by gleaning grass blades and selling them to families that raised rabbits for fur and meat. Malnourished, she had become less and less able to move around. "Then last year's grain harvest ran out. There was not much foreign food aid. It is the start of the harvest season now but drought has halved what we normally would be harvesting. Neighbors and relations like me who would have helped her could not. We are all hungry." The woman looked apologetic.

I walked back to where Mi-song was standing. "With nothing at all to eat," she said, "the girl collapsed out there by the road. I gave some money to this ajumma to buy some food and try to restore the girl's health. She is one of the worst cases. Maybe she will live, maybe not." She lowered her voice so that only I could hear, and spoke in English: "But there are so many who do not have enough to eat!"

Mi-song's eyes were blazing with anger. "The United Nations says more than 40 percent of our population is undernourished; more than thirty percent of our five-year-old children have had their growth stunted. You will not hear the government confirming that for public consumption, but my agency has its own figures. They are worse."

Mi-song held a whispered conversation with the auntie, who then left. "She is going to buy provisions," Mi-song said. "I said we would stay and watch the patient. I told her not to mention to anyone that we are here."

She walked around checking windows and doors, making sure there was no one within listening distance. "I can answer further questions now."

I gestured at the sleeping young woman. "I guess you see her situation as an example of misrule. But can you spell out a closer connection to what we were discussing?"

Mi-song stooped to dab salve from a tube on the eye socket of the still-sleeping patient. "I brought some antibiotic ointment from the Number One Villa," she said. "You cannot get it anywhere else around here."

She stood, placed the tube of salve on a table and replied, "The ajumma told you there had not been much foreign food aid this time. Cutting food aid was a predictable response by foreigners to our barrage of provocations — which were even more intense than usual, in view of the CDS scheme. The scheme has worked brilliantly on one level. Piles of money have come in. But Jong-un" — she shook her right fist — "has used virtually none of it to help people who need help. I had to face the fact that it is past time for at least one Kim to try to clean up the intolerable mess my family has made of this country."

I respected her passion, but I still had questions. "Where is the money going?"

"Following in the footsteps of his father, Jong-un spends a billion dollars a year for luxury goods to pay off his allies. I have been on each of their gift lists. Kim Jong-il gave me my motorcar, complete with a license plate whose number started with two one six — which represented his birthday, February sixteenth. He attached that self-advertisement to every automobile he gave as a present. I received mine after I returned from New Zealand, when he promoted me to deputy director of the agency."

"What did you get from the Young Whippersnapper?"

She held up her wristwatch so I could see the signature, engraved on its face in calligraphic style, of Kim Jong-un. "He gave me this to thank me for the CDS idea."

"It's odd you wear it, considering your opinion of the giver and his motives."

"I wear it as a constant reminder of how he perverted my plan. Whenever I glance at it I vow once again that I will defeat my nephew *in time*."

She always came back with the right answer. More and more I was inclined to trust her.

"Jong-un has added cash rewards for loyalty. I get eight hundred bonus U.S. dollars a month, which I am saving for the revolution."

"So Kim doesn't keep the money for himself?"

"He has built new villas, like the one you visited. Typically they are equipped with pistol shooting ranges and other amenities depending on location: a ski slope here, stables and bridle paths there. He has had them built so fast that the construction has sometimes been faulty. The roof of the villa at Wonsan collapsed."

"Guess a fellow needs a place to call home."

"He ordered a super-luxury submarine yacht with velvet curtains over the main stateroom's picture window. The curtains are to block the view of dolphins, which otherwise might become jealous and attempt to break in while he and his companions of the day try out all the positions in the *Kama Sutra*."

To hell with the dolphins. Such talk was intensifying my own arousal. I struggled to focus on urgent business and managed to get back to the main thread of the conversation. "Now I understand where all the money washing through the Koryo Hotel came from. How long can they keep it flowing?"

"While they have almost completed my list of proposed military provocations and other market signals, surely, in view of the scheme's success so far, they have added others."

"And they have the capital to keep going."

"I had suggested spending only a portion of the profits — enough to feed the people — and using the rest to increase the size of the successive bets. Jong-un ignored the part about making massive food purchases, but he seems to have followed my advice that he keep raising the ante. The biggest money is yet to come. By now it is clear that using it for the people's benefit is not high on his list of priorities."

Hearing moaning and mumbling from the pallet, Mi-song knelt and mopped the young woman's brow with a wet cloth. Rising, she spoke to me again. "I keep wondering what set Ri's people on your trail."

"Maybe they made the same comparison you made, realized I was Joe's friend and colleague — so they were afraid I knew what Joe knew. Maybe they also decided there was no way they could kill me while I was on the same tour Joe had taken and have it be seen as a coincidence."

"Perhaps." She looked and sounded doubtful.

"In any case my boss, the university president, got it wrong when he said I'd be safe on campus."

"My opinion was that you might not be safe. That was one reason why I sent Ms. Yu — to protect you."

That made me smile. "She's on the small size for a bodyguard, but I guess you know what you're doing."

"Yu completed the full course at spy school. She is as deadly as those United States Navy Seals who terminated Osama bin Laden. Not only does she work for me officially, but she is also a member of the resistance organization. Unfortunately she had not been on the Posey campus for long enough to develop suspicions about the man who attacked you last night. After the incident she alerted me that you were in trouble. I came immediately."

"Thanks for that. To tell you the truth I'd been feeling considerable doubt that there was any use staying on campus. Obviously the place is far from being the headquarters of some nefarious international financial scheme. But I've learned there's something else going on there that's supposed to be a big secret."

She leaned forward, excitement in her eyes. I have to admit it was a pleasure to be able to reveal a secret to someone whose job was keeping and unearthing secrets.

"The university students' families live and work somewhere near the campus, but we foreign faculty members are not supposed to know that and the students aren't supposed to speak to us about it."

She closed her eyes for a moment as she thought that over. "This is fascinating precisely because the first part is no secret among North Koreans in China. Recruiters emphasize that the students' families are welcome. I wonder why they want to keep the American professors in the dark about that."

"When one professor accidentally found out about it, his notes on the matter *and* his passport promptly disappeared from his room. He told me about it this morning. After what happened last night, he figured Min had taken them. Without a passport, or a phone or Internet connection, he's in no position to spill secrets abroad."

"We need to find out just where the families are and what they are doing."

"I may have a way to do that. I tried to establish rapport with the students by telling them my grandfather and uncle had disappeared trying to escape south from Kaesong during the Korean War."

"That came up when I compiled your dossier."

"One student, named Pak, told me his father thinks we are first cousins. He wouldn't tell me where the father lives, but I plan to push for an answer and try to meet the family."

"Yes, it would be helpful for you to stay on campus for the time being and find the compound. That might help us learn what sort of quid pro quo exists between the university and the regime."

"Ever since Robert Posey told me he'd founded a university here I've been trying to figure out just that: What's in it for the North Koreans?"

"Even what we already knew about the university represents a suspicious policy shift by the regime. There are many possible implications. By the way, I learned this afternoon that Min had been attached to the Posey organization staff since planning for the university began — long before there was any need for kitchen help."

"What do you think that means?"

"It suggests that someone very important — most likely General Ri's agency — had a long-term interest in the Posey project. I do not know why. This is another situation in which I was kept out of the loop."

"Against your will, no doubt."

"I began to watch the Posey people's DPRK operations just before your tour group arrived — not because I suspected them of plotting anything that I should worry about. Rather, I wondered what some person or agency on the North Korean side, unbeknownst to me, might be up to with the Posey organization. That was my man whom you twice encountered upstairs in the Koryo Hotel. He left the notebooks in your room."

I remembered my glimpses of the business-suited man lurking on Reverend Bob's floor and then, on my last night in Pyongyang, walking toward me on my own floor.

"With both you and Ms. Yu on campus I had been hoping to

learn a good deal more. Your possible relative at the family compound — wherever that may prove to be — gives you an in. Of course we now know that staying could be dangerous for you. I would not suggest you take that risk if it did not seem important."

"No point stopping now. But what about you? Isn't there a chance General Ri's people, besides looking for another shot at me, will be suspicious about your presence here today and start watching you more closely?"

"I am not meant to know anything about how they carry out the CDS scheme, or about Min's assignment. Your having been on the tour that I accompanied gives me jurisdiction over you, up to a point. They would have a difficult time pinning anything on me, merely on the basis of my having had you released this morning. Just as I have my spies in their agency, though, they certainly have theirs in mine. If they were to learn that we had spent the greater part of the day together, their suspicions and machinations would go into overdrive. It was necessary that we talk today. Now that we understand each other, you and I had better avoid direct contact."

I wanted contact with her — a lot of it, as direct as possible.

"We can exchange messages via Ms. Yu. She is equipped to communicate with me. Because of what you just told me, we have a promising direction in which to . . ."

A god-awful sound interrupted her. It was the last sound the stricken young woman would make, her death rattle.

Covering her patient's face, Mi-song kept her own facial expression even. But I saw the tears in her eyes and heard her muttering angrily under her breath. Of course helpful Heck would have been available to hold and comfort her, but even I was able to realize that this was neither the time nor the place.

The auntie, returning with her bag containing vegetables and a little meat, reacted matter-of-factly. She'd seen this script play out before. Mi-song gave her more money, to take care of burial, and the woman reported on her shopping trip. Gossip in the market that afternoon was focused on the arrival of a container load of Chinese consumer goods, she said. She added that her fellow villagers apparently had not noticed the Benz in the shed of her out-of-the-way house.

Mi-song turned to me. "Before they do notice, let us leave now."

It was dusk when we arrived at the spot where she'd picked me up earlier. Shifting the transmission into park, keeping the engine running, she looked at me with a concerned expression. "This is a terribly dangerous undertaking. There can be no turning back. I should like to collaborate with you in exposing the scheme, if you are willing. Otherwise . . . "

"I know. You'll have to kill me. But what the hell? In for a dime, in for a dollar."

She smiled, and clasped my left hand briefly before letting it go. I wanted more of a demonstration of our newly intertwined lives. Her body language was signaling that she did, too. We kissed. I'd been right about her lips. So much for the journalism ethicists' advice to avoid getting emotionally involved with your sources.

Finally she pulled away. "We are risking too much," she said breathlessly as she gave me a push. I got out.

As I found my way across the darkened campus, I reflected that we were taking on one of the toughest, meanest regimes in the world. The two of us very soon could find ourselves up the proverbial Shit Creek in a chicken wire canoe. But the mission was worth the risk. *She* was worth the risk.

I returned to my room and knocked back a bourbon. It helped. I downed one more for the road to the dining hall. Arriving with only a moment to spare, I looked around and made sure there were no new faces I needed to worry about before taking my seat and bowing my head for grace.

I SEEMED to be in a race with General Ri — and who else? Sable had contended the campus security rules were for our protection. Father Paul had given me a different version: the authorities wanted to keep outsiders from seeing the reality of the country. So far, on my morning runs I had stuck to the prescribed paths. I did the same for one more run, to lull the guards back into complacency after the Min incident. I used that time to plan.

A narrow path led off one of the roads. It snaked up an adjoining hill where twenty or so mature trees, like those I'd seen inside the Kim villa's grounds, had escaped the massacre of the forests. I would check it out the following day. I'd already sat still for enough frustrating restrictions. Sooner or later, any self-respecting newsperson must test the limits.

The next morning, as planned, I veered off course and ran up the path. While I knew I wouldn't find a securities trading floor or similar temple of high finance hidden away in those mountains, I wanted to know where the family compound was.

My first guess proved correct. At the top of the hill I saw, in a cleared valley below me, scores of men and women. I stepped behind a tree in case anyone should look up. Dressed in dark blue Mao suits, they were passing single file through a stone-faced arch built into a barren hill opposite the hill on which I stood. Except for the lack of a conveyor belt or a railway backing up to it, it might have been the entrance to a mine. I saw no buildings. Preschool and school-age children ran around, getting their energy out, on the packed dirt of the valley floor. I didn't watch for long before returning to my usual route.

That day I asked Pak to stay after class. "There are people in the next valley. Is that where your father is?"

He looked troubled. "We are not supposed to talk about it. The university has arranged for the families of students to move to this area. There is work for our parents in the underground factory."

"What sort of factory?"

"It is called the One Eight Tractor Factory."

"Why would a tractor factory be underground?

"My father told me the authorities anticipate American and South Korean bombing attacks, so they try to protect important installations by placing them underground."

The country indeed had a high level of tunneling technology. The North had built invasion tunnels under the DMZ. The South had discovered several. I'd visited a couple, including one that had been turned into a tourist attraction. Photographing it, I'd felt amazed that so many hundreds of people, a large percentage of them Chinese tourists, showed up each day to experience claustrophobia first hand.

"When can I meet with your father?"

"I will ask, the next time I see him."

⸻

Before the week was out, as I'd been halfway expecting, Sable called me in for a perfunctory lecture. "You're a role model for the students. If I may make a suggestion, you might want to pray over whether drinking whiskey is really a behavior you want to model for them."

Without waiting for a reply, she then passed the word from

Reverend Bob that he expected me, in due course, to lead the singing at Sunday services. To scope out what the song leader role would entail, I decided to attend church.

The next Sunday, following the Fatback rule, I made sure to sit in a back corner of the auditorium where I could watch the largest number of churchgoers at once, just in case anyone might want to target me during the service.

The auditorium filled quickly. Most students were present, but I didn't see Pak. I hoped he had special permission for a home visit.

Bartow Toombs came in and sat beside me. His sour expression made clear that his situation and mood hadn't improved. "Look who's in the pulpit today."

I looked. Wearing an aloha shirt over pressed red trousers and white buck shoes, the Rev. Darley Scratch was preparing to do a guest turn in Reverend Bob's absence. Scratch was one of those young true believers who'd been chosen on the basis of charisma and athletic good looks to go to Hawaii for intensive training in the wiles of converting other young people.

His day job at the university was physical education, but everyone knew that Reverend Bob was grooming him for bigger things. Still single, he was closely attuned to what younger people wanted — and what they did *not* want, the old conservative Sunday-go-to-meeting garb and sedate services. It was prophesied that televangelism was in his future.

Coach Scratch, as he liked to be called, exerted a magnetic pull on many of the students, female and male alike. I had chatted with him briefly about our mutual interest in motorcycles, after noticing a full-color "Biking for the Bible!" poster tacked to a bulletin board. It pictured him tank-topped astride a gleaming hog, his seductive smile highlighting clenched white teeth, his tanned biceps bulging, blond mane flying in the wind, as he tooled past a venting Big Island volcano. A rhyme had occurred to lyrics-minded me: Darley on a Harley.

Rock 'n' holy-roller — that was Coach Scratch as a preacher. Not even waiting for the sermon, he began his oratorical fireworks while reading the scripture of the day. He didn't announce what verses he would quote, but once he'd started I realized they were from Ezekiel, chapters 38 and 39. That's where the prophet quotes God as foretelling a great battle with Gog, the enemy of God and the people of Israel. With rhythmic emphasis the coach screamed through his microphone:

" 'THUS saith the LORD GOD' — huh! 'It shall ALso come to PASS' — huh! — 'that at the SAME time shall THINGS come into thy MIND' — huh! — 'and thou shalt THINK an evil THOUGHT to turn thine HAND upon the DESolate PLAces that are now inHABited' — huh! — 'and upon the PEOple that are GATHered out of the NAtions that DWELL in the MIDST of the LAND.' Huh! 'It shall be in the LATter days, and I will bring THEE against my LAND' — huh! — 'that the HEATHen may know ME' — huh! — 'when I shall be SANCtified in THEE, O GOG' — huh! — 'before their EYES.' "

Hardly still for a nanosecond, his voice hoarse from shouting, he went wild for the Lord. At one point I thought he was about to levitate. The show didn't offend me the way it obviously did Toombs. I was used to that sort of worship. Since moving to Asia I'd confined my churchgoing to times I was back home visiting my folks in Mississippi. As I'd told my students on the first day of class, instead of going back to either Calvary or the Korean church, I would seek out black Pentecostal congregations — the more demonstrative, the better.

Experiencing their uninhibited gospel music, sermons punctuated with speaking in tongues, dancing in the aisles and passionate amens could only help me pursue a professional standard I liked to describe using a line from Barbara Hambly's novel *Bride of the Rat God*. In 1920s Hollywood, a gramophone is wound up to produce the sound of a woman singing the blues "gay and sad at once, like a stranded angel who had traded holiness for humanity but remembered what it used to be like to know God."

As Darley Scratch raved on, though, I looked at North Koreans present and sensed from their expressions that most of them didn't get it. Lost on them was whatever the coach was shouting about when he made a joyful noise unto the Lord. As Scratch continued — quoting the part about how God will turn Gog back "and leave but the sixth part of thee and will cause thee to come up from the north parts and will bring thee upon the mountains of Israel" — I glanced at the windowed booth where three Korean interpreters sat.

The coach hadn't been stopping for the women to take their turns translating. Whether that was according to plan or not, it left them to attempt simultaneous interpretation — which is exhausting work and requires special training. Seeing a frantic expression on the face of the one who was speaking, I pulled a translation earpiece from the hymnal slot.

Switching on the earpiece, I heard the poor woman jabbering incomprehensibly in Korean. She would correctly translate the occasional English passage the coach uttered but then miss several more before translating another. Evidently there'd been a screw-up. She'd failed to get advance notice of what he planned to quote from the Word.

Employing the same rhythmic shouting and interjections, Darley moved directly into an apocalyptic sermon. " 'GOD will release his STORED UP WRATH' — huh! — 'paving the WAY for the triUMphant return of JEsus.' " After he had offered further graphic description of the shit storm at the end of time, he paused and flashed his trademark smile before quoting Revelation 20: " 'I saw an ANgel' — huh! — 'coming down out of HEAven' — huh! — 'having the KEY to the ABYSS' — huh! — 'and HOLDing in his HAND a great CHAIN' — huh! 'He seized the DRAGon, that ancient SERpent' — huh! — 'who is the DEvil, or SAtan' — huh! — 'and bound him for a THOUsand years.' "

Scratch boomed on, swaying from side to side, walking in circles, raising his arms for hallelujahs — heedless of the puzzled looks from Koreans. He quoted Peter's second epistle.

" 'LOOKing for and HASTing unTO the COMing of the day of

GOD' — huh! — 'whereIN the heavens being on FIRE shall be disSOLVED' — huh! — 'and the ELEments shall MELT with fervent HEAT' — huh! 'NEvertheLESS we, according to his PROmise' — huh! — 'look for NEW heavens and a NEW earth, whereIN dwelleth RIGHTeousness.'"

Younger foreign faculty and staff members were getting into it, shouting "Amen!" and dancing around in the aisles. Sable and Ezra — but not Shirley, I noticed — spoke in tongues. That completely stopped the interpreter.

Nevertheless, gradually more and more of the Koreans in the congregation, most of whom were students, tried — or at least looked tempted — to respond in kind to Darley's call to arms. I remembered how at the Pyongyang mass games, when the thousands of colored cards flipped into place to create portraits of the leaders, thousands of North Koreans on the field jumped up and down like dogs on their hind legs begging their master for bones. It couldn't be too hard to transfer that sort of worship from the country's triune dynastic godhead to Jehovah, Jesus and the Holy Ghost.

Toombs looked my way and rolled his eyes. But eventually he became the odd man out as Scratch with his infectious cries and whoops and leaps and grunts had the whole place jumping. Even I did some arm-waving to get into the spirit of things.

When the ecstasy reached fever pitch, the coach gave his altar call, an impassioned plea for sinners to walk down front, confess their sins and either accept salvation or — if they were among the majority who had done that already — rededicate their lives to Christ. "Not a ONE of us — huh! — is free of SIN — huh! — and only JEsus can SAVE us! Come down the aisle NOW — huh! — and throw yourself on HIS MERCY!"

I'd been painfully aware from the start of the service that the lugubrious music on the program failed to match Darley's preaching style. I figured the listed numbers were typical of the selections for the usual Sunday services, chosen by Reverend Bob and the woman who played the electronic organ. To my dismay the invitation hymn, which followed the altar call, turned out to be "Just As I Am."

> *Just as I am, without one plea,*
> *But that Thy blood was shed for me,*
> *And that Thou bidd'st me come to Thee,*
> *O Lamb of God, I come! I come!*

Once, at a Calvary Church revival during my senior year in high school, the guest preacher reported having been assured by God that someone would come down front that night. But even after we'd gone through all six verses of that hymn twice and almost gotten through them a third time, not a single soul had stood to make the trek down the aisle. Only after seventeen verses did the preacher give up. "Just As I Am" in its standard arrangement had always struck me as downright ugly. The lyrics were naggy; the melody, draggy. By the time Joe and I filed out after those seventeen verses, I was filled with the devout hope that I'd sung it for the last time.

But now here I was singing it in the Posey Korea University worship service. As music director I was going to have to make sure this sort of disconnect wouldn't happen again on Sundays when Darley filled in. I might even want to ask Reverend Bob whether he'd care to have me pep up the music on days when he preached, as well.

We had plodded through five verses of "Just As I Am" and started on the sixth when I looked up and realized that a chubby female student bearing one of the few two-syllable Korean family names, Namkung, was walking toward the altar, her mouth set, the bangs of her severe pageboy haircut covering her forehead but failing to hide the tears that streamed down her cheeks. I reflected that this was a positive development to the extent it made it unnecessary for Darley to have us repeat the verses.

"There she goes again," Bartow muttered in my ear. "She rededicated the other time I came to church, too, so today makes at least twice this term. Wonder what her sins could possibly be. I'd figured she was like the Norfolk High School cheerleaders: 'We don't drink! We don't smoke! Norf'k! Norf'k! Norf'k!' "

The old joke was still funny, but guffawing at the most emotional moment of the service would not have helped me meld into the university community.

On Monday Pak stayed after class. "I spoke with my father. He does not worry about himself if you meet — he is accustomed to risky situations. He worries about you. They send people to political prison camps in this country. Few get out, ever. They even shoot foreigners sometimes. There was such a case just a few weeks ago at Panmunjom, we are told, although we have heard no details."

"I'm also pretty accustomed to risky situations."

Pak grinned. "*Abeoji* told me you would respond that way, after he heard what happened in your room the other night." As soon as he'd said it his face turned red. He felt he'd said too much. Besides Bartow's morning-after camaraderie and Sable's admonition, the response of the community had been to pretend nothing had happened.

"If you go over to meet him, you will need to blend in," Pak continued, glancing at my jeans, brightly checked shirt and wide leather belt with the big brass John Deere buckle embossed with a picture of an ancient tractor. I assured him I could manage to blend. We settled on Wednesday night, after supper. With a prayer meeting scheduled, few people would be out and about.

I found Yu studying alone at a dining hall table and we compared notes. She'd been living in the dormitory with other students long enough to wear down their distrust of the newcomer, and she'd started to hear a little about the campus's parallel universe. Of course she'd reported all our new tidbits to Mi-song.

I had my hair cut again, to standard North Korean length. Then I washed the people's clothing I'd bought in Pyongyang, to wear off the new. On the appointed evening I donned the outfit, complete with portrait pin and Lenin cap. The image in the mirror startled me. I could've been looking at one of the taller cadre in Kim Jong-un's entourage.

⸻

It was a moonlit night. Without using a flashlight I could make my way, first on the familiar gravel roads and then all the way up the hill on the dirt path and down the other side. Sneaking around in disguise to get to a place I wasn't supposed to know even existed — that gave me a rush, I admit.

I was so eager to meet a new cousin that I failed to notice an armed guard standing where the path I'd taken fed into the field. I came out from behind a tree and there he was, a few inches from me. Another man standing on the field called to him just then and the guard walked over to talk. I crept back behind the tree until the guard finished his conversation and headed across the field.

Taking a chance, I emerged then. The man who had distracted the guard was still waiting on the field, in people's clothes but with no portrait pin. Instantly noticing his strong facial resemblance to Mama, I exulted. We had to be related. "That was close," he whispered. He motioned for to me to walk beside him, keeping his expression impassive as we passed a few other people. Mostly men, they were standing in small groups smoking and talking.

My escort guided me through an opening in the same hillside I'd walked down. Inside was a dank but clean and well-lit tunnel punctuated by the doors to living quarters, each unit carved out of stone.

As we entered the main room of their apartment, with its whitewashed walls, his wife greeted me. She ushered me toward the main item of furniture, a low Korean table. Then she closed the door to the public corridor. Finally, she closed the connecting door to the second room, in which their two younger children were sleeping — but not before I had glimpsed them on their pallets. Pak's father and I sat on the floor before the table, which was set with a steaming teapot and three palm-sized mugs without handles. Ignoring the tea and with obvious relish, he opened the bourbon I'd presented him and poured some into two of the mugs.

Their windowless apartment didn't give off the unpleasant smells you might expect in an underground dwelling, even though the exhaust fans seemed not to be working very hard. Pak senior explained why. Gesturing toward the passage, he told me that the kitchen and dining hall as well as the bathrooms were communal and far down the hall.

The floor was covered in the traditional lacquered paper, which gave off a yellowish sheen. It was a heated floor, in the Korean *ondol* style. It felt toasty against my butt. I adjusted my haunches to get comfortable. "Is the furnace wood-fired or coal-fired?"

"Electric."

"Unusual for the DPRK, isn't it."

"Unlike most places in the country, we have a good power supply. That is done to keep the factory running."

We quickly established that the elder Pak, whose given name was Shin-il, liked a drink and was indeed my first cousin.

"Mama will be thrilled I've met you. I wish I could phone and put you on to speak to her. I'm sorry to have to tell you that Halmeoni died a couple of years ago. It was her abiding regret that she still didn't know whether her husband and son were alive or dead. She only knew they hadn't made it south. She guessed they'd been killed or captured."

"Halmeoni guessed right." Shin-il closed his eyes and beamed as he sipped at the bourbon, as if he'd never tasted anything so wonderful. "After the family was separated into two groups in the confusion of the escape, the two males stumbled into a communist camp after dark. The communists killed Halabeoji. After that, they were sitting around their campfire discussing what to do with Abeoji, who was only ten years old then. He heard one of them say they should kill him, too, so he ran for his life into the woods. They fired some shots at him."

"Obviously they missed, or you wouldn't be here today."

"Yes, but it was only a temporary escape. They recaptured him the next day. A party commissar who was with them said they should spare him because he could run fast. Once the war ended, the country would need strong young men to rebuild. They took him back to Kaesong and turned him over to some relatives until after the war, when they were all banished to a coal-mining district."

"Halmeoni was a devout Christian. She must have raised your father that way and maybe that's how your family got to the Posey compound."

"Actually what my father was exposed to, before finding himself a citizen of a country that banned religion, was not much more than the version taught to young children in Sunday school. Then, after the war, he was brought up as a Kimilsungist. That's the way I was brought up, too, as was Joung-ah, my wife. We learned to bow at every meal and thank the Great Leader for all the bountiful blessings he had bestowed upon us."

With that he turned, raised his cup and gave a nod to a blank wall where, I gathered, in a normal North Korean home the leaders' portraits would hang. The guy had a sense of humor.

"Nor were our children brought up to be Christian believers — although they, like Joung-ah, have been receptive to Christian teachings since we came here. Before that, we all suffered the consequences of the family's half-successful escape attempt and history of Christian belief."

"You had a lot of difficulties, I gather."

"Although the security services eventually upgraded us from the 'hostile' class to the 'wavering' or unreliable class, we were never considered 'loyal.' I was stuck working down in a mine shaft with no chance to better my prospects because of the supposed sins of my ancestors."

Joung-ah brought communal bowls of three kinds of kimchi from their dining hall and put them on the table, with three pairs of long metal chopsticks. She joined us, drinking tea. I told them a little about the life of Halmeoni and Mama in Seoul, where they'd first settled, and then in Mississippi. Then I returned to my hosts' story.

"As non-Christians, how did your son end up at Posey Korea University and you and the rest of your family in this compound?"

"The coal mine where I was assigned to work wasn't producing. Still I was expected to show up for work every day. To survive, we grew vegetables around our house and in a secret forest plot. Joung-ah sold them in the market. But the authorities put an end to that when they started yet another crackdown on the markets. We fled to China, fearing starvation if we stayed in the DPRK."

"Were things better in China?"

"We both managed to get low-paying work, so we were all eating, but it was a rough life. We were illegal aliens, hunted by the police of both countries. When a recruiter put the word out in the Chinese village where we were hiding that any North Korean of Christian belief *or* background could come here, we revealed ourselves and volunteered. Here we do not even have to wear those." He pointed at my portrait pin. "The rules of this place recognize that belief in God is inconsistent with belief in Kim Il-sung."

"Isn't there a catch? I've always trusted Dr. Posey, but he's not the only one involved in this strange arrangement. Why did the regime bring people it considered dissidents here and feed you quite well — judging by this kimchi we're eating — when even members of the 'loyal' class were hard-pressed to get enough to eat? Why did the authorities let the Posey organization build a university and preach Christianity not only to the students but also to their families? Am I wrong to think there could be something fishy about the whole deal?"

"We were so eager — so desperate — that we banished doubts at the time. But now I lie awake at night wondering whether that offer was too good to be true."

"Do you both work in the tractor factory?"

"Yes, we are assembling metal parts into subassemblies."

"Which are then made into tractors?"

"So they tell us, but . . ."

"You doubt it?"

"My friend who works with me used to be a farmer on a big cooperative farm. He drove a tractor until the Russians and Chinese gave up communism and stopped supplying us with highly subsidized fuel. That was when farms in this country had to resume plowing with oxen. He has difficulty figuring out where in a tractor the items we make would fit. 'That must be quite some high-tech tractor,' he said once. The supervisor looked hard at him and he has not repeated the remark down there, but when I see him up here he shakes his head and says, 'Quite a tractor!' Then he laughs."

"He thinks you're making weapons."

Shin-il nodded.

"In that case, keeping enemy countries from targeting the site could be the reason for putting the factory and your living quarters underground."

"And the railroad spur. That is underground, too, terminating in a big siding in the factory tunnel where materials and supplies come in and the finished products go out."

"I wonder if Dr. Posey has had similar doubts. Has he spent time down in the factory?"

"He sometimes comes over to preach. But the church in this compound is in a different tunnel. I have never seen him in our factory."

"A church in a tunnel . . ."

"Yes, that is where they are holding the prayer meeting right now. It is really something to see — a cathedral carved out of limestone. You should have a look some time, whether or not you believe in the religion."

"That last part could be said about a good many churches around the world, but count on the DPRK to put everything on a lower plane." I chuckled but Shin-il didn't. I'd had enough to drink, was enjoying my own joke too much. Anyway, it was time to leave before the end of the prayer meeting when the faithful would pour forth from another hole in the ground, watched by camp security. I thanked the couple and headed back.

As I walked up the hill my feelings were mixed. I had found a cousin. That was a cause for rejoicing. But it appeared that North Korea had managed to get Reverend Bob's organization tied up with something that was not listed among its spiritual and charitable purposes — something that I feared would, in the end, deeply hurt my old friend and mentor.

I cringed as I imagined the headlines:

ARMS PLANT HIDDEN AT EVANGELIST'S UNIVERSITY CAMPUS IN NORTH KOREA

Hearing something rustling behind a tree, I froze and waited. Nothing happened. It must have been a breeze stirring up some vegetation. The scare reminded me: I had to assume I was still on General Ri's hit list.

I STOPPED by the dining hall, where Yu was studying, and alerted her. "The students' parents have been told they're building tractor assemblies, but some suspect they're making weapons components instead."

She looked up from the statistics textbook and gave me her full attention.

"I'm afraid the people here are being used as a tool for the regime. I'm pondering whether I shouldn't go over right now and warn Reverend Bob."

"If I may, permit me to suggest that you wait until I have made a report before you pass along your suspicions to others."

She came to my door a few minutes later. I stepped outside to hear her convey Mi-song's advice that I not speak with university officials about the matter. Before I could protest she said, "My boss has confirmed that your attacker was working for General Ri."

I considered the implications. "And Ri, besides being connected with the plot on my life and thus, presumably, with the CDS scam, probably was involved with any arms manufacturing as well. I'd feel pretty bad about sitting on that kind of information."

"My boss says she cannot imagine that arms could be made

here without the knowledge of at least one person in the Posey organization. Someone must know, and it stands to reason that whoever that is was also in on the plot against you. She says that even if you tell only Dr. Posey, it is simply human nature that he would wish to share the information with one or more of the people working with him — perhaps tipping our hand to our adversaries."

I pondered. "That makes sense. For now I won't speak with Reverend Bob about it — but I'm at a loss trying to figure what our next step should be. Did Ms. Kim offer any ideas on that?"

"No."

It occurred to me that our side needed to do some brainstorming. The university's upcoming long weekend would provide enough time for me to travel to Dandong and Hong Kong. The students would be holding an intensive religious retreat — as if their daily life on campus didn't already amount to just that with all the religion courses, morning prayer sessions and church services. I stuck my head into the dean's office and told Sable I wanted to leave for a little R&R. She wasn't happy. Darley Scratch was there with her, planning the retreat, and they'd just been talking about asking me to handle the music.

Resignation showed on her face as she evidently decided she shouldn't begrudge me a vacation after the unsettling experience in my apartment. "Ask Byon to work out your travel arrangements."

Back at the bar in Arirang, seated with Paul, my Catholic priest friend, I picked up where he and I had left off: "You didn't tell me the Posey Korea University recruiters were bringing not only students but also family members."

He thought for a moment. "Oh, yeah, as I recall I was getting ready to mention it, but that was when Ms. Kim came over and we never got back to the subject. What I've heard is that this is something that they want to keep secret from the faculty for some reason. Let me guess: You found out what that reason is?"

"Not sure yet, but I'm working on it. On another matter, what's your take on the third-generation successor?"

"The longer he sticks around without pushing through real reform and opening, the more likely it becomes that malcontents among his own subjects will tear him limb from limb. He doesn't feed even his soldiers, much less the ordinary civilians. And it isn't just bad economic policy. Whatever money does come in he diverts to the benefit of himself and other top elite."

He took a sip from his drink. "On my dad's side I'm ethnically Chinese. I grew up understanding the idea — which the Chinese gave to the rest of East Asia — that bad rulers eventually lose the 'mandate of heaven.' The sell-by date of the Kims' mandate is close at hand, I'd guess."

"Do they teach North Koreans about the mandate of heaven?"

"Textbooks and the propaganda outpourings that pass for news do explicitly describe the Kims as rulers sent from heaven. In no way do they acknowledge that the 'peerless' dynasty's heavenly mandate could ever be withdrawn."

"Too bad."

"Yet people have started to connect the dots and revert to their ancestors' view that if heaven gives, it also takes away. They've had some help in that from smuggled South Korean TV historical drama series."

"Do Northerners dare talk among themselves about such things?"

"Some have started to venture such remarks — more often one on one than in larger groups. When Kim Jong-un had his uncle put to death, there were economic consequences. Trade with China declined; inflation rose. The young ruler got a lot of the popular blame. In a patriarchal society, there's enough of the traditional cast of mind left that not a few North Koreans saw the country's economic problems as inevitable punishment."

"Hope that wasn't the end of it."

"It wasn't. There was more of that sort of talk when the Chinese cut off coal imports and agreed in the United Nations to a cap in fuel exports. Of course Beijing adopted those measures in connection with international sanctions regarding the nuclear and missile programs. But the timing suggested it was also in retaliation for Pyongyang agents' assassination of Kim's elder brother Jong-nam, who had been under Chinese protection. Choking trade certainly hurt the North Korean economy. And in the traditional view of things, fratricide is right up there with avunculicide as a cardinal sin."

A waitress came by, and Father Paul stopped talking until she was out of our hearing.

"Jong-un's father was a nasty fellow. Even during the great famine, though, as unattractive as he was, Kim Jong-il managed to stay in power — because he was cunning and vicious, and everyone feared him. This youngster is at least as brutal, maybe more so. He had not only his uncle but also the uncle's close associates killed, and then applied guilt by association to kill or otherwise punish their families — people who in many cases had been this close to the Kim family."

The priest held up two fingers to indicate how close. Then he continued. "It may be that the uncle really was plotting to bring down Kim Jong-un and replace him with the elder brother, and that Jong-un got wind of the plot. There have been such reports, and they suggest compelling reasons for getting rid of the uncle and brother. But we've also seen other reports of killings that suggest Jong-un is simply brutal by nature. A general is said to have been put to death for showing 'disrespect' by falling asleep at a meeting in the presence of Kim Jong-un, for example. Farther down in society a terrapin grower supposedly drew a death sentence for losing some of his animals — due to the state's failure to provide enough power to keep the tanks pumping."

"I hadn't heard those stories before. Sounds like Kim's on the Stalin end of the bloodthirstiness scale. Any chance of a revolution?"

"It might be wishful thinking to call the situation pre-revolutionary. But what I hear is that when the peace process collapsed, people were really disappointed — to the extent that more of them untied their tongues and spoke ill of Kim. He had gotten their hopes up — they'd felt change was coming — and then he went back to emphasizing the military over the economy. Sanctions started biting again in people's everyday lives."

"You feel sorry for the kid?"

"I've seen enough of what the Kims have wrought that I feel sure if the task fell to me I would pull the trigger myself. Why do you ask?"

"Just like to know where people stand. I'm a newcomer here, you know." I looked up. "Here comes Byon. Do you know where he stands?"

"I think he's a good guy but I wouldn't bet my life on it," he said in a soft voice.

"Same here." I remembered how critical of the regime Byon had been on our first trip and how loyal to Reverend Bob he seemed.

As Byon arrived at our table Father Paul changed the subject. "So, Professor Davis, are you going to make music for us again tonight?"

I turned and gave the new arrival a welcoming look. "Pull up a stool, Byon. Well, I'm a little tired from the long drive — as I imagine Byon is, too. After the cocktail hour I think I'll just go back to my hotel for a quick bite and then read myself to sleep." I didn't mention that I had an appointment.

"That probably would be a wise move since Ms. Kim, the star of the show, took the evening off. She won't be here to liven things up, and there's no replacement yet for that bouncy little harpist, Ms. Yu. I'm anticipating a fairly sedate performance." He looked up. "Meanwhile, here's Quentin McLoughridge joining us." Father Paul introduced the broad-faced fellow, squarely built inside his gray tweed suit, as a London-based businessman.

McLoughridge gave me a handshake and ordered a Scotch. He told me he'd begun commercial involvement with North Korea

decades before, had handled the country's substantial gold shipments. "Business has ebbed and flowed. Before the peace process
collapsed I was setting up a fund so that foreigners could invest in
enterprises in North Korea. Since there is no stock market, I was
arranging for our fund to form joint ventures with official DPRK entities in such fields as mining. Anything on that scale is, of course, on
hold for the time being. The sanctions — counterproductively, I
believe — scare everyone away. I'm heading for Pyongyang tomorrow,
by train, but my purpose this trip is merely to check in with my
network. I must keep contacts open until circumstances become more
promising."

It was pretty obvious that Father Paul, Byon and I were not
prospective investors. McLoughridge changed the subject. "I understand there is rather more going on at Posey Korea University than
meets the eye."

Byon sucked orange pop through his straw. I said nothing.

McLoughridge continued. "I hear the Posey organization has
something to export and is in contact with one of my competitors —
someone with far less experience than I have in dealings with the
DPRK. Next time you see the good reverend let him know that I'm
available. Whenever my competitor makes a cock-up of it, as he is
certain to do, I'm the man to put things to rights."

Byon put down his pop. "Dr. Posey is concerned with souls,
not sales."

"All I'm telling you is what I hear, something about tractors."

That certainly got my attention. Maybe I was about to learn more
about what Shin-il and his co-workers were manufacturing in the
tunnel.

Instead McLoughridge knocked back the remainder of his Scotch
and stood to leave. "Well, gentlemen, carry on. I have an appointment
down the street."

He wasn't getting away from me that easily. "I'll head out now,
too." As we walked together toward the Renmin Hotel I asked
McLoughridge for more detail on what he had heard.

"The competitor I mentioned, a Lebanese named Maloof, is staying in the Renmin, as I am. When I came down to the lobby this evening he was sitting in a chair with his back to me, talking in Arabic on his phone. I suppose he had assumed no one else in the lobby would understand him. He knows of my modest capability with the language. Turning around, he could see that I would have overheard his end of the conversation. That got his knickers in a twist, as I easily determined from the scowl on his ugly face. Tractors are small change, but in view of the unpleasant history of our competition I do enjoy irritating him. Every small triumph is to be relished. Well, cheerio."

I had eaten a bowl of room-service noodles by the time I heard the sound of someone moving around outside in the hall. Not sure whether it was Mi-song or a less welcome visitor, I took note that my available weaponry consisted solely of the minibar's miniature bottles. Then there came a tapping on the door. I asked who was there.

"Mi-song." There was an edge in her voice. "Please open the door."

I opened it, and helped her off with her coat. Her face was pale and she was trembling. I moved to embrace her. That seemed the right thing to do for an agitated lady who, when last glimpsed, had been kissing me.

She brushed me off and pulled herself together. "I feared you were dead."

"What's this about?"

"A hotel guest has been murdered in his room directly above yours, two floors up, a British businessman. Apparently the killer was waiting in the man's room and suffocated him with a plastic bag."

"British?"

"Yes. He was a big man, I'm told, and he put up a struggle and made a lot of noise."

"Quentin McLoughridge?"

She looked at me. "You knew him?"

"We met this evening, in Arirang. My god."

"By the time hotel security arrived at the room he was dead and his killer had escaped."

"The usual suspects?"

"It seems likely the assassin misread a digit in the room number." She looked hard at me. "I was afraid whoever did it had realized the mistake and come after you. You must have been the real target."

"Not necessarily. Is it safe to talk here?"

"This hotel assigns certain wired rooms to guests whom the authorities wish to spy upon. You are not in one of those rooms. I had thought that this would be a good place to talk with you about what we must do next."

I told her what I had learned from McLoughridge. "The fact he had overheard Maloof's conversation in Arabic probably got him killed."

"Assuming that Ri was behind tonight's murder, they may still be planning to come and kill you. It is possible that they had intended to do so but McLoughridge jumped the queue." She pulled out her phone, dialed and instructed someone to keep an eye on Maloof, as well as any others, locals or foreigners, who might be working with him, and to watch my room.

"And that brings us to the purpose of my current trip." I indicated the room chairs with my arm and we both sat. I let her begin.

"We still do not know who has taken the broker role in the CDS scam," she said. "And we have yet to prepare a counter-scheme. Although I devised the swaps plan, my knowledge of the financial markets is wholly academic. I gather you have contacts who are qualified and perhaps willing to help us, people in the industry who have practical knowledge."

"Helmut Fassler's the guy. I tried to call him earlier in the evening, but his phone was turned off. He's the one who taught me about the CDS market and how easily it could be manipulated, *if* traders willing to help could be brought into the scheme. He's had enough further time to think about this that there may be a break-through idea lurking in a corner of that big brain. I'll call again in the morning and arrange to meet him."

"Is there anyone else?"

I could understand her evident disappointment that I'd come up with no better a plan than to return to an old advisor. "Before you brought me the news tonight, I was thinking Quentin McLoughridge had the expertise to help if he wanted, and I might not need to use my Hong Kong ticket. But we can scratch his name from the list. Anyhow, I doubt McLoughridge would have wanted to get involved since his business depended on good relations with the powers that be in your country."

"You are quite right. My agency watches the handful of European businessmen who have invested time and money in the hope of making deals in my country. We maintain dossiers on all of them. They are not the sort to be diverted into political intrigues. Is there anyone else?"

"Do you know the name Zack Nodding?"

"The Goldberg Stanton Asia CEO, who works with Dr. Posey — yes. We keep a dossier on him, too, but there is little in it other than open-source information. He does, of course, have the expertise that we need."

"He might be willing in principle to help, so he could show the U.S. regulators what a straight arrow he is and maybe get a few extra million in his annual bonus from Goldberg Stanton."

"You dislike him."

Good thing we weren't playing poker. I had broadcast my feel-ings. "I wonder if he could manage to pull his head out of his ass for long enough to seriously consider what I'd be telling him."

Apparently unfamiliar with the image, she looked confused but then broke into a laugh. "If as seems likely you and he should experience a 'failure to communicate,' to use the terminology made famous by Cool Hand Luke, Nodding might start chattering in the wrong places. As I asked Ms. Yu to tell you, I assume that not all of the Posey people are kept in the dark about the so-called One-Eight Tractor Factory. By the way, do you know what that number signifies?"

"You tell me."

"The current Supreme Leader's birthday, January eighth. That name alone suggests the factory could be very important in Jong-un's plans. And that would also help to explain why General Ri's agent killed a British businessman who showed an interest in it."

"Right. I prefer to leave Nodding out of it, for now. By the way, how does a North Korean spy know about Cool Hand Luke?"

"Kim Jong-il used to invite me often to film-viewing parties in his palace. He had thirty thousand movies in his private collection. That one was among my favorites."

"Got it. Even my thoroughly married and righteous mother fell in love with Paul Newman."

<hr>

Figuring that there was little more we could do that evening about the bad guys, I moved on to another pressing matter. "You seemed upset when you first came in."

"Yes."

"You're a pro at what you do and I have no doubt you've seen people killed, maybe killed some yourself."

"Yes . . ."

"Would you have been broken up if they'd killed me instead of McLoughridge?"

"Yes. I have developed feelings for you, and there are unmistakable signs that they are mutual." She laughed. "When I came in and you started hugging me, the insane thought occurred to me that I should borrow a great Mae West line: 'Is that a gun in your pocket, or are you just glad to see me?' That is from another movie that Kim Jong-il showed in his palace. What a hoot!"

It was also a hoot to hear Mi-song with her posh British accent trying to mimic Mae West.

"If you care to resume comforting me now, I have no objection."

There was no need for her to say more.

When I got around to undressing her, she stopped me. "Can you please turn off all the lights? Showing my breasts embarrasses me. They are not symmetrical. The right is bigger than the left."

"Who cares? I don't."

"It did not bother me until the staff members of the spy school that I attended made me self-conscious. They wanted junior agents to become more glamorous, so that we could be sure of seducing espionage targets and potential abductees. When they stripped me and saw these, they told me to go to the Nine One Five Hospital — that is the same hospital whose surgeons made Jong-un look like my father — and have them adjusted to be the same size. I did not wish to have surgeons cutting on me as long as I was healthy. If the spy school director had not known I was Kim Il-sung's daughter they would have forced me to have the surgery."

I couldn't help smiling. "When I first met you I thought you were too perfect to be real — probably had gone under many a plastic surgeon's knife. Now that I know you're no Barbie doll, I'm even more mightily smitten. Let's see those beauties."

She lifted her bra and let me gaze upon them for a second before replacing it and reaching for the light switch.

"They're lovely as can be," I said, and meant it.

———

The latest signal of danger, far from interfering with our concentration on lovemaking, seemed only to focus us. At one point I mentally speculated that her training in spycraft had included use of the female body to bring on heart failure in imperialist Americans, puppet South Koreans or, as in my case, a mixture of the two.

I awoke a while later to find her nestled in my arms, gazing at me. "Tell me, how did you come to be called Heck?"

"I grew up in a strict church, went down front at age twelve and got baptized by full immersion. Initially I think I was motivated by a sense of obligation — peer pressure. I was at that age when it was time. But they enrolled me in intensive religious training and soon I really bought into the program. We were supposed to fight against our sinful natures and try to become worthy, now that God had forgiven us in exchange for our belief in Jesus. As I got on with puberty I often promised God in my bedtime prayers that I'd give up a couple of chronic sins. The private sin, to put it in biblically euphemistic terms, was lusting in my heart."

"Oh, you mean like President Jimmy Carter?"

"Another sin-obsessed Southern Baptist, yes. And my public sin was cussing. When Joe figured out I was trying to avoid strong language, even to the extent of saying 'heck' instead of 'hell,' he made fun of me and pegged me with the nickname. It stuck."

She smiled. "So you were a good boy?"

"I tried — stayed a teetotaler all through high school. At the end of senior year when I was getting ready to go off to college, a class-mate bet me a fifth of Jack Daniels Tennessee whiskey that I'd be drinking by Christmas vacation. He turned out to be right about that — although I've always greatly preferred the Kentucky product. I saw him ten years later at a class reunion and made good on the bet."

"I had some brief encounters with religious people in Switzer-land but the exposure did not really take. Did your religious training stay with you?"

"What I'd learned failed me on two main counts. First, taken literally — which was the way I'd been taught to take it — it fell short of providing up-to-date understanding of the cosmos. Second, the higher being it pointed to had a personality disorder that increasingly, as I read the scriptures that defined him, made him a nasty, brutal fellow. Eventually I could no longer believe in him, much less worship or even respect him. But I could see that, for a great many people, that belief system's rules provided a needed social order in the here and now. And — with its rites of passage and its emphasis on good works — it helped get them, individually, and the larger society through times of crisis. At two out of four it was pretty much a wash. I couldn't believe, but I didn't feel I needed to go around carrying a sign telling other people they shouldn't believe."

"That all sounds rather theoretical, I must say."

"OK, I'll put it another way. Aside from the music and the literary influences — the powerful cadences of the King James version of scripture — only what I still consider the real basics of Jesus's teachings have stuck with me over the long haul: the Golden Rule and the Sermon on the Mount. Oh, and from the Old Testament some of the commandments still resonate, especially Thou Shalt Not Kill." I paused. "I'm still trying to rationalize what happened with Min."

"Self-defense. Put it out of your mind."

"I guess you're right, but . . . anyhow . . ." I thought of something and chuckled. "In college I developed other non-puritanical behaviors besides drinking. My roommate was the campus distributor of free samples for a cigarette company. Instead of passing them out at parties as he was hired to do, he let me help him smoke up all the samples. The two of us acquired major tobacco habits but saved untold numbers of classmates from doing the same."

"And did you continue lusting in your heart?" Mi-song mischievously chose that moment to take matters in hand. Becoming aroused again, I sensed I had only a moment or two to finish my story.

"You bet. There was a likewise pious girl I'd been sweet on in high school. She was two years younger. As devout Southern Baptist boys are supposed to do, I had placed her on a pedestal as a chaste prospective wife."

"How *upright* of you." She stroked me and laughed wickedly.

"When I came home after my college freshman year, though, I

took her to a drive-in movie and tried to get her to French-kiss. She broke up with me on the spot. 'Oh, Heck, you've changed. You smoke and you drink and you cuss and all you ever think about is sex, and I don't want to see you any more.' "

"And she stuck with her decision?"

"Yep. And I have to admit, of all the vices she berated me for, the only one I eventually gave up was smoking cigarettes."

Mi-song laughed. "Don't ever give up the others." With her free hand she ran her fingers through my hair and stroked my face. "Was it in your university days that you grew your braid and whiskers?"

"Yep."

"You're handsome with or without, but when I saw that you had cut them I admired the sacrifice for your mission. It reminded me of the Chinese nationalists who sliced off their braided queues before they overthrew the Qing Dynasty, early in the twentieth century."

That's when she mounted me.

―――

"You mentioned you'd studied in Switzerland," I said when conversation resumed. "Is that where you learned your English?"

"Yes, and French, German and Italian as well. It turned out I had a flair for languages."

"That's handy for a future spy. Did you graduate from high school in Switzerland?"

"No. I returned to Pyongyang — to Mangyongdae Revolutionary School, which I pointed out to you from the tour bus."

"Now I remember."

"It is a highly elite school that prepares youngsters for careers in the military and in the security services that are at the heart of the regime. From there I went to Kim Il-sung University, also in Pyongyang."

"You stayed in a dorm?"

"I lived at home with the Shin couple through college. But when

I enrolled in a post-graduate program at the spy and commando school I was required to move to a campus dormitory. Most of the enrollees at that point had to cut all ties with their families permanently so there would be no danger that they would reveal state secrets. Because of who my father had been I was an exception, permitted to go home on weekends."

"What mission were they training you for?"

"Broadly, to protect our leader and ensure that eventually he would rule all of the Korean peninsula without challenge."

"Really? I've often wondered if the top guys in Pyongyang still believe that's possible. Lots of Western pacifist types claim the leadership is focused purely on defense."

"The people who trained us argued that we could and would take over the Southern territory one way or another. General Ri put in an appearance and gave the most dramatic — actually, shocking — presentation. He said we had stockpiled enough chemical weapons to wipe out the South Korean population. In his view, taking over the whole peninsula would require killing all of the South Koreans because there was no way they would adapt their ideology to ours."

"Is that when you started to dislike Ri?"

"He was repulsive. He reminded me of Dr. Strangelove. I had just seen the movie at another viewing party that Kim Jong-il hosted in his palace. Peter Sellers was funny. General Ri is not. In fact, it is hard to find anything to smile about in our military — and especially at the spy school."

"Were you supposed to take part in the conquest?"

"Yes. You had better stop what you are doing if you care to finish this conversation."

I rested my hand on her warm haunch. I did want to continue the conversation and find out more about the person who had joined me in an enterprise in which she and I both were risking all. I fervently hoped her abilities were up to what she'd signed on for.

"We trained in a tunnel using a scale model of downtown Seoul with exact replicas of shops, restaurants and bars. That was important not only to commandos who might lead an invasion but also to those of us spies who might be infiltrated into the South for information gathering and subversion."

"Did they also train you to go against other countries?"

"We were expected to have overseas assignments, too. So that we could blend in, each of us studied a foreign language and culture with a native speaker who had been abducted abroad and brought over to teach us. When General Ri spoke to us he said we must be prepared to wreak havoc on Japan, in particular. Japan became my focus in spy school because they decided that my European languages were already good enough."

"So spy school was heavy on brain work?"

"Yes, but you cannot imagine how grueling the physical training was. Because I was already a university graduate I did not have to stay for the full six years, but I am stronger than many men."

I reached across the pillow and felt a bicep. Suitably impressed, I had to kiss her again.

⸻

In the morning I took the train to Shenyang. All the way to and through the airport I watched for possible malefactors — and plastic bags; I'd never be able to view one of those with equanimity again after having heard of McLoughridge's horrible end. I visualized his face turned purple, his eyes and tongue popped out, as the last flicker of life left him.

On the plane I relaxed a bit and caught up with the news. It was amazing how much someone stuck in North Korea could miss, even though the rest of the world was hearing daily about North Korea.

The lead story described Pyongyang's most worrisome provocation to date. An unidentified U.S. government official, flying northwest out of Honolulu in a window seat on a passenger plane, had whipped out his iPhone to photograph a ship that he thought looked suspicious. Anchored in the French Frigate Shoals, an uninhabited atoll designated as a wildlife preserve, the ship when checked turned out to be a trawler that North Korea had used for mid-ocean monitoring of intercontinental ballistic missile tests.

Everyone remembered Pyongyang's threat to unleash an electromagnetic pulse attack. For Washington pundits it was but a short step to predicting that the regime was about to make good on that threat, by exploding in the atmosphere near Honolulu a thermonuclear warhead delivered by one of its missiles. An EMP could wipe out unshielded electronics in Hawaii. Modern cars wouldn't start. Cell phones would go dead and computers kaput. Key military communications would survive, but the damage to the civilian infrastructure would presage a huge problem in the continental United States whenever Kim might get around to targeting farther east.

What the analysts suspected North Korea was contemplating would have seemed an insanely suicidal act — on the order of the Japanese bombing of Pearl Harbor. Meanwhile, another news item was a reminder that North Korea's leaders couldn't be assumed to be free from mental quirks.

A high-level defector recently arrived in Seoul, a former North Korean police general, was quoted as claiming that Kim Jong-il's December 2011 death on the Number One train had come moments after he'd summoned his aides to report a ghostly appearance by his late father. The second-generation ruler had insisted he'd seen Kim Il-sung standing on the railroad right of way and making the universal crossed-arms gesture for "no entry." South Korean intelligence before Kim's death had reported an earlier such ghostly sighting, suggesting it showed a deterioration of the ruler's mental faculties. The police general's account was the first indication that a second sighting had triggered the heart attack that killed the Dear Leader.

Meanwhile the war in Honduras was still uncompleted, and other irate Latin American countries threatened complications. Although talk in Washington of launching a preventive attack on North Korea intensified, officials in the Pentagon and elsewhere in official Washington worried that an immediate and vigorous response to Kim's provocations would risk opening a second, much bigger war front halfway around the world.

Old differences of opinion in the U.S. had not been fully resolved following the failure of the peace process. One op-ed item that I read returned to the debate among North Korea specialists about whether Kim Jong-un was a closeted reformer trying to out himself in a big way. Reverend Bob's sweet-tempered board member John Hyon argued that the U.S. president ought to have persisted in negotiations despite difficulties. Hyon wrote that all Kim needed was a peace treaty and withdrawal of U.S. troops to make him feel secure enough to turn North Korea into the newest Asian economic tiger.

Iran, also, was back in the news. According to a background analysis piece, the Iranian in the street wanted to put struggles in the past and focus on living well. A faction of the powerful Revolutionary Guard, on the other hand, wanted to struggle further against the Great Satan.

———

I met Helmut in the Kowloon bar and brought him up to date, leaving out only the part about possible weapons manufacture at the university. I wasn't sure what, if anything, the connection might be. Besides, the problem I had come to pose to him seemed sufficiently intractable on its own.

Helmut racked his formidable brain and came up with no ideas on how Kim and company might have enlisted financial industry people willing to carry out the CDS scheme. "Bankers would know full well they risked ruining their banks and going to prison."

What proved easier for him was giving me the basic concept of a counter-scheme. "Markets move on news developments. Bad guys often try to manipulate prices by manipulating the media, and that's the sort of scheme we think is involved here. The way to stop them is to fight news with news. There are at least three problems: knowing when they're going to try unleashing a particular story on the market,

232 / BRADLEY K. MARTIN

coming up with a story that counters theirs and, finally, getting the counter-story out so that major market players will see it in time to act."

"Makes sense, Helmut, with one caveat from a news purist who's working for an ethical outfit. Even for the purpose of bringing down bad guys, we wouldn't be able to justify joining them in using the news media to fool investors. What we need is not just any old story that counters theirs but an *accurate, true* story that counters theirs. But I don't see how we can get a true story, one fit for engineering a twist like that, without being on the inside of their conspiracy."

"It might work if you stayed in North Korea for a while longer and learned the details of their plans. But since they've already tried to kill you three times, you might well prefer not to. Joe was the bloodhound, after all."

I let Helmut's comment pass. I knew where he was coming from, but I was on an adrenaline and testosterone high.

We went through various scenarios of how things might work out. Helmut tended to think the North Koreans' scheme was flawed and would be discovered. The swaps traders were likely to figure out they were being used. They might blow the whistle to protect their own hides. But then again, that might not happen if the traders' bank management was consciously part of the scheme and able to manage the huge risks it involved.

Vague as our conclusions were, the session had made the trip worthwhile. At least I had a clearer idea of what our goals should be.

━━━

When I got to my hotel I phoned to give Evelyn an update. She sounded strange when she answered.

"Sorry to call so late. Didn't have phone access earlier but tonight I'm in Hong Kong on a quick weekend trip. Everything OK with you?"

"No," she gasped, sounding as if she could burst into tears at any moment.

"Uh oh. Is that insurance investigator — Hashimoto? — bothering you again?"

"Yes," she whispered. After a moment she pulled herself together and explained. "He says unless new evidence turns up before a week from Monday the insurance company will determine that Joe committed suicide."

"What's Hashimoto basing this on?"

"Joe had gone to Panmunjom on assignment earlier from the southern side. Hashimoto learned about that and went to interview the public affairs officer, Major Player. He found out that media visitors always stop at Camp Bonifas and hear the same lecture mentioning the Soviet diplomatic trainee who ran across in 1984."

"What does that have to do with anything?"

"Hashimoto is arguing that Joe would have known, from hearing the lecture, that the North Koreans would definitely shoot at him if he ran."

"And that's supposed to make his run a suicide?"

"That's Hashimoto's theory. Grady Edwards, who's advising me, says there's a line of legal thinking that permits the suicide clause to be triggered if the deceased did something that had a high probability of causing his death — even if he didn't intend to kill or injure himself."

I knew Grady, a lawyer with an American firm's Tokyo office. "You mean negligence?"

"Something like that but with closer awareness of the danger than in the usual negligence case, it seems. Grady says two behaviors that meet the test under that theory are playing Russian roulette and shooting at police who have come to arrest you."

"Would the insurance company's ruling be final?"

"Grady says we could sue the insurance company, asking the Hong Kong courts to determine it wasn't suicide and order the company to pay up. It seems courts usually aren't satisfied there's been a suicide without knowing the motive."

"And what does this Hashimoto slime-ball claim is the motive?"

"His theory is that Joe was a closet alcoholic, deeply depressed; impending fatherhood drove him to desperation."

"Alcoholic! Where's he get off with that?"

"You know Mandy Willins at the Foreign Correspondents' Club? The P.R. woman pretending to be a journalist who ran against him for vice president and has had it in for him ever since he won?"

"Yeah. Mandy's obsessed with club politics. She should get a job that leaves her less spare time to assemble factions and foment conspiracies."

"Hashimoto took a deposition from her, and she painted a dark picture of Joe's drinking. The way she described him, he was a veritable wino whose behavior was a grave embarrassment to the club."

"She's the embarrassment."

"I don't know if you noticed on the night of the memorial gathering, but when Joe's parents and I were leaving I saw her lurking around at the edge of the crowd. In her deposition she testified that you sang two of Joe's favorite songs from your repertoire, 'Duncan and Brady' and the other one that's also about someone getting shot to death."

"'Louis Collins.' I saved those two for after you'd left."

"Thank you for that. I wasn't ready to hear those again yet, especially that line about angels handling the body." She paused, probably to compose herself. "But now Hashimoto is using Mandy's testimony about the songs to argue that Joe had dreamed of dying in a hail of bullets."

"Why, the goddamned bitch! Listen, I'm working on getting proof that Joe had reason to run. I don't have the goods at this point, though. Is there any way to make the insurance company hold off on its determination?"

"Apparently not."

"Well, I'll work as fast as I can. Let's hope we get a break soon."

＝

In the morning I met Langan Meyer. "Lang, I've decided to leave you with just a quick oral report. First, Joe didn't commit suicide. I can't prove that yet — and if you've been talking with Evelyn you know time is of the essence. Second, Joe was headed in the right direction. Third, the case may involve more complications than even he imagined."

"Sounds like you're making progress. Why don't you want to tell me more?"

"If I did, you'd have to agonize over whether you should run with what I already know. Just take it from me: I need you to sit on it while I let this develop. In due course I hope to be able to offer you a big story."

"I can't squeeze the information out of you." He looked resigned.

"I'll tell you this: I'm getting material from a high-ranking North Korean source who needs to be anonymous, for now. I've written that person's details here, in this sealed envelope. Please lock it up and open it only when you need to, if and when the story comes in."

"Watch your step."

Lang's concern was contagious. Lulled by the civilized comforts of Hong Kong, I'd been slow to notice an ebbing of my bravado. When I came out of the restaurant, I looked around to see if anyone might be following me.

Byon was supposed to be waiting for me in Dandong, but there was a message from him at the hotel front desk. He'd been enlisted to escort some visitors; I should stand by for further instructions. I headed for Arirang with my harps in my pockets, in the mood to make beautiful music with Mi-song. There was no sign of her.

I drank for a while with Father Paul. Recalling the latest news report about the circumstances of Kim Jong-il's death, I couldn't resist teasing the priest a little. "So do you think maybe Jong-il's enemies got a Kim Il-sung double, somebody like you, for example, to stand there by the tracks and scare the Dear Leader to death?"

Father Paul gasped and blanched. "Don't even joke about such a thing. Someone might overhear and report."

I changed the subject and we had supper. Concluding that Mi-song wasn't going to show up there, I called it an evening.

Back at the Renmin, I unlocked the room door — carefully. Sure enough, someone was waiting for me. Fortunately it was Mi-song, in bed, the sheet pulled up to her neck. "I thought we'd better not be seen together, even in Arirang."

I didn't bother asking how she'd gotten into the room. Keeping the lights off, we talked about what I'd done in Hong Kong. I left out the part about the insurance company, since I knew there was nothing she could do and I figured she had enough on her mind.

When I mentioned Byon's delay, she told me the new group of campus visitors included Maloof and two other men from the Middle East. Then we took care of another urgent matter.

About a half hour later there was a knock. Moving deftly and swiftly she took her things and hid in the bathroom. I went to the door, naked as a jaybird, and glanced to make sure the chain was set. "Who's there?"

"Mr. Byon sent me," someone said. The voice was low, masculine.

When I cracked the door, the guy jammed his steel-toed workman's shoe in and applied a wire cutter to the chain.

"Son of a bitch!" All I had time to do as I heard the chain snap was run past the bathroom and dive over the empty bed. Crouching behind the bed, I heard him close the door and move toward my side of the room. Once there, with the aid of the low light filtering through the closed window curtain from the neon signs outside, he'd be able to get a clear enough look at me to aim the snub-nosed revolver he was now holding.

Behind him Mi-song emerged naked and silent from the bathroom. With a flying leap she crossed the distance between them and cold cocked him with the butt of her own gun. His head lolled as she picked him up from the floor and sat him in the desk chair.

It's funny how odd sayings pop up in your memory at times of stress. "Everybody needs a chance to be told to *sit down*," I remarked. "Old bluesman friend of mine used to say that."

Standing behind him, she crossed her arms, looping the left one around his head to grab the right side of his jawbone and placing her right hand on the left side of his head. She twisted his head sharply to the left while simultaneously pushing forward. He showed no sign of life after that. To make sure, though, she reversed her grip and turned his head in the other direction.

I had to admire her handiwork. "You're obviously good at what you do. Tell me, who's the biggest notch you've carved in your gun belt — or is my security clearance not high enough to hear the answer?"

She laughed. "I will not tell you but perhaps you can guess if I provide a hint. Imagine whose life it would have given me the most pleasure to end and you will have your answer."

I knew the answer immediately. "Kim Jong-il."

"Sometimes it makes sense to give nature a push. He was ill for a long time and I grew tired of waiting for him to die. Toward the end of 2011 a story went around in Pyongyang circles that our father had appeared to him. Jong-il had told people close to him that he could not be sure whether he had seen the old man or only dreamed it. That was when South Korean intelligence put out reports that his mind seemed to be going. I calculated that another sighting could be just the thing to send him on his way forever."

"Earlier this evening I was kidding Father Paul, suggesting he was the double who stood by the tracks. He didn't much care for that line of discussion."

"I should think not."

"But he wasn't the one, was he?"

"If he did not tell you so himself, it is not for me to say that it was he — although I can say that I had come to know that Father Paul hated Kim Jong-il as much as I did."

"So, whoever the mysterious doppelgänger was, how did the caper work?"

"I persuaded . . . someone to dress up as Kim Il-sung in people's clothing and wait with me beside the railway tracks outside Dandong when the Number One armored train came through from Beijing. Jong-il had been undergoing treatment there — secretly, but it was part of my job to know his entire schedule. We hid behind some trees until the locomotive passed us. Then the double stepped close to the train, posed as I'd instructed him and uttered a ghostly cry of 'Woooooo wooooooo woooooo.' As I had anticipated, Jong-il was seated at his table with the window shade open, enjoying the scenery.

Although of course the double's cry was not audible inside the train, the overall performance had the desired effect."

"Details?"

"Screaming for his bodyguards, Jong-il keeled over from a heart attack, according to a an intelligence report I later received. He just managed to tell them what he had seen. They pulled the emergency cable and sent in his doctor. The train screeched to a halt and the bodyguards leapt off to investigate — but we had driven away."

I snorted, and then burst out laughing. "I love it. And that's the heart attack that killed him."

Smiling impishly, Mi-song nodded. "No one else had seen the apparition and investigators could not find any evidence, so they finally concluded that Jong-il had not seen anything real — he was hallucinating, as he had done earlier."

She frowned as she picked up the dead hit man's gun, looked it over and then showed it to me. "I wondered why he was carrying a revolver. Generally they are so noisy that he would have been at great risk of being apprehended before he could leave the hotel. However, this is a Russian Army OTs-38 Stechkin, a rare silent revolver. External silencers do not work properly on revolvers. The Stechkin uses a special cartridge. The propellant gases are retained inside its case, so that there is no flash or bang when the weapon is fired."

"Retrograde ejaculation."

"What?"

"Your description sounds like a diagnosis an older friend got. As a side effect from a prostate pill his urologist had prescribed, the guy's semen wasn't going out via the urethra but headed in the opposite direction, to the bladder. The doctor changed his prescription."

"Where is your *mind*?"

Seeing the twinkle in her eye made me smile. When she quickly reassumed a serious expression and dressed, I followed suit to the extent of putting on my undershorts and t-shirt.

"Whether the previous attempt at the university was planned as a simple burglary or not, now they are determined to kill you. If it were not so important that you be there, I would discourage you from returning to the campus. General Ri's agency is certain to infiltrate another first class agent into the campus to replace Min. Let us hope there has not been enough time for that. Meanwhile, at least Yu is there."

She pulled my shoulder toward her and looked me hard in the face. "But I am wondering now what to make of Byon."

"So am I. That note of his looks suspiciously like a setup."

"Possibly Byon works for them. But he does not display the moves of a trained assassin. Perhaps he is innocent and what happened was that one of General Ri's people saw the note that Byon left for you and took advantage of his absence. In any case, you had best be on your guard and find out as much as you can before someone tries again."

No kidding. I didn't say that, but I thought it. Three men trying to kill me earlier had all struck out. This had been the fourth attempt. For the North Koreans, apparently, it wouldn't be over until the fat leader sang.

Maybe Mi-song read my mind. "Do you have any experience firing a pistol?"

"Not lately, but Joe's father, the colonel, used to take us to a firing range. Seemed I was a natural. At the range they called me Hawkeye. Who knows? I might have grown up to become a card-carrying Second Amendment zealot if I hadn't turned my eye to photography instead. But that was decades ago."

"You had better carry this bloke's weapon when you return to campus. I shall have it, and a Chinese cell phone, left at the front desk in the morning, the package disguised as spirits. The Posey campus is close enough to the border that you can receive a signal from the China side. That is how Ms. Yu and I communicate."

She used a manicured fingernail to cut the plastic wrap sealing a box, containing a fifth of duty-free bourbon, that I'd just brought from Hong Kong. Then she removed the bottle, set it on the desk and slipped the empty box into the voluminous bag she carried. After cutting loose the remaining bit of door chain, to tidy up and hide the evidence, she placed all the chain and the wire cutter in the bag.

She handed me a pad and a pencil. "It is better to save your phone for backup. In due course you can use it to communicate with your editor, whose number you should write down so that I can program it."

"Carry the gun with the hammer pre-cocked, the manual safety on. Here is how to disengage the safety before you shoot." She showed me and then checked the cylinder. "It is fully loaded. You have five shots, with a range of up to fifty meters. Do you think you can manage if you must shoot someone?"

I nodded. "You already owned my heart, Mi-song. Saving my life puts a seal on it. If I live through the next few days, we need to plan on being together on a long-term basis." I kissed her.

Extricating herself from the embrace she held me at arms length. She spoke tenderly, tears in her eyes. "Darling, with so much at stake, with the risk so great that evil will prevail, this is no time to plan for the future of a couple of mere individuals."

"Don't amount to a hill of beans in this crazy world."

"What?"

"You watched Casablanca at another of Kim Jong-il's palace movie viewing parties?"

"Yes, but this is serious." She looked at the sitting body of the would-be assassin. "Please open the window and help me carry him over there."

We heaved the body far enough to the left that it would land beneath someone else's window. "The police will think he jumped or fell from the roof," she said.

I closed the window and she headed out into the corridor toward the emergency stairs. As I locked the door and turned to pour myself a double shot, I could hear people below raising an unholy cry at the package the heavens had delivered.

"I THINK we need to change your hotel next time you come through Dandong," Byon said when we met the next morning. "Two men have died while you were staying here. One, last night, was ruled a suicide, a Korean guy who jumped off the roof. But the other, immediately before you left to fly to Hong Kong, was that British businessman you and I had just met at Arirang. He was murdered in his room."

"That's terrible. Who did it?"

"The Chinese police are saying they have no idea who, or why. But I don't intend to stay here again, and I imagine you would also be more comfortable somewhere else — especially after your encounter with Min, the fellow you . . ." Byon looked embarrassed. "We still don't know what that was about."

Looking at his face I found no sign that the concern for me he'd expressed was anything other than sincere. In the end, though, you could never tell what someone else was really thinking.

"So what kept you away? Your note said something about escorting visitors. Anybody we know?"

"Dr. Posey's financial advisor, Mr. Nodding, is one. I don't know much about the others. They're a group from the Middle East — a Lebanese and a couple of Iranians."

"Why did Zack show up? He'd just come for the Pyongyang meeting. It's amazing he can spend so much time away from the job that pays his enormous salary." As soon as I'd said it I reminded myself that I should be more sparing of my disapproval — try to learn from Reverend Bob, see the good in people like Zack even when they themselves didn't make much effort to show that good.

Byon gave me a look. "Mr. Nodding believes in the mission. I'm not sure why he came. Dr. Posey is back from his trip to the States. He and Mr. Nodding may need to discuss finances, but I really don't know. None of the visitors talked much on the drive up. Except for the driver, we all napped. They were jet lagged from their flights and I was exhausted from traveling back and forth."

Byon had been forthcoming; I didn't think he was involved in dirty tricks. On the other hand, there couldn't be much time before another agent from General Ri's outfit would show up. Then I'd have to either flee or start spending full time watching my back. With Iranians joining the Lebanese, I figured I had considerable nosing around to do as soon as we got back to the campus.

First we had to get through customs. I doubted even Reverend Bob's organization could save me if I got caught for weapon smuggling. A different official was running the booth this time. He had a lean and hungry look that made me nervous, especially when he told me to put everything on the table. I made an effort to keep my eyes off the disguised weapon. The agent pointed to one of my Hong Kong purchases. "What's that? A comb?"

"A tuning fork." I struck it against the heel of my hand and moved it close to him so he could hear it vibrate.

He nodded. His hand moved toward the whiskey box. My heart rate soared. Byon's cell phone rang. The light on the phone screen glinted against one of my harmonicas, the shiny, brand new F-sharp. That's a rarely needed key. Only time I ever heard anybody performing on one was when Mickey Raphael soloed in Willie Nelson's version of "Georgia on My Mind."

The agent stared, transfixed, at the harp, neither picking it up nor dismissing us.

Byon read the body language as he turned off his phone and put it back in his pocket. "He wants you to give it to him."

I picked it up, blew a few bars of the Georgia number and handed the instrument to the fellow, bowing my head. He grinned, pocketed the harp and waved us through.

"I could have argued," Byon said as we left.

"It's OK. Seems I wasn't meant to own an F-sharp."

Tired after the events of the night before, I decided to follow the delegation's example and get some shuteye during the ride up.

An hour or so after we set out, Byon shook me awake. "You must have had a nightmare. You were moaning."

I rubbed my eyes. "Thanks for waking me up."

"You are a sound sleeper. The driver got a call on his mobile phone a little while ago and the loud ringing didn't awake you. This is his last trip driving us. That call was to tell him he is being transferred. His replacement arrives day after tomorrow."

I had a feeling my nightmare was nowhere near over.

━━━

When we reached the campus in the late afternoon there was no sign of either Zack or the Middle Eastern visitors. Sable told me Reverend Bob had asked that I see him as soon as I returned, so I headed over. It was after four and his staff had left for the day. From the outer office, I saw that his door was open. I figured he'd be back soon so I went in and sat down in front of his desk.

With nothing else to occupy me while I waited, I glanced around the room. It was a combination of a preacher's study and a politician's lair. Books on scriptural interpretation lined the shelves, while the framed photos showed him in Korea with Kim Il-sung, Kim Jong-il,

Kim Jong-un. In one picture he was shooting hoops with Jong-un. In that photo he looked much more like the young, athletic Reverend Bob I'd known at Calvary. The picture was dated only two years earlier. He'd aged too suddenly, I thought.

Another photo showed him praying at the inauguration in Washington. I thought back to Bartow Toombs's reminder that photo ops with U.S. presidents had been far more a specialty of the elder Posey. But even if Reverend Bob had additional U.S. presidential photos, I figured, they would be hung on the walls of his U.S. offices. I was willing to bet he hadn't displayed copies of the Kim photos there. After all, a big shot's photographic displays are for the benefit of visitors and in North Korea those would be mainly the North Koreans.

On the desk were some medicines with the name and logo of Mayo Clinic, next to a glass of water. One of the containers was labeled Nivolumab. *Damn! His cigars ended up smoking him.* I thought of Fatback, in Mississippi, washing down the same cancer drug with Four Roses. It appeared Reverend Bob had been about to take his meds when he'd needed to go out. How sad to think of my two old mentors, the saint and the sinner, facing off against the same deadly enemy and using the same weapon.

Under a pile of paper on Reverend Bob's desk I spotted a familiar leather-bound volume: his Souls Ledger. Normally I was a respecter of privacy, but I knew this book had my name in it. I slipped it out. Leafing through, I was astonished to find that it contained not only the tens of thousands of entries, starting in the front, for people who had made religious commitments under Reverend Bob's direct personal influence; there was also another, much less extensive set of entries starting from the back, entitled "Fallen Away." I thought for a moment and remembered that an accounting ledger shows both credits and debits.

Joe's name, I saw, was one of the earliest ones in the debit category. The entry noted his letter of resignation from Calvary Church and the date of the letter. I gave some thought to that. Was Reverend Bob simply listing failures? Knowing him, knowing that he didn't give up easily, I figured he put the names down to remind him to pray that the fallen would reconsider. There were only twenty or so unused pages between the two sections of entries; it seemed he'd need to start a fresh volume pretty soon — if the cancer let him live long enough.

Turning the debits pages, I quickly found my own name. The entry, with the notation "universalist heresy," was dated a couple of months into my sophomore year in college. That was around the time I had written to my parents approvingly quoting Thomas Starr King, a nineteenth century Universalist preacher, on the difference between what were then two separate non-mainstream Protestant Christian doctrines: "Universalists believe that God is too good to damn people, and the Unitarians believe that people are too good to be damned by God." If there was a supreme being, I informed my parents, I hoped the Universalists had been right in worshipping a God who embraced everybody.

Reverend Bob, keeping in touch with his old Calvary Church friends even after his move to North Carolina, must have heard about that and seen no choice but to make a debit entry in his ledger. Nothing inconsistent there — Reverend Bob was Reverend Bob.

Smelling cigar smoke and hearing coughing, I replaced the faded brown ledger under the stack of papers, picked up another book and opened it as if I'd begun looking through it.

Reverend Bob seemed taken aback to find me there but smiled when he saw the volume I'd just placed in my hands. "That's the second most important book ever published."

I looked at the cover. The book I held was Johnny Posey's *Gird Up Your Loins*. It was about prophecies of the End Times. Out of the corner of my eye I saw Reverend Bob sitting down and trying to seem casual as he covered his medicine containers with a copy of the *International New York Times*.

"Thanks for coming in, Heck. I was horrified to hear of the trouble you had in your apartment while I was gone. Don't know what got into that fellow, why he burglarized you, why he would attack you with a knife. The DPRK authorities assure me they don't know, either. We paid him more than decently by local standards. I've told our official contacts I expect them to see that nothing like that happens again. When I heard you'd left us to go abroad, I was a little concerned you might decide to make it permanent. It's good you're back and I hope you'll stay for a while."

"I enjoy the students As long as it's feasible for me to stick around, I want to do my best for them."

Reverend Bob looked pleased. "I'm told you've proved to be a champ in the classroom; look forward to hearing the results. In fact that's why I wanted you to come in. We've scheduled a special service for tomorrow night and I'd like you to handle the singing. Here's the order of worship. If you could have your students practice these hymns in class tomorrow that would be a big help."

"Happy to do it."

"This service won't be held here on campus. Near here we have another facility where the families of our students live while they work in a tractor factory. I've been preaching both places on Sundays, but I hadn't told the faculty about the other location earlier because the DPRK authorities didn't want us to make it known yet. Now matters have developed to the point where there's no harm in letting you all know."

It was easy for me to look confused, as if I were hearing about the other place for the first time. After all, the whole thing still puzzled me. Who in his organization had allowed Reverend Bob's university complex to land in a site that seemed likely to include an arms factory? And why would the North Koreans permit a community of security risks to live and work in such a sensitive zone?

"I think you'll be impressed to see the combined worship hall and auditorium. It didn't take all that much money to fit it out, but largely because it was hewn out of solid rock it turned out to feel a lot churchier than the university auditorium. I call the place our cathedral. One of our donors offered us a pipe organ and we decided that was the place to set it up. All you need to do is bring us a student choir to lead the hymn singing. That way we can let the family members — especially the ones who normally sing in the choir over there that's directed by the organist — hear a bit of what their kids have been learning to do. Aside from faculty members like me who don't know the language, people will be singing the hymns in Korean. They'll have the words printed in the program."

"No problem. We'll get the students accustomed to those hymns for sure."

"One other request: That was a terrific arrangement of 'Saints' on your CD. If you could do that with a small ensemble like the one I hear you took to perform for the young leader, it would fit perfectly as an interlude between the two parts of my sermon. I know it's a bit of a push to work up a number in one day, but I hope you can manage it."

"Love to do that."

His smile turned almost imperceptibly to a frown. "You made any progress tracking down that business you and Joe were talking about?"

I had no choice but to deceive Reverend Bob. It wasn't easy to be cagey with him on this. Our long relationship entitled him to a timely heads-up that his people weren't producing tractor sub-assemblies, whereupon he could take steps to protect his organization and himself. But I could see Mi-song's point that we shouldn't yet risk telling him.

"I'm no Joe Hammond. I'm a musician and photographer, not a financial reporter. I've found that stuff pretty much beyond me."

He nodded slightly and I went on.

"Now that I've faced up to my limitations in that department, the urgency is gone. I can focus a hundred percent on my music and my teaching."

Reverend Bob may have had other things on his mind. Uncharacteristically, he didn't seem to detect my discomfort at having to lie. "Sounds like a plan." He stood to signal I was being dismissed. "Byon probably told you we have some foreign visitors. They're prospective contributors to our God-given mission here. Zack invited them. That man is amazingly dedicated. It's a great blessing that he manages to

juggle our spiritual concerns with his practical responsibility to Goldberg Stanton. He's invited the visitors to supper tonight in my private
conference room, starting at six. I have about an hour's worth of work
to do here in the meantime, and then I'll give them a quick welcome
and turn it over to Zack before I go over to the dining hall to join the
rest of you. Sorry we can't chat longer."

As I walked to my apartment I reflected that all this was going to take
some sorting out. Reverend Bob's right hand man was up to serious
no good. Zack had invited some guys from the Middle East to
contribute? Give me a break. McLoughridge had been killed for over-
hearing one of them, Maloof, talk about being in the market for
tractors.

Mi-song had mentioned that Yu had surveillance equipment on
hand in case of need. When I got to my room I scribbled a note saying
we needed a listening device planted in Reverend Bob's private
dining room, right away. I inserted my note into a printed instruction
pamphlet, with a black and white drawing of a harmonica on the
front, and walked to the music classroom. Yu was there, as I'd
expected, practicing with some other students.

"You guys are going to have to go pro if you keep this up." That
got a chuckle out of them. I handed the pamphlet to Yu, the only
harmonica player in the group. "This may help you."

She thanked me and put it in her purse.

At six I took my seat in the dining hall. Yu, at another table,
nodded at me, just once. While we all waited for Reverend Bob to
arrive and say grace, Sable made the announcements. It was movie
night and the remake of the first installment of the *Left Behind* series
would be shown, with commentary by faculty members before and
after the showing. I had seen the original of that End Times thriller,
released in 2000, in which born-again Christians were suddenly
"raptured" — taken up to Heaven, their clothing left behind.

Sitting next to me was the theologian Lindsey Harrold. The elderly Texan and I struck up a conversation as we ate our supper. One thing he told me was that there was controversy over an issue of sequence. "The *Left Behind* view is that the Rapture will happen suddenly, before the Tribulation."

Although that was the first I'd heard about the theological debate on the issue, I understood when Lindsey explained. If the Rapture should happen first, that would spare the faithful from having to live on earth during the prophesied period of war, disaster, famine and disease that would wipe out the majority of the world's population in the run-up to the return of Christ.

"Johnny Posey pointed out, correctly, in his book *Gird Up Your Loins*, that the scriptures don't settle the timing question," Hal said. "The Posey view is that additional testing by the Tribulation before the Rapture is likely to be God's plan — and that Christians who buy into the more optimistic *Left Behind* version and count on being able to sit out the Tribulation from the comfortable vantage point of Heaven are cruising for a huge letdown."

He grinned. "Just between us, there's also the matter that the Poseys were somewhat bent out of shape when Tim LaHaye and Jerry Jenkins hit the bestseller lists with those books."

The difference of scriptural interpretation would be the focus of the evening's faculty commentary before and after the movie's showing. I'd been hearing from students about Tribulation — not the Christian version but in the context of a recent and horrible period in North Korean history. I was intrigued, but instead of staying for the movie program I went to the library and checked out a copy of *Gird Up Your Loins*. In addition to Johnny Posey's name in big letters on the jacket, I saw that Robert Posey's name was printed beneath it in smaller letters. He had contributed updated material for the latest edition. The back of the jacket featured a photo of the two of them together.

I took the book to my apartment and skimmed it all the way through, stopping to read certain parts carefully. Learning how the last days would play out according to the Poseys was a revelation, if not quite in the sense intended. This was a subject that Reverend Bob had become deeply interested in back in his Calvary Church days. I was fascinated to see how real-world events and trends before and since then had fit together to inform his and his father Johnny's fully developed theology.

Right after I put the book down, I heard a knock. I went to the door. It was Yu. Without coming in, she asked me in a low voice to meet her in Music Practice Room B. I waited a couple of minutes and headed over.

"This practice room has sound insulation and it's not bugged." Yu shut the door. "I did manage to plant a microphone in Dr. Posey's dining room before the meeting. Here is the recording."

"Let's listen together."

The recorded dinner session was another revelation. Reverend Bob welcomed the visitors, thanked them for coming such a long distance and expressed hope there could be mutual cooperation. "Please accept my apologies that I can't join you for the meal that our staff has just served. I hope you'll enjoy it. Thank you again."

The sounds of footsteps and a door closing followed. Adrenaline surged. My mental computer accelerated, rearranging information.

"The sound's really clear," I told Yu. "First class recording device."

"Japanese."

My concentration was total as we waited to hear what would come next. I had never been more attentive to an auditory experience. For a musician to say that is something.

Zack's tinny voice came through the speaker. "Let's wait a moment for the servers to finish." We heard the door closing again and Zack resumed talking. "The servers have left coffee, tea and dessert on the sideboard for us, so they will not need to return. We will not be disturbed. Please feel free to talk frankly."

A man with a guttural voice spoke up in heavily accented English. "We liked what we saw today during the factory tour, but we were simply double checking. After observing the missile launch test and the underground test of the nuclear warhead, we had already decided that your weapons would suffice to fry the enemy and season the dish with a cloud of mushroom."

He chuckled at his joke and so did one or two others in the room. I was appalled that anyone could so blatantly make light of mass destruction.

"Therefore we wish to go ahead with the purchase. Before we do, I would like to ask General Ri to go over the details of delivery so that we can be sure that all the arrangements are synchronized."

I hadn't known that Ri was on campus. A man translated for him, but the general referred the question to Zack.

"Thank you, General Khorsandi, for your question." Zack replied. "As I mentioned during the tour, the Posey organization is handling delivery so as to avoid detection by your enemies. Your shipment is waiting on the dock at the DPRK port of Nampo. After we send word in a few minutes that the deal is sealed, the cargo will be loaded overnight onto one of our aid ships, which is tied up at the dock. Our vessels call at Nampo often, bringing food, medicine and other relief goods, and always return empty except for water in the ballast tanks. General Ri's people will load your merchandise and adjust the volume of ballast water accordingly. The ship should have clear sailing tomorrow. The Posey organization's vessels are well and favorably known to the navies of the United States and its allies. They can enter the Persian Gulf without interdiction or special attention, having sailed there before. We would like to offload your cargo at Bandar Abbas at night, not leaving our ship in your port past dawn."

"Will your crewmen not have suspicions?" another questioner asked.

"The officers and key crew are trusted members of our organization, General Farahani. They follow orders. They have been told that what we are doing fits with the mission. We hired Filipino sailors who understood that they were signing on only for a one-way voyage to Myanmar. They were released in Yangon, told that the ship would be going into a repair yard for maintenance. For the remainder of the voyage here, and on to Iran, we replaced those men with North Korean crewmen supplied by General Ri."

"Excellent," said a new voice — also accented. "My clients were surprised that your organization was willing and eager to deal with us, in view of Dr. Posey's well publicized denunciations of Islam. But we all suppose you have your reasons. As for what might go wrong, I wish to personally thank General Ri for taking care of that busybody McLoughridge."

This must be Maloof, the Lebanese middleman.

"Are there any other snoops around that we should know about?" Maloof continued. "Frankly, I was concerned to see that you have American professors living so close to the factory. Any of them could be a U.S. spy."

"Your concern is quite understandable, Mr. Maloof," Zack said. "Our security has been close to flawless. One faculty member, a professor of English, caught wind of vague information about the existence of the other compound. But he has no means of communication — and no passport — so there has been no chance for him to share the information with anyone in the outside world."

We could hear grunts of approval, as Zack continued.

"General Ri's people checked him out and found he is by no means a spy. And what he knows has become useless because it is no longer a secret. From now the only secret we need to keep about the other compound is what the 'tractors' really are. And of course the factory tunnel is closely guarded and remains strictly off limits to anyone without clearance to enter. From your point of view we need to keep even that secret for only a short time, while you take delivery and make use of the product."

"The professor of English is the only one?" the Lebanese asked.

"Another American showed some curiosity about a different matter that doesn't concern you gentlemen. When I heard that Dr. Posey had an opening on his faculty I encouraged him to hire this fellow as a visiting music teacher. My thinking was that General Ri's people could keep a close eye on him here — and deal with him in due course. I assure you he has learned nothing and is no threat to you. Having met him, I can attest that he's a fool. You needn't worry."

General Ri, after hearing his aide's translation, offered his own brief assurance that everything was under control.

The guests had run out of questions, and Zack suggested everyone concentrate on supper. I thought he was being a smooth salesman. He could have simply lied that everything was perfect in the security arrangements, not mentioning Bartow and me. Probably he'd calculated that those Middle Eastern hard cases would be more likely to believe in near-perfection.

I, on the other hand, was not reassured by Zack's bland version of the non-threat I posed to their scheme. Unlike Toombs I still had my passport, and I had a phone. I even had a gun. But I assumed that number five of Ri's killers, the new driver, was on the way. Toombs! My colleague's name was too evocative. I felt a sepulchral chill as I contemplated the great likelihood that the cryptic prophecies I'd been reading earlier in the evening, prophecies interpreted as warnings that the end was near, applied literally to me.

"Pause the machine for a moment, please, while I think about something," I said to Yu.

I realized, looking back, that I should have figured out Zack's involvement right after interviewing him in Hong Kong. He hadn't told me "CDs" was a misreading. Once I'd realized Joe had meant to write "CDS," I should have smelled a rat. But Zack had done a good enough acting job, pretending he had to rack his brain to recall — dimly — his conversation with Joe. He'd fooled me into thinking he was just full of himself, as busy big shots often are.

Out loud I said, "The big question is why Zack Nodding would want to team up with North Korea's thuggish regime to sell nuclear missiles to some other thugs from the Islamic Republic of Iran. He had to have a huge reason to risk the world's richest investment bank *and* the biggest name in evangelical Christianity. Goldberg Stanton didn't need the money, and neither did the Posey organization, that's for sure."

Yu nodded.

"Besides," I said, "You heard Maloof, the Lebanese guy, allude to the fact that Dr. Posey has no use for Islam — has publicly denounced it as an 'evil religion.'"

"Maybe Mr. Nodding is a secret Muslim militant who was infiltrated into the Posey organization?" Yu ventured.

Tense as I felt, I had to laugh. "Like the way President Obama's opponents said he was a Muslim — and Reverend Bob chimed in on national TV to say he couldn't rule out the possibility? I don't think so."

"I was surprised to hear Mr. Nodding say that he had encouraged Dr. Posey to bring you to teach here, so they could watch you and 'deal' with you."

"So was I. I'd imagined it was all Reverend Bob's idea, and for only his reasons, the ones he gave me."

"Hearing that from Mr. Nodding, I started to wonder if Dr. Posey himself might be knowingly involved in the scheme. But that would not make sense — and, as we heard, he left the meeting at the very beginning."

"He sure did. Didn't stick around with those sleaze bags even long enough to say grace."

I had her turn the machine back on, but we already had the substance of the conversation. We were now hearing more chomping and slurping than talking. In a little while Zack dismissed the group. We heard squeaking sounds as they pulled their chairs out, footfalls as they exited and then silence.

I stood to leave. "We don't have all the evidence we need but it's time to get started carrying out our plan. I'm going to make a quick visit to the family camp while you give your boss a full report of what we've just learned. Please tell her I will draft the story and send the draft to my editor when I get back. Also, ask her to check out a Korean-American preacher named John Jae-ho Hyon. He serves on two boards with Nodding and I'm wondering if there's a connection with what's happening."

THE FACTORY COMPOUND almost certainly would be among the first targets of U.S. bombs once Washington learned about the nuclear arms export scheme. A passel of innocent Koreans including my cousins faced grave danger, and neither Mama nor I would forgive failure to warn them. Besides, for my story I needed more information about the factory.

It was darker than the night of my previous foray. A flashlight would give me away, so I imagined I was blind, closed my eyes and felt my way up and down the hill. I'd had some success with that technique a couple of times at my mountain place when I'd stayed out too late without a light. It worked as it had before, my few missteps from the path into the brush quickly corrected.

Once inside the factory camp, I found that the darkness was on my side. Maybe because there was no prayer meeting that evening, more people than before were out and about. It was hard to make out anyone's features, though, even within a foot or two, because only a few dim lights burned.

I walked into the residential tunnel and knocked on the door of the Pak family quarters. Surprised to see me, Shin-il hurriedly ushered me inside and locked the door. I set the bottle I'd brought on the table. He seemed in need of a drink, looking almost as haggard as Reverend Bob.

"How have you been?" I asked, as he opened the bottle and poured for us.

"Things are not so good. Our supervisors tell us we are doing a rotten job. The parts were supposed to be machined to extremely close tolerance but as we assembled them it was clear we had not managed to achieve the accuracy they demand. Last Friday we stopped work entirely and we haven't been called back to the factory since then. Daily criticism sessions in the cathedral have lasted all day and into the night. Everyone is exhausted. I just got back from today's session."

"What's their specific complaint?" This could be important.

"They told us, 'The tractors run backward, just like the first one our country's engineers put together soon after the liberation from Japan. Clearly your attitudes are wrong and you are not devoting yourselves to the *Juche* ideal.' Then they made us stand in the front of the room, one by one, and list our individual failures and those of our fellow work group members."

"Juche — that's the name for Kim Il-sung's ideology."

"It means what we Koreans do without depending on foreigners — our thing."

"*Cosa nostra.*"

"What?"

"That's a Sicilian term for our thing. Crime families around the world seem to think alike."

Shin-il didn't get my quip.

"So the 'tractors' don't work," I said. "If that's true, I hope the news gets out in time — and I hope Washington believes it."

"In time?"

"The 'tractor subassemblies' you and your friends are producing fit together to make nuclear-tipped missiles. As we speak, a consignment of them is being loaded onto one of the Posey aid ships at Nampo to be shipped to Iran. Are your tunnels set up as bomb shelters? If we don't play our cards right, this site is likely to be in the crosshairs of the U.S. military before you know it."

"Maybe that explains why they had us using stencils the other day to paint large Russian markings on the biggest subassemblies."

"Interesting. They try to think of everything, don't they. But still they've left too many loose ends. Those markings may fool someone for a while, but you should have protection. After all, you and I already know the missiles are North Korean made. It won't be long before that news will get out to the whole world." I didn't mention that it was my job to get that news out.

"The residential tunnel wasn't dug deep enough to serve as a bomb shelter. But the factory tunnel was, and so was the auditorium/cathedral tunnel, which is where we're directed to go in case of emergency."

"Be ready to run down there on short notice. Do you have any co-workers you can trust with what I'm telling you? People who won't lose their cool, who will act to save the people here?"

"There are several. Tomorrow is a special work holiday with no criticism session, and I can talk with them privately."

"Is the holiday on account of tomorrow night's church service?"

"If so, that's only part of the reason. They told us we have done such a poor job we should stay home and reflect on our inadequacy. It seems they are preparing to reorganize the factory."

———

We hadn't been talking more than two minutes when there was a knock on the door. Shin-il looked alarmed. He obviously wasn't expecting more company. He hushed me by putting a finger to his lips, but whoever was out there was not going away. We heard a key turning in the lock. It was an inward-opening door. Shin-il motioned for me to hide behind it as he moved to open it. "Ah, Comrade Ja," he said, affecting a yawn. "We were asleep already."

"No you weren't," came a deep, gruff voice. "You have an unauthorized visitor. I was behind him as he walked in. I went to my apartment to get my rifle. Put up your hands and move backward. Now, where is he?"

I pulled the revolver from my pocket and released the safety as the intruder closed the door. A very large woman, built like a pro wrestler and wearing people's clothing, spotted the bottle and two glasses on the table. Then, seeing me, she started to swivel her weapon toward me. Not waiting to see what would happen next, I aimed for the double portrait pin on her breast and fired. She fell without getting off a shot.

While I grabbed her rifle, which likewise had fallen to the floor, Shin-il knelt and examined her. "She's dead."

"Then so are we," Joung-ah exclaimed with a muffled cry as she joined us from the second room. She pressed her hands against her temples. But she was a woman thoroughly accustomed to danger and hardship. Pulling herself together quickly, she went to get rags to clean up the scene and a blanket to wrap the body. Thanks to the Russian designers of the revolver, the children hadn't awakened.

"Comrade Ja was a factory supervisor, party member, army veteran and reservist who served as hall monitor for this section of the residential tunnel," Shin-il told me. "Her apartment is three doors farther down."

"Anybody likely to miss her right away?"

"No, she was a widow — and she, too, was given tomorrow off."

"Maybe you'd better not wait till tomorrow to confide in those like-minded pals of yours."

"Right. The first thing for us to do, once everyone else is asleep, is get rid of the body."

"Hide her rifle — and any ammunition you can get from her pockets or her apartment — someplace where you can get to it easily. You may need it." I turned to go. "See you in church?"

"Yes. We are expected to attend the service."

It would be an understatement to say I was nervous as I left. If the authorities caught me in the factory compound, of course they'd find my gun and quickly learn what I'd just done. All the Swedish diplomatic representation in the world wouldn't save me from standing before a firing squad as a murderer and spy. The Pak family would be punished as accomplices. And all of Mi-song's and my efforts would come to naught.

In the end, my departure from the compound was as uneventful as it was stealthy. I'd been inside my apartment only a moment when Yu brought word that I should phone her boss, who was back in Pyongyang. I went to the practice room to make the call.

"My sources say loading is already under way at Nampo and the ship sails at dawn." Mi-song's calm voice belied the fact she was talking about a shipment of nuclear missiles that could set off wars in the Middle East and Korea — the Third World War, if the Americans and Russians started nuking each other.

"Were you able to find anything on John Hyon?"

"That was a good call on your part. I researched him on line, saw his photograph and recognized him as one of Kim Jong-il's unofficial offspring, another nephew of mine. Real name: Kim Song-chol."

"He went into the bastards' honor guard?"

"Yes, we were in spy training together. He was notable then for his baby face. When he graduated he went abroad immediately on behalf of the agency that General Ri now supervises. I never heard of him or from him until tonight. Working backward, I learned he was smuggled into South Korea and, with the help of local undercover agents, stole the identity of a dead eighteen-year-old named Hyon Jae-ho. With his native nationality thus laundered from North to South Korean, he emigrated to the United States, enrolled at Posey University's U.S. campus and studied for the ministry. It seems he was sent to become a mole within the evangelical Christian community in your country."

"I figure he may have served as go-between when his masters made their arrangements with the Posey organization."

"That seems likely. I suppose you are ready to start writing, while I attempt to flesh out the main strand of the story further?"

"I'm ready. Yu's recording of this evening's meeting is devastating evidence, just the sort of thing to convince people this nightmare is real. And I got some more information just now." I told her about the "backward tractors."

Fearful of the consequences if she were caught, I hated to ask for more — but I asked anyhow. "I doubt there will be stamped and sealed official documents available this soon to back up what I write. Please record any potentially incriminating conversation if you can."

I sat alone in my apartment drafting the piece on my laptop. In my nervousness, I realized, I'd forgotten to tell Mi-song about Comrade Ja. But adrenaline helped more than it hindered my labors to render a complex story succinctly.

Two hours later, expecting Mi-song's call, I went back to the practice room. She rang almost immediately. She'd gone to Kim Jong-un's office. Her recording device had been built into one high-heeled shoe so cleverly that she'd made it through the patting-down that even royal family members had to endure. It was her first time to use the shoe device; she'd saved it for a top-priority occasion.

Hugely relieved that she'd gotten out safely afterward, I focused as she played back the recorded conversation with her nephew. Her voice came through first.

"Here is the report I promised, pinning down the whereabouts of remnant members of the Jang Song-taek cabal who have avoided arrest for so long."

"Thank you," young Kim replied in a voice now familiar to me. "I'll read it and we'll put out a global dragnet tonight. You were right to bring this to me immediately instead of waiting for regular office hours. We don't want any of the traitor scum to escape."

"I shall leave you to read it, but before I go I must congratulate you in person on launching the ultimate move of the CDS exercise —

and also on having procured with my nephew Kim Song-chol's help the collaboration of the Posey organization and, particularly, of Mr. Nodding of Goldberg Stanton."

The tone of Kim's voice revealed that he was furious. "How did you find out?" he sputtered. "If you know, then others must know."

Her voice was soft and comforting. "My job is finding out about secrets."

"True, that is the job I gave you, and I cannot blame you." His voice took on an ominous tone. "It was General Ri's job to keep it absolutely secret."

He recovered the ebullience I remembered from our meetings. "You deserve credit for devising a great idea. This last act of the drama will be by far the most spectacular."

"With the export of nuclear missiles, I should think so."

"We are dealing with some militant Revolutionary Guards who opposed the nuclear agreement and were ecstatic when Washington backed out of it. This group is determined that Iran will deploy nuclear missiles at any cost. We're more than happy to facilitate that."

His gloating sickened me.

"Once they set them up, the news that Russian nukes are ready to launch from Iran against Israel will be leaked to Western news media. The design for the missiles was Russian in the first place. We have had them painted with large markings in the Cyrillic alphabet. U.S. satellite photography will spot those, validating the leak."

"Ah, I get it," said Mi-song. "At that point, Israel will begin final preparations to fire its own missiles and destroy not only the newly deployed missiles in Iran but also any infrastructure that could be used for Iranian nuclear development. Of course the country you are really focused on is Russia, because its economy is so much larger than Israel's or Iran's."

"Correct. Events will occur with lightning swiftness. The Western news media will report that the Ukraine episode and the U.S. election sabotage, in retrospect, were mere preliminaries to the main event that's now beginning. NATO will go on high alert and deploy troops and weapons. The U.S. and the Europeans will add exponentially to the economic sanctions already in place against Russia. They'll prepare blockades to choke off its economy. Putin, of course, will not sit still for that but will fuel his tanks for an adventure he's been eager to set out on, such as invading Baltic states. Pundits will warn that the Third World War may be beginning, with Russia and Iran shaping up as likely losers."

"I see where this is headed."

"Yes. Nodding has had his traders at Goldberg Stanton place nearly all of my CDS bets, most of them against Russian government bonds and the bonds of the biggest Russian companies. When those news stories hit, investors in a mad capitalist scramble will bid up the prices of the swaps I hold. I will collect my billions — a vastly larger payoff than you envisioned when you drafted the original scheme."

Her musical laughter came through the phone. "I can already hear the champagne corks popping in the palace."

"After my profits are in the financial pipeline — and before the Americans realize that the missiles were ours and punish us for selling them — my agents will leak additional news: We sold the missiles, *but* they are duds."

"Are they?"

"Of course. Do you imagine we'd have been so foolish as to entrust manufacture of our real nuclear missiles to a bunch of Christian dogs with no previous experience in the machinery industry? We're making the real ones for our own use elsewhere, at sites that are familiar to you. The One Eight Tractor Factory was designed like the other sites, and will be used to make real weapons eventually, but its initial function has been to assemble a shipment of missiles with a built-in design flaw for this Iran export deal."

"You had invited the Iranians to view a launch test of the missile and an underground test of the nuclear device."

"Those Iranians watched tests of the real ones. My engineers have observed Iranian rocket launches. They even obtained a copy of the Iranian launch manual, which sets forth the parameters. Knowing the procedures that will be followed, they assure me that if the Iranians try to fire off one of the defective ones they've bought it will suffer an electromechanical failure after launch."

"What does that entail?"

"All the massive sound, vibration and acceleration of the launch must be accounted for. Our engineers have developed a way to use those forces to disable the payload, even the rocket itself, by intentionally weakening the device so that a key part will shift or break free at the worst possible moment. This will at the very least make the device useless — and the shifting will affect the rocket's trajectory."

"Could it still fly all the way to Israel?"

"If Iranian launch control should fail to push the button for a command detonation first, in response to data showing the rocket was going out of control, the rocket would be expected to tear apart at the moment of maximum dynamic pressure, early in the flight."

"Tear apart!"

"Yes, there are a couple of ways this might happen. The payload while shifting could poke a hole in the shroud. Or it could produce a load that the rocket guidance system could not compensate for. In either case the rocket would break up over Iran, not far from the launch site. Its warhead, ripped apart by aerodynamic forces, would scatter radioactive material over a relatively small area of Iran. Most of the core would land in lumps."

"I take it that Nodding, like the Iranians, is completely in the dark about this engineered flaw."

"No American has been let in on the secret — yet. At just the right time, Washington will be tipped off that the missiles we sold were designed to fail. After confirming that fact, the American bastards once again will start to look at us in a different way."

"I suppose you have plans for mollifying Iran."

"Remember that we're dealing with an Iranian faction — not the government as a whole. The government should not mind too much. Even if it does object, our profits from the CDS scheme will be so vast it won't matter to us even if we can never sell another weapon to Iran."

"What about the Russians? Are they not likely to be seriously peeved?"

"They need us more than we need them. Gazprom is eager to build a pipeline across the DPRK to South Korea, and of course that's why the Russians have written off most of our Soviet-era debt to them. They're flirting with pariah-state status themselves, and cannot afford to alienate additional countries. Putin understands the need to make money — you probably saw the news reports when Obama was still in office saying the American bastards were going after his personal fortune, estimated to total forty to seventy billion dollars. And what if Russia does get upset at having been cast — only briefly, after all — as the villain? The Russian government and Russian corporations will not actually go bankrupt and default on their borrowings. They will simply look, for a short time, as if they were likely to default — just long enough for me to cash in on the CDS price rise. Look at it as payback time for us. The Russians since Stalin's death have been no better than fair-weather friends."

"Your grandfather certainly felt that way. So how will you spend all the loot from this enormous CDS haul?"

"To modernize and build up the military in support of the eventual armed liberation of the South from its puppet rulers, in case we fail in our current first-choice plan. Plan A, as you know, is to form a peace confederation with South Korea and use our superior political unity and propaganda skills to dominate the fractious and often naive Southerners. Not recognizing my intentions, the puppet masters in Washington will be so happy with the way I have stuck it to Iran that once again they will be ready to join us in direct talks toward a peace treaty. When the treaty is signed all U.S. troops will leave the peninsula, clearing the field for us."

"So it will not be long before you, like King Taejo starting in the year 936, will rule over a unified Korea — and thus you will achieve the dream that for decades eluded your grandfather and your father."

Mi-song must have been steaming — Kim had made no mention of using any of the windfall riches to feed the people. But she had kept up her sympathetic pose. She sounded convincingly obsequious. What an actress. "The generals and the people will be happy," she said. "Your reign will be a long one."

"I could not have summarized it better myself."

"I suppose you will have no further use for the Posey organization."

"I intend to play them along, let them keep the university — for a while. That will help us disarm the authorities in Washington."

"For a while?"

"Once the American troops are gone from the South, Posey Korea University will be closed down, the foreign faculty sent home. Swiftly and secretly, all the Korean Christians and Christian sympathizers who have been studying there or living in the factory complex will be sent to rot in prison camps."

"I assume that was the plan from the start. The difficult part must have been bringing Nodding's bank and the Posey shipping line into the plot."

"It was only after Comrade Song-chol devised the general outlines of this final act that he was able to approach Nodding and persuade him to go along with the program from the beginning of your proposed list. Then Nodding handled our bets timed to each provocation in sequence."

"I had wondered about that. The earlier provocations that I outlined for you were not designed to appeal to religious people's particular interests. I do not understand how this last one is, either."

"That's where Song-chol came in. He had studied with Nodding and other Christians under the Poseys and had spent his entire career interacting with them. Understanding their mind-set so well was what enabled him to devise a way to persuade Nodding to trade their help with the CDS and arms export scheme for our tolerance of their religion — tolerance in a limited sphere. I admit that I still don't quite get why they went along with us. After all, Song-chol is the one we assigned to spend all those years reading their Bible. But he assures me the transaction somehow goes to the very heart of their religious beliefs."

"Well played, indeed."

"Meanwhile, having the faulty missiles assembled by the students' family members was my own idea — presented to the American Christians as a means to assure ourselves that their side would not double-cross us. What we did not tell them was that the real purpose was to use the prospects of university studies and factory jobs to lure disloyal, religious-minded termites out of the woodwork and make sure they would never cause further trouble."

"Or as Mao Zedong put it: 'Let a Hundred Flowers Blossom.' Then plow them all under."

"Kim Il-sung was the author of the Hundred Flowers metaphor," young Kim replied frostily. "As with so many other great ideas that my grandfather originated, non-Koreans falsely attribute it to Mao. There has never been any need for us to borrow ideas from the Chinese or anyone else."

"Sorry. I must redouble my studies and refresh my understanding of Juche."

"If you had not volunteered so quickly to handle it on your own, I would have sent you for a year to a reeducation camp to carry out that very task. Meanwhile, it's undeniable that the Christians' factory skills are marginal. And the site where they are working cannot remain secret for much longer. If our timing should turn out to be off, conceivably the Americans could even bomb it before realizing the missiles are no threat."

"And save us the trouble of sending them to the camps," Mi-song exclaimed, in a tone that suggested she stood in awe of his brilliance.

He chuckled. "But assuming those workers survive the next few days, we'll sideline them to a simpler task. They will sew military uniforms for as long as we need to wait before we imprison them. They have been informed already in no uncertain terms that their work on 'tractor assemblies' is highly unsatisfactory."

I would have given my last bottle of bourbon for a chance to tear that smug son of a bitch apart. I got hold of myself, though. He was not to be underestimated. I had to acknowledge that the scheme wasn't totally crazy. A better description would be brilliant in a crazy way. Contrary to Father Paul's actuarial calculation, the kid might even be smart and quick enough to enjoy a long reign and die peacefully in bed — if the news I was about to send failed to get out, or even if the news did get out but somehow failed to dislodge him as Mi-song hoped it would.

I would need to be totally focused to deal with what was coming. My first precaution was to ask Mi-song and Yu to phone in their recordings to Lang in Hong Kong, right away, with notes saying I would be following up. We couldn't risk the chance that persons unknown would destroy or confiscate our main evidence before we could transmit the story.

Crossing the campus to return to my apartment, I passed the presidential office and apartment. The windows of both were dark. Considering his illness, Reverend Bob probably needed a good night's sleep. And what I needed to do was file what we had, get the editing process moving in Hong Kong. I'd talk to him the next day.

With young Kim's straight-from the-horse's-mouth corroboration and elaboration in hand, I rewrote the draft and my proposed headlines. Phoning Lang from the practice room, I dictated the story draft. More than once he gasped in amazement to hear details of the plot we'd uncovered.

N. KOREA SELLS DUD NUKES TO IRAN FACTION IN MULTI-BILLION-DOLLAR MARKETS SCAM

Evangelicals ship missiles to Revolutionary Guard; Goldberg Stanton trades derivatives for Kim Jong-un

By Heck Davis

An AsiaIntel investigation has revealed that an aid ship owned by an American religious group founded by the Rev. Johnny Posey is en route from North Korea to Iran carrying a cargo of medium-range nuclear-tipped missiles that the North Korean regime — knowing that the missiles are defective and will malfunction if launched — has sold to a militant Iranian faction.

The exporters painted Russian-language markings on the Russian-designed missiles. That was a ploy to shift the blame to Moscow, North Korean Supreme Leader Kim Jong-un acknowledged to another regime official in a palace conversation. AsiaIntel has obtained a recording of the conversation. [[LINK TO AUDIO & ENGLISH TRANSLATION]]

In the conversation Kim Jong-un boasted that he had plotted to create an international crisis that would undermine the creditworthiness of Russian government and corporate bonds, so that he could cash in via trading in financial derivatives called credit default swaps.

Aiding Kim in the scheme, he acknowledged, is Zacchaeus J. Nodding, who is both Asia chief of the investment bank Goldberg Stanton and vice-chairman of the Johnny Posey Evangelistic Mission Board. . . .

━━━

Lang's newsman blood was up. He said he'd check the piece, run it past AsiaIntel's lawyers and get back to me with questions. He planned to release the story the morning after next, which I thought was just right.

I'd need that much time to plug holes. The tentative schedule would give Goldberg Stanton traders working for Zack Nodding another day in which to sink any remaining unallocated North Korean money into Russian CDS positions. The ship would have time to reach the open sea, where the U.S. Navy could interdict it.

Also benefiting from the schedule could be some of us who fit Mi-song's description of mere individuals whose fate didn't matter all that much under the earth-shaking circumstances. Shin-il — assuming he hadn't been caught while hiding Comrade Ja's body — would have the day to organize his buddies. Mi-song, I hoped, would position herself outside Kim's grasp. And Yu would have a little time to look for an alternate way to get me the hell out of Dodge, now that Ri's newly assigned assassin almost certainly would be the one driving the university van.

20 / WHAT IF IT WERE TODAY?

SAYING GRACE THE NEXT MORNING, Reverend Bob asked God to "bless the food to the nourishment of our earthly bodies on this uniquely special day." Then he left hastily, once again carrying his breakfast in a takeout box.

Sable, making the day's announcements, explained that he was closeting himself somewhere outside the campus for the day to put the finishing touches on his sermon. "Of course you'll all see him at the service."

She sat down at our table and Darley Scratch spoke to her. "I want to pass along one more idea to Dr. Posey for tonight's sermon."

"Sorry but I have no idea where he is, Darley." She smiled. "If he told us, it wouldn't be a hideout, would it?"

My plan was to make my own escape only after leading the singing at the service as scheduled. The evening's event would be my chance not only to talk with Reverend Bob but also to warn Shin-il and Joung-ah about Kim's intention to send them and others to the gulag. Then they could get the word out. The students and their families could respond accordingly. I didn't dare go over to see them in broad daylight, especially after what had happened the night before.

I devoted the day's class time to preparing the music. That required an effort intense enough to provide welcome distraction from stress that more than once threatened to get the better of me.

The special service's program of worship called for us to lead off with the Posey organization's trademark hymn:

> *Lo, He comes with clouds descending*
> *Once for favored sinners slain;*
> *Thousand thousand saints attending*
> *Swell the triumph of His train:*
> *Alleluia, Alleluia!*
> *God appears on earth to reign.*

Then, just before the sermon, the congregation would sing another hymn with a closely related theme:

> *Jesus is coming to earth again.*
> *What if it were today?*
> *Coming in power and love to reign,*
> *What if it were today?*

"What If It Were Today?" had been published in 1912 but it was new to the students. We ran through it several times to get it down.

I'd always had a thing about the need to understand lyrics' meaning in order to sing with the appropriate attitude. Yeah, it's disappointing that not only The Who and Moody Blues but even true greats Ray Charles and Aretha Franklin performed Coca-Cola jingles. But to my ear the superstars when singing about a sweet fizzy drink didn't invest their performances with the totality of the sacred power of their artistry.

I was pondering that second hymn when it occurred to me to say to the students, "Here's a mental exercise. How would you feel if the End Times were upon us? What if it really *were* today."

There was silence, at first. But my students' shyness had dwindled during the time I'd been teaching them. Some of them had started to volunteer observations during class – usually slipping into Korean when they had complex sentiments to express, which I thought was OK at that stage of their English training. So it was that, before the silence could become uncomfortable, one especially articulate woman spoke up to critique the second hymn's focus: "I hope it isn't today, or tomorrow, or even in this century. I don't think many among us are ready for that. We have it pretty good here, for the first time since we were born, and a lot of us are in no hurry to give up our earthly lives."

"Anybody else want to talk about that?"

A male student in his twenties chimed in. "Dr. Posey keeps preaching about the Great Tribulation he tells us will precede the Second Coming of Jesus. Most of us are old enough to have experienced the DPRK's national March of Tribulation. After coming out of that horrible period only to slip back into something not much better, we volunteered to move here because we looked forward to living in peace and getting enough to eat. If entering the End Times means that all of us — or at least those among us who aren't quite as repentant, or faithful to Jesus, as we should be — have to suffer even worse, I say put it off for as long as possible."

Some others spoke up to agree. Only one student — Ms. Namkung, the campus's serial public penitent — proclaimed that Jesus couldn't come back too soon to suit her.

Next we ran through the night's invitation hymn, which the congregation would sing after Reverend Bob had warned that those who were not right with God had better accept salvation. *And that means you, Heck Davis.*

OK, I knew it wasn't Reverend Bob's style to single me out by name. But I sensed that giving me another chance at salvation could have been one reason he'd made sure, by asking me to lead the music, that I would attend services. He wanted to cancel out that debit in his ledger with a new credit if possible. I found it affecting to think he still cared.

The students were almost as familiar as I was with "Just As I Am," but to be on the safe side we sang it one time, all the way through verse six:

> *Just as I am, poor, wretched, blind;*
> *Sight, riches, healing of the mind,*
> *Yea, all I need in Thee to find,*
> *O Lamb of God, I come! I come!*

I dismissed most of the students early but kept back a small group, basically the ensemble I'd taken to the villa, and we practiced "Saints" for the rest of the allotted time. Then, in the afternoon, I phoned Lang.

"We've got problems, Heck. Your draft doesn't sufficiently explain the motivation for Nodding to participate in the scam. Is he personally making enough money out of it to justify the risks he's taking? More importantly, the story blames two huge, powerful organizations and our lawyers want more evidence. Those guys you're writing about have deep pockets. They can pay their lawyers to sue us for libel till kingdom come. Meanwhile, we go bankrupt."

"I knew I needed to give you more. I'm still working the story but I wanted to file last night to let you have something to work with, then fill all holes later."

"That might have worked out, under other circumstances, but the really bad news is the new publisher, a Hong Kong Chinese bean counter. Ever since his appointment a few weeks ago, he's been complaining on a daily basis that this story or that story would offend Beijing. The lawyers' red flag made the publisher happy for reasons of his own. He keeps quoting Mao as having said China and North Korea are 'as close as lips and teeth.' He wants me to spike your story."

"Oh, man."

"Yeah. It's the last straw for me with this publisher. I'm about ready to resign. But before I do, is there any way we can nail the story down tighter so the lawyers can pass it and the publisher won't have their objections to hide behind? If you can do that, I'll put it up on the site regardless of his instructions and take the heat *after* the rest of the media pick up the news."

"I'm positive I know the answer to your first big question, on motivation, and I expect to have enough evidence to plug that hole by the end of the day."

"OK, but what about the reverend's place in the story? Robert Posey is the association's president, and has his family name on it, yet we don't have a comment from him. Of course we need to give him a chance to respond, make sure we don't tar him with guilt by association. Looks to me like the conspiracy could boil down to the dealings of a rogue banker who happens to be on Posey's board and is using the association for logistics and cover, taking advantage of Posey's trust."

"Reverend Bob's been unavailable for comment, but I'll see him tonight for sure. Stand by for his statement and the rest of what you need to fill those holes."

━━━

I met with Yu to check signals. The visiting Middle Eastern delegation and Nodding had left for Dandong early that morning in the van — the old driver's last trip. Nodding had wanted to get back to Hong Kong that same night. Ri had left in a separate car, for

Pyongyang. Yu asked if I had any experience operating motorcycles.

"You bet."

"Then your escape vehicle is a two-wheeler. To get a start on Ri's new assassin, we'll need to leave right after you've finished essential business here and at the family compound. We need to have you out of the country before he can catch up with you."

Otherwise I was dead meat, as I knew but didn't say.

⊏⊐

The students formed up to hike over to the faculty compound. I thought about how close I'd gotten to quite a few of them — and how precarious their futures looked now that I had learned of Kim Jong-un's intentions.

My story — assuming I could do enough additional reporting tonight to finish documenting it, and assuming Lang could upload it to the site despite the publisher's objections — might prompt Kim to speed up his plans. He might decide to truck the students and their families off right away to the living hell of the labor camps.

On the other hand, American bombs could start falling on the factory compound if everything didn't go according to either my scenario or Kim's. The students might be staying with their parents and siblings by then. Even running into the deeper factory and church tunnels might not save them if the Americans used smart bombs.

I gritted my teeth as we faculty members boarded a bus to take us from the university parking lot via an outside road. Tonight was the key.

The factory compound's front gate proved to be as tightly guarded as our own. Alighting from the bus and reaching the church tunnel, we joined the students and walked down a steep, spiraling ramp for ten minutes or so.

Knowing this could be my last night alive, I wanted to savor each moment. Darley Scratch was beside me. In manic fashion — no doubt inspired by my conversation with Yu — I observed, "It's OK walking down, but coming back up wouldn't you rather have two wheels and a big V-twin under you?" That got a wide, toothy grin out of the coach.

At several points we passed through doorways where massive double doors — obviously constructed to provide tight seals — had been left open for us. As we got closer we could hear the organist playing the processional, an arrangement of "Onward Christian Soldiers" that was even more martial than usual. By the time we entered the sanctuary, the sound was deafening. The organist surely was pulling out all the stops; you could have closed your eyes and imagined yourself in the midst of a stupendous cosmic battle.

And what a sight the cathedral was: a commodious chamber hewn out of solid rock, its walls and high ceiling covered with huge slogans and pictures exhorting the faithful to prepare for the final struggle with Satan and for Christ's return — all painted in the garish style of North Korean propaganda posters. The painter must have enjoyed a previous career as a socialist-realist artist working for the regime.

I imagined the cathedral decor might represent a consciously ironic turning of tables. After all, the North Korean regime's visual propaganda style, as I'd read somewhere, owed much to the Christian Sunday school literature that Kim Il-sung had studied as a boy.

My student choristers filed into the choir loft, which overlooked the pulpit and the gigantic pipe organ. Behind them was a glass-fronted baptismal pool. It was full. The water looked clear and fresh. Apparently Reverend Bob planned to dunk any converts without delay.

On the stone wall behind the pool was painted a giant cross on which Jesus was depicted as a determined-looking, square-jawed worker straight out of a poster designed to whip the masses into a frenzy of overproduction. With the exception of the pipe organ, the fittings and furniture — including pews and pulpit — were simple and didn't appear to have cost a huge amount. Still the effect was spectacular.

I was relieved to spot Shin-il sitting at the center aisle end of a pew, Joung-ah next to him. He and his pals must have succeeded in hiding Comrade Ja's body. We pretended not to know each other.

I led the congregation in the first hymn, singing into a microphone and backed by the choir. Reverend Bob prayed for blessings on this very special, momentous occasion. Then, putting on his reading glasses, he read — as Darley had done during his turn in the campus pulpit — from Ezekiel's prophecy about a great attack on God's chosen people by combined forces of enemy countries, with Magog and Persia in the lead.

This was going just as I'd expected based on my reading of *Gird Up Your Loins* the night before.

" 'And thou shalt come from thy place out of the north parts. And thou shalt come up against my people of Israel, as a cloud to cover the land,' " Reverend Bob intoned, quoting the prophet's channeling of Jehovah's warning to Prince Gog of Magog. " 'Surely in that day there shall be a great shaking.' "

"Amen!" Darley Scratch shouted.

" 'And I will plead against him with pestilence and with blood; and I will rain upon him, and upon his bands, and upon the many people that are with him, an overflowing rain, and great hailstones, fire and brimstone.' "

"Amen," shouted Darley, along with two or three other congregants seated near him in the front of the room and to my left.

" 'I will give thee unto the ravenous birds of every sort, and to the beasts of the field to be devoured. Thou shalt fall upon the open field, for I have spoken it, saith the Lord God. And I will send a fire on Magog and they shall know that I am the Lord. So will I make my holy name known.' "

More amens followed, and the singing of the second hymn. Then Reverend Bob launched into his sermon. "What if it really *is* today?" he began — just as I had anticipated. "There are vital reasons why we must ponder this question, right now, today, and that's why I asked you all to come here." He paused, as he had done while reading the scripture, to let a Korean interpreter translate. When she had finished, he coughed and resumed speaking.

"Sending his only begotten son to the earth, the almighty God offered his kingdom to any and all who would accept it. It has been two thousand years since the Lord made that offer, and still most of mankind has been too stubborn to accept it."

"Tell 'em, brother!" Darley shouted.

Reverend Bob smiled thinly and continued. "Jesus knew rejection. In fact, he expected it. He knew that even many who thought they were listening to his words did not really listen. They didn't pay attention when he said, as recounted in Matthew 10:34, that he had *not* come to bring peace to the world — he had come with a *sword*."

A chorus of loud amens issued from Darley, Sable and Ezra, all of whom were nodding in emphatic agreement. Shirley, who was seated with them, wearing light makeup for the occasion, failed to match her parents' enthusiasm. In fact she looked downright bored. Goodness and Mercy hadn't followed them down to the cathedral — they must be upstairs in the family tunnel with the other young children.

"But didn't Isaiah say the coming messiah would be called 'Prince of Peace'? Yes, he did, but you have to read carefully what the prophet says in that verse, Isaiah 9:6. 'For unto us a child is born, unto us a son is given, and the government shall be upon his shoulder. And his name shall be called Wonderful, Counselor, the mighty God, the everlasting Father, the Prince of Peace.' "

When he paused, I heard more amens and saw more heads bobbing.

"Only the first of those conditions has been fulfilled. The child Jesus was born on earth; the son was given. Jesus won't be called Prince of Peace until the government is on his shoulder. Only *then*, as we learn in chapters 19 and 20 of the book of Revelation, will Jesus rule the earth. *Then* shall his name be called Prince of Peace!"

Reverend Bob's pause this time was longer than required for a translator to render his words in Korean. He dabbed at his mouth with a handkerchief before resuming. The amen corner was quiet — maybe out of concern for the preacher, who looked unwell.

"Bible prophecy foretells two great battles for control of the earth. Those will be the battle of Gog and Magog and the final battle of Armageddon. The two great battles will be at or near the beginning and the end, respectively, of the seven years of Tribulation." He paused again for more mouth dabbing.

"The signs that the prophets pointed to are now all in place. The Temple in Jerusalem is being rebuilt as we speak. Red heifers are being born in Israel. There is nothing left but for Israel's enemies — Gog and Magog, Persia and so on — to do their part."

"Yes, Lord!" cried Lindsey Harrold. The normally staid old theologian was starting to get into the spirit of the occasion.

"What does this mean?" Reverend Bob asked rhetorically. "The scriptures are clear that it means the patience of Almighty God is exhausted and he is ready to judge the sinful of the earth and show his glory to all human beings, the saved and the unsaved alike."

"Amen!" Darley Scratch shouted louder than before. Ezra Pugmire seconded the motion.

"Reading the descriptions in the Bible," Reverend Bob preached, "we see that the coming warfare will employ horrific weapons of mass destruction."

A chill went down my spine. *Here it comes.* I reached into a jacket pocket and felt to make sure the recorder was still switched on.

Reverend Bob dabbed his mouth again before continuing. "The book of Revelation says, 'The fourth angel poured out his vial upon the sun, and power was given unto him to scorch men with fire. By these three was the third part of men killed — by the fire, and by the smoke, and by the brimstone.'"

"We trust in thy wisdom, Lord!" Darley Scratch shouted.

"The prophet Zechariah tells us that Armageddon 'shall be the plague wherewith the Lord will smite all the people that have fought against Jerusalem; their flesh shall consume away while they stand upon their feet, and their eyes shall consume away in their holes, and their tongue shall consume away in their mouth.' "

Reverend Bob's face consumed away into a scary mask.

"The prophets who foresaw that future for us had never heard of today's nuclear, chemical and biological weapons, but they described with perfect accuracy the effects of such weapons."

Ms. Namkung got into sync with Darley and company by shouting "Yes, Lord!" in Korean from the choir loft. No other Koreans appeared really pumped. Reverend Bob didn't seem to notice. He just continued on, coughing more often, his voice becoming raw.

"Ezekiel tells us that enemies of Israel involved in the first battle will include the land of Magog led by the prince called Gog. We know that those are code words for what is now Russia and its ruler. President Ronald Reagan knew that biblical truth. Ezekiel tells us that Persia is also involved. Persia is the old name of Iran. Surely you all know that for quite a while a huge argument has raged over how much time will pass before that country turns itself into a nuclear weapons state, with or without international agreements, sanctions and so on. I have prayed over this. Today I can tell you that the matter is no longer subject to dispute. Persia is within a few days of playing its prophesied role, using Russian-designed nuclear missiles."

I glanced behind me at Yu with a questioning look. I wanted backup. She nodded toward her handbag, a signal that her own recorder was running.

"Israel already has its own nukes," Reverend Bob said. "God's will be done. By the end of the two battles, all the works of man will be destroyed. Will the world end then? No. Rather, as Peter tells us in his second epistle, it will be remade by holy fire."

He turned to me and nodded. Playing guitar, I sang about the saints who'd go marching in when the sun refused to shine and the moon turned to blood. The students of the ensemble did me proud — particularly Yu on harmonica. It was a shame I wouldn't be able to work with them after that night.

Reverend Bob resumed preaching, launching into his altar call: "Sin and human failure have horribly tainted the world as it is now. The earth must be returned to the pristine state that Adam and Eve found when God created them in his image and placed them in the Garden of Eden. Then Christ will reign over human beings, who will lead sin-free lives for a thousand years under his perfect system of government."

"Come, precious Lord," Darley interjected.

"His return will be a great comfort to true Christians. Nonbelievers make fun of us. In the final judgment the tables will be turned; we believers will be vindicated. The nonbelievers will choke on their laughter in the face of the horrible wrath of God."

I looked at Reverend Bob's face during the translation. Although his preaching was not especially powerful — to tell the truth, it was on the tedious side — he looked mighty pleased with himself. His eyes wide and unfocused, he gazed out over the congregation, toward the invisible hills and mountains beyond, in a fair approximation of the look for which his far more eloquent and charismatic father had been famous in his preaching days.

At the same time I had to note that he appeared more than slightly unhinged. His mouth was twisted. Spittle had formed around his lips, but he didn't wipe it away with his handkerchief.

"What about you?" he inevitably asked. "Where do you stand? When the trumpet sounds its call, when the new world is revealed, will you be one of the saints privileged to march in?"

Some people were fidgeting. The message was so overpowering, so challenging to the worldly hopes and dreams of even the most faithful, that it was sorely testing Reverend Bob's delivery capabilities. It seemed he had actually begun to bore people, if not turn them off.

"You won't be in that number if you haven't accepted God's offer, if you haven't confessed your faith in Jesus Christ, letting him wash you clean. You won't be in that number if you were once right with

God but fell from grace and fail to get right with him again before it's too late."

Damned if he didn't look briefly over at me as he said that. Then, without pausing for translation, he thundered on to the climax.

"Do you really want to be left behind, left outside? Revelation tells us, 'Outside are the dogs and the sorcerers and the immoral persons and the murderers and the idolaters, and everyone who loves and practices lying.' "

A student just behind me in the choir loft whispered to her companion, "Coach's preaching is better." Reverend Bob didn't hear the remark. I couldn't tell whether he sensed that he wasn't getting through.

"I can't make the choice for you. God won't make it for you. If you have not made that choice, make it now. Come down the aisle and throw yourself on the mercy of the Lord as we sing the invitation hymn."

He nodded at me, my cue to be ready to start "Just As I Am" at the conclusion of the translation.

I turned on my microphone. When the time came I stood. Instead of singing, I spoke: "Reverend Bob, I always admired and loved you, and I deeply appreciate your concern for all our souls, so it pains me to have to point out that you are perpetrating a fraud."

I stopped for the translator and saw that my first words had shocked the English speakers in the congregation. Darley Scratch, looking somewhere between outraged and confused, spoke up. "Where are you headed with this, Heck?"

I couldn't come out and explain, at that point, that I needed more details to be confirmed in the preacher's voice while Yu and I recorded, so I continued speaking to Reverend Bob: "Russian-designed, Russian-marked nuclear weapons are on the way to 'Persia.' But it was not through communing with God, as you implied, that you learned about that. You and your organization are the ones who are sending them, and those nukes are in fact put together from the 'tractor subassemblies' that you've had these good people manufacturing in the next tunnel. You not only look forward to the Tribulation, the final battles and the Second Coming; you can't wait. You're determined to make them happen right now."

The Koreans in the congregation were listening carefully to the translation coming through their earphones, and the expressions on some of their faces suggested they understood what I was saying.

"You and Zack Nodding are helping the North Korean ruler make huge profits so he'll play his part in your scheme."

Lindsey Harrold pulled himself up straight. "Sit down, Heck. We all thought you had a good mind, but it turns out there's nothing in the attic but cobwebs."

"Zack is brokering a fraud scheme that involves investing through his bank in financial instruments called credit default swaps."

"Can you prove that?"

"I can."

Reverend Bob marched over and tried to wrest the microphone from my grip. No longer the man he'd once been, he was no match for me. Desperate, he spun around to face the choir. "Sing!"

Dumbfounded, the choir remained silent, as if the lamb had opened the seventh seal.

"I said SING!"

Only Ms. Namkung obeyed: She didn't have much of a voice, and faltered and stopped after a couple of bars of "Just As I Am."

I kept talking, addressing Harrold and Scratch. "I have a recording of the meeting in Dr. Posey's private dining room last night with Iranian generals, a Lebanese arms merchant middle man and General Ri of the DPRK People's Army. The scheme is laid out there." I turned to Reverend Bob. "I can play it back for you if you want."

He shook his head, as the translator did her work.

"You and Nodding planned for the North Koreans to supply the weapons that 'Persia,' allied with other Islamic forces, would deploy to attack Israel and start the battle of Gog and Magog. Meanwhile you would pass those weapons off as Russian so you could implicate the country you identify as Magog as the aggressive facilitator."

Sable Pugmire spoke up from her front pew. "Heck has made some extremely serious allegations, Dr. Posey. I'm sure you have a response and I think we all need to hear it."

"Yes, please answer the charges, Bob," Lindsey Harrold said.

Reverend Bob returned to his pulpit and used his own microphone to answer. "I — we — did those things, for God," he croaked. "It's altogether right and proper for the Lord's people to help his plan along. The Lord helps those who help themselves."

Lindsey Harrold looked stunned. "There's nothing in the pages of the Bible to justify such actions, Bob. You're presuming to decide God's timing, and Matthew tells us that Jesus specifically warned against that. 'But of that day and hour knoweth no man; no, not the angels of heaven, but my Father only.' "

"I have not violated Christ's admonition by presuming to specify the *precise* time."

Darley Scratch seemed to be struggling to make sense of things while Bartow Toombs smiled his thin smile as his clever mind sorted through what he had heard.

Toombs spoke. "You're talking like a lawyer, not a pastor, Dr. Posey. Sooner or later somebody — whether mortal intelligence agents working for the CIA or the angelic operatives of a heavenly spy network — would have figured out your trick. You must have realized it would be clear then that if any country fit the role of Magog, enemy of God's chosen people, that would be North Korea."

Harrold picked up the attack. "Yes. If I understand correctly you've shipped those weapons — in Ezekiel's words — 'from the north parts.' It's impossible that you would fail to realize you risk bringing down terrible retaliation upon this country — not by the almighty God, who wouldn't be fooled about the origin for an instant, but by the mighty enough United States. Were you really willing to sacrifice the lives of untold numbers of North Koreans, starting with the people here who made the weapons, and their children studying in your university? I'm deeply grieved to have to say that, from what I've heard, it seems that way."

———

I couldn't help reflecting — not for the first time — that Reverend Bob's plan for the evening clearly had been to save as many souls as he could before the fires came. It was possible to see that as a kindness, of the sort that had contributed to making him an admirable man and teacher. On the other hand, I couldn't help feeling that such sincere concern for the smaller picture, when set off against the enormity of the overall catastrophe he planned, called his sanity into question. Was he simply an example of the extent to which religion can drive a certain type of believer to extreme behavior? Or was the man stark, raving mad? Hard for me to decide; I was too close to the situation.

Either way, I would have preferred to think that this was a recent phenomenon — that, late in his life, he had somehow slipped over the edge. But I couldn't be sure he hadn't been that way all along and managed to hide it, from me and from others. Incidents from the past, especially the reported self-crucifixion I'd heard about from Father Paul, came back to my mind.

Regardless, I realized that I was feeling in my gut an ineffable sense of personal loss. As Fatback Hawkins had once remarked, "Nothin' worse than a preacher gone bad."

I kept those thoughts to myself as Reverend Bob put on his reading glasses and bent over to consult his Bible.

Darley, whose own preaching suggested he wasn't always able to distinguish between pious and loony, found his voice and stood to defend Reverend Bob. "Let's not be too quick to draw conclusions. 'Judge not, that ye be not judged.'"

Reverend Bob continued poring over the printed scriptures.

The confrontation between us wasn't over. I had more to say: "What you didn't know, Reverend Bob, is that the missiles are duds, and the North Korean authorities planned it that way. Let me ask the people who work in the factory: What have your supervisors been telling you about the 'tractors' you're supposed to be helping to assemble?"

Shin-il listened to the translation, then shouted, "The 'tractors' run backward. They're no good!" Several men seated near Shin-il, and then Koreans from other parts of the congregation, joined the chorus: "That's right! They don't work."

I spoke again. "General Ri and his boss, Kim Jong-un, have double-crossed you, Reverend Bob. They want money, all right, and they get it — from the missile sales and even more so from that financial markets scam your right-hand man is helping them carry out. But even though they proclaim that North Korea is a 'nuclear power' they know they're not ready for the United States to come after them with everything it has."

Reverend Bob looked up from his Bible, his eyes wild, as I continued speaking.

"Meanwhile, I have learned from an impeccable source that they plan in due course to shut down Posey Korea University and send all of this flock to rot in prison camps. You provided the bait that lured these refugees back into the country. Whether you knew it or not, their fate is to be sent to the gulag. That's what Kim Jong-un had in mind all along."

I had needed to get that said, to warn the Koreans.

Startled, Reverend Bob grasped both sides of the pulpit. A buzzing erupted in the congregation as the translator relayed my remarks to the shocked and frightened Koreans.

At that moment a Korean man in people's clothing rushed through the tunnel door and ran down the cathedral's center aisle, pointing a handgun in my direction. *Of course* the plainclothes security detail, up in the guard house with a listening device, would have sent someone down when I started talking about nuclear weapons being made at the site. And by the time he got down that long passage he and his colleagues were able to hear me commit a far worse North Korean sin, taking the ruler's name in vain. No doubt reinforcements were assembling upstairs.

I reached for my pocketed revolver. Before I could extract it, Shin-il and some other Korean men seated on the aisle grabbed the security man and wrestled him for his weapon. It discharged into the cop's belly. He fell.

Just then the entire cathedral began to sway as if it were a porch swing. "Jesus Christ!" My irreverent cry was lost in the general hubbub. The lights went out. One by one, the students switched on their flashlights. Turning, I saw the illuminated organ. Its pipes vibrated; some bent as I watched. Waves formed in the baptismal pool, sloshing over the edge. People who had been leaning forward slid off their pews onto the floor.

The swaying continued, left and right, increasing in intensity. It turned into lurching, and then things got out of control. Ms. Namkung screamed, in Korean, "Come, Lord Jesus!" Others panicked and joined her in yelling. Some attempted to maintain calm.

As the shaking started to subside, parents including the Paks and the Pugmires moved stumblingly toward the exit to check on the young children they'd left under adult supervision in the residential tunnel. I signaled Yu to go in the same direction to phone in her recording, which contained everything Lang would need for filling the holes in the story.

The microphones were dead but I raised my voice. In English and then Korean I said it appeared we had experienced an earthquake. I advised those with no urgent business above to stay. Since we were in what had been built as a bomb shelter, we should be relatively safe below. Ezra and Sable conferred at the tunnel entrance; she turned back while he headed up. Shin-il, along with a co-worker who carried the dead security man's pistol, continued upstairs while

Joung-ah remained behind. Before reclaiming her seat she covered the security man's body with her coat.

I reached down and, by feel, released the safety on my revolver, to be prepared if more security men should come down. Then I checked to make sure my recorder, in a different pocket, was still running in case Reverend Bob might say anything else of importance. For the moment he was silent as he stood at the pulpit, leafing through his Bible.

The upstairs contingent had been gone for just a few minutes, and small groups of congregants were standing around talking excitedly, when the earth moved again — an aftershock almost as strong as the first shock.

"You see!" Reverend Bob exulted. "As prophesied, the sin-cursed earth is screaming. 'The whole creation groaneth and travaileth in pain.' Romans 8:22. The great war is starting!" Even without a microphone his husky voice carried. The three Korean interpreters who'd taken turns translating the proceedings were no longer in their booth. The two who hadn't rushed upstairs translated Reverend Bob's words for knots of congregants.

"Not likely," I said. "If this isn't a standard earthquake, maybe Mount Paektu has erupted on account of the nuclear testing"

Reverend Bob started reading aloud from Psalm 59. " 'The mighty are gathered against me, not for my transgression nor for my sin, O Lord.' " He coughed and wiped his mouth. " 'Visit all the heathen; be not merciful to any wicked transgressors.' "

People stopped their conversations and turned to look at him as he raised his voice to a scream. " 'They return at evening; they make a noise like a dog and go round about the city! Behold, they belch out with their mouth; swords are in their lips. For who, say they, doth hear? But thou, O Lord, shalt laugh at them; thou shalt have all the heathen in derision.' "

He looked over at me. There was hatred in his eyes and in his twisted mouth. " 'God shall let me see my desire upon mine enemies. Slay them now, lest my people forget; scatter them by thy power and bring them down, O Lord our shield. For the sin of their mouth and the words of their lips' . . ."

He stopped reading, looked at me again and shouted, "Who are you, Heck Davis, to question the motives of a man of God? You're worse than a heathen. You're a heretic. Worse still, you're an apostate!"

I couldn't help reflecting that, for better or worse, he no longer saw me as a pleaser. "You didn't finish reading that last verse, Reverend Bob. I happen to recall the line that follows and I'll recite it for you: 'Let them even be taken in their pride.' "

Lindsey Harrold, who had remained seated, nodded thoughtfully as he asked, "Is that what it's all about, Bob? Your pride?"

Reverend Bob frowned. Ignoring the professor's question, he bellowed at me: "Look to *your* sins. There's not much time left before it's too late."

I realized I'd done, that evening, what I had to do. Not wanting to kick a man when he was down, I let his last remark go unanswered. Bartow Toombs glanced at me with what I took to be a sympathetic expression. Reverend Bob sputtered, looking frantically to the rest of the congregation for support. No rescuer appeared.

Instead, Lindsey Harrold directed a question to me: "What do you imagine are the chances that Bob's blasphemous dream — the world's nightmare — will be fulfilled?"

I didn't know whether Yu had managed to phone in the new material — or, if she had, whether the AsiaIntel publisher would persist in blocking publication. I needed to give an honest answer, but one that wouldn't discourage them to the point of inaction.

"Much of my working experience is as a newsman, as Reverend Bob and some of the rest of you know, and I've done my best to see to it that what you've heard here tonight will go out tomorrow to everybody on earth who cares to know. If that effort succeeds, I hope international society will put the quietus on the various schemes. But that's a best-case scenario. All of us ought to be prepared for sudden changes, which I can't predict."

Most of those remaining in the congregation looked at Reverend Bob, some whispering among themselves. As they waited for his response, a fit of coughing seized him. Maybe it was a result of the movements of the earth; maybe it was his late-stage cancer's delayed reaction to the pressure that all that preaching had put on his throat and vocal cords. Then again, hearing that his grand scheme might be going for naught could have been the signal for his body to follow.

Blood spewed from his mouth. He collapsed into his chair behind the pulpit. He was losing consciousness.

Sable rushed to attend to him. She removed the white pulpit cloth and dipped it in the baptismal pool, whose water continued to sway slightly. "Here, let's get you cleaned up," she said gently as she began dabbing at him.

Congregation members who had gone up to ground level had yet to return and I worried that, with the subsidence of the earth's movements, security men would appear momentarily in the tunnel. I decided the appropriate thing for me to do, while keeping one hand on the pocketed pistol, was to start singing — not "Just As I Am" but a much prettier invitation hymn, its message more closely keyed to Reverend Bob's immediate needs. The choir and then the congregation joined in. Korean and English lyrics blended together into a mixture that would have been incomprehensible to a listener who didn't know the words.

> Softly and tenderly Jesus is calling,
> Calling for you and for me;
> See, on the portals He's waiting and watching,
> Watching for you and for me.
>
> Come home, come home,
> You who are weary, come home;
> Earnestly, tenderly, Jesus is calling,
> Calling, O sinner, come home!

Some of the faculty members who'd been particularly close to Reverend Bob joined Sable in a vigil at the pulpit. Grieving the hardest, judging by the tears streaming down his face, was Darley Scratch. I empathized with the coach. Both of us were losing a key figure in our lives and it was going to take time and thought — and in Darley's case, certainly, prayer — to come to terms with the way that was happening.

As we began the third verse, Reverend Bob's breathing grew shallow.

> *Time is now fleeting, the moments are passing,*
> *Passing from you and from me;*
> *Shadows are gathering, deathbeds are coming,*
> *Coming for you and for me.*

He slipped away as we sang the last lines of the fourth verse:

> *Though we have sinned, He has mercy and pardon,*
> *Pardon for you and for me.*

The expression on his face could have been a standard-issue rictus but I hoped it was a smile of peace, understanding and contentment.

YU RETURNED. Whatever the disturbance had been — ordinary earthquake or volcanic eruption — it had caused much more damage on the surface than in the cathedral. The only aboveground structure in the factory camp, the camouflaged guard house, had fallen down. All the uniformed and plainclothes security men inside either were crushed or had fled. Broken rocks and other debris partially clogged the entrances to the tunnels.

Yu had managed to get a cellular signal after the first wave and had succeeded in sending the new recording to Lang Meyer. Then the aftershock had cut her off while she was talking to Mi-song, but not before she'd learned that her boss had crossed into China.

Ezra Pugmire, the second to return, reported that it had proved possible to get through the debris to the residential tunnel. The room serving as a nursery had held up well, even though some of that tunnel's other rooms had caved in. Some children were asleep again already and others were nodding off.

The university bus had survived intact. So had some factory trucks parked out in the open but under camouflage tarps. That came as good news to the Koreans. Shin-il proposed making a run for it back across the river to China. The others agreed. By now, the

Koreans all realized, they knew too much to be of any further use to the Kim regime.

They'd leave before the inevitable arrival of security heavies. If they stayed, some might face a firing squad; the rest, prison camp. There was no reason to assume Kim Jong-un and General Ri would delay in dispatching new security forces tasked with their capture, even if doing so interrupted disaster relief efforts.

To have a decent chance of getting through, the Koreans needed weapons in addition to Comrade Ja's rifle and the slain plainclothesman's pistol. Shin-il and his pals sifted through the ruins of the guardhouse, accumulating a sizable pile of weapons and ammunition. A military veteran in their group distributed the pieces, instructing the non-veterans in their use. Then a half dozen of the newly armed fellows acted as bodyguards for Sable and a few faculty colleagues who went over to check conditions on the university campus.

Another group removed Reverend Bob's body and carried it over for temporary burial at the university. Yet another group left to retrieve the body of Comrade Ja from a little used storeroom at the end of the residential tunnel, where she'd been temporarily stashed, and bury her, as well as the security man, in an unmarked grave well away from the path that led to the campus. At Yu's suggestion, that work detail cleaned the blood off the cathedral floor so that the next cops to arrive would not immediately realize there'd been shooting and killing.

Our migrant caravan formed up as we received a tearful sendoff from the foreign faculty members, who had decided not to cross the border illegally. They would wait, hoping I could manage to reach China and alert the U.S. government to the need for an official evacuation. That seemed to make sense for them, although we who were fleeing lacked the luxury of choice.

The teachers would bide their time in a couple of campus buildings that still stood. The campus's security men, like those attached to the family compound, were dead or missing, their weaponry added to our stock. Plenty of canned foods and dry staples that had spilled out of the pantry were still edible, and some of the water tanks and fuel tanks remained full.

I made it a point to speak to Bartow Toombs. "You seem to have nailed it with your psychological analysis."

"Lucky guess, but it does seem to have been on target. My current theory —— Shakespeare and Freud would approve — is that Robert Posey wanted to make sure prophecy was fulfilled while his father was still alive. That way the old man could participate, as the End Times unfolded according to the son's version of the biblical plan. Johnny Posey would realize, finally, that Bob was as big a man as he was."

The Koreans who once again were refugees piled their portable belongings into the bus and the trucks.

Yu, the day before, had stashed nearby a pair of North Korean highway patrol motorcycles. Darley Scratch looked them over with a connoisseur's eye — "Chinese-made?"

"Wish we had an extra one to offer you, Darley," I said. "You'd be a good man to have along on this expedition."

Over our regular clothing, Yu and I put on uniforms bearing the insignia of the Ministry of Public Security. My costume was tight. Hers was loose enough that it didn't reveal her feminine figure. Her helmet provided enough extra space to hide her hair, which she tied up as I explained to her puzzled fellow Koreans that she brought some training and experience to what we were attempting.

"Westward ho!" I said as she and I mounted up.

She looked at me quizzically. "It will be a minute or two before everyone is settled into the large vehicles, and that gives me a chance to ask you something. Judging from the assured, direct and efficient way you drew that confession out of him, I am guessing that you had arrived at the service believing that Dr. Posey was in the thick of the plot. You didn't look surprised at all when he started preaching about weapons of mass destruction — which is the point at which I began to realize where the sermon was heading. Dr. Posey hadn't stayed to talk with the arms buyers. He had left his private dining room before Nodding and General Ri and the Middle Easterners made incriminating remarks. How could you be sure that Nodding hadn't kept Dr. Posey out of all the nastiness? Or were you bluffing, to draw him out?"

"I wasn't bluffing. I knew. Reverend Bob hosted those visitors for dinner after telling me they were prospective contributors to Posey Korea University's God-given mission."

"Yes?"

"That mission as he saw it was Christian. Of course there are Christians among the Lebanese and Iranian populations. But when Reverend Bob announced that dinner was served he didn't say grace."

"Oh, I get it. Even I dined with him often enough to know how out of character that was. He never neglected to say grace."

"We didn't have to listen for very long before the visitors made clear they weren't by any stretch of the imagination Christians. Reverend Bob already knew who those men were and what they had come for. I could see he must be up to his neck in the whole rotten mess."

"Even the efforts to kill first your friend and then you?"

"Killing's all in a day's work for General Ri, but murder wouldn't have been Reverend Bob's first instinct. Still, as time went on, he'd have had to work hard to push aside the suspicion that Ri — and, I imagine, Nodding, as well — had wanted Joe and me dead."

I actually choked up a bit at that point and paused to compose myself before continuing. "Maybe it's better for me if I never know for sure whether, at some point, Reverend Bob confronted his dilemma. Did he come to see that his priority was not observing the commandment against killing but fulfilling the End Times prophecies? To him, after all, those prophecies meant raining death on humanity."

"You look sad. I know it must hurt you to find that someone you admired so much was pursuing an evil scheme."

"Well, I had some preparation. 'Man is conceived in sin and born in corruption, and he passeth from the stink of the didie to the stench of the shroud. There is always something.' " After reciting the words in English I translated them.

"Is that from the Bible?"

"Pretty close. It's from a novel, *All the King's Men*, by Robert Penn Warren."

"In any case," Yu said, changing the subject as we chugged over to join the rest of the motorcade, "I hope the earthquake, or whatever it was, has put a crimp in the travel plans of the university's new driver. We have enough to worry about, trying to get past what lies between us and the other side of the river."

"Tell you what. This is your turf. You lead and I'll bring up the rear."

———

For the first several hours of our journey we remained, both figuratively and literally, in the dark about whether Mount Paektu had erupted. Meanwhile, though, we could easily determine that the movement of the earth had been widespread and devastating.

A town we passed through came as close to hell on earth as anything I'd ever seen. As we drove in pitch darkness we saw that everything our headlights illuminated had been flattened. It was such a ghastly sight that hardly anyone noticed at first as a gang of little boys and teenagers, filthy, stunted, ragged and emaciated, approached us from off to our left. Before we knew it they were climbing on the running boards and beds of the trucks, hanging onto the window frames of the bus, attacking like Somali pirates, yelling and pounding, demanding food.

In the darkness they had missed seeing Yu's cop uniform. When she fired a couple of warning shots, the marauding youngsters turned to look at her. She ordered them to climb down, but sweetened the demand by telling them we'd share our supplies with them. They complied and Shin-il handed over three bags of food.

"*Kotchebi*," Shin-il said. "Homeless. The disaster last night did not make them the way they are. It started during the March of Tribulation. Later, in 2013, Kim Jong-un had them rounded up and put into orphanages. The orphanages turned out to be sweatshop workhouses where they didn't get enough to eat. A lot of them have run away and resumed hanging around stations begging and stealing, sometimes robbing."

When we left them, the young beggars were divvying up our donated provisions. We headed out of town and soon began to cross steep mountains. The going was tough — but it beat trying to traverse the sea of molten lava below, the glow of which confirmed that the volcano had spewed.

As dawn broke we were navigating a stretch of mountain road, poor to begin with, that had partially collapsed at one point. We stopped, took the precaution of emptying the passengers from the vehicles and had them walk ahead while the drivers picked their way slowly along what remained of the road, constantly within inches of tumbling into a gorge on their right. It would have been a long tumble. We were getting enough early morning light for me to estimate that the gorge dropped straight down a thousand feet or so.

About fifty feet farther, just past the place where the landslide damage ended, the drivers stopped to let the passengers back in. Then, from behind us, I heard the roar of an engine and the crackle of gunfire. An olive-green Jeep-like vehicle sped up the road after us, its driver with his free hand holding a rifle — automatic or semi-automatic, judging by the volume of bullets being expelled. I was the closest to him, and saw him swing his weapon in my direction.

I pulled out my pistol and fired twice. One bullet hit him in the head or neck, I couldn't tell which. Blood splattered on the shattered windshield. But he kept coming, shooting as he drove.

Everybody else was diving for cover except Yu. She took aim and blew out his right front tire just as he was negotiating the washout. Seeing him and his car spinning in mid-air over the abyss, the whole bunch of us clapped our hands and cheered.

"Nice shooting, Ms. Yu. An appropriate welcome for General Ri's new man on campus."

I'd relaxed too soon. As we neared the bottom of another mountain, the last on our route, Yu halted the column. She had spotted a roadblock, set up between us and the river border. The uniformed guards remained standing in position, their lack of agitated movement indicating they didn't realize their quarry had arrived.

Shin-il gathered the factory workers and university students for a conference. We considered waiting all day and trying to sneak around the roadblock after nightfall to get to the river. Refugees typically crossed at night, after all. But because General Ri might send backup forces swiftly, we figured our better chance lay in pressing ahead in what was rapidly becoming broad daylight.

Even that was going to be a highly risky operation. We'd be foolish to assume that the guards, before arresting or shooting us, would be conscientious enough to take any time eliminating the possibility we were innocent evacuees from the disaster area. A few of our men, whose expressions of interest in Christianity had come late in life, had previously served in the army. An ex-sergeant drew up a battle plan. We left the children and most of the women — Namkung and two female factory workers chose to bear arms — to wait there out of the guards' sight.

Yu and I in our police disguises, our goggles fixed, rumbled ahead, rounding a bend in the road. When we arrived at the roadblock, the leader of the guards gestured for us to stop. As we had anticipated, he demanded our police credentials. At that moment, from around the same bend where the larger force was waiting, our former sergeant fired a grenade launcher. The explosion of the grenade off to the side of the roadblock created a diversion.

As the armed men blocking our way turned around to look toward where the explosion occurred, Yu and I pulled our pistols.

One of the guards swiveled back and started to aim at me. I fired and missed. Yu dispatched him with a single bullet. I fired at another guard and watched him fall to the ground. Yu and I gunned our motors and drove on past the checkpoint while our larger vehicles, the bus in the lead, plowed through with rifles and pistols blazing. I had used up my ammunition.

Surprise and superior numbers won the day for us. All the guards were dead. Our side had quite a few wounded. Fortunately we'd brought along first aid supplies from the campus infirmary. We'd lost one fighter. A former military man who was the father of the student body president had been firing a semi-automatic weapon from a standing position in the bus's doorway, where he'd made a big target. Attended by his sobbing wife and children, he lay dying of multiple wounds. His last words: "I'm glad I finally had a chance to stand up against the Kims."

FOLLOWING YU'S ADVICE, we wiped down our weapons, ammo clips and motorcycles for fingerprints and piled them on the ground. She and I added our uniforms to the pile.

The convoy forded the river to China. It was shallow at that point, the water coming only halfway up the wheels of the trucks and bus.

Wearing her black dress and, as I could see because her coat was open, no loyalty pin, my favorite spy stood on the other shore next to Father Paul. "I had a feeling that you two would manage to bring the entire crowd with you," Mi-song said.

"What shall we do with them?"

"We had better get them away from the river bank before the Chinese authorities spot them. Ms. Yu, in the boot of my motorcar are some Chinese license plates. Father Paul will guide you to his rural retreat, via back roads. He will send for his discreet doctor friend to care for the wounded. The group can hold a funeral and hide out while we wait for the situation to calm down." She turned my way. "Heck, you should come with me."

As the Koreans changed the plates on their vehicles, I said my goodbyes. I assured Shin-il and his family that Mama and I would do whatever we could to help them settle in Mississippi. Then I loaded my things into Mi-song's Benz — noticing in the process that she, too, had switched to Chinese plates. I sat in the passenger seat. She drove away, fast.

"What's the latest?"

"My sources say that when Jong-un tuned into CNN, KBS and BBC this morning, your story dominated the programming. One of his first moves was to have General Ri brought in, then taken to a field and killed with anti-aircraft fire."

"Couldn't have happened to a nicer guy."

"Jong-un also sent a squad of heavies to my office to arrest me, but I wasn't there."

"That explains these?" I pointed to a silver-gray wig and a pair of eyeglasses poking out of the center console.

"Yes, just in case of need. News broadcasts are still sketchy but the developing international story soon should become clearer. In Shenyang, where we are proceeding, I shall tap into secure communications to catch up further on domestic developments."

"Shenyang?"

"We must deliver you to the airport so that you can fly out of China."

"I was kind of hoping for a hoedown in Arirang with full orchestral backup, but I guess you're right. General Ri's successor is sure to be on both our tails."

"And the Chinese authorities will be more than curious when they realize that a major shootout involving an American has occurred just across the border."

I yawned and she looked at me. "Since you have been straddling a motorcycle all night, my guess is that you will sleep within seconds. By all means, recline your seat and close your eyes while I play some lullabies." She reached for the button on her sound system.

We reached the outskirts of Shenyang. First stop was a shop whose front part sold Chinese brushes and ink, for traditional painting and writing, and related paraphernalia including seals. Mi-song took me into the back. A stooped old man hovering over a workbench took my passport. He stamped it to indicate I'd re-entered the country normally at Dandong.

"This should be sufficient to get you out on the first flight tomorrow," Mi-song said.

On her way to a safe house, where she would check on the latest Pyongyang developments, she dropped me at the U.S. Consulate-General. There I handed over the faculty roster that Sable had entrusted to me.

"At last we have a list," said the consul-general. "The Posey organization's spokesman issued a statement from old Johnny Posey. He was praying for members of the Posey Korea University community, including the students' families and the faculty — and including his son Robert, although in no way could he condone attempts by mere humans to decide the timing of Christ's return."

"I'm glad that's not the old man's style." I didn't mention that Reverend Bob was dead. The government could find that out very soon, at the same time as AsiaIntel's other readers, after I'd had a chance to file my follow-up story.

Without going into detail about how they'd escaped or where they were hiding, I urged that the United States fling open its gates for any of the Koreans who might want to immigrate, specifically including Shin-il's family.

The consul-general called in an aide and instructed her to pass the word that Washington would need to gear up some fancy diplomacy to extract the Posey Korea University faculty. Then he turned back to me.

"You've reported the news story of the century. I congratulate you."

Although I couldn't think of anything graceful to say, that was OK since the consul-general was in a talkative mood. "I'm afraid we'll always have maniacs trying to blow up the world for reasons that make sense to them. The pessimist in me says that one day one of them will succeed. The optimist hopes people, from reasonable and resourceful private citizens like you all the way up to the president of the United States, will maintain vigilance and stop them every time."

He took a sip of coffee and urged me to do likewise.

"Speaking of presidents," he continued, "did you know that George W. Bush during his time in office was much attuned to Bible prophecy?"

"Really?"

"When he was trying to get the French to join him in Iraq in 2003 he did his best to explain to President Chirac that Satan was about to unleash Gog and Magog in the Middle East."

"Maybe it's a good thing he has different responsibilities now — his library, his painting."

"Every four years, others like him apply for his old job. Every four years presidential hopefuls of that stripe appear at an evangelical convention in Iowa to answer questions put to them by a panel of preachers. The very first question always is, 'What is your favorite passage in the Bible?' At one of those affairs, three candidates all gave the same answer: 'The time is at hand.'"

"Revelation 1:3."

He sighed. "Fortunately, the time is at hand for my retirement from government service."

I changed the subject, to a matter of more urgent personal interest. "I've been out of earshot of the news so don't know much about what happened after the story broke."

The consul-general picked up a stack of printouts from his desk. "Your story hit too late for the evening news on the east coast back home, but it led the late-night news. The repercussions began immediately. Our Navy seized the ship, after a shootout with the North Korean crewmen. Even if the missiles are faulty, they're needed as evidence."

"Did the government talk with Kim Song-chol, a.k.a. the

Reverend John Hyon"?

"Feds had been watching him since they saw he was tight with the North Korean mission to the United Nations. Your story provided the ammunition needed to smash an espionage and propaganda network he had assembled. A federal judge got out of bed to issue warrants and FBI agents fanned out to arrest almost the whole ring. Unfortunately the mysterious Hyon-Kim himself seems to have given them the slip."

"What about the CDS scam?"

"Markets haven't opened yet in Russia, Western Europe or the United States. But Goldberg Stanton headquarters in New York issued a statement saying it had frozen the North Korean investments at the order of U.S. regulators, pending investigation into securities fraud and banking sanctions violations."

The consul-general's phone rang. He picked it up and listened, then spoke to the person on the line. "It's my guess we have a little time before the dust settles in Pyongyang and the people in charge start thinking about what to do with a crowd of leftover aliens in their midst."

Hanging up, he turned back to me. "Coming out of this we'll probably see a strong push for tightening the regulatory rules for Wall Street banks generally."

"I gather it's been tried before."

"Yes but your revelation that Nodding placed massive bets against Russia and other earlier targets of the scheme — and somehow managed to avoid arousing the suspicion of his bank's compliance department — has made a difference. Senator Macon made a midnight announcement calling for tougher regulation of trading in credit default swaps. He apologized for having opposed earlier attempts to legislate that. Nodding had misled him, he said. Goldberg Stanton, along with other banks, had lobbied massively against major reform."

Information overload and returning fatigue were starting to get to me, but the consul-general continued.

"Instant pundits on CNBC and Bloomberg TV wonder if Goldberg is doomed to go the way of the late lamented Bear Stearns and Lehman Brothers. Our economic desk people in Washington are having a hard time figuring out how a hotshot like Nodding could have imagined he'd get away with such a harebrained scheme. I mean, North Korean missiles disguised as Russian missiles? Give me a break. For a kid like Kim Jong-un to go for it is one thing — that's why the U.S. Constitution sets a minimum age of 35 to be sworn in as *our* Supreme Leader." He pointed to a portrait on his office wall. "Not that the requirement guarantees we always have a mature incumbent, but at least we made the effort."

"What does Nodding say?"

"He isn't talking, apparently. But, for heaven's sake, he's a top-level financial professional with two university degrees and a world of experience."

"Nodding believed what his lifelong spiritual guide believed. They both figured that, before anybody caught on, the scheme would spark the war that would bring Jesus back to earth. Then it wouldn't matter if Goldberg Stanton went down the tube."

Of course the story would have explained that, but I thought reminding him couldn't hurt. I shouldn't expect people removed from the cultural context to grasp it immediately. Not everybody'd been raised the way I had.

Being so close to retirement, the consul-general may have figured he had little to lose from speaking frankly and ironically, rather than diplomatically. "I can't help thinking of Wernher von Braun's explanation of why he turned the Nazi rocketry advances over to the Americans," he said as he tapped some search parameters into his computer. After a moment he read this aloud:

We wanted to see the world spared another conflict such as Germany had just been through and we felt that only by surrendering such a weapon to people who are guided by the Bible could such an assurance to the world be best secured.

⊏⊐

Mi-song picked me up outside the consulate, so excited she had to struggle to catch her breath. She was in a hurry to get somewhere and shushed me when I asked her where. She wove her Benz into a tiny gap in the evening rush hour traffic. Finally, as she waited at a red light, she briefed me: "After Jong-un had watched the foreign telly news, his aides gave him an update that made him even more upset. The tremors from the Mount Paektu eruption had reached as far as Pyongyang. The shaking had cracked Kumsusan Palace, the mausoleum where the dead leaders' bodies were lying in state."

"Oh, I'm sorry." I knew she didn't like it that her dad had been stuffed and put on public display.

"Kim Jong-il's body spilled out of its glass case and onto the mausoleum floor. Jong-un needed to settle on someone to blame for that horrible indignity. To make things far worse, his aides told him that at several places around the country security forces were fighting with armed citizens who retained enough traditional mindset to see in the eruption an evil omen. Perhaps the dynasty's obsession with nuclear weapons had disturbed the sacred mountain."

"Where did the rebels get their arms?"

"Most coal miners are military veterans, retained in the reserve forces. In several towns the miners were so fed up by an accumulation of grievances that they emptied their local armories to join the struggle. Hearing this, Jong-un was boiling mad, raving mad. That was the context for the especially brutal method of executing General Ri."

"I wonder where this is leading."

"You'll see, now." Turning sharply she whipped into the parking lot of a Korean restaurant similar in décor to Arirang but larger. "General Ri's agents in Northeast China run this establishment and his agency has its regional headquarters in another part of the building. We must be discreet, but we can watch DPRK television here."

The establishment was standing-room-only, packed with portrait-pin-wearing North Koreans. The reason immediately became obvious: There on each television screen was the young leader, in people's clothing, forelock hanging down, no earring or tattoo visible. Pacing like a caged animal around a luxurious office fitted with maps, screens and other command apparatus, his face mottled, he shrieked abuse at underlings. Behind him stood his unsmiling chief bodyguard, wearing the same striped tie I'd seen twice before.

Kim turned to a fiftyish general who was standing at attention in front of his desk. "The People's Army must shoot all the protestors," Kim ordered. "Shoot to kill." The general saluted, wheeled and left the room.

"The security camera was running in his office," Mi-song whispered in my ear. "This is footage from that camera, transmitted now by national television."

The video showed a man in a business suit entering the office. When the camera focused on his round face I recognized Choe Ryong-hae, the only survivor among the designated regents.

"I'll speak bluntly," Choe said, wearing a stern expression as the two stood facing each other. "You have failed so miserably that if the protests cannot be put down, and if money cannot be found to replace what you have squandered, the top elite will be lucky to get out of the country alive with the clothes on our backs."

"How dare you talk to the leader this way?" Kim demanded, looking as if he would explode. "You will die and I'm sending three generations of your family to our worst penal labor colony. I will assign them all — down to your infant grandchildren — to be guinea pigs in the scientific and medical experiments that we perform there."

"Your orders mean nothing now. Your elders have met and decided that henceforth you will make ceremonial appearances but no substantive decisions. A group of us with more experience will rule."

"You don't have the authority to make such a decision." Kim Jong-un's blotched face showed his anger. Quick as a horse-opera gunslinger — all his practice at shooting ranges in his villas had paid off — he pulled the pistol from his shoulder holster and shot Choe dead.

Kim then turned to his chief bodyguard and said, "Call General Dong back. I have new orders for him. As my grandfather taught us, the best defense is a good offense. We'll finally make use of our nukes. Our first targets are Seoul, Tokyo and the American bases on Guam and Okinawa. A final war fought to the bitter end is what the People's Army and the people need, to restore unity at this dangerous moment."

The bodyguard dialed, but advised Kim that the general's phone didn't answer. Kim named two other generals, and the bodyguard dialed twice more but said he was unable to raise them, either.

Kim changed his mind on the spot. "I don't like the looks of this," he barked. "Prepare the Number One plane and guard the route to the border with maximum air escort from the bodyguard service — *not* from the regular military. I have a destination in mind, where we will be welcomed on short notice. Assemble the Number One household and my other usual traveling companions immediately, for departure within the hour. "

"Yes, sir. For how long an absence from Pyongyang shall we prepare, sir?"

"Perhaps a long one. It appears things here are getting out of control. I don't know who is trustworthy — besides you, of course. Where are the generals when I need them?" He raised his voice, his wattles swaying as he spoke.

The bodyguard had no reply.

Kim continued. "Starting a nuclear war is not simply a matter of pushing a button, it turns out. I have a feeling the generals who aren't taking my calls are turncoats, busy joining traitorous reservists and elderly civilians to move against me." Looking down on the floor, he kicked Choe's blood-soaked body so hard it flipped over and we could see the dead man's face.

"If I cannot take the honorable warrior's way, winning or losing on the battlefield, the best I can do as the third-generation Kim ruler is to continue living to fight another day. I didn't invest everything in the CDS market. I have enough secret funds stashed abroad to finance a long absence while we await a signal that my bad luck has turned good."

The bodyguard nodded and stooped at a desk to begin phoning instructions.

Watching this on the TV screens, many of the Koreans in the restaurant looked uncomprehending, stunned.

"Jong-un is superstitious, like his father and like those protestors in the provinces," Mi-song whispered. "He thinks he is having bad luck."

As she walked off to speak with one group of officials, I glanced at another group, sleek-looking fellows huddled in one corner who appeared deeply grief-stricken. I guessed they might be Ri's security operatives, whose futures now suddenly looked bleak. Would they have to answer for having operated the regime's system of oppression — including the gulag to which so many North Koreans had lost friends, neighbors, relatives, schoolmates and coworkers?

Mi-song returned after a couple of minutes. "Jong-un already left the country. He has wrecked his reputation with the majority of the elite by slinking away like this. And letting the news out that he has turned tail is going to prove more effective in solidifying public opinion than if we had caught him and brought him back to face the music. We may count upon him to set up housekeeping abroad so lavishly as to provide our citizenry with an endless supply of unflattering news about his life in exile."

"What if he gathers resistance forces around him, wherever he lands, and returns to fight?"

"Off the record" — she looked into my eyes with a hint of amusement — "you should not assume that everyone on the plane with him is loyal."

Some of the people in the room were responding to the ruler's behavior by smiling nervously as they swapped comments with their companions.

"Are the soldiers out shooting protestors now?" I asked Mi-song.

"General Dong Chung-hee, leading member of our secret group, was the one you saw receiving that order. He ignored it and staged the coup that we had been planning for some time. He is chairing an executive committee drawn from our group of reformers."

As if on cue, the TV announcer introduced General Dong, speaking from military headquarters as the country's new top leader. The short-haired, uniformed, square-jawed military man spoke briefly. "Kim Jong-un has fled abroad after betting many billions of dollars of the country's money on a scheme that my spokesman will describe. He lost his bet. The country must move quickly to avert financial catastrophe. The Committee for National Regeneration, of which I am chairman, is in charge. As my first official act today, I have canceled the former leader's order to shoot civilian protestors. As my second, I am ordering the military storehouses opened. We will distribute a million tons of war-reserve rice to our long-suffering citizens — soldiers and civilians alike, with priority going to victims of the volcanic eruption and earthquake."

That elicited scattered applause from around the room. The expressions and demeanor of around half of those present suggested guarded approval while a smaller percentage showed poker faces, probably keeping their options open. The sleek, worried fellows in the corner continued to huddle.

"We all need to eat well and restore our bodies because we have a huge task ahead rebuilding what almost every countryman realizes is a sick and broken economy," General Dong said. "We need every pair of hands for this task. We cannot afford to waste our energy and resources on antagonizing other countries. Thus, while keeping enough strength to guard our borders and maintain our independence, we will shrink the military. The discharged soldiers will go back to school or switch to productive labor. Discharged officers will be retrained for important roles managing the civilian economy."

He took a sip of water and continued. "We welcome assistance from international institutions and from other countries, including our neighbors. We need to develop our own economic strength before even thinking about discussing reunification with our Southern brothers. In exchange for appropriate assurances of non-intervention and the withdrawal of sanctions, we are prepared to halt the nuclear, chemical and biological weapons programs and shift our resources to programs for peaceful development."

In the restaurant there was more applause. At the same time a couple of uniformed officers with rows of ribbons and medallions on their tunics exchanged downcast looks. Maybe they suspected that the extra perks they'd been receiving were a thing of the past.

The television screen switched to scenes of provincial North Koreans knocking down propaganda boards that praised the second- and third-generation leaders. The crowds conspicuously exempted the founding Kim. "In response to an appeal by General Dong, these people have now gone home to prepare for participation in the new society," the announcer intoned.

Mi-song turned to me. "Let us go." We squeezed our way out of the room. As we drove off, she resumed talking. "Most of the military is coming around. Some ten thousand armed security officials from General Ri's agency are resisting. They calculate, correctly, that they would fare poorly under the new administration. General Dong's soldiers will make short work of them. The lucky ones among them are those with foreign postings, like those fellows we saw in the corner of the restaurant. Being in China already, they have a head start to seek asylum in Eritrea or some place."

"Is democracy on tap?"

"First things first. For now, what the people would really appreciate is not democracy. They have never experienced such a thing. Cut off as they have been from the rest of the world, they have practically no idea what 'democracy' means. What they want is economic competence and an end to officials' constant demands for bribery. Nevertheless, the new ruling group is made up of relatively cosmopolitan people whose own inclination is to end our isolation — to open up. When the people feel enough of those subversive breezes from outside and decide it is time for democracy we shall work with them to achieve it."

"I heard General Dong say you're not ready for reunification."

"That is mutual. On the one hand, until we close some of the economic gap with South Korea there is no way the South would wish to take on the horrendous costs of reunification. Fear that the South would bankrupt itself by bearing that burden is why the sketchy early news of the collapse of the Kim regime was extremely bearish for Seoul markets today. That was totally predictable. Too bad we had not bought up a large CDS position. We could have made a killing."

"You're incorrigible."

"On the other hand, Northerners are proud people who are unwilling to become a menial underclass wiping South Korean babies' bottoms in a unified Korea. South Koreans who are competent in business, especially including defectors from the North, will be welcome to come up and help us achieve a level of affluence that would make such subordination unnecessary — but only if they refrain from taking advantage of our people's naiveté through such predatory behavior as property speculation. We shall remain separate for the foreseeable future, drop our claims to sovereignty over the entire peninsula and ask the South to do the same, negotiate peace treaties with South Korea and the U.S. and in due course propose turning the Demilitarized Zone into a public park and wildlife preserve, keeping Panmunjom intact as a living museum."

"Do you think it would be OK if I raised some money to install a modest statue, in the Joint Security Area, of Joe running for his life?"

"Why not? It would help remind visitors of the historical significance of the place."

"Well, congratulations! I don't suppose you have any ideas on how we might celebrate."

"I have reserved a suite for us. We are almost there."

In the hotel, I booked a flight leaving the following morning. I wrote a very short email to my parents telling them I was safe and hoped to send a nephew and his family their way. Then I phoned Lang and asked if he still had his job.

"You better believe it. The owners are delirious. Every other news organization in the world is crediting you and AsiaIntel for the original scoop. The publisher's the one who will be looking for a new job. How did you leave Robert Posey?"

"Gone home to his Lord. I'll give you the details in a minute. But first, what about Zack Nodding?"

"I reached him on the phone just before we put the story up and told him what we had. He blustered at first, saying that by the time his lawyers got through with us AsiaIntel would be a wholly owned subsidiary of Goldberg Stanton. He'd make sure you and I both were fired and would never work again."

"I can't be fired. I'm a freelancer."

"I told him that. Then I started playing excerpts from the recordings. He went quiet, hung up on me. By the time his work force started arriving for the day, the news was out and he wasn't in the office. Nobody knew where he'd gone. Someone checked with the border authorities and learned he had crossed over to the mainland. The trail turns cold in Guangzhou."

I dictated all the new developments for a second day story recounting the events surrounding the coup and describing the new rulers' plans.

Then I rang off and turned to Mi-song. The hotel mattress had a nice bounce. She and I made excellent use of it.

"How about if you join me?" I asked. "Since Japan was your spy school specialty, I bet you have a passport you can use to get on the plane to Tokyo with me tomorrow. The new North Korea will concentrate on making money, not war, so there shouldn't be a requirement for a whole lot of spies. My band needs a keyboardist and my life needs you."

"Thank you for thinking of me that way, Heck. I should like to go with you. But it is not to be."

"Why not? You're not married, are you?"

"Officially I am. A year before I went to New Zealand for my studies, Kim Jong-il decided it was unseemly for a woman of the age I had reached to remain unmarried. He arranged a marriage to a naval officer who likewise had waited longer than was considered proper to find a spouse. I thought it could work. He is bright, charming and very handsome. But he turned out to be gay. On the positive side, knowing him has helped develop my political awareness. The pressure for homosexuals to remain closeted is another cruel aspect of the old regime with which we shall dispense."

"Can you just get a friendly divorce?"

"We shall do that. But, sadly, I cannot accept your flattering offer. There is another man, An Jae-ik. We were students together in New Zealand."

Having no words, I let her talk on.

"He is the smartest of the group by far, absolutely brilliant. When it came time for him to return to Pyongyang, he wanted very badly to continue his studies. We staged a fake drowning accident and the New Zealand authorities certified him dead. He defected to the United States under an assumed name, enrolled at Stanford and earned a Ph.D. in developmental economics before starting to teach there. When several of us began plotting regime change, I alerted him and he told me to count him in. His hope was always to return and use what he had learned for the benefit of our people. Jae-ik will be flying over tomorrow to serve as General Dong's chief economic advisor and planner."

"So he'll bring about the complete economic overhaul that Kim Jong-il and Kim Jong-un never delivered?"

"We shall work with South Korea, China, Japan, the United States, Russia, the European Community, the United Nations, the World Bank, the International Monetary Fund, the Asian Development ment Bank, the new Chinese-sponsored Asian Infrastructure Investment Bank — anyone who is willing to help us reform and open our economy. We shall jump-start our economic development by focusing on mining our mineral deposits. Jae-ik thinks we can move quickly into a period of double-digit growth, adapting the Japanese, South Korean and Chinese development models to create a market economy with guidance from the center."

"Look out, Samsung."

"Yes. The officials who have learned to run trading companies will be shown how to turn those into world-beating corporations."

She halted the flood of words to look at dejected me.

"I fear this is my last time with you, so let us make the best of it," she said, using her hands to reawaken my resting member. "Things are more passionate with you, I admit, but I shall stay with Jae-ik. He and the country need me. First I shall set up security for General Dong — a totally new system designed to root out corruption and keep the revolution pure, focused on what is good for all the people. At the same time, while I still can, I shall bear children, who will be part of North Korea's first free generation. I hope you understand."

Still polishing my engorged organ, she paused, looked me in the eye and added, "Besides, I suspect that your full-time musician days are over."

───

At Shenyang airport I neared the gate. Passing a sign for a Muslim prayer room I noticed another sign — brand new, as I could see from the clear plastic packaging that had yet to be peeled off it. "Christian Prayer Room," it said.

I remembered Reverend Bob's publicized complaint that airports were appeasing Muslims by building prayer rooms for them. He had announced a worldwide initiative to match the Muslims, room for room. Shenyang, where he'd often flown in and out, was the first. There was no Chinese translation of either the Christian or the Muslim sign — I supposed because of the Beijing regime's policy of discouraging religious worship by its subjects.

A no-entry tape blocked the bottom of the doorway but the door was open. I had only a few minutes before my flight, and I was eager to get on the plane and put constant danger behind me. Still, I couldn't resist walking over to take a peek inside. Tools and materials were strewn about but I saw no construction workers. Maybe they were on break. But Zack Nodding, in pinstripes and shined shoes, was standing on a folding metal chair, facing the far wall.

Yeah, it's a small world. Too small. Shaking my head, I stepped over the tape, dropped my carry-ons just inside the door and went over to see what the hell he was up to.

I detoured around a pile of galvanized scaffolding tubes and stood behind Zack as he finished propping up a seven-foot wooden cross. Not noticing my presence, he bent, picked up a gas-powered framer's nailing gun that had been dangling from the chair's back and slammed a dozen nails through the cross to affix it to the wall. With his free hand he pulled the two ends of his Armani necktie up over his head — I could see the label on the short end — and held them in place while he nailed the tie to the top of the cross. Then he reached into an inside jacket pocket, pulled out a sealed envelope and dropped it on the plywood subfloor.

Realizing that the obnoxious son of a bitch was about to hang himself, I was sorely tempted to turn around and leave – maybe with a parting shot like "Bon voyage, asshole!" But all the relentless training in altruism got the better of me. I crept up on him and clamped my arms around his legs.

Turning his head with a jerk, he tried to kick free of the hold as he glared down at me, his eyes wild. Having some angry thoughts to get off his chest, though, he stopped thrashing while he mustered the requisite sarcasm. "Well. 'Bring hither the fatted calf.'"

"Luke 15:23."

"Might've known you'd show up. It was always about you."

"Let me hold the chair while you pull off your necktie. Your life doesn't need to end now." I squatted and, with one arm still around his legs, grabbed the rickety chair with the other hand to steady it.

"In all those decades, Reverend Bob never could stop talking about you, the wild rover who'd lit out for faraway lands to lead a sinful life."

"Maybe that's who I am. Maybe not."

"You were his all-time favorite apostate project. I went along with his idea of hiring you to teach — thought that would let General Ri have his way with you. Turned out Reverend Bob was determined to protect you."

"His protection seemed to have some holes in it."

"Yeah. Min screwed up when he drew his knife on you. His assignment was to steal your passport so you couldn't leave, same as Toombs. You screwed up when you left campus and gave Ri's people a clear shot at you. You weren't supposed to die until yesterday."

"When the new driver showed up."

"Right. I kept pleading with Reverend Bob — the last time after the supper meeting with the Iranians — to let the general find a quick and permanent remedy for your nosiness. We needed to stop you from endangering the mission. He wouldn't listen. He was too excited by the thought you might return to the fold at the last minute, coming forward at the cathedral service and repenting."

"Washed in the blood of the lamb — and worthy to be sacrificed."

That smart-ass remark brought out the same synapses-popping response I'd seen from Zack in his Hong Kong office.

Now that I knew — despite the fact I'd have preferred not to know — precisely how long Reverend Bob had planned for me to remain alive, I should've shut up or changed the subject back to the reasons why suicide would be a bad career move for Zack. Should'a would'a could'a – but didn't. "I was grateful Reverend Bob always looked out for my soul."

"You call that *gratitude?* Destroying a great man's dreams? Think about it as you burn in hell for all eternity." He turned toward the cross and jammed the gun barrel's surrounding contact-compression spring mechanism against the oak, to switch off the safety. Spinning back to face me, he aimed.

I let go, dived and rolled away as he pulled the trigger. The gun spat a long framing nail deep into the plywood I'd been squatting on.

A loudspeaker out in the corridor crackled a warning. "Last call for China Southern Airlines Flight six two seven to Tokyo."

Zack turned to jam the safety off again. I'd rolled several feet away from him but not quite far enough that I could take cover behind the scaffolding pile in time to avoid getting nailed.

Fatback's advice came back to me. *Use anything handy.* Scrambling to my knees, I slid the top length of scaffolding off the pile and clasped it between my right arm and the side of my chest. As Nodding swiveled to fire again, I swung my improvised jousting lance. The nail gun flew out of his hands and clattered onto the floor. The chair teetered but didn't fall.

I got to my feet. "What you're trying to do to yourself can be really painful. I suggest you pull your tie off, carefully, step down and walk away. But it's your call. I gotta catch a plane."

━━━

Back in my cabin I gazed out the window at the farming hamlet nestled in a mini-fjord across the lake. I wouldn't stick around long. I'd keep making music — had a performance gig the next week. Meanwhile, Lang was working up an assignment. I'd stay freelance, wouldn't be a company man. Just needed a little while to lick my wounds. So I listened to the kettle rattling on top of the kerosene stove, played my guitar and wrote lyrics like these:

> *Reverend wanted to give a push to*
> *Gog, Magog 'n' Persia.*
> *Yeah that preacher thought he'd give a shove to*
> *Gog, Magog 'n' Persia.*
> *Light the world up like the burnin' bush*
> *So Jesus'd shout, "I heardjya;*
> *I'm comin' back — in glory!"*

See that woman yonder tootin' the walls down?
She a musical spy.
Woman tootin' the walls down, yeah,
She a musical spy.
Now Armageddon gotta wait
For the sweet by-and-by.
Take your time. No hurry.

But I lost that woman to another man.
Don' like it one bit.
Yeah I lost that woman to another man.
Ain't that some shit?
Knock me way, way down —
But no use to th'ow a fit.
Like them Eye-talians say, that's amore.

Could handle all that but the preacher in question,
He was my hero.
That crazy evangelist tried to blow up the world,
Preachin' at ground zero.
Bob wadn't the right name for him.
Should'a' been Reverend Nero.
What can I say? It's my story.

That's why I got them nuclear blues,
radioactive.
That's why I got them nuclear blues,
explosive.
Them blues got me so low, low down,
Don' see how a man can live.

THE END

ACKNOWLEDGMENTS

In *Nuclear Blues*, I imagine a best-case scenario for an atrociously ruled country with which past denuclearization and peacemaking efforts have consistently foundered. Let's hope current efforts succeed. If that comes to pass, then you may read this book as a work of alternate history — what *might* have happened. It's fiction in any case, but informed by a great deal of reporting, research and news analysis done before and after publication of my nonfiction history, *Under the Loving Care of the Fatherly Leader: North Korea and the Kim Dynasty*.

While credibility is my sole responsibility I owe gratitude to providers of inspiration and help, starting with two fellow members of the Kamiyama Writers' Collective.

Beloved wife Susan Rose Stanga Martin has been my indefatigable and highly skilled chief editor *and* my brilliantly focused instructor in the ways that fiction differs from nonfiction. Couldn't have done it without you, honey. Meanwhile, old friend Collin Piprell, a.k.a. the Bard of Bangkok, has checked in on an almost daily basis, leading by example and constantly encouraging me with his never-failing wit.

The extremely talented Rambling Steve Gardner, a real Mississippian photojournalist-turned-bluesman, served as a partial model for main character Heck Davis. Son Alexander Martin, also an excellent musician-journalist, helped among other ways by modeling up close some bicultural aspects of the Heck character.

As for the major character called Kim Jong-un, any resemblance to a real person, living or dead, is purely coincidental . . . OK, strike that. Of course there's a real Kim Jong-un, but as of the time of writing we know very little about him — so little that even if I should put everything I know into a biography I wouldn't feel good about charging for it. I've used my imagination to fill out this character's personality, starting with what we do know about the historic Kim Jong-un. As far as I know, he has not yet bought a submarine yacht equipped with curtains to keep jealous dolphins from smashing the windows when they become aroused by watching him frolic in bed with members of his Pleasure Corps.

(By the way, I had drafted *Nuclear Blues,* and my agent had started looking for a publisher, well before the Sony Pictures movie *The Interview* came out, also featuring a fictional version of Kim Jong-un. Pants-wetting in the thriller industry when hackers alleged to be Kim's agents attacked Sony computers — causing by some estimates as much as $100 million in damage — factored into the delay in publication until now, as did the untimely death of my agent.)

The young Reverend Bob who mentored the teenaged Heck is partially modeled on two fine young Southern Baptist pastors I knew when I was growing up, the Rev. Hoyt G. Farr and the Rev. Posey Davis, Jr. It was another young pastor I knew then, the Rev. Jimmy Garrett, who proclaimed that he had become a missionary in order to convert the Catholics (in Brazil, in his case) to Christianity. When it came to depicting the mature Reverend Bob, there was no shortage of well publicized real-world evangelistic careers to help set out the general outlines — but, again, this is a work of imagination. Reverend Bob is a fictional creation.

Moving on to minor characters, a real-life visiting revivalist who required the congregation to sing seventeen verses of the invitation hymn "Just As I Am" was the Rev. Chester Schwartz, preaching at the Marietta, Georgia, First Baptist Church in 1960.

The starved young woman with one eye pecked out is based on a real person who, before her death, was interviewed and videotaped by Kim Dong-cheol, a member of Jiro Ishimaru's *Rimjingang* team of daring undercover journalists.

Some of Heck's and Joe's most remarkable adventures as "tourists" in Pyongyang I actually experienced during one of my seven visits, a tour on which my companions included Mary Ann Jolley and Stephen McDonell of the Australian Broadcasting Corporation. Their video "North Korea: Parallel Universe," currently available on YouTube, captures those adventures for posterity.

I knew a real yakuza who with his girlfriend kept a small white dog as a pet and who over the years had chopped off three finger joints from his left hand in separate gestures of apology to his boss. Although we were friendly and he never tried to kill me, he did on one occasion in 1979, from across his living room in Kawasaki, propel his throwing knife up to its hilt into the upholstery of his sofa, about an eighth of an inch from my shoulder. That was his way of responding when I asked about his role in the boss's organization.

Choe Ryong-hae, North Korea's Roger Stone, is a real person. I wrote about him in my earlier book. (Attention index-users: the customary romanization back then was Yong-hae.) I have no information suggesting he's disloyal.

The originator of Heck's trick of showing up in sweats and sneakers, announcing to his North Korean minders that he simply must run each morning for his health – and letting a minder run along with him until blisters hobble the man, leaving our hero free to roam – was Mike Tharp of the *Wall Street Journal*, when we spent three weeks in Pyongyang in 1979 covering the world Ping-Pong tournament.

It was the venerable Asia correspondent Donald Kirk who, to pass himself off as an ordinary tourist, claimed to teach at the School of Hard Knocks.

If anyone wonders, "Where were you when you learned about

credit default swaps?" I have no trouble recalling that I was sitting at the feet of Oliver Biggadike and Uwe Parpart.

Contemplate Lance Gatling's name and you have to suspect he was born to be a fount of knowledge about weaponry. So he has proven in his generous advice to me.

For several years before Kim Jong-il's death and Kim Jong-un's succession to the leadership I worked with other Bloomberg News journalists to cover North Korea. Thanks to Hideko Takayama, Peter Langan and Allen Cheng for great teamwork whose fruits are reflected in this novel — in, for example, the descriptions of Dandong and the examination of the treelessness of the mountainsides.

Reading Hal Lindsey's *The Late, Great Planet Earth* helped me understand how interpretation of End Times prophecy developed in the nuclear age.

Whenever questions about photography have come up, I've been able to turn to Charlie Cole and Bob Kirschenbaum for enlightenment.

I'm extremely grateful for useful and encouraging comments from early and perceptive readers Rui Parada, Mark Schreiber, Charles Smith, Don Huse, Grant Newsham, Bob Whiting, Donald Baker, James Brown, Peter Montalbano, Jeff Purser, Melissa Wheeler, Oliver Hockenhull, Susan and Thad Riddle, Michael Breen, Bob Neff, Jack Swinney, Eric Eason, Sean Desmond, Hank Morris, Peter Jaeger, Larry Kelly, Rich Read, Rich Meyer and Sara Vagliano.

Thanks to Michael Johnson and Charles Kelly for rescuing me from computer glitches; to Barry Lancet, Greyson Bryan, Wanda Jane Maddox and Iain Wilson for sharing publishing lore; and to Geoffrey Tudor, Matt Aizawa and Ken Moritsugu for help in the home stretch.

After Jack Scovil died, I found that he was literally irreplaceable as my agent. Rest in peace, Jack. Eternal thanks for believing in my work, starting back when publishers showed almost zero interest in Korea.

Growing up in the U.S. South, Bradley K. Martin weighed career goals ranging from preacher to president. After majoring in history at Princeton, studying law at Emory and serving as a Peace Corps volunteer in Vietnam War-era Thailand, he settled on journalism and spent decades as an Asia correspondent. The two-time Pulitzer nominee was bureau chief for the *Wall Street Journal, Newsweek,* the *Baltimore Sun, Asia Times* and *Asian Financial Intelligence.* For Bloomberg News he was chief North Korea watcher. He has taught journalism as a visiting professor at Ohio University, Louisiana State University, the University of Alaska Fairbanks, Fresno State University and the University of Iowa. His earlier book, *Under the Loving Care of the Fatherly Leader: North Korea and the Kim Dynasty,* won the Asia-Pacific Special Book Prize.

For further information:
  http://greatleaderbooks.com
  https://www.facebook.com/GreatLeaderBooks/

how ruthless, effective and evil men can oppress their neighbors . . . .
It reads like a medieval court, the Ottoman sultanate or imperial
China.

Doug Bandow, *The Washington Times*

The sensational extravagance of the leadership; the dreadful
sufferings of the common people; the ludicrous personality cults
thrown up by both Kims; . . . the systematic destruction of normal life
and language in North Korea — all this is laid out here for inspection.
If I may be permitted a book reviewer's cliché: I couldn't put it down.
. . . By sheer relentless accumulation of detail, Martin succeeds here
in giving us a full portrait of the Kims and their filthy little tyranny.

John Derbyshire, *National Review*

The book is terrific. Bradley Martin has solidly and vividly recon-
structed North Korea from the inside, through his extensive interviews with refugees, much as Mike Oksenberg, Doak Barnett and
Ezra Vogel did with China during the Cultural Revolution.

Yoichi Funabashi, *Asahi Shimbun*

The mother lode. Ferociously detailed, lengthy account of the
world's only communist dynasty.

blogjam

This is journalism at its best — nothing so comprehensive and
authoritative has been written about North Korea for thirty years. It
is frankly amazing that a non-Korean could produce such a work.

Nicholas Eberstadt, author, *The End of North Korea*

Under different circumstances, North Korea could be the subject of a Marx Brothers satire, with the elements of a pompous, ego-driven patriarch, a worshipful population and a general aura of fantasy and illusion. But North Korea has a superbly equipped million-man army and an expanding nuclear weapons program. So this comprehensive examination of this totalitarian society and the two men who have dominated it is often terrifying. . . . Using newly available material from Russian and Chinese sources, Martin offers surprising insights into the career and character of both Kim Il-sung and his son, Kim Jong-il.

Booklist

A careful, penetrating analysis of North Korea. Given the levels of secrecy which surround the Pyongyang regime and the danger it poses to its neighbors, Brad Martin has rendered a considerable public service to us all.

David Halberstam

A remarkable book, and probably the most important on North Korea for many years . . . a mine of insights that are both fascinating and alarming.

Howard Winn, *Finance Asia*

So it's been confirmed. North Korea has nuclear weapons. . . . The hawks versus doves debate won't help us much. What might help us, though, is reading the best book ever published about North Korea.

Eamonn Fitzgerald's Rainy Day